THE BODY SNATCHER

The donor slipped in and closed the door without even a click. It seemed to Watly that they had stopped breathing. The donor reached into the workervest and slowly removed the surgeon's cutting blade from its case. They took a silent step toward the chair. Then another. The boards creaked.

The occupant of the chair, a middle-aged woman, stood and looked over the winged back. "What do you want?" she said.

The donor kept advancing. "I want *you*, my dear. You don't know how long I've waited."

The woman's eyes were frantic. She was trapped. Watly wanted desperately to help her, but he was powerless, trapped like her. "Stay back!" she screamed.

The donor kept coming, Watly's body a savage thing, unstoppable. The first stab went into the woman's shoulder, and it was Watly who had done it. The donor came down again with the blade, and again and again. The donor slowly stood up.

"Mea culpa," the donor said. "Mea culpa, Watly Caiper. I'm afraid you've been a bad boy, my friend. A very bad boy."

Bantam Spectra Science Fiction
Ask your bookseller for the titles you have missed

THE HOST

PETER R. EMSHWILLER

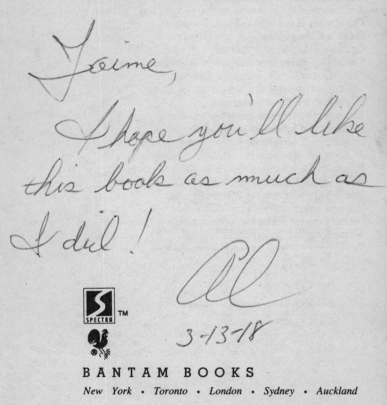

Jaime,

I hope you'll like
this book as much as
I did!

Al

3-13-18

BANTAM BOOKS
New York • Toronto • London • Sydney • Auckland

THE HOST

A Bantam Spectra Book / May 1991

SPECTRA and the portrayal of a boxed "s"
are trademarks of Bantam Books, a division of
Bantam Doubleday Dell Publishing Group, Inc.

ISBN 0-553-28984-5

Published simultaneously in the United States and Canada

Bantam Books are published by Bantam Books, a division of Bantam Doubleday Dell
Publishing Group, Inc. Its trademark, consisting of the words "Bantam Books" and
the portrayal of a rooster, is Registered in U.S. Patent and Trademark Office and in
other countries. Marca Registrada. Bantam Books, 666 Fifth Avenue, New York, New
York 10103.

PRINTED IN THE UNITED STATES OF AMERICA

OPM   0 9 8 7 6 5 4 3 2 1

Dedicated to my incredible poovus, Margaret, for all her help, support, and love; my wonderful new family, Rich, Vicky, Melissa, and Mary; my great and talented sisters, Eve and Susan; and both my mothers, the genius Carol and the late, great Ed. (Miss you, Dad.) And to Amy, for thinking I had something here.

Who says there's no such thing as family anymore?

PROLOGUE

Something about California.

Something curious happened out there, word had it. Something interesting, they said. Something big. All official channels were silent on the subject, but word of mouth was buzzing with vague, strange tales. By the time these stories traveled across the continent, across the entire United Countries of America, through the borders of Arizonia and the Nuclear Nations and the Drug Zones and Jesusland and Pennyork and all the other countries, by the time they reached from the Republic of California to Brooklyn, they had become nebulous and blurry. Amorphous gossip. People talked on street corners. People speculated and elaborated. Whatever it had started out as, it was distorted, mutated— probably bore little resemblance to the truth. Or to the facts, either.

California. Something about the Republic of California. Something had happened out there. Something those here weren't supposed to know about. Something those in power wanted to contain. Something involving violence, perhaps. Little people, big changes.

Some said it was mass destruction. Earthquakes, the bomb, war. . . . But most said it was an uprising—a takeover of some kind. *Revolution*. No one used the word *revolution*—no. But it was there, unspoken, floating just beneath the surface of every conversation. *Revy*. It was a tough word to say out loud. A tough word to think about. The connotations of that one simple word . . . *enormous*. So no one said it. But it was there.

And during this, during these drifting rumors and quiet mutterings and murmurings, perhaps *because* of them, something *moved* in the people. Something shifted slightly. Tilted. Twisted. It was not a specific, tangible thing, but even in Brooklyn you could feel it in the air. A vibration. An electricity. A charge that went from negative to positive. An excitement that . . . *something* was going to happen soon here. *Here*. People felt a pulling together.

The news reports said nothing. The news reports always said nothing. There were hardly ever any real bulletins anyway, except about the local countries. Once in a while you'd hear something bland about the other, more western ones. Nothing important. And there was never anything at all about overseas. The distant lands outside of the UCA had been totally out of bounds since well before Cedetime. Shut out completely. For all anyone knew, things might have become very nice over there in the Outerworld in all this time since Euroshima. But nobody knew, or cared, really. There were probably lots of low wars going on there. There always were. Fights over territory, economics, or religion—all of which really were the same thing in the end. But this California talk, this was different. It made people hinky. Uneasy. Fidgety.

There was unrest about. Unspecified, unfocused unrest. Lots of it. The streets were thick with it. Clogged with it. The streets of Brooklyn, and even the streets—the bottom ones—in the country of Manhattan itself.

Watly Caiper didn't care. Not at all. He had more important things to think about. Personal things. Things involving his goals, his ambitions. His life. Things were moving for him. All that rumor stuff was of no concern. None at all. Let other people think on it.

He didn't care. Caring was something Watly used to do. That was his mother's influence. That was *her* way. Now . . . now he cared about himself. Now he cared about his dreams, his plans.

His plans.

Tiny toenails and hyperventilating cries. Fine wispy locks and contented gurgles. Small toothless smiles and first words. The pink cheeks, warm to the touch, and that bubbly cooing. Grasping hands—always grasping. Eyes focusing, tracking, gazing lovingly. Hiccups. Spit-up on a towel. The smell of shit—somehow sweeter and less offensive than your own. Hugs and cuddles and tiny feather kisses. The laughs, the incredible impossible giggles. Dependency goaded, prodded, nudged into a painful independence, like you'd coax out a burp. Someday. Somehow. Raising another self until that self can do it alone. And on. Babies. Children. Kids. Being *in* on it. In on the formation of another person. A different person. Better, maybe. A person to carry on. The new wave. The pass-along.

"You don't pay back," Watly's mother would say. "You pay forward." And so.

This is where Watly Caiper's mind was. This was the nature of his thoughts. The Republic of California was not a concern. Unrest was not a concern. Revy was not a concern. Leading a revolution was the last thing on his mind. The last thing. If you had mentioned it, he would have laughed and slipped quietly away. There was a time he would not have laughed. Or slipped away. There was a time he would have cared. But that was long ago. That was then and now was now. Now he was out for himself. And for his passion.

Mothering.

PART ONE

THE SETUP

The me is a movable thing.

WATLY CAIPER

CHAPTER 1

Thump thump thump.

He was a real pig of a man. Size of a house, with little tufts of black and gray hair peaking from each nostril. The sign in front of his desk said his name was Mr. Oldyer and that he was Examination Five.

Thump thump thump.

Oldyer. Ol-die-yer. That's how the clerk had pronounced it. Ol-die-yer. Rhymes with *mold buyer*.

Thump thump thump.

He had no hair to speak of except for that nose stuff and, Watly suspected, an ugly mat of it all down his back. He didn't just look fat, he looked bloated—inflated, pumped up with fluid or jelly or something. His eyes seemed almost buried amid little puffs and folds of extra lumpy flesh. The two thick lids looked permanently bruised. And beneath it all—beneath these pinkish flaps and lumps—two glistening pupils could still be seen. They watched coldly and aloofly, with that special mixture of hatred and condescension that always appears when one gives a little scrap of power to a little scrap of a mind.

Watly shifted from his left foot to his right.

Thump thump thump.

Mr. Oldyer hadn't said one word yet. He just sat and stared at Watly, thumping that No. 2 pencil proudly on his plasticore desktop. *A real wood pencil like that must've cost him a full week's pay,* Watly thought. *He's really showing it off.*

Thump thump thump.

Watly wished he could think of something to say—something witty or sarcastic. A quip. Where the hell was a quip when you needed it most? Needed it for your own sanity. Watly's brain was dry. This Mr. Oldyer—this unapproachable *building* of a man—stood between Watly Caiper and his future. This was it. Watly didn't want to blow it. Not now. Not after coming this far.

Thump thump thump.

Even before the enormous man finally broke down and spoke, Watly suspected this was the kind of guy who could make every word in existence a curse. Watly braced himself for it. Everything this man would say was going to sound like an obscenity. And curses—rape, bolehole, subspawn—would sound worse than ever slipping from this man's sloppy flesh wound of a mouth.

But nice, positive words—good words—would be tainted with fatty toxins. Words like *pretty, happy, wonderful, kind* would be corrupted when spewed from those two lopsided lips. Even wholesome, positive words like *fuck* would end up tainted. *Fuckhead, fuckable, fuckface*—all would sound like bad things instead of good when they escaped from this blubber-puss.

Watly stared at Oldyer's mouth. He remembered hearing once about how in ancient pre-Cedetime, pre-history, the word *fuck* was indeed considered a curse: something harsh, something one couldn't say in polite company. Whereas, back then, *rape* was not considered a curse word at all. Pretty strange, that. It was like they had everything backward in those days.

Thump thump thump.

Mr. Oldyer broke his stare and turned his massive head down to look at the papers on his desk. The facial blubber trembled for a moment and then the man laid his pencil carefully before him. No more thumping. There was a palpable release of tension.

Watly exhaled slowly through his teeth and focused on the toes of his shoes.

"Watly Caiper, huh?" Four swinging jowls shuddered with the impact of speech on Oldyer's face.

The brown half-walls of the small office seemed to close in around Watly. He felt as if something was tightening around his neck—pressing, squeezing. Yes, Watly had been right. This man made even Watly's own *name* sound like an obscenity.

"Yes, sir. That's me."

"Come a long way, haven't you, Caiper?" the big man said in a monotone.

Watly smiled but kept his mouth shut, not sure what was expected of him. It hadn't sounded like a question. *What do you want, fat man? Tell me and I'll give it to you.*

"You've passed through four examinations and two physicals, right?" Oldyer looked up from the papers and resumed his scrutinizing gaze. "You know how to talk, firstface?"

"That's right, sir. Been here all day." Watly's hands were damp again. They'd been going damp like that on and off since he'd first gotten on line at five that morning. The whole thing had been much more an ordeal than he'd expected. The enormous queues, the tension, the waiting, the shuffling, the forms, the prodding, and the *endless*, endless questions. . . . Yes, sir-ree, the admissions procedure at Alvedine Industries' Hosting Building was . . . less than soothing.

Watly surreptitiously wiped his clammy palms across his pants legs on the pretext of smoothing the fabric. A conspicuous dark stain of sweat was left behind.

"So you want to be a host—is that it, Mr. Watly Caiper?" Oldyer's voice now had a tinge of sarcasm to it.

"Yes, sir. That's it exactly."

"A fade-out host? A final host?" Oldyer's sunken eyes gleamed.

Watly's stomach did a complete half turn. Something bubbled in his throat. "No, no, Mr. Oldyer. Not a fade-out host, sir. Just a host. A regular host."

The huge man was playing with him. Any other circumstances and Watly would have socked him in the jaw. The guy was a secondkissing bolehole. But it was all too important. This was the big time.

"We're always in need of a good *fade-out* host, Mr. Caiper," Oldyer said slyly, leaning back in his chair. He was smiling. The man was showing off his power. He was threatening Watly—trying to intimidate him, trying to make him hinky and more.

Watly allowed himself a tight little smile back. "I'm not interested in dying just yet, sir. I understand fade-out hosting pays very generously but I'd have no one to leave the money to. Right now, sir, I'm just interested in hosting."

"And why would that be, Mr. Watly Caiper? Why do you want to be a host?" Mr. Oldyer lifted his pencil again and began to slowly—almost sexually—caress it with his fingertips.

Watly picked out a particular Oldyer nose hair to focus on before answering. A gray one. "I need the money, sir—Mr. Oldyer. It's the only way I know of to make a lot of it fast."

The huge jowls reared up to form a smile again. A big one. "Oh, you're a treasure, Mr. Caiper. A real treasure. Need the money, do you? That's precious. I'm stunned. Imagine my surprise. *Kelgar!*" Oldyer's voice boomed out—directed over the half-wall to the next office. "Kelgar! This unique fellow's in here because of financial considerations! He needs the money!" The big man rose with great exertion. His fat wobbled asymmetrically over the top of his pants as he rounded the desk toward Watly's side. The floor shook slightly under Watly's feet. "Imagine that!" There was clipped laughter from beyond the half-wall. "Needs the money!" Oldyer moved closer and held his face just a few centimeters away from Watly's. Watly could smell the stale alcohol-infused breath, the rancid skin. He saw that Oldyer's swollen nose and cheeks were covered with a fine latticework of blood vessels that grew more engorged by the minute. A map of blood. The guy was flushed. "Mr. Caiper," he said. "Mr. Caiper, in the entire history of hosting—since it first began—there has never been a sofdick subspawn of an applicant like you who came across my desk, or any other terradamn desk . . . who *didn't* need the raping money." Oldyer accented each of the last few words by poking Watly in the stomach with his blunt index finger.

Watly Caiper remained as still as possible. He wanted to

strangle this Mr. Oldyer. This bolehole. He wanted to knock him
down and see how high he'd bounce. He didn't. He didn't budge.
He breathed. In-out. In-out.

Oldyer moved even closer and Watly thought for a moment the
big man meant to kiss him.

"You'd like to hit me, wouldn't you, catbreath?" Oldyer asked
softly. "You'd like to knock me over. I've read your file. There's
more than a streak of prideful violence in there." Again a sharp
poke in the solar plexus. "You don't dare, though, do you? 'Cause
you want this real bad and it's all in my hands." Oldyer backed off
a few inches. "Do you know what my job is, Mr. Caiper? My job
isn't to *accept* you. Oh, no. My job is to *weed you out*. My job is
to turn you away. My job is to send you out of here on your bole.
Just because you made it this far you think you're second shit.
This department *alone* sees over a thousand people a day just like
you. *Just like you*. You know how many of those people get by
us?" Watly shook his head. "On a good day? *None*. On a good
week? Maybe one, if you're lucky." Oldyer moved back to his
side of the desk. "So, Mr. Watly Caiper, the odds are against
you." Oldyer paused and sat his huge form back down. "That is,
unless you want to be a fade-out host. . . ."

Watly clenched his teeth. The guy wouldn't give up. "I do not
want to be a fade-out host, sir."

"Then give me a reason I should make you a host, Watly
Caiper. I've got your file and papers in front of me and there's
nothing special there. Give me a reason"— Oldyer's eyes smiled,
though his mouth showed nothing—"why I shouldn't kick you out
right now."

Watly felt his mind go blank. Somebody must have pulled the
stopper and let his brain drain out. *There's gotta be a puddle of it
somewhere down there. . . .* He openly wiped his hands on his
pants this time. *Give him a reason, dammit!*

"Well, Mr. Oldyer, I'm, uh . . . I'm in good shape. I'm strong.
Uh." Watly groped for something—*anything*. "I'm relatively attractive to either sex. Pretty fuckable-looking. I . . . uh . . . can take
a lot of punishment. I've got a lot of stamina and endurance. . . ."

Oldyer started shuffling the papers around on his desk. "You're
not helping yourself, Caiper," he said offhandedly. He pulled

aside one particular form and began inspecting it. "Says here you did factory maintenance work in Brooklyn and that you just moved to Manhattan last month. Are you a tenter or are you staying someplace?"

"I'm staying with my Uncle Narcolo. He has an apartment."

Oldyer seemed to perk up for a moment. "Narcolo?" he asked. "Narcolo Caiper?"

"That's right," Watly said, his hopes rising a notch at Oldyer's perky tone.

The man scratched his large bald scalp. "He used to work here a few years back—Narcolo Caiper . . . Narcolo Caiper—he worked in files, I think. Retired now, I believe." Oldyer grinned, ignoring Watly. He seemed pleased with his own memory.

"Yes, sir. He's a real fuck, a great guy. He—"

"Subspawn," Oldyer snapped. "Connections will get you nothing here, Caiper." The cavernous eyes turned back to the form. A thick vein near one oversized ear bulged outward. "So you're staying in an apartment. Near here, is it?"

"It's very convenient, yes, sir."

There was a long moment of silence from Oldyer. Over the half-walls, Watly caught snatches of conversation from the other interviews and examinations going on all around him—insecure mumblings from applicants and self-confident bellowings from interviewers. It was the same everywhere.

"Let me guess, Mr. Caiper. You want the money because you'd like to save up and someday move to Second Level. The good life, and all that? Gave up on playing the Level Lottery, huh?"

"No, sir."

"Dying relative out in Jersey Commonwealth needs an operation?"

"No, sir."

Oldyer looked annoyed he hadn't guessed right. The nose hairs actually seemed to bristle. "Then what's your sad story, Caiper? What's your tale?"

"Antiprophies, sir."

The fat man looked confused for a second, as if he'd never heard the word. "Antiprophies? You want to be a mother?"

"That's it, sir."

"A mother? A mother, huh? Had a calling?" There was new respect in Oldyer's voice.

"Yes, sir."

"You have a female? Volunteer or mate or anything?" Oldyer's face transformed into that of a pouting child for a moment. "You have a poovus?" he asked.

"No, sir."

Oldyer inhaled and let out a long, drawn-out whistle. It started high and descended slowly, the sound of someone falling off a cliff. "Gotta give you credit for trying, Caiper. You'd need a rape of a lot of money—antiprophies, a female, a license. A *lot* of money." Oldyer's eyes glazed over as though he'd slipped into a daydream. He was gone.

"That's why I'm here, Mr. Oldyer," Watly said as firmly as possible. *Wake up, Mr. Fat Man.*

Oldyer still looked like he was drifting, his mind far away. "That's fine, Caiper." Without looking down, Oldyer gathered the various papers together on his desk. "Application denied."

Watly thought he hadn't heard right for a moment. "What?" he said softly.

"Application denied. You know the way out. Follow the blue arrows."

"Denied? Just like that?" Watly felt his face getting hot.

"Just like that." Oldyer was sealing up the papers in a plastic sanifile. He finished quickly and pulled out another file from behind his desk. The next person's file.

Just like that.

Watly stood still. Breathing. In-out. In-out. *Just like that a man crushes another man's dream. Just like that.* Watly felt dazed. He cleared his throat gently. "Are you asking me to leave?"

Oldyer snorted. "I'm *telling* you to leave, rapeface."

Watly started to back slowly out of the cubicle. This couldn't be happening. This man *arbitrarily* decided to deny Watly's application. *Arbitrarily. Just like that.*

Watly stopped at the doorframe and scanned the small cluttered office. *There must be some way to change this huge man's mind.*

Watly wouldn't give up without a fight. This was too damn important. This was his *life*.

"Mr. Oldyer?" Watly let his voice go louder than he had all day. It felt good. It felt right.

"I thought I told you to leave, Caiper." Oldyer spoke without looking up from his new set of papers.

"Two minutes, Mr. Oldyer. Two more minutes of your time. Just two." Watly found himself pacing wildly back and forth in front of Oldyer's desk like some crazed salesman. "Two little minutes—that's all. Humor me for two minutes, Mr. Oldyer, and then I'll get out of your life forever."

Mr. Oldyer glanced up from his desk and manipulated the pockets of flesh around his mouth to form a sneer. It was not a pleasant sight. "Why the hell should I?"

Watly swallowed and stopped his pacing. "Entertainment," he said deliberately. "Think of me as a minor diversion."

Oldyer smiled and leaned back. His chair squeaked as if in pain from the change in weight distribution. Watly wondered if it was reinforced. "You've got *one* minute, Caiper. Make this good."

"Okay. Okay . . ." Watly was trying to think and talk at the same time. "Supposing, sir, just supposing I owed you a certain sum of money. Let's say one thousand New York dollars . . ."

Oldyer rolled his eyes. "A bribe won't get you anywhere with me, Mr.—"

"No no no." Watly started pacing again. "Not a bribe—not a bribe. Just suppose I *owed* it to you. Legit. Hypothetically, of course."

Oldyer smiled again. "How the hell would—"

"Just humor me for a second. If I owed this to you . . . there'd be virtually no way for you to get it. You know *why,* Mr. Oldyer? Because I've got zip. I've got nothing in my pockets and nothing in the bank. No savers. Nothing. I've got no job, and any job I *could* get—it would take me years to pay you back on the best salary. Except one job. Hosting. Hosting's the only job. If—hypothetically, of course—if I owed you that thousand, I could easily pay you back with interest after only a few *minutes* of hosting."

Oldyer was looking impatient. "What's the point, Caiper? You don't owe me nothing."

"No, that's true, that's true . . . but bear with me a second." Watly pressed his fingertips together. "If—hypothetically—I had, say, *stolen* the money from you or owed you because I *wronged* you in some way, it would pay for you to turn me in. No, it wouldn't pay. If you had me arrested there'd be even *less* chance I could ever repay you. You'd *never* see the money. No, the best thing for you to do would be to make me a host, right? Then I'd pay you right back, because basically—" Watly smiled, "basically I'm an honest fuck."

"Are you threatening me, Caiper?"

"No, sir. Absolutely not." Watly stood opposite the big man, right up against the desk.

"Sounds to me like you're either trying to bribe me or threaten me. I can't figure which. Either way I don't like it and either way I've had enough of this. You've had your minute."

"I'm not bribing you and I'm not threatening you, sir. What I *am* doing . . ." Watly reached over in one swift movement and snatched up the No. 2, "is breaking your pencil." Watly snapped it neatly into two pieces and then broke each one again with a loud *pop*.

All four of Oldyer's chins dropped. "You bolehole! Do you know how much that thing cost me?" His huge features seemed ready to explode. Watly leaned back and let the wooden pieces fall through his fingers.

"Exactly," Watly Caiper said with a smile.

CHAPTER 2

The daylites were down to half by the time Watly Caiper left Alvedine Industries' Hosting Building. He walked down the front steps to the street, looking upward. Even after a month of living on First Level Manhattan, Watly still wasn't used to the absence of sky above. It remained uncomfortably disorienting—even claustrophobic—to step out of a building and still be under cover. The stagnant oily air, the thick upright girders, the oblong daylites, constant drips, hollow echoes—all took some time getting accustomed to. Not to mention that constant mildew stench. . . .

And where is the sky? Where has the sky gone?

"Spare a dollar, boss?"

Watly turned to look at the bum. There were ten or fifteen others right behind him, looking like a gauntlet of derelicts. This was a prime area for begging—right outside Alvedine's Hosting Building. The guy who had asked first looked relatively well kept for a bum. More likely he was a tenter out for extra cash. His clothes seemed pretty new and his face looked washed. Watly gave him a buck anyway and moved away quickly, walking down the center of the street.

Fifty-seventh Street was full of tenters down both sidewalks and in the gutter. Some of them looked packed so close they seemed edge to edge. Street cats ran between rows of tents, looking for food. Watly heard a police cruiser, so he stepped aside and let it pass. He gave out three more bucks before hitting Second Avenue. It was all right to be extravagant, Watly thought, considering they'd given him a two hundred New York dollar advance toward his first hosting. Quite a fuckable amount. He patted his right pocket where the wad of bills sat comfortably. It felt good. He felt good. Tired, but good.

He headed downtown at First Avenue. By his estimation, Watly had at least two hours before the daylites would go to night. He walked slowly, enjoying the exercise. It'd been too long since he'd had a chance to move much at all. His muscles had cramped up from almost fourteen hours of bureaucratic shuffle. "Follow the orange arrows. . . . Follow the green arrows. . . . Name? . . . Age? . . . Turn and cough! . . ."

There were fewer tenters in the forties but a lot of people walking. The occasional whine of a bus or police cruiser cleared them all toward the sidewalk. A few lowtrucks and bicycles passed slowly. The eateries, sunbean cafés, bodegas, music tube stores, and used clothing shops were full of brousers, if not customers. Someone was hawking hot birdhats from a cart. The dripping was pretty bad, so Watly took out his own plain hat, unfolded it, and put it on. At least it wasn't raining up above on Second. Then the drips and falls and flooding here below would *really* start. This was mild. This was tolerable. Almost pleasant.

On Thirty-eighth a strong breeze started as Watly neared one of the major exhausts. He clamped his hand over his hat to keep it from being sucked up into the huge fan. Those near him did the same. Everyone's loose clothing whipped and danced around their bodies. A few people held their ears to protect them from the fan's steady roar.

Directly below the fan some old guy stood staring up, his white hair blowing wildly. Whatever it was—hat, bills, whatever—he hadn't held on tight enough. Poor old guy would have a hard time recovering whatever he'd lost up there. That was next to impossible. As Watly understood it, the guy would have to fill out requests, affidavits, and a million other forms out the bolehole. Then, after all that, a few months later he'd probably see some policeman wearing whatever he'd lost. Can't fight the system.

The old guy was shouting something now, cursing up at the fan. Watly couldn't hear the words, but it looked like he was saying something like, "The time is coming, you sofdicks! The time is coming!" And then there was more Watly couldn't make out. Maybe the man hadn't lost anything up there after all. Maybe he was just standing there yelling up toward Second Level. Maybe.

Clamping his hat down even tighter, Watly passed quickly underneath the exhaust and moved on. The wind and noise lessened rapidly. *Something about California. The old guy had said something about California. . . .*

Watly made a pit stop at a corner W.C. Aside from the obligatory urine test, he'd been holding it in all day. Usually Watly avoided streetcorner water closets, but at this point he had little choice. The W.C. experience was survivable. They weren't so bad if you breathed through your mouth.

Back on the street the people were starting to thin out as night approached. Watly continued on leisurely, enjoying the lack of crowds. It had been a day full of crowds. The lines at Alvedine had been enormous. Bodies mashed against bodies. From one examination or medical to the next, one room to the next, one floor to the next, Watly had spent most of the time staring at the backs of different heads. It had been quite an ordeal. Questions, questions, questions. "Name?" *Watly Caiper.* "Mother's name?" *Pepajer Caiper.* "Ever broken a law?" *No.* "What do you think of when I say the following words: Hot?" *Cold.* "Sex?" *Good.* "California?" . . . *Beach.* Questions and more dumb questions.

And then, of course, came Oldyer. Ol-die-yer. What a nightmare. Watly almost lost the whole deal on that one. But it worked out after all. Somehow. The pencil idea had been desperate, but in the end Watly guessed it had served its purpose. Not as he'd expected, yet—strangely enough—everything had worked out in the end.

The fat man was a real cipher. His reaction had been unexpected. Oldyer had frozen in what looked like shock after his initial outburst about the pencil's cost. Then he seemed about to burst once again. Suddenly and with absolutely no warning the man began to shake with laughter. He clutched his enormous sides and howled, almost tipping his chair backward. His belly bounced with it. Tears poured down the puffy cheeks. His jowls flapped. The laughter was so loud a security guard stuck her head through the doorway to see if everything was okay. Oldyer just waved her away.

When the laughter finally subsided Oldyer spoke again. "Okay, Caiper. Okay. You got me. You got me good, Caiper—so far as you're concerned. You pulled what you thought was a fast one. You can be a host. Don't ask me why, but you got it, Caiper. You got guts, little man. Little man. You got *oves*. *Huevos*. You got eggs, I'll give you that. Didn't think you'd go for it. I'll make you a host, Caiper. And you know what, Mr. Watly Caiper? I hope you make it. A mother, huh? You haven't a chance in hell, but I hope you get your little dream. I hope you do. I could almost feel sorry for you, considering what's in store. But then, what do I know? Here's a booklet for you. Follow the green arrows to registration."

Oldyer started laughing once more when Watly turned to leave the office. Watly stopped at the doorway when the big man spoke one last time to him. "Oh, and Watly. . . . Watly, about that pencil," Oldyer said between short, panting breaths. "That pencil—it's a fake. Made out of placene and paint. Sells for five New York dollars down on Fourteenth. You think I'd keep something expensive in *this* office? In *this* raping shithole?" A fit of laughing once again overcame him. "You kill me, Caiper. You kill me."

Watly walked out of Oldyer's office feeling dazed. He registered and picked up his advance. The woman in registration smiled mechanically and told him, "Congratulations and please report tomorrow at nine o'clock A.M." Watly smiled back and left the building feeling like he was part of some enormous practical joke he knew nothing about. Life itself was a practical joke. *But he'd won.*

How the subs did I pull that off? he wondered. *Or* did *I pull that off?*

Either way he was glad to have the job. Either way he'd somehow done it. He was a host.

As Watly continued down First Avenue, he realized there was only one thing about the whole day that really disturbed him. The pencil turning out fake didn't really bother him. Perhaps it was just some kind of standard ingenuity test or something. "Is the applicant smart enought to break wood?"—that sort of stuff. No, the thing that bothered him—really bothered him—was Oldyer's *attitude* at the end. Even the words he used were strange. He called Watly "little man." "You've got guts, little man. . . ." If anything, Watly Caiper was on the tall side. Tall and solid—that was Watly. "Little man." Watly supposed *anyone* was little next to the bulk of that interviewer. But that's not how he'd said it. He'd said it like Watly's *part* in life was little. His *role*. It was said like Watly was a sunbean headed for the breakfast table.

There was a tone in Oldyer's voice—and even in his bone-rattling laughter—all through those last moments, that seemed to imply Watly had done *exactly* what was expected—that he was just an overgrown key on a jumbo-sized keyboard who'd been pressed as planned. A trace of something in Oldyer's manner said, *Watly Caiper, you just fell for it.* When Watly had glanced back one last time and caught Oldyer's eyes, he'd witnessed a frightening sight. Truly frightening. Worse than the condescension, the loathing, the superiority, there was *pity* in those buried, officious little pupils. It seemed to Watly that Oldyer thought he was staring at a dead man. In fact, Oldyer looked sure of it.

Watly shuddered the thoughts off and tried to relax as he continued to walk. Things had gone well. He was in. He was a host and that's all that mattered. Work started tomorrow. Money would start coming soon. More money than he'd ever had before. After a short while hosting he'd be able to save up enough to fulfill his dream. His calling.

The word *calling* was common when referring to motherhood. Watly didn't like the expression. To him it implied something mystical or spiritual or religious. *You want religion, move to Jesusland,* he thought.

There was nothing supernatural about his ambition. Parenting was not exactly a new idea. Granted, it was next to impossible for a person of Watly's station to achieve motherhood, but that didn't mean he was "blessed" to want it. Or cursed. Watly was more realistic than that. His desire since youth to be a mother was no different than someone else's desire to be an office worker or technician. In some ways, Watly thought his goal was more reasonable than those of the Manhattan dreamers who lived on First Level but wanted to work on Second. Or worse, those who thought they'd work their way up to living permanently above. Talk about your bad odds. Winning the Level Lottery was probably more likely to happen.

Watly always knew the chances were slim. But he couldn't remember ever wanting anything else. As his mother used to say, "A life without dreams is not worth living." And now Watly's dream was closer to being a reality. If anything could get him what he wanted it was money, and—now that he was a host—*that* was no longer a fantasy. After five or ten hostings, Watly should have enough to buy antiprophies, and then it was a matter of finding and hiring a willing female—just to father the kid—and, of course, getting a license. The license part was the hardest. If hosting went well—and he could stay in good shape through it—then the biggest obstacle ahead would be fitting the requirements for his mothering license.

But Watly was getting ahead of himself. *One step at a time, Caiper. One step at a time. First concentrate on earning the money, then worry about the other problems. You've got to take off the covers before you get out of bed, and all.*

The most difficult thing about this whole mothering idea was that Watly knew nobody who *was* one. He had no role models—at least not of his age. The only successful mother he'd ever known personally was his own (a female), and she'd had him before the population laws were enacted. He'd come in just under the wire. She'd had Watly two years before they implemented the controls: prophy-laced water, the mother licensing, high-priced antiprophies, and so on. There was no one Watly could emulate. No rule book to follow. Watly hadn't seen a kid in person since he was a kid himself. But this just reinforced his desire. He was all the more determined. Back in the old neighborhood in Brooklyn, the other kids used to say, "If you want Watly Caiper to do something, just tell him it's impossible." In a way, they were right. Watly smiled at the memory. Perhaps he did have a calling. Anyone in his right mind would never try to be a mother. Maybe there was some deeper reason Watly needed a child. Watly laughed. *Yeah, maybe. And maybe if I flap my arms hard enough I can fly.*

Watly looked up just in time to stop himself from walking into an upright. His mind had been wandering so much he hadn't been watching his step. He'd drifted from the center of the street to the side, where the huge support girders stood every thirty feet or so. He glanced around, embarrassed. A few pullers passed by, pulling an empty lowtruck. No one was staring. *That's right, Caiper. Walk into a plasticore upright and break your raping face the day before you start hosting. Real smart.*

He was in the Stuyvesant area, coming up on another exhaust. He cut across Eighteenth Street and headed down to Second Avenue to avoid the fan this time. The wind didn't bother him but he wasn't in the mood for the noise.

Second Avenue was more crowded than First had been. Lots of police cruisers passed by loudly, and even a few unmanned coppers. Bicycles clogged the sidewalks. There were many tenters here, and the street was full of workers heading home for the day, as well as bums hitting them all up for money. Watly ignored the beggers this time. *I gave at the office.* The thought made him smile.

At Second and Fourteenth was one of the seven existing tubes to the Second Level. A few lucky workers came out of it. They were getting off for the day, returning down here to the real world. (Or perhaps what they *left* was the real world. Or maybe neither.) Passersby stopped to gawk at them. They were extremely well dressed by First Level standards. The men had crisp, clean-looking black jumpsuits with yellow workervests and the women wore the same with buzbelts and higher boots. Everyone looked on enviously. The Firsters with their tattered, dirty clothing, unkempt hair, gaunt faces, and generally slumped shoulders stared at the special ones but kept a polite distance. These descending ones were the chosen few. Next best thing to Level Lottery winners, they lived below, yes, but they worked above. Every terradamn day they were up in the sun. Watly smiled to himself. He'd be perfectly happy staying on First Level all his life as long as he could get his dream. Make that his "calling." Watly's smile broadened. That was all he wanted. A baby. A little life to help along. This was the only important thing, the only thing worth caring about. Mothering.

He was a few blocks from Uncle Narcolo's place. He wondered if he should use his advance money to pick up some expensive tidbit for dinner. A surprise. Bird meat, even. No, Narcolo Caiper would already have a complete meal waiting. The man loved to cook. He could do culinary wonders on minimal retirement pay, plus whatever he had socked away in savers.

Instead, Watly settled on picking up a good bottle of booze for forty bucks. As an afterthought, he returned to the store and bought another one. This was a night to celebrate.

He tucked one bottle under each arm and strolled on, thinking of children. A police cruiser zipped by, cutting close to him, and Watly had to jump back to avoid its fender. He lost his grip on one of the bottles and it fell. Some passing woman dove and grabbed it just before it hit the street. Great reflexes. She handed it back to him smiling, her eyes dark and shiny beneath the hood of her threadbare cloak. Watly smiled back. "Thanks," he said. She raised a fist in the air at him, as if in a secret signal or salute.

"California," she whispered, and walked off.

CHAPTER 3

Little Uncle Narcolo was bustling about in the kitchen, chopping things into pieces and tossing them in pots on the stove. His wrinkled features were tight with concentration.

"Oh, good, Watly. Oh, good. Perfect timing. Just perfect. Couldn't've asked for better. Things'll be ready in just—almost perfect timing, Watly. A few more minutes and we'll sit down to a—be ready in a few minutes, Watly. You have a seat and put your feet up."

Watly smiled. Uncle Narcolo had tidied the one-room apartment since Watly had left early that morning. The six worn cushions were neatly lined up on the couch with careful symmetry. All the leafs and books were back on the shelves or stacked carefully in the coffee table. The music tubes were in their holders. All the clothes had been picked up and put away someplace—probably folded. The old cable-vidsatt and the keyboard looked freshly dusted. Narcolo Caiper was always keeping himself busy. Even when he didn't have something to do, he'd find something to do. There was a certain charm to the old guy's frenetic, obsessive cleanliness. The only place in the apartment that didn't look freshly swabbed was the kitchen area—and that was currently in use. It too would be spotless eventually. In the living area, the faded chromells depicting glamorous Second Level Life were bright with polish. Even the windows looked like they'd been wiped down—which was silly because they were sealed up from the outside. Narcolo had a front apartment near street level (down four short steps), and so it was safer to seal the windows with placene sheeting than leave them exposed. Watly had commented on it when first arriving and Narcolo had snapped at him for being naive.

"Besides," the old man had said, "you tell me what I've got to look at out there. Someday, when I win the Level Lottery and I'm living in luxury on Second Level, *then* I'll have windows. Windows are for *nothing* here, kiddo." That was the end of that conversation.

Watly set the two bottles on the coffee table and sank comfortably into the couch. He watched Uncle Narcolo dance around the kitchen, adding dashes of this and touches of that. He really liked the old man. The guy was a fuck. If it weren't for him, Watly never would have made it into Manhattan. Nowadays you not only needed a clean identicard, travelpass, and visa to get into Manhattan, you also needed a recommendation from a current resident and proof of some kind of legitimate housing waiting. Narcolo had vouched for Watly and promised to supply lodging for him. Watly still couldn't thank him enough. It was amazing how the old man had helped out to such an extreme. Watly barely remembered meeting him more than a few times as a kid.

"Say hello to your Uncle Narcolo, Watly," and, "Say goodbye to your Uncle Narcolo, Watly." They hadn't been in contact since. Yet here this old guy takes in a nephew he hardly knows, feeds him, shelters him, and gives up his solitude. Of course, Watly suspected the guy had been more than a little lonely all by himself. It was pretty obvious Uncle Narcolo enjoyed the company. On Watly's arrival, the old man had hugged him tightly and his eyes had watered some. "Ain't hardly such thing as family anymore, Watly Caiper," he'd said quietly.

But, whatever the reason, Watly still felt he owed Uncle

Narcolo Caiper a lot for his help. As soon as the money started coming in, some of it was going to the old man.

"It's a stew I'm making, Watly." Narcolo carefully stirred as he spoke. "And we've got a hardloaf and some sunbeans and stuff. Be ready in just a—be done soon here. What'ya got on the coffee table, Watly? Bottles?" The old man strained to see. Narcolo had neither the money nor the patience to keep his eye care up to day. His sight was probably a good deal worse than he let on, and he tended to squint at anything more than a few yards away.

Watly raised the two bottles and held them out over his head in a rough imitation of a police victory salute.

"Booze, Uncle Narcolo. I bear booze."

The old man's stirring hand faltered. "Booze?"

"Not just *any* booze . . . *expensive* booze. Forty New York dollars a bottle!"

"Where'd you get— How did you get that kinda . . ." Narcolo stared at Watly. His right hand continued stirring as if it had a mind of its own. To Watly's surprise, the old guy looked suddenly sad. Maybe even disappointed. The strong creases in Narcolo's wrinkled face all sagged downward, pointing toward the placene floor tiles. "You went to Alvedine today?" he asked.

Watly let his mouth spread into the smile he'd felt coming a long while—the smile he'd held inside ever since he got the job. He'd spent all day smiling, but not like this. This was not a polite, subservient grimace of a smile. This was a *real* smile. It stretched out his lips and pushed his cheeks up into his eyes. It was a smile that came from inside.

Narcolo stopped stirring altogether. "You mean . . . you mean you're *in*, kiddo? You're a host now?"

"Damn right," Watly said, still grinning, waiting for his uncle to jump up and down, to race around the counter, to grab Watly and spin him in a dramatic circle punctuated by bear hugs. He waited for the love, the admiration, the pride, maybe even a touch of good-natured jealousy. He waited for that friendly old face with the wide mouth and the broad nose to break into a glorious smile that folded all those character lines around the thin edges and gathered them into deep folds of amazement on the sloping forehead. He got none of this. The old guy just stood there, frowning.

"Yes," Narcolo said quietly. "Yes, I see."

"I *did* it, Uncle," Watly said, jumping up. "I terradamn *did* it. You know the odds? You know the raping odds? I'm a host! I'm on my way!"

Narcolo turned down to look into the stew. "No surprise to me, kiddo. No surprise."

"No surprise? *Nobody* gets to be a host. I don't even know how *I* did it." Watly ripped off one of the bottle caps and grinned widely again, hoping this excitement would be contagious. "One minute it looks like it's all over and the next thing I know, I'm *in*. I did a song and dance and thought I could weasel my way in, but it turns out that had nothing to do with it."

Narcolo finally put the spoon down on the counter next to the stove. He looked up, made a little questioning expression with his eyebrows, then exhaled slowly and went back to his somber frowning. "I always knew you'd get in, kiddo. No question. You're host material."

"Maybe they just liked my style," Watly continued. "But it almost seemed, looking back, like they wanted me all along. Wanted *me* specifically. I got a funny feeling they just wanted it to *seem* like they were giving me a hard time. Nothing I could put my finger on."

Narcolo walked slowly around the counter toward the living area. Under the worn checkered shirt, his bony shoulders were slumped and defeated-looking. It was more than your standard First Level slump. "Of course they liked your style, Watly. You've got something special, kiddo. They must've seen it in you." He stepped up near Watly and looked at the expensive bottles. "What're . . . what're they paying these days?"

"Ten thousand New York dollars a hosting," Watly said, passing by his uncle to the kitchen. This was not what he wanted. Not what he *needed* from his uncle. Right now, he needed that charming boyish giddiness he'd seen so often the past month. He needed his uncle to express the excitement and joy that Watly himself so often had trouble expressing. Maybe a drink would help.

Narcolo whistled breathily. "Those are big bucks. Big bucks indeed."

Watly rummaged in the pristine kitchen cabinets until he came up with two cloudy glasses. He crossed back to the coffee table with them and splashed a healthy dollop of booze into each one.

"What's the deal, huh, Uncle?" Watly asked, passing one full glass to a withered right hand. "This is what I came here for. This is good news. I'm on the way to getting my dream now. I'm doing the impossible. Hey"—Watly touched Narcolo's shoulder—"what the sub's the deal here? You look like somebody died."

Narcolo tossed some of the liquid to the back of his throat and swallowed hard. He sat down—almost fell down—on the worn pillows of the couch. "I just thought we might have more time like this."

Watly took a sip of the strong booze himself. It burned roughly on its way down the pipes. "More time?"

"I didn't think it would happen so fast—the hosting." Narcolo gulped down the rest of the glass and coughed away a booze bubble. "You've only been here a month, kiddo."

Watly smiled. "I'm not going anywhere, Uncle." He saw fear in Narcolo's eyes. Fear for Watly's safety, or maybe just fear of being alone again. Or maybe a little of both.

"We've been having an okay time, haven't we, kiddo?" Narcolo asked, reaching forward and pouring himself another brimful glass of booze. "Downright fuckable time, huh? You and me? Roommates. Send me to the Subkeeper if I'm lying." He leaned back limply into the cushions and took a sip from the glass. Some of it missed and ran down the side of his chin. A smooth, pink tongue peeked out and lapped up the dribble. "We shop, we walk, watch CV, eat good food." The gray-blue eyes focused directly on Watly now. "Just didn't think everything would move so fast, kiddo. So damn fast."

"This doesn't change anything, Uncle," Watly said. "I'll still be staying here. I'll just be working as a host now—finally earning my keep. This is still my home here, Narcolo. I'll stay as long as you can stand me."

Narcolo looked around the room angrily. "Some home this is. Some raping home."

Watly thought for a second and then spoke again, softly. "I won't leave you, Narcolo."

Narcolo gulped down still more booze. He seemed to be drifting away someplace. "Family used to mean something once," he said. "Long time ago, kiddo, family meant something. Before Cedetime. Loyalty and love and stuff like that. People stuck together. Family. Relatives. The country fell apart and the family fell apart. It's the same thing. Nobody wants to be a part of anything—anything big, kiddo. Everyone's out for themselves now. Everything's all split off. Family don't mean shit."

Watly sipped a little more and enjoyed the warm burn this time. "Does to me," he said. "I'm staying, Uncle."

"Well, you're full of catshit. It shouldn't. Stick up for yourself, kiddo. Go ahead. You're the only one that counts—in the end. You die alone." There was raw, naked fear in the old guy's eyes now.

Watly smiled gently. "I'm not planning on dying for a while."

"What do you know about it?" Narcolo snapped. "You're a raping host. A *host*."

"I know," Watly said. "I'll be careful."

"You're gonna hafta be more than careful, Watly. This is dangerous work, kiddo. This is no game you're into. You'll need luck. A lot of luck."

Watly noticed how with each sip the booze tasted milder. "So far I haven't done bad, old man," he said with a wink.

"I'm not kidding, Watly." Narcolo's expression was hard now. "People get hurt bad. I've seen it. I worked at Alvedine, remember? I was in records. I know what goes on. And the second you get hurt bad, Watly, you're out. Out on your bolehole. Any *real* pain and you can't host, you know that." He poured himself more and stared at the bottle's label. "Worse part of it is, it's out of your hands. You've got no control. You'd *damn well* better hope you're lucky. You'd better have nice donors, Watly. Perfect donors. One lousy donor and you're dead, kiddo. It ain't just fade-out hosts that die. It happens all the time. You'd better hope your donor ain't no pain-freak."

Watly was silent a moment. He watched as Narcolo began to peel the bottle's label. "I'll be all right," he said, not at all sure.

"You know why they pay so much, Watly?" Narcolo's voice was acid. Angry and bitter. There was something animal about it. Something cruel. "You know why they give out such a fortune? To subsidize Future Mothers of Manhattan? Not on your life. They pay so terradamn much for hosting because no one in their right mind would *do* it if they didn't." The old man released a loud belch and waved it off.

"I'm not sure I want to hear all this now, Uncle. Tonight's for celebration." Watly reached for the bottle but Narcolo's hand lashed out with surprising speed and grabbed Watly's wrist. The old guy was still strong and his grip hurt.

"You're not listening to me, Watly Caiper. This is serious stuff here. Hear what I'm sayin'. You haven't been listening." Narcolo's eyes were piercing and made Watly want to hide. There was amazing strength to his hold. "When do you start?" Narcolo asked coldly.

"Tomorrow."

"Tomorrow when?" His nails were digging into Watly's wrist.

"Morning. Tomorrow morning."

Narcolo threw Watly's hand back at him like it had been a ball he was holding. "You drink more of that and you go in there with a hangover and you're *out*. You understand? *Out!*"

Watly looked down at the red marks around his wrist. They looked like four little new moons. "Okay, Uncle—take it easy," he said.

The frightened look came back to Narcolo's eyes. His voice softened. "No donor wants to vacation in a painful body, Watly. You got to be careful. And you'd better hope your donors don't mess you up so you can't do it again. And that's the other thing: Things are strange out on the streets lately. I feel it. Something's up. It's dangerous out there. Even if you're *not* hosting. But that's not even the point. *Hosting's* the dangerous thing. *Hosting itself*."

Watly tried to make his voice calm and soothing like he remembered his mother's voice. "I'm only going to host long enough to buy antiprophies and pay a female to carry the baby and all. That's it, Uncle. Then I quit."

"That's all it takes, Watly. It only takes one bad donor. Just one." Narcolo poured himself another glass and left Watly's dry.

His hand trembled slightly. He now looked small and weak—a little old man on the verge of death. This was not the real Narcolo. Not the energetic boy of a man Watly was used to seeing. Watly turned away.

"Have you thought about why there's a call for hosting, Watly Caiper?" Uncle Narcolo's voice sounded as weak and feeble as his body now looked. Watly wished he could cover his ears to shut that off too. "Have you ever considered it? I'll tell you why. It's because all those fat, rich Second Level donors want some excitement. They want a thrill. They want the sense of danger and adventure without any risk. If you're really lucky, Watly . . ." Narcolo gulped down some more booze and put his hand on Watly's shoulder. The old voice was weaker still. Watly pictured flimsy vocal cords shredding and ripping under the wrinkled neck skin. He cringed. ". . . If you're really lucky, all your donors will find the mere idea of being on First Level with us scum for a few hours excitement enough. Or maybe screwing a few lowlifes and walking around sexsentral. That's if you're lucky."

Uncle Narcolo tried to turn Watly to face him but Watly wouldn't move. The old hands were easily resisted now. "If you're unlucky they'll want to see what it's like to do something else. Something dangerous. Why do you think fade-out hosts are so popular, kiddo? Why do you think? The crazies up there want to experience death without dying. They say it's the ultimate high. Best vacation you can have. Well, regular hosts die too, Watly. They do. They also get hurt bad sometimes."

Watly turned to face Narcolo. The weathered old features looked more frightened than ever. The eyes were sad and liquid. Watly tried again to calm him. "Uncle, they have laws and rules —"

"Oh, sure, they've got rules out the bolehole," Narcolo interrupted, "and they'll slap a fine or penalty on the donor who breaks one. They even imprison some, in theory at least. But none of this means the rules aren't broken. And it doesn't mean you won't get hurt. It ain't hard to make accidents happen. Not on First Level. Not hard at all." He reached over and took a swig directly from the bottle. "Not at all." The old guy's voice trailed off some. "It's easy to find hurt out there nowadays. There's a lot of hurt about. . . ." The words faded to nothing, lips still moving slightly.

Watly didn't feel much like celebrating anymore, but damned if he wasn't having another drink. He slowly and deliberately poured himself a short one. Narcolo kept his peace now. His eyes looked glazed over and seemed fixed on some middle distance between the colorful Second Level chromells and the coffee table. Watly wished to the subs that he had an apartment all to himself. A tent, even. A pothole. This wasn't exactly how he'd planned it. Why had the evening gone so sour? Where was the party? The congratulations? He took a small sip and felt the renewed burn. *Two drinks does not a hangover make,* Watly thought. It tasted good and the slight beginning of a buzz was more than welcome. Narcolo continued staring into space. He seemed convinced of Watly's doom, convinced he would be alone again soon. *Why is everyone so sure I'll mess this up?* Watly took another tiny sip and tried to think of something comforting to say as the booze slithered warmly downward.

"I've heard," Watly started quietly, "that it's usually just sexual stuff. Experiments the donor wouldn't have the guts to do himself. Things that would ruin a reputation up on Second. Fantasies lived out, and all. You know how they are on Second about appearances—"

Narcolo blew out air between his lips and made a dismissive *peh* sound. "Fantasies, all right," he mumbled. The old man's nose twitched and he started sniffing in short breaths like an asthmatic cat. "You smell something? Somthing burning?" He leaned forward and his eyes widened. "Oh, no! Damn damn *damn*! Dinner! I've ruined the terradamn dinner!" He rushed to the kitchen area and peered into the pots on the stove. "Oh, damn. I can't believe it. I ruined it. It's all raped now."

Watly stood and walked forward to look at the charred mess in the pots. "It's no problem, Uncle. We'll just have something else," he said.

Narcolo's eyes blazed insanely. He hurled one of the pots across the room and it clattered loudly against the wall before dropping. Watly stepped back. Shit, his uncle was really overreacting.

"I ruined it! I ruined it!" Narcolo yelled. The tendons of his neck stood out tautly. "I ruined the damn dinner!" Suddenly the old man was crying, weeping like a baby. He covered his face and his shoulders shook. Each sob was as piercing as a shout. They came out fast and powerful: *"Igh! Igh! Igh!"*

Watly put his arm around his uncle and gently led him back to the couch. Narcolo Caiper turned his body toward the back of the couch and buried his face in one of the tattered pillows. He was curling into an almost fetal position, still crying loudly. *The booze and the excitement are all too much for him*, Watly thought. *And he's worried sick about me*.

"I'm sorry. I'm sorry. I'm so sorry, Watly." The old man choked the words out between sobs. Watly got a blanket and covered Narcolo carefully, tucking it around his thin shoulders and spreading it down over his shoes—scuffed-up old office shoes with holes in the toes. The fetus was rocking slightly now. Rocking himself. Watly loved this old man. He loved him a lot. He loved him even though he'd ruined the celebration. He loved him *because* he'd ruined the celebration.

The sobbing continued awhile before it changed to snoring. The transition was hardly discernible. Noisy sadness into noisy sleep. Watly watched the old guy awhile and then raised his still half full glass.

"Cheers," he said softly to himself.

CHAPTER 4

People disappeared. Out on the Manhattan streets, it became almost common. Like the Skyfinders.

A small group of friends—seven or eight folks, ten at the most—would gather every Tuesday night. (This started just before Watly Caiper moved to Manhattan.) They'd gather and they'd talk. They called themselves the Skyfinders. Just for the sub of it. It sounded good. Couple of roofers, a few tenters and some apartment people, meeting on a Tuesday for a chat. No big deal. Their talk wasn't all that special. Nothing serious, nothing earth-shaking. They exchanged gossip, recipes, even a few ideas. Silly stuff, mostly. "Wouldn't it be nice . . ." kind of stuff. "In a perfect world . . ." sort of talk. "If I had my way . . ." prattle. Fantasies and silliness. And California conversation. There was a lot of that: California conversation. The usual stuff. Speculation, wild guesses. This, that, and the other thing about that far-off land. The Republic of California.

And then one day—the very same day Watly Caiper was busy interviewing for the job of host—the Skyfinders disappeared.

Nobody knew what happened. One day they were there, the next day they weren't. All gone. One woman left for her job at a sunbean deli and never arrived. One man went to the store for a bottle of cheap booze and never came back. One just never showed up for a regular breakfast date at a café. They all vanished.

Friends and relatives had no clues to go on. None. Except maybe the most obvious clue of all: what these missing ones had done. They had called themselves the Skyfinders and had met every Tuesday night. That was the clue: They had organized.

If you could have asked them—these friends and relatives of the Skyfinders—If you could have asked them one by one, late at night in their small apartments with the shades drawn, leaning close over one floating pinlight and sipping low-grade booze, they might have told you what they thought. They might have confided their *true* guesses: that the Skyfinders were eliminated. Killed and quietly melted down while no one saw. They had *organized*. That was a threat to those in power. That was dangerous.

People had been disappearing all over, all around, for years. It was usually the vocal ones, the ones who dared to raise their voices above a whisper. Recently, it was the ones who wondered a bit louder than the rest about California.

Watly knew little of this. The disappearances weren't publicized and he had no personal contact with those types. He'd heard a few rumors, but he'd ignored them. If he'd heard more, it wouldn't have mattered. It wasn't his problem. He had his own concerns. Send them all to the Subkeeper. This political stuff was of no interest to him. Leave that for people more like his mother had been. He was too busy. He had his hands full.

He was hosting for the motherhood.

CHAPTER 5

The room was white and sterile-looking. One corner was full of equipment. A large hanging metal bundle that looked like a prehistoric monster or some medieval dragon was the most prominent piece. Cables dangled from it in a tangle of poisoned tendrils. Everything was brightly lit and very well polished.

Watly Caiper felt out of place. He felt his own pitifully human body was grotesquely organic compared to his surroundings. He was . . . too *living*. He was lumpy and soft and unevenly colored and hairy and lined. He was porous and weak and dirty and constantly changing. He was not pure—not solid and shiny.

If I were made of steel or plasticore or even placene, if I were hard and full of angles, he thought to himself, *I'd feel much more comfortable here. This is not a place for people. Not a place for imperfection.*

Watly sat in the center of the room in an adjustable reclining chair with cushioned head and neck brace. It was a relaxing position, but he was anything but relaxed. He was in a small room on the fifth floor of the Alvedine building. It was a hosting room.

Just a few minutes before, he'd been unconscious. Since it was his first day as host, they'd had to do the initial implants. Watly arrived early but the doctors whisked him along and put him under anesthesia to perform the simple operation. Afterward, he was reassured that all had gone smoothly. The two creosan implants had been inserted behind each ear and the area resealed without a hitch.

Watly felt no pain or tenderness. The only physical hint that anything had been done at all was a slight tingling at the corners of his jaws. After the implantation, they'd sat him in this hosting room and told him he'd have a half hour of recovery time alone. Then the hosting would begin.

To Watly this "recovery time" did nothing but give him a chance to reintroduce the butterflies into his belly. It was not a comfortable sensation. Every so often his stomach would get so bad he thought he might throw up. Fortunately he didn't, especially because he saw no receptacle to aim his breakfast toward.

The queasiness and fluttering had been going on since early morning. He woke at five A.M., feeling really hinky, and was unable to go back to sleep. Skimming through the Alvedine Hosting Brochure didn't exactly help relax him. Uncle Narcolo was dead to the world. Small favors. Watly snuck out of the apartment silently and wandered around the Village until the daylites came on full. His mother had once told him the best thing for nerves was a long walk and a hearty meal. It might have been good advice once, but this time it didn't work. After a terrible sunbean breakfast on Houston, he headed uptown, feeling sicker and more nervous than ever.

Now, as he sat waiting in the firm recliner, his mind kept fixing on those two small implants. They did not affect him in any *physical* way, but the thought of them was still unsettling. The creosan wafers would only act as a receiver when activated—otherwise, the two were inert and undetectable. But Watly knew they were there. It bothered him. They were in his head and that wasn't a pleasant idea. *In his head. Inside*.

Maybe this whole thing wasn't a good idea. Uncle Narcolo had soured Watly's optimism some. The old guy had been so damn downbeat. He'd looked at nothing but the dark side. *If it wasn't for*

him, I wouldn't be so damn queasy, Watly thought. *Stage fright.*
Full-fledged stage fright.

If he leaned forward and turned to the right, Watly could see a
complete reverse-corrected mirror. It took up most of the side
wall. There was Watly Caiper looking back. "Hello, Watly.
Nervous? *Damn right.* Scared even? *No kidding!*" Watly was
wearing his usual outfit. He had on his brown veneer pants
(carefully folded by Narcolo the day before) and a clean pocket-
jacket with no shirt underneath. He was a study in chic
casualness—poverty style. Watly stuck out his tongue at the
reflection.

You're a fine-looking fellow, Watly. Tall, dark, and near to
handsome. A close second. If it wasn't for a slight crookedness to
the nose and that damn high forehead, you'd be just about perfect.
Well, a crooked nose showed character and a high forehead
showed brains. You're a prince, Watly. A prince among
paupers—or something like that. Anyone would be dumb to hurt a
body like that (and so damn well dressed!). It would be an act of
stupid vandalism. Irresponsible destruction of private property.
Now, come over here to the mirror, Watly Caiper, and kiss your
sweet gorgeous face goodbye—this may be the last time you get a
chance.

Watly pinched up his face into a tight little grimace to shake off
the notion. This was not the time to be a pessimist. Narcolo be
damned. This was his chance to make something of himself. *Be*
brave, Caiper. Be a person. Have some eggs, already.

The door folded open and an extremely dark-skinned woman
wearing all white walked briskly in. The contrast was incredible.
The all-white jumpsuit in an all-white room under the intense
lights canceled each other out. All that stood out was a deep brown
face and two deep brown hands floating in the bright void. She
smiled and Watly was newly blinded by a set of perfect teeth. He
felt love. Lust.

She held up the monitor she was carrying and clicked past
several of its screens.

"I see here you are Watly Caiper, first-timer. I'm Dr. Tollnismer, and I'm going to read you the List of Hosting Rights and
Regulations." Her voice was light and wispy. There was a

singsong lilt to it that reminded Watly of a child reading nursery
rhymes. She continued without checking to see if Watly was
listening. " 'Number One,' " she read. " 'You are a Host now.
You are a highly paid professional who has taken on a heavy
responsibility. We welcome you to the Alvedine Hosting Family.
Without you and others like you, there could be no hosting. We
thank you for your commitment and loyalty to our fine company.
We are confident you will live up to our reputation.' "

She glanced up blankly for a moment and then went on.
" 'Number Two. For each hosting you will be issued a coded wrist
hosting cuff. This will identify your donor. It will also inform any
general population member you contact that you are in the process
of hosting. It can be removed by neither you (the host) nor the
donor. If any crimes or infractions are committed during the
wearing of this cuff, you (the host) will not be held accountable.
If any serious injury or damage to your person occurs during the
wearing of this cuff, there will be a formal inquiry and the then
identified donor will be duly fined or punished if found negligent.
It is the donor's sole responsibility while the hosting cuff is in
place to use good judgment and common sense regarding the
protection of the host's (your) body. Of course, true accidents and
natural disasters are the exception.' "

Dr. Tollnismer paused to wet her lips carefully. Watly felt
another surge of love for her. Or maybe just lust. Or maybe just
fear's flip side.

" 'Number Three. Hosting is a limited process. The average
length runs five to seven hours. When your creosan wafers lose
the donor signal, the transmitter in the creosan will electronically
release the wrist cuff. You will not be able to relock it. Naturally,
at that point the host becomes responsible for his own actions,
both literally and legally. You must carry the wrist cuff and return
to your original point of departure (the Alvedine Hosting Building). Failure to do so will result in withholding of payment and
expulsion from the hosting program. You will be awarded full pay
only upon completion of the successful hosting and return of the
assigned hosting cuff.' "

The doctor paused once more and Watly waited eagerly for a
repeat performance of the lip-wetting. He was left disappointed.

" 'Number Four. We at Alvedine Industries put every effort into making the hosting process comfortable and interesting to both donor and host. It is, however, the nature of the activity that we can offer no guarantees. All donors are carefully screened prior to our acceptance of them, but we promise nothing. You are hosting at your own risk. In accepting a job as host, you are also agreeing to take no action at any time, legal or otherwise, against Alvedine Industries or any of its subsidiaries. This includes any action regarding the host's (your) demise.

" 'If by some fluke of nature the *donor* should pass away during the hosting procedure, Alvedine Industries shall use its best efforts to track you down and remove the creosan implants. Until that time the deceased donor's projection would be unfortunately trapped in the wafers. This is however, an unlikely occurrence.' "

Watly cringed. He'd never heard of it happening, and it was probably just a formality that they mentioned it at all, but it still wasn't a pleasant thought. Too weird to even consider. A nightmare scenario: Donor gets overexcited during the hosting process and drops dead of a heart attack or something. Host is stuck with a dead guy's personality in his head until somebody can track him down, identify the cuff, and remove the wafers surgically. A corpse's personality projection embedded indefinitely in Watly's brain. Yuck. Damn good thing the odds were against it. A pretty beanheaded thing to get hinky about, statistically speaking. In fact, odds were, if anyone was going to die during this catshit . . . *Ah, rape.*

The doctor clicked to a second screen. She looked somewhat bored, but her voice remained bright and childlike. Watly noticed for the first time that the whites of her eyes were as dazzling as her teeth.

" 'Number Five. At this time, as we begin final preparation for your hosting, we ask you to listen carefully. Take stock for a moment. Become conscious of all your physical sensations. You are now to relate to the doctor present any discomfort you might feel. If you feel any pain at all anywhere, or anything that could be *misinterpreted* as pain, let the doctor know. This is very important. You will not be disqualified for pain as long as the situation is treatable, but you *must* inform the doctor so that he may attend to the discomfort. The hosting process can be initially traumatic for the donor, and therefore your body must be as comfortable as possible when the donor enters it. Be thorough. After seeing to this matter the doctor will administer a mild euphoric. This will impart a gentle feeling of well-being. It is only temporary and intended to ease the transition. When the doctor is through, barring any difficulties, your hosting session will commence. We wish you the best of luck and thank you once again. Happy travels.' "

The doctor lay the monitor down on a white table Watly hadn't even noticed before. She faced Watly dead-on and crossed her arms. "Well?" she said, the childlike voice gone.

"Well, what?" Watly asked.

"Any aches? Pains? You heard the deal."

Watly smiled as ingratiatingly as he knew how. "Do you have a first name. Dr. Tollnismer?" he asked.

The doctor took a step forward and kept her expression deadpan. "You're changing the subject."

"I like the new subject," Watly said.

"Let's stay on the old one," she said with just the beginnings of another devastating smile forming.

"I'll answer your question if you answer mine."

The doctor's teeth began to show. "I'm not here to play games."

"I thought *everyone* was here to play games," Watly countered.

Dr. Tollnismer took a deep breath and let it out in a wispy sigh. "Okay, Watly Caiper. I'll answer yours if you answer mine."

Watly shifted in his seat to a more comfortable position. "Sounds good to me," he said.

"Promise?" she asked.

"Promise." Watly replied firmly.

"All right," the doctor said. "In answer to your question . . ." She stopped and her smile broadened. "Yes. Yes, I *do* have a first name." She paused and waited for Watly's response. He was busy making a sour smile. "So if that's *all*, Mr. Watly Caiper, I'd like you to answer *my* question."

"You're a pip, Doctor." Watly grinned.

She was back with her arms crossed and a look of satisfaction on her face. And what a face it was. It was almost as if it took this long for Watly's eyes to grow accustomed to the lighting contrasts. Her features were exotic and strong. There was something regal about them, something elegant. The skin looked so smooth and velvety Watly wanted to reach over and touch her cheek to see if it was real. But she was all business now.

"So. Any aches? Pains? Sore spots?"

Watly tried to form a witty reply but the doctor gave him a look that said the party had ended. *Play time's over.*

"Think seriously, Mr. Caiper. It's important," she said.

Watly pondered it a moment. *No pain here, ma'am.* Dr. Tollnismer stared him down. He closed his eyes and tried to become acutely aware of all the sensations he felt. There was nothing he could call a pain, but now that he thought about it, there was a slight twinge at the back of his right ankle. Also he felt a very, very slight soreness where Narcolo had squeezed his wrist. And of course his stomach still didn't feel great. And his neck felt just a touch stiff and maybe even his lower back and . . .

Watly listed everything he could think of for the doctor. As the process continued, he was amazed how many tiny points of discomfort a person could have and never really notice. To be alive, he supposed, meant to hurt. He continued on as specifically as possible until he ran out of discomforts. She seemed pleased with his honesty and carefully tended each complaint— temporarily numbing the individual nerves with what looked like a sonic device of some kind. Watly wasn't familiar with it. All this high-tech medicine was new to him. As a boy, the most common treatment had been a hug from Mom and some gentle rocking, with a song or two thrown in. As he grew older, expensive treatments were still out of the question. This was the closest Watly had ever come to a real hospital—not counting seeing them on the cable-vidsatt.

Dr. Tollnismer treated everything but the butterflies. She said the euphoric would take care of them. She followed the statement with another dazzling smile that made Watly weak. He wanted . . . he wanted . . . he wanted her to want him. And he wanted . . .

to touch that soft-looking skin—just below the cheekbone. And he wanted—real bad—to see what was under that all-white uniform of hers. He was sure she'd look real neat without it. Real neat. Fear seemed to heighten his desire.

"How about a quick one beforehand, Dr. Tollnismer?"

She kept smiling. "Not allowed, Mr. Caiper. And neither are you—if you read the pamphlet." She leaned close and Watly smelled a clean, powdery scent. "Besides, save some for the donor. That's the idea."

She turned and began fiddling with the equipment in the corner. After a moment she brushed her hands together and, almost as an afterthought, pulled a small shoulder bag out from behind the equipment. She handed it to Watly and motioned for him to put it on. He sat up and slung it over his shoulder.

"Don't tell me," Watly said. "The donor has some goodies he wants to have with him."

"That's usually the case," she said, looking preoccupied with the machinery. She nudged the hanging dragon-shaped thing and it glided easily forward. Removing two of its cables, she brought them to either side of Watly's chair.

"All set to go, Mr. Caiper. Now for the euphoric and your cuff."

Watly suddenly became aware that he was sweating in spite of the carefully regulated air. The back of his neck felt distinctly damp and his nausea was growing worse. Dr. Tollnismer ripped open the euphoric's package and stuck the pad to his forearm. She pulled it off after only a few seconds.

Watly wondered how long it would be before it took effect. He was still aware of his sweatiness, but it really wasn't bad at all. Not bad at all. Not at all. His stomach, in fact, felt fine. Just fine. Pretty fuckable. This was all going to work out fine. Fine. Yes, the beautiful, spectacular, gorgeous doctor took a long cuff from its wall mount and began securing it to Watly's wrist. Right wrist. The *right* right wrist. She was a real cutie. Potential poovus. And she was putting that cuff on *just* right. Not too loose, not too . . . uh . . .

It was a spectacular cuff. Colorful and intricately designed.

From the top of his wrist it extended out on a complicated hinge involving many tiny ball sockets to clasp the bases of Watly's two middle fingers. The body of the cuff itself was almost as long as his whole forearm. Watly had, of course, seen them before, but only from a distance. You couldn't go a day in Manhattan without seeing at least a few. He had never imagined they were so complex, though, and so carefully designed. It was a work of art. There was a fine layer of thin wires just below the surface forming curlicues, geometric designs, and other seemingly intentionally aesthetic shapes. If he stared at them, Watly could almost imagine pictures. A house. A flower? A sleeping cat. A foot? A breast. You could see anything you wanted in them. Lots of breasts. Brown breasts.

And of course the most prominent feature of all was the large cuff number. 9703. Each numeral was about two inches long and bright yellow. 9703. This figure represented whoever his anonymous doner was. It was, most probably, the only thing Watly would ever know about his donor. Of course, that wasn't counting any personality traits Watly picked up from watching the guy's behavior from the *inside*.

Oh, rape on a half shell.

Suddenly Watly felt dizzy. Dr. Tollnismer had finished locking the cuff on and was now adjusting the two cables. They held whatever position she moved them into. Watly thought maybe he didn't want to do this after all. Maybe he'd just like to go home and forget all about it. It struck him he really didn't know enough about all this. Too hasty, he'd been. Much. He needed more data before he could make an informed . . . Maybe he could still be a mother if he raised the money by . . .

At the end of each cable was a brass-colored rectangular plate. Dr. Tollnismer touched these plates to either side of his head—just behind his ears. They rested there gently, tickling a little right outside where the new implants were.

"Are you ready, Watly Caiper?" she asked. Her voice had returned to that lilting, childlike tone. It was intoxicating.

"I love you, Dr. Tollnismer," Watly said quietly.

The doctor let another gut-wrenching smile loose and patted

Watly on his high forehead. "And I love you, Mr. Caiper. And now it's time for your first hosting." She let her voice go to almost a whisper. "Don't worry, Watly. They always find a mild one for first times." She patted his cheek. "You'll be fine."

She turned to the hanging dinosaur and talked into its mouth. "Are you ready up there? Is the donor ready?"

Watly gave a start. *Up there?* It never occurred to him the donor was in the same building. It hadn't crossed his mind. It made sense, of course: Wealthy donor goes to Alvedine Building on Second Level. Meanwhile the first five stories of what really is the *very same building* are on First Level. How convenient. He'd never really thought it out. At this moment right above Watly was his donor. Maybe *directly* above him. Maybe just a few feet away. *Have a good vacation, big fella,* Watly thought. *And . . . make nice.*

Watly didn't hear any reply from the monster's mouth, but the doctor nodded into it and released three ringlets from its side.

"We're starting now, Watly. Here we go." Watly got the joyful impression she wouldn't have said that to just *any* host. He was special to her. She connected two of the loose cables and released another ringlet from its casing. It dangled freely. "I'm going for it now, Watly. Try to relax," she said.

Relaxing wasn't all that hard. The expression *mild euphoric* had been, perhaps, a touch understated. Watly felt a renewed tingling where his jawbone met his skull.

And then . . . then it started.

Watly Caiper felt the strangest sensation he'd ever felt in his life—horrifying and fascinating simultaneously. It was like some drug-induced distortion of perception. It began with the feeling of being removed—of being one step away. It was dreamlike, foggy. It felt to Watly as though he had pulled back from himself—as though he'd moved back from his usual place at his window to the outside world. His body seemed far away. Drifting off. He was smaller—shrunken down and receding into a corner within himself.

And then, while he receded as if down a long mental hallway, he sensed—he *tasted*—another coming in. From behind. A stranger coming in.

This mental hallway was confined—narrow and dark. The tingling sensation of another person neared and neared and neared and then brushed by him in the darkness. There was no feeling of it being another body, another full being. Not at all. It was a metallic taste, an antiseptic smell, an electrical feeling of another *consciousness* passing swiftly by. Nothing more came through. No sense of *who*, just the sense that it was an "*I*." A different "*I*."

Fear washed over Watly, and it seemed whatever euphoria had been there was now gone. He felt panic. He seemed to sink back farther down the corridor—farther and farther away from . . . *life*. Away from existence. And then this other being—this other person—was taking over. The other one was in charge. It was as if Watly had been pulled away and someone else had replaced him at the controls. All power was gone. He was impotent.

He wanted to at least *comment*. He wanted to say something—anything—but he couldn't. He had the words but no place to put them. It was like some insane nightmare. He couldn't even make himself twitch. He could see and hear clearly but it was more like seeing a monitor and hearing through a hollow tube. Echoey and astigmatic. Reality was at arm's length. He felt lost.

Whoever was in charge flexed Watly's right elbow slowly. To Watly, the sensation was almost familiar. It was similar to a trick he'd tried as a kid. Back then, he'd stood in a doorway with his arms straight down and pressed outward on the doorjamb with the backs of his hands. He pushed with all his might for a full two minutes. When he finally stopped and stepped out of the doorway, his arms spread upward like a bird's wings. It was totally involuntary—something to do with muscle tension. It made him feel strange and foolish, puppetlike. Out of control of his own body.

Now was worse. Now there was no control over *anything*. Someone else was telling his arm to move. This was no kid's game. Someone else bent that arm. Watly had no say in the matter. Watly didn't even have a say over which way to move his eyes or what to focus on. When to squint—to flinch—to twitch—to blink. Nothing. Watly wanted to scream. He wanted to bail out. *Where's the escape hatch? Dammit!* Nobody had warned him properly. Nobody had said it was like this. Five to seven hours of this? *I'll go mad*, he thought. *Worse than mad. I'll raping die in here. I want out!*

Watly felt his hands grip the armrests. His body leaned forward slowly. After a brief pause, Watly felt his body carefully stand up. And he had nothing whatsoever to do with it.

CHAPTER 6

Watly knew something of history.

Not a whole lot, but enough. Enough to fake it. Enough to think about, to concentrate on, and to ponder over. He'd learned some of it from the CV, some of it from books and leafs, some of it on keyboard, but most of it from stories. You'd always hear stories.

When he put it all together it was impossible for him to tell how much of the history he knew was true, how much was conjecture, educated guesses, and outright lies. And there were a lot of holes.

Nobody knew much about the time before Cedetime, about the time when it was called the United States instead of the United Countries. All Watly knew was that they fought like crazy, those "united" states. Economics, politics, laws, religion, medicine, the bomb, drugs, sex, everything. Mostly money, though. That, Watly knew, was always the bottom line.

They fought and they fought, and the government just got larger and more lumbering and more unwieldy and more out of control. So they started breaking the thing up; dismantling the bulging hulk. Everyone wanted to be isolated, separated, and in control of themselves. They formed their own little countries. Watly figured it was like Narcolo had said about the family. Everyone just wanted to be left alone. They pulled away from each other, and—most of all—they pulled away from the rest of the world. Away from the bigness of it all.

International trade and relations were just about cut off completely. Isolationism. The last straw was that Euroshima thing. Watly had no idea why they'd called it that—somebody probably thought it was catchy once.

But, whatever the name, it sealed the UCA up tight. People were fighting some war or other in the Outerworld and the United Countries of America was staying neutral. Then somebody dropped a bunch of big ones somewhere over there and messed everything up bad. Watly didn't know exactly where—somewhere in Europe or Asia or Affrika or someplace like that, or maybe all over the place. Maybe it was a couple little big ones or big big ones or maybe it was a whole pile. But it was a big mess. People dead, people sick, the air all over raped up bad. Euroshima. And the good ol' "You See of Aye" said, "Okay, that's it. Have fun. Play all you want. We don't want nothing to do with your boleholes." So we hung a big KEEP OUT sign, closed up shop totally, and let them be.

Some of the midwest UCA countries still had bombs and stuff, so, Watly supposed, that help keep the Outerworld from messing with us. That, and the fact that those countries got protection money from the other ones, and that there were all kinds of complicated treaties and contracts tying us UCA folk together. But that was about as much as Watly knew of it. You never heard anything much about the Outerworld growing up in Brooklyn. And Watly sure hadn't heard anything consequential about it so far during his one month of Manhattan. Hard enough to hear news of *Brooklyn* on the island country.

Manhattan was a special country. Watly knew more about *its* history than Brooklyn, even. No other UCA country, as far as he knew, was bi-level.

The development of the bi-level system was not a planned one, the stories said. No one ever sat down and designed it that way. It was never laid out on some blueprint. Referenda and polls and votes were never taken. No, Watly had heard that it grew all by itself. It evolved not long after Cedetime. There was some disagreement even among the historians Watly had read on keyboard, as to how it all got started. The general consensus attributed its inception to Walker Gavy, real estate baron.

Mr. Gavy was a wheeler-dealer. They say he devoured plots of land like another person would eat a meal. Gobble, gobble. Each day enormous areas of the island country would change hands, and they almost always passed through Walker's hands first. At one point he owned a large piece of prime real estate in mid-Manhattan. It was a Fifth Avenue section in the fifties, and full of very profitable retail businesses. He'd been holding on to it for some time. One day, one of his many lackeys made an off-the-wall suggestion. A crazy suggestion. Gavy liked it. He never turned down an idea that might yield a profit, and this idea sounded good to him. He began work on the project right away. The central concept amounted to nothing more than a glorified mall. It was a way to attract more businesses, more people, and—he hoped—more money.

The idea was to build a second "street" five stories above the first. This higher street would be for pedestrians only and would be accessible through numerous elevators. New stores and other businesses could be put in up there. Where there once had been only windows and ornaments and ledges and air conditioners, Gavy would cut out doorways and install elaborate storefronts. So that the lower level wasn't too dark, he designed the upper street with a center strip of clear glass to let sunlight down.

They say his many critics had called the project absurd. Walker Gavy never denied it was absurd—not at all. The point was, he thought it would work anyway. And it did. After changing a few zoning laws, fighting a few noisy groups and associations, and greasing more than a few palms, Gavy built a small "sample area." A couple of shops and restaurants, far above the maddening crowd. Yes, it did work. It worked fabulously. People flocked to the area as much for the novelty of it as anything.

An embryo had been concieved, or a fungus, or perhaps a cancer—depending on one's viewpoint. Watly thought of it as a

fungus. Whichever, the idea caught on and others tried it and
added to it. It seemed a good investment to many, and so it
continued. Second Level expanded. People hardly noticed any
change, though it was not all that gradual. In just a few years, 25
to 28 A.C. or so, large areas of the city became bi-leveled. It was
unpopular among the rich and the powerful (usually one and the
same) to live in the lower or "dark" level, as it was called. No
matter how many glass panels or gratings in the upper level, the
lower was still largely in shadow.

As more and more of the city was covered, the technology
involved progressed. The upper "streets" were reinforced and
braced to handle private vehicles. A somewhat primitive (by
modern standards) system of suspension support poles was set up.
The idea of permitting sunlight to pass down to First Level became
impractical and was abandoned. Artificial sunlight (daylite) was
tested and eventually installed throughout the First Level. These
lights supposedly mimicked exactly all healthful qualities of real
sunshine, though Watly had his doubts. In addition, they were
timed to three convenient brightnesses: bright for day, half power
for evening, and low for night. All the comforts of Sol. The
exhaust fans and intake ducts were added. Gradually, First Level
was literally being sealed up tight.

It became more and more difficult to travel from one level to
another—or at least from the lower to the higher. Identicards were
issued and checkpoints instigated. Those in control decided to
limit the number of "undesirables" permitted above. First Levelers had to have an approved reason to go up to Second Level.
Eventually virtually no reason was approved, except for the select
few who worked up there. And most of the labor in Manhattan,
though done *for* the Second Level, was done *on* the First.

The rich succeeded in isolating themselves almost completely.
If the CV was any indication, their world was clean, bright,
uncrowded, and crime free. A beautiful environment for the
beautiful people. Watly figured that this boringly serene existence
was probably a prime motivation in the creation of hosting: the
restless rich seeking safe excitement. In any case, there was a
sharp contrast between life above and life below the "fifth-floor
line."

The First Level was overpopulated and dirty. Ironically, expressions like "the lower classes," "the underclass," and "below the poverty line" took on literal as well as figurative meanings. People were poor down below. Those who couldn't find space indoors moved to the streets and sidewalks. Tenting became popular. Tenting was considered just a short step above bumming, even though many tenters had jobs. A tenter had to be ever prepared to pick up and move on a moment's notice. The police would often shift them around arbitrarily.

Then there were the roofers. They fell on the social scale somewhere between tenting and apartment dwelling. These were people who'd set up a house or shelter on the roof of a building that was four stories high or shorter. Quite a few Manhattan buildings had less than five floors, so there was a lot of space between their roofs and the Second Level "ceiling." Some of these roofers set up quite elaborate homesteads up there. Others were just glorified tenters.

The Second Levelers would give an occasional nod of the head to those below in the form of repair or maintenance. But more often than not, those below had to fend for themselves. If the "upperfolk" did help with a problem, it was only when they foresaw it affecting *their* lives adversely. They would repair and maintain decaying buildings when it affected the stability of the upper floors. When escaping odors became a problem for them, the Second Levelers funded public W.C.s on street corners and an extensive garbage disposal and air filtering system. It appeared they were free with money as long as it was in their own interest to spend it. But if the people needed something on First Level that had no impact on Second, those above did nothing.

A perfect example was the underground. Years before, the subs were called the lifeblood. No more. As time progressed, they decayed and corroded, gradually falling apart. Eventually they broke down altogether from neglect. The upperfolk had no interest in repairing them. Why should they? They left them to rot. Over many years the barren tracks and filthy tunnels became home for the worst sort of person. Criminals of all kinds gathered there. Murderers, rapists, thieves, muggers. It was the last outpost for humanity's rejects. An island-wide hideout for sociopaths. The police wouldn't go down there. Even the toughest and most streetwise of First Levelers never ventured below. Eventually, First Level authorities brought military personnel in and held a massive cleanup. The system was purged. The criminals were flushed out in one bloody massacre and all of the sub's entrance-ways were sealed. It was over. Done. Since no one went down there, nothing more was heard, but the rumors and tall tales continued. Stories circulated of an evil subculture that still existed below. "Go to sleep, Tinny, or the Subkeeper will get you!" "Eat your food, Mesipi, or I'll send you to the Subkeeper." Watly had heard these fairy tales all his Brooklyn childhood. As time went by, the underground was all but forgotten. The fairy tales were all that was left. Transportation for Firsters was either on foot, on bicycle, or on the occasional bus. A good subway system would have been welcome. But Second Level said no, and Second Level was the boss.

The flip side of the bean was Central Park. Unlike the subways, the upperfolk *wanted* it. They wanted it bad. It was their style. As construction spread, those in charge realized something drastic would have to be done. Already people were complaining that the park was "down there with the dirty ones," and how unfair that was. Meetings were called. Further construction was delayed. At first they were going to build their own elevated park above the real one, but the logistics were too complicated back then. A few trees here and there up above were easy, but this was too much. And too damn expensive. Besides, Second Level wanted the *real* Central Park. It was a matter of principle.

So they took it. They claimed the park. Central Park became the only place in Manhattan where Second Level dipped down to First. Starting around a half block away—all around the park—the upper streets sloped down to the lower level. If Second Level was thought of as real land, then Central Park was its green valley. They built a gentle incline all around the park down to its level. Of course, it therefore became inaccessible to First Level people. On First Level, the result was an angled ceiling in those areas, narrowing to pointed corners where bums slept. And no park. Watly had visited the park's edges when he first moved to Manhattan. It was cramped and claustrophobic, not a nice area at all. This was to be expected. This was the way of the world. The way of Manhattan, the island country.

It was said—said quietly—that at various points in time attempts were made to liberate the Second Level. There was nothing about it in history lessons. No one taught it in school. Nothing on the CV. But Watly had heard the stories: Attempts were made. And failed. Failed real badly and real consistently. It may have been propaganda or it may have been truth. Who was there for Watly to ask? But there *were* stories. The tubes were stormed, they said. Uprights and girders were bombed. Hostages taken. Riots and rebellions. Violence. Uprisings. *Unrest*. Maybe even Revy. But it never worked. None of it. They said nothing like it ever *could* succeed. And, if these things really happened at all, Watly knew they had only resulted in stricter security and tougher laws. Crackdowns. Punishment. Discipline. Execution. Actions against the bi-level system were useless. Against the greater good, and all. So it was said. And Watly believed it, or—more accurately—he accepted it.

The upperfolk always had a favorite response to unhappy Firsters: "If you don't like it, you can leave!" It was hard to argue with. You *could* leave. No one was forcing anyone to stay on First Level. Not at all. In fact, it was always much harder to get *into* Manhattan than to get out. Getting in was complicated and required all kinds of approval. But you could always leave the country easily. No problem. Few did. Manhattan had the money. Manhattan had the jobs—what there were. Those above had wealth and power—investments and businesses in various countries all across the UCA. And if any of that money was going to trickle down, it seemed logical that it would trickle down in Manhattan.

By and large, people were resigned to their station on the island country. They knew their places, high and low. That was the history. In spite of obvious inequities and an almost comically literal split between the classes, the levels of Manhattan kept lumbering along. To Watly the extreme opposites of Manhattan's parts somehow balanced into a functional—if uneven—yin–yang symbiosis.

Over those early post-Cedetime years, the bi-level system

continued to grow. And it continued still. Watly knew Second Level, even now, had not reached capacity. There were still areas of construction way uptown and a few places on the West Side. It would be years before all of the island was completely covered. So the building continued. On First Level, people could always get a job in construction. The pay stank and the injury rate was high, but the work was steady. And in the back of most everyone's mind, like a fairy tale wish, was the dream that they might somehow, in some way, make it to Second Level. Watly recognized this wish even in his own uncle. It was an almost universal First Level dream. Work your way up, save your way up, win the Level Lottery, or whatever. It was the carrot. It was all that kept some people going. The dream of Second.

That and, lately, something new. Something about California. Whatly had heard that something happened in the Republic of California. Maybe . . . maybe something *worked*. Maybe things *were* possible. Maybe change was in the fetid wind.

CHAPTER 7

Euroshima. Cedetime. The bi-level system. Walker Gavy. Central Park. The subs. Ah, yes.

Watly just let his mind wander on all this. It was a good way to kill time. He'd mentally covered just about all he had ever learned about history. Reviewing it. Modifying it. Even letting himself think about California. Just a little. It was calming to let his thoughts drift. Relaxing. Every so often a claustrophobic sense of helplessness crept up on him, but now he seemed able to control it. It was all a matter of mental control. Concentration. As soon as he felt the beginnings of panic he would force himself to mentally explore some subject or other. The more complex the better. This distracted him whenever the reality of the situation was difficult to accept.

The reality of the situation at the moment was that his body was leaning casually against a girder on East Fifty-seventh Street. His eyes were scanning the pedestrians who passed by. Occasionally, his left hand would swing over and hang on his right wrist, as if trying to surreptitiously cover the hosting cuff. *The donor must be self-conscious,* Watly thought. *People do tend to look at our cuff.* It was like a big sign that said, I MAY LOOK LIKE ONE OF YOU FOLKS, BUT I'M NOT.

They had been standing there, host and donor (Watly and the Stranger), for almost half an hour. They were only a block from the Alvedine Hosting Building. There was a rag store, a laundry, a used clothing store, and a CV repair shop on the street opposite. Some guy was on the corner trying to sell broken buzbelts—quite unsuccessfully, it appeared. The Stranger just gazed at all this lazily. Watly wondered when things would get started. *Perhaps it's the first time for the other guy, too,* he thought. The humor of that did not escape him. Two virgins.

A police cruiser passed and the donor focused on its taillights until it disappeared around the corner. A few cats streaked across the street. More people passed—on foot and bike. The donor inhaled and exhaled slowly. Things were not exactly hopping right along here. Not that Watly was complaining. He'd just as soon it continued on like this, thank you. So far the hosting had been surprisingly uneventful. The most frightening moment yet had been one of the first.

After slowly and shakily getting to his feet, Watly's donor had trembled for a moment while Dr. Tollnismer looked on, and then carefully tried to take a step. It didn't work. Watly's right foot did not behave as the donor apparently had expected, and the already precariously balanced body flipped forward, head first. To Watly it seemed to happen in slow motion. As the floor came closer and closer he tried everything he was accustomed to doing to break his fall. Of course, nothing worked. His body wasn't responding. It was like a pet who'd stopped doing tricks. The floor neared. Watly let out what he would later call a thought-scream. It had no physical manifestation but, at least mentally, Watly was screaming insanely—hysterically. The floor kept coming. Just before Watly's already slightly crooked nose would've been mashed beyond recognition against the tiles, his donor clumsily shot both hands out to break the fall. It was an awkward, last-minute attempt, but prevented serious damage.

There was no movement for a while.

"You all right?" It was Dr. Tollnismer's voice coming through.

"*Fine.*"

Fine was just one word. It was a simple word. No big deal. Four letters. One syllable. Unfortunately, it was still enough to send Watly into another period of mental hysterics. Yes, it was his mouth; and yes, it was his tongue; and yes, of course, that was his voice—but, subs help us, that was someone else telling it what to say!

Dr. Tollnismer was checking Watly's body over for any damage. The somewhat distanced sense of her hands gently examining him was soothing and helped calm him. He could still smell her powder scent when the donor inhaled. There was another smell in there too. Something baser and more primitively female.

"If you want to use the bathroom, the W.C. down the hall will be just fine," she was saying as she worked. "That W.C. will be just fine."

What was that all about? It struck Watly as a somewhat odd statement. What did going to the bathroom have to do with anything? He'd just gone a short while ago. It was at that moment Watly noticed how much concentrating on some mental problem helped to relax him. If things got out of hand, Watly discovered, you just needed the willpower to focus on an absorbing topic. Think narrowly.

The doctor had finished checking the body over and helping them back into the chair.

"To be sure the process was completed properly," she said, "I'm required to ask you the password."

"*Bluebird,*" Watly felt himself say.

"Ah, very good. Welcome, donor. I'm sorry about your first few moments in this body. I'm afraid you tried to stand too quickly. As you know, sometimes it takes a while getting used to balancing." As she talked there was a slight hint of distaste in her voice and expression. Her eyebrows turned up as if mildly disgusted. Her words were unfeeling, mechanical. Little crinkles around that broad brown nose made her look as though she smelled something unpleasant, sour. Watly felt hurt and rejected until he reminded himself that she wasn't talking to him. Not at all. She was talking to the donor. It was apparent to Watly that she didn't like donors. He felt a renewed sense of closeness to her. She was on his side. She was a fuckhead.

"To your right," she was saying, "is a reverse-corrected mirror. I'd recommend you take a few minutes to acquaint yourself with the body. Take it slowly—it won't take long to get the feel of things. If you need any help, just yell—I'll be nearby. If not, when you're ready to go, turn left outside the door and follow the yellow arrows. I hope you enjoy your hosting. Remember, take your time standing up and walking for the first time." Suddenly the disgusted look lifted from her face and the Dr. Tollnismer Watly liked best showed herself. She smiled warmly. The teeth flashed, glaringly white. "Don't forget," she said. "That W.C. will be just fine. Just fine."

Again the strange bathroom topic. And then it hit Watly. W.C.—Watly Caiper! She was talking to him! Him alone! She was giving him a secret message! *You're gonna be okay, Watly Caiper,* she was saying. *That W.C. will be just fine.* Watly felt a surge of joy. He felt almost safe for a second. She kept talking, her features relaxed. "In fact, on reconsidering, I may avail myself of its services after all." Her smile broadened. If Watly could have smiled back, he would have. And then he would have kissed her. And whatever else came to mind.

The fixed mask of disapproval returned to the doctor's pretty face. "I'll leave you now," she said curtly. "Again, if you need anything, yell. And *donor*"—Her eyes blazed for a second—"be careful, would you?"

Dr. Tollnismer walked quickly from the room.

With some difficulty, the donor swiveled the chair to the right and Watly found that his eyes were carefully scanning his own body in the mirror. Whoever the donor was, he used Watly's vision differently than Watly himself would have. The focus jumped from one part of the upper body to another. Shoulders, chin, ears. . . . The movement was at times so rapid it was dizzying. This was not how Watly looked at things. After this somewhat frantic overview, the eyes inspected Watly's face in minute detail—traveling along lips and lashes and cheekbones— and spent a long moment on the somewhat receding hairline. Then the eyes moved on. Watly felt a brief feeling of embarrassment and shame. *I'm sorry the hair isn't perfect,* he wanted to say. *I've always had a high forehead, but I find if you brush it forward, you can camouflage it a good deal. . . .*

By now the donor was not only looking, he was gently moving—poking, prodding that, flexing this, wiggling his jaw, raising his eyebrows, and generally "breaking in" Watly's body. Watly realized he had nothing to be ashamed of. Right now the body was as much the donor's as it was Watly's. No—*more.* "Buyer beware," and all that.

The body sat forward in the chair and Watly felt his donor *very* carefully ease toward its edge. The donor was being much more cautious about standing this time. No more pratfalls. After about five minutes of extremely slow edging, Watly found himself standing upright.

It did not take long for the stranger to get "land legs" once standing. Whoever it was held the arm of the chair for support and took a few cautious steps. It was amazing to Watly how differently the donor used his body. Things Watly had always taken for granted—the set of his shoulders, the angle of his head, the swing of his arm—all these things were slightly different now. The donor used Watly's whole physical being differently. Totally. Watly's body was an instrument being played by a different performer with a subtly different style. It was eerie. Watly could even feel that the muscles of his face were set in an unfamiliar way. His brow felt tight and strained as if stretched from either side, and his bottom lip was bent in slightly and seemed to be trying to grip hold of his teeth. His lower back was overly arched and his head tilted down a bit. From the outside he probably just looked like good old Watly Caiper. From the inside it was obvious someone foreign was in charge. Very obvious. Watly felt another wave of vertigo and panic approaching. He tried to shut it out by concentrating. *Concentrate, Caiper! Concentrate! Think narrowly! Now, what's this donor fellow up to? Come on, Caiper—pay attention!*

Watly became aware that the donor had developed an enormous erection and was now uncovering it for inspection. The panic attack subsided as the removed-Watly watched his own genitals come into view. Well, well. The donor turned to the mirror and unashamedly inspected the rigid organ from every conceivable angle, giving it a few hardy—almost painful—tugs for good measure. The erection was one of those super solid ones Watly usually connected with the loss of virginity or the beginning of an affair or maybe even a bloated morning bladder. It was so hard it practically hurt.

The humor of the situation was enough to quell any last vestiges of the attack Watly had felt. Here he was, Watly Caiper, floating around powerlessly in his own head while his body was being mentally aroused by some unknown person. The farthest thing from Watly's mind was sex, but there bobbed Watly's own penis in contradiction. *Down, boy.* Whoever this donor was, he seemed pleased with the alotted equipment and, after playing with it a bit more, replaced it under cover of the veneer pants where it still bulged noticeably. *I have a feeling,* thought Watly with a mental smile, *that this guy plans to have sex. Call it a wild guess.*

The donor spent a few more minutes alternately staring into the mirror and walking up and down on his new legs. He seemed to be getting the hang of it rapidly. There was still an awkwardness and tentativeness to his movements but it was lessening. At first every action involved with walking had been overexaggerated to the point of some distorted military march with the knees being raised way too high. Gradually, the donor gained more control. It wasn't graceful, but it no longer looked and felt as foolish.

Meanwhile—as the lump in his pants receded—Watly continued to ponder the erection. The idea of it. His erection. *Their* erection. Who's erection had it been, anyway? Whose penis? He'd never viewed his own sex organ in such a removed fashion before. There had always been something intrinsically *important* about the little fellow. It was his. Yes? It was a part of him—an extension of his personality. A manifestation of his private sexuality. But no. Suddenly it was just another one. Another schlong aimed skyward—aimed to the Second Level. It could have been *anyone's.* In fact, for the time being at least, it wasn't Watly's at all. It was the donor's penis. And it was the donor's face. And the donor's hands. And the donor's high forehead and crooked nose. The body is, after all, just a thing. *We are not our physical beings,* Watly realized. He'd known it before to some degree, but it had never *really* sunk in until now. The body is a shell. The body is a vessel. We are merely the "I" inside. (Inside for the moment, at least.) And even our most private parts—or our most public—are still not "us." They are just another "it" that can, it turns out, be transferred. Thus the principle of hosting. It was all the principle behind hosting. Obvious, perhaps—and yet it just then solidified for Watly.

He made up a little something—a chant or mantra. It was just a few simple phrases, but Watly took comfort in them. He concentrated and repeated the words mentally. Thinking narrowly.

> *The me is not the body.*
> *The me is not the body.*
> *The me is neither hand nor face nor sex.*
> *The me is Watly Caiper, I.*
> *(A sense of self.)*
> *The body is an it.*
> *The body is a that.*
> *It could belong to another.*
> *For the me is a movable thing.*
> *The me is a movable thing.*

Watly had repeated it then over and over. He somehow found solace in it. He ran through it again and again as his donor finished assessing and breaking in. He continued the chant as his body left the building with cautious steps, following the yellow arrows. Dr. Tollnismer—the lovely and wonderful Dr. Tollnismer—was nowhere to be seen on the way out. Watly broke his concentration for a moment to hope she would be there when he returned. *If* he returned.

> *The me is not the body. . . .*

And so here they stood, donor and host, Watly and the Stranger. They were still leaning against that same East Fifty-seventh Street upright, occasionally covering the hosting cuff with a casual brush of the hands. Watly had gone from acute awareness of his situation, to his mental chanting, to reciting history, and back to awareness again. Hard as it was to admit, he was actually growing bored. Who knows how long they'd been standing there. The donor seemed quite content to lean back and watch the First level world go by through Watly's eyes. Occasionally he'd fix his borrowed vision on a passing rear end or thinly covered bosom. Both sexes were ogled. Again Watly would sense a twinge in his donor's rented genitals and an unfamiliar tensing of the groin muscles. The fellow was hot to trot. *All right already—let's get on with it*, Watly thought. *Don't be a chicken!*

At that moment, the donor leaned forward from the girder. The movement was so abrupt Watly at first thought the donor had heard his thinking. But no. There was a wall between them. It was an impenetrable mental shield. They had a sense of each other's presence but nothing more. In fact, Watly was at the advantage in this department. At least he had the donor's behavior to go on. The donor had nothing but the body.

Watly realized they were turning and had begun to walk swiftly. The donor's pace and footing were strong and sure now. After a few blocks it became clear what direction they were heading. Watly and the donor were going southwest—into the heart of sexsentral.

CHAPTER 8

It took Watly's donor only a few minutes to walk from that girder on Fifty-seventh to an entrance into sexsentral. They headed rapidly down Sixth Avenue, wending through the thickening crowds. During the short walk, Watly wondered if he should feel happy for the change of scenery, or nervous about what might happen next. He settled on an uncomfortable combination of the two.

Watly had never been in sexsentral. In his one month of Manhattan living he had avoided the entire area. It extended from the Riverwall on the west over to Fifth Avenue, and from Fiftieth Street down to Twenty-third. Of course, there was some spillover into other neighborhoods, but that was basically it.

A rusty old banner announcing the zone stretched from upright to upright above them as they entered. There was an abandoned guard box standing to the left of them as they passed under the banner. It looked like someone had made the box into a home. Watly knew there were banners across ever street and avenue that entered sexsentral. Now ENTERING SEXSENTRAL, they said in glowing red letters. NO ONE UNDER PUBERTY PERMITTED. In the old days, the police had enforced that. There would have been guards posted in the boxes, ready to check for authentic pubic hair on anyone who looked too young. Now, it was just silly. Watly couldn't remember the last time he'd seen someone who looked under twenty-five, let alone near puberty. There was no need for guards now.

Entering sexsental was like entering a different country. The crowds were much heavier, but there were no tenters at all. Gaudy signs and drifting floaters of increasing explicitness became more prominent overhead. Watly's donor had to duck more than once to avoid them. Some of the floaters had lost their program and never been repaired. These bounced about overhead out of control. Mangy-looking cats scattered as Watly's body approached. Street vendors sold porn and high- and low-tech sexual devices. A lot of the daylites had been vandalized or shot out, so the lighting was sporadic. One got the feeling of a perpetual evening lighting setting. Lots of hosting-cuff-wearers meandered by. This made Watly feel better. All around him he could see others with trapped consciousnesses inside—consciousnesses praying fiercely that theirs was a wise and gentle donor. A donor with a lot of luck. Naturally, the area was bustling with men and women who didn't have cuffs, as well. Some locals and some probably from outside of Manhattan on visitor's passes. Sexsentral was a very popular place and attracted all types.

Watly's donor went quickly past the crowds near the Rockefeller Center area and cut across Forty-eighth Street to Seventh Avenue. On the corner of Forty-seventh and Seventh was an enormous bar called The Prick. The door to the saloon was shaped like some generic thick-lipped human orifice. Vagina or sideways mouth—hard to say. Probably vagina. Every ten seconds or so a gigantic phallus the size of a bus came thrusting out of the opening onto the street. The donor stood staring at it for a moment, obviously taken with the display. Watly was equally impressed. It was an incredible effect. The phallus was very realistic. It must have been made of some kind of heavy-duty neoskin. The doorway was flexible and would bow outward slightly with each lengthy thrust.

The donor watched for a while longer as a few customers went inside. They were not having an easy time of it. To enter the saloon, one had to wait for the phallus to withdraw and then, at just the right moment, dive through the hole. Watly supposed that if you missed you'd either be shoved outward or crushed against the side of the opening. Dicked to death.

Watly's donor stepped forward and approached the entrance. It was apparent he intended to go inside. *I hope your reflexes have improved,* Watly thought. The donor's eyes tracked the huge thrusting organ for a few moments in what seemed like an attempt to gauge the timing. In-out. In-out. Standing that close to the gigantic display gave a strange impression. It felt to Watly as though they were all inside an enormous woman. Inside a vagina, looking out. The street, everyone here, Manhattan *itself*, were being screwed. And not very delicately. *We are being raped, not fucked. This is not a niceness, this is a nastiness.* That was probably the effect intended, Watly realized. And then Watly felt his body leaping into the almond-shaped doorway. It was an awkward, sideways dive—flying out of the womb—both arms outstretched, hands fisted. They landed with a thud on a hard metal floor and felt the blast of air as the penis sped behind them. *Cleared it by a mile,* Watly thought. *That's my donor!*

In the next few hours, Watly's donor—and by association Watly—had three strong shots of booze, two women, and one man. Quite an afternoon.

The same-sex sex had thrown Watly. When his donor had purchased a male's services, he had mentally cringed. In principle it was fine with him, but he was troubled by the approaching reality of it. Watly had always been comfortable with his heterosexuality, but he wondered if what his body was about to do would somehow compromise that. Was this some kind of threat to his masculinity? His straightness?

Apparently it was a very common thing for donors to try. Though not illegal, among the upperfolk homosexuality was considered bad form compared to straight sex. It was not officially sanctioned. It was accepted and ignored up there, as long as one did not engage in it openly or admit to it publicly. Very First Level kind of behavior, don't you see. So naturally, anyone on Second

Level who was so inclined would give it a shot while a donor, so as to keep his/her reputation intact. Watly had been prepared for this. On some level, he'd expected it. He'd felt a tad hinky about it, but he'd expected it. And, as it turned out, the experience was not as devastating as he'd imagined. It was actually quite mundane. Boring, even. Though not aroused by it, Watly certainly didn't find it sickening. It was just another body and another empty sex act. The smell of sex, the heavy breathing. One more sweaty person and one more sweaty climax.

The me is not the body. . . .

The straight sex was no better. Watly thought his donor's technique was surprisingly unimaginative. He found himself mentally coaching. The donor's style was rough and simple. There was no joy involved. *Don't be so serious. Have fun with it!* Watly wanted to say. *This isn't supposed to be work. This is play. Slow down, fella.*

It was remarkable how differently the stranger used Watly's body—especially at a time like this. There was an awkwardness to the movements, an extreme clumsiness, and an almost brutal aggressiveness involved in the whole act. Beginning to end. It was all about genitals and nothing more. *Look at her face, my friend. She's pretty. Look into her eyes. Kiss her. Inhale her. Make some kind of contact. You don't do this to her, you do this with her. See her. Celebrate the sex. And look! Breasts! Aren't breasts wonderful?* But the donor kept his borrowed eyes closed and his face buried in the pillows. Eventually Watly gave up the cheerleading and let his mind drift away. He settled, finally, on an image of Dr. Tollnismer and her brilliant smile.

Watly sensed each physical orgasm as if it were far away and belonged to someone else. After all, it was and it did.

The donor had paid for sex with the man and the first woman. Watly had glimpsed a huge pile of bills in the shoulder bag as his own hands pulled out payments and tips. The second woman had not been a professional. No money changed hands. She and the donor had engaged in a sexsentral "layperson's lay." With so many different types out seeking pleasure, this was not uncommon.

After the drinking and the sex, Watly's donor rode the big prick out of The Prick and began to wander the streets of sexsentral. It was dripping heavier than it had been earlier. Had Watly been in charge, he would have pulled out a hat for protection, but he really didn't mind going without. The donor didn't even know Watly *had* a hat, having never checked the pockets. Oh, well. If the donor didn't mind getting dripped on every few steps, then neither did Watly. Find and bolehole dandy.

The booze had left Watly slightly light-headed, but fortunately not drunk. When the drinking first began, Watly had had another panic attack. *Don't get us drunk, my friend. Please keep your head. Our head.* But the three drinks spread over time (and a lot of bouncy-wouncy) had only loosened them up a bit. Watly had been deeply grateful the donor hadn't gone further. That could have been dangerous. The moderation probably hadn't been out of any sense of responsibility. No, more likely the donor hadn't wanted to jeopardize his sexual gymnastics. Three times in as many hours could sometimes be difficult enough sober. As they walked, Watly wondered if maybe this hosting would be wearing off soon. It must have been over four hours already. Maybe it would end shortly. Maybe he'd get out.

The thought of being free soon—of being in control again—gave Watly another powerful spasm of claustrophobia. *Think narrowly, Watly.* He pulled his mental reins and started the chant.

> *The me is not the body.*
> *The me is not the body.*
> *The me is neither hand nor face nor sex.*
> *The me is Watly Caiper, I.*
> *(A sense of self.)*
> *The body is an it.*
> *The body is a that.*
> *It could belong to another,*
> *for the me is a movable thing.*
> *The me is a movable thing.*

The donor was heading west to a more desolate area of sexsentral. He seemed to be wandering aimlessly. Killing time. Looking for action.

There were fewer daylites in this area, and those that did work were in bad disrepair. It was obvious no one—person or machine—had been around to clean in a while, if ever. The streets were filthy and there were piles of garbage in huge drifts against some of the buildings. Wild cats were everywhere. A few floaters careened wildly overhead, bouncing against buildings, girders, against the dark, corroded-looking ceiling, and against each other. There were hardly any other pedestrians in the area. Unattractive people of both sexes (and some in-between) stood in the shadows of doorways and whispered, "Sets! Good sets! You wanna have sets?" as the donor passed. When they were a few steps behind they'd yell up ahead to their associates, "Hosting comin' up on ya! Cuffer comin' up with a bag!"

Watly was getting hinky. They were on Forty-fourth Street approaching Eleventh Avenue. This was not the best of neighborhoods. *Don't get any stupid ideas, donor. How about we turn back?*

Watly became aware that his body was sweating and his breathing was shallower. At first he thought it was his own fear showing. Then he realized it was the donor. The donor was scared. Or was it excitement? It was hard to tell. The two emotions had similar manifestations. Watly saw the dark street zip back and forth as the donor began scanning rapidly. The eyes blurred some.

"Cuffer comin' up wit' a bag!"

"You wan' sets, mister?"

"Hey donor! Wan' some sets cheap?"

"Low-tech sets right here on the street? I make you happy good."

An unmanned copper whizzed by, going too fast to do anyone any good. Watly's feet kept walking. *Where are you heading, you sofdick beanhead?* he thought. *You want to get us killed? At least try to cover the cuff. And the bag.*

"Donor moving up on ya!"

"Sets?"

Just when Watly thought the donor might reconsider the dangers of the neighborhood, they turned and headed down an alley that was even darker than the street. A few shadowy forms moved about up ahead. The donor squinted but kept on. To the left and right were more piles of garbage and pieces of scrap metal. Chunks of broken cemeld lay in powdery mounds. The shadowy figures moved closer. Soft mewings of a new litter came from some far corner.

"What you got inna bag, cuffer?"

"The bag for some sets?"

"You a pain-freak, donor?"

Watly felt trickles of sweat dribbling down his back. Still more drops came down his forehead and stung his eyes. Whatever the donor was feeling, the guy was feeling it strongly. *For rape's sake, don't turn into a pain-freak on me, fella. I like excitement as much as the next person—dangerous neighborhoods, strange characters—but I've had my fill today, thank you.*

Watly was on the verge of another chant recital when his donor tripped over a pipe and fell head first into an oily puddle. There was a soggy splash. And thump. Watly was temporarily stunned. Nothing seemed to be seriously hurt. Then there was a frenzied sound of footsteps rushing forward and within seconds Watly could tell they were closely surrounded. Lots of them. A terradamn crowd. The shoulder bag was violently ripped from his arm.

Watly's donor turned and half sat up, leaning on one arm. Watly's eyes slowly scanned the faces. All around were strange and frightening people. They wore tattered clothing in browns and blacks and grays, but all had extremely ornate makeup on. Bright splashes of abstract shapes in vivid colors covered each face. Masklike. Most of these creatures were of indeterminate gender. They looked dangerous—coiled. Behind the paint they had hatred in their eyes. They seemed to be waiting for Watly's donor to make a move—any move at all. One of them was ripping open the shoulder bag and spilling out what remained of the donor's money. It looked like a lot—thousands, maybe.

"Well, look here, girls and boys. Mucho dinero. Look at all this, will you? Isn't that nice."

The one speaking turned and looked directly into Watly's eyes.

"What're we gonna do with you now, huh? You like this stuff? You a fade-out? You a pain-freak? You've got Second Level eyes, fella. I can tell. I hate them Second Level eyes. You want me to take those eyes out?" He/she opened a long blade that looked well worn and squatted in front of Watly's splayed body. "You want me to take 'em out?"

Watly could feel the donor try to clear his throat and move his tongue. The mouth was bone dry. No sound emerged. The person with the knife leaned forward. The knife's heavy plastic handle was stained a dark color and there were flecks of something brownish dried on the blade itself. The point was just a few inches from Watly's face, hovering there, swaying gently back and forth. Watly's donor seemed frozen in position, going cross-eyed staring at the chipped metal.

A piercing female voice cried out back at the mouth of the alleyway.

"The Ragman!" she yelled. "The Ragman's coming!"

The crowd surrounding Watly turned to look. The one with the knife backed off. Watly could hear mumbling and whispering.

"The Ragman. Ragman comes here?"

"Here he comes!"

"Here comes the Ragman!"

There was respect—almost reverence—in the way the group pulled apart to let the short, dark figure pass through. Watly's donor kept his eyes glued to the man. The Ragman. He was bearded, stocky, and only about five feet tall. His eyes were dark and his skin smooth and free of makeup. He wore clothes similar to the others, but here and there—at a seam or torn edge or wrinkle or cuff—tiny points sparkled and glittered like gold or brass. His eyes held them. Held them all. There was a charisma to the man, an intensity you couldn't quite put your finger on. He seemed brighter, somehow. Lit from within. The Ragman approached.

"What's going on here, Tavis?" The voice was deep and resonant. It was the voice of a superior—a commander.

The one with the knife spoke up. "Nothing, Ragman. Just a cuffer with a wad."

The Ragman looked at Watly and then down at the pile of

money. He turned back to the other. "You were gonna knife him, huh, Tavis? Gonna knife him up good?"

"I was thinking that, Ragman." He/she held up the blade. "Yes." This Tavis creature appeared to have the shadow of facial stubble under the thick makeup, as well as an obvious swell of large breasts under the dirty rags. The voice sounded too deep for a woman, yet too high for a man.

The Ragman knelt next to Watly. "You a donor, mister?"

Watly heard his own voice respond. "Yes, I'm a donor." The accent that came out was definitely Second Level.

The Ragman looked Watly's body up and down. "You realize we're gonna take your money?"

"I realize that."

The Ragman glanced at the hosting-cuff. "You a fade-out?"

There was a pause. Watly thought he'd die. *Answer the man! Tell the truth!* "No, I'm not a fade-out." *Thank you for that response, my friend.*

"You a pain-freak?"

Again a pause. *Please,* thought Watly.

"Not really, no."

The Ragman turned to the others. And to the one he had called Tavis. "You were gonna hurt him. Kill him, maybe. Look at his shoes, children. Look at them. Never forget the host. Never forget. Somewhere in there"—Ragman gestured to Watly's head—"is another person. Watching us right now. You've got to judge the host as well as the donor. This host is one of us. You can tell by the shoes. Those are class-one poor man's shoes. The pocket-jacket's used. The hands are working hands. You don't hurt a cuffer till you judge the host. The host could be you. Look at the face, children. It's the donor's expression but the host's face. The face is one of us."

Watly felt his donor prepare to speak again. "Then you're not going to hurt me?"

The Ragman stood and turned away. There was a pause and then he spun, reared back, and kicked Watly full force in the thigh. He threw his whole weight into it and it tumbled Watly's body over on its side. The crowd roared with approval. There was laughter. Watly's donor grabbed the leg and grimaced with a pain

Watly shared. The whole leg felt like fire. Searing pain. The Ragman leaned in and the donor cringed with fear.

"I'm sorry to the host," the Ragman said, breath close. "I'm sorry to the one inside. It was for *you*, donor. It was a lesson to you. The pain is real. The pain hurts. Tomorrow the host will have a bruise and you will not, but you will still have the memory of the pain. Do not take the idea of pain so lightly. I see in your eyes you don't like it. You're no pain-freak. Next time don't be foolish."

The Ragman straightened. Suddenly he seemed the tallest one there. "Again, my apologies to the host, but you are not beyond lessons yourself. There is a softness to your features that tells me you were not made for this. A good host is hard. Reconsider your occupation, child." The Ragman reached down and touched Watly's forehead with a warm palm. His voice grew soft and Watly was mesmerized by the beauty of it. There was compassion and lightness to it. "Some say I have the sight. I do. The sight is mine. It is how I've survived this long. The sight tells me things. Of you, the host, it tells me pain. More pain than this. Much. A thousandfold. And death. Death all around. Blood will come. Be apprised, child."

The Ragman swiveled dramatically on one foot and left the alley. His strides were long and fluid. They seemed out of place on such a small figure. The money was gathered up by Tavis and the crowd quickly dispersed.

Host and donor, Watly and the Stranger, slowly rose and limped out of the alley. Two blocks later there was a tingle in the jaw, a click of metal shifting, and a loud clatter as the hosting-cuff fell to the street.

Watly was free.

CHAPTER 9

When Watly Caiper finally arrived home at Uncle Narcolo's apartment that night he was more than a little tired. He was beat. He was weary. He was at the point of physical and mental collapse. He was badly bruised and very stiff. And he was shook up. Real shook up. But . . . he was Watly Caiper and Watly Caiper alone. And he was alive and without major injury. For those things he was truly grateful. (He was also grateful for the eight hundred in New York dollar bills and the balance of nine thousand in titled and untitled credit pieces stuffed deep in his pocket-jacket.)

"That you, Watly? Good to see you. Good to see you. I'm making a pie for dinner tonight. A big pie. High in protein and full of good things. This and that. But that's not all, Watly. Oh, no. There's more than pie for us. More than pie. Lots of things, kiddo. But it's a heavy pie, Watly, so we mustn't spoil it with too many extras. Can't fill up too much. It's almost a stew pie—you might call it. But not really."

As usual, the apartment was spotless. Narcolo Caiper had kept up his well-earned reputation for cleanliness. At the moment he was racing around the kitchen as usual, doing his cooking ballet. Watly smiled, enjoying the sensation of controlling his own muscles, and crossed over to the couch, limping slightly. He sat down heavily and put his feet on the table. Rape, he was tired. Everything ached. And that damn leg. . . . But it was nice to be home. It felt safe. Comfortable.

"Could you turn on the cable-vidsatt for me, Uncle?" Watly said without energy.

Narcolo looked up. "Oh, no. Oh, no, Watly, not the CV tonight. Not now. First off, the damn thing's half broke. Never been fixed. Everything comes on cockeyed and fuzzy. The mist goes crazy. No, no. No CV. Secondly . . ." The old man paused and his features went soft. "Secondly, I gotta ask you how you are. You've had a big day, kiddo. You've had a big one. I was worried. I was a little worried, you know? I want to know—I want to know if you're okay. Are you okay, kiddo?" Narcolo's face looked pained. He seemed to be bracing himself for the bad news.

"I'm okay," Watly said with some effort. "I'm fine. Tired but fine."

Narcolo's face lit up. "Oh, that's good. That's good to hear. I was worried sick about you, Watly. Worried sick. I feel—I feel bad about the other night and all. I feel real bad. I was a sofdick bolehole. I was a beanhead." He turned the stove down and rounded the counter to Watly's left. "The thing is—it's just that . . . point being . . ." Watly saw a tiny splash of wetness under each of Narcolo's eyes. His uncle's throat seemed to catch before he could continue. "It's just that I feel responsible."

Watly tried to lift his head but he felt too weak. Emotionally drained. Physically drained. "You're not responsible, Uncle—"

The old man jumped in. "Oh, but I am! I am. Weren't for me you wouldn't be here—it's true! In fact it was my idea in the first place—this hosting thing. My idea. You wrote me—remember? Asking your big-time uncle if he had any ideas how you could be on the road to motherhood. And like an idiot I wrote back. 'Watly,' I said. 'Watly, you come here to Manhattan. You stay with me. I'll vouch for you. Come to the big time. Manhattan's where the money is,' I said. 'Maybe we could get you a job hosting,' I said. I remember saying it—like I was some big shot with connections. Well, I didn't have no connections, kiddo. I was never a host or anything. Sure, I worked for Alvedine. Sure. I was a terradamn *clerk,* I was in *records,* for subsake. I was a nobody. So I really didn't know nothing." Narcolo's hand worked the front of his shirt into a tight ball. "I thought you'd come here and . . . and keep me company and after a few tries at Alvedine admissions you'd give up. I thought you'd settle in and get steady work—construction, maybe. We'd have a ball, you and I, kiddo. Maybe if . . . maybe if, you know, I won the Level Lottery— silly, I know—but maybe we'd move up together. You know?"

Watly leaned forward. "I appreciate that, Uncle. I do. And, to tell you the truth, I'm not sure I ever thought I'd make it myself. It was a surprise to me."

Narcolo Caiper began to pace back and forth in front of Watly. "I know you think I'm a crazy old man, Watly, and I'm sorry. It's just I don't want to be responsible. I don't want to be responsible if you get hurt."

"I haven't gotten hurt yet," Watly said. "Not really."

"You did *one hosting.* And I'm proud of you. You did good. You look okay. Tired but healthy." He stopped walking and turned to face Watly directly. Watly noticed the old guy had missed a few spots shaving. There were little tufts of gray hair on his chin and neck. "But that was just *one.* Just one hosting. You never know what happens next, kiddo. You were lucky so far. I don't want to be responsible. I couldn't live with that."

"Uncle—"

Narcolo cut him off, his eyes clear and honest-looking. "I couldn't live with it, Watly."

"You are not responsible!" Watly was getting angry and he felt renewed strength in that. Narcolo was pissing him off with all this fear. He didn't want to get angry at this old, lonely guy, at this "family," but there it was. It was nice that his uncle cared. It was nice that his uncle worried. But this was too much. This was getting silly. "Who made you responsible?" Watly said, his voice coming out louder and more forceful than he'd intended. "I came to Manhattan on my own power, Uncle. *I* signed the waiting list at Alvedine and waited the month—*me. I* stood in line all day. *I* got the job. I *accepted* the job, Narcolo, *me*. Just me. You helped me out—that's all." Watly slowed and took a breath, trying to regain his composure. Sometimes talking to his uncle felt like talking to a child. Maybe that was part of the appeal. Maybe that was one of of the reasons he felt so close to Narcolo. He was a shriveled old child. Sometimes giddy and out of control, sometimes whiny and tantrum-prone. A surrogate infant. Watly's baby substitute.

"I'm grateful, Uncle," Watly said soothingly. "I thank you. I love you. I appreciate your concern and all that, Uncle. But it's not your fault *or* your responsibility!"

Narcolo Caiper seemed to weaken and his shoulders slumped. He looked deflated. A major pout seemed imminent. His small frame sagged inward. "How much did you make today, Watly?" he asked.

Watly pulled the cash and credit pieces out of his pocket and scattered them over the table. His arms felt tired, almost numb. "Just what they said I'd make. Ten thousand minus the advance."

Narcolo looked at all the money for a moment. "That's a lot of money, kiddo. A lot." The pout disappeared. There was some of that giddy, childlike excitement washing over the old guy that Watly liked to see. But this time it wasn't particularly welcome. Watly was tired. Watly had been through a lot. He had no baby-sitting energy.

"Listen, Watly," Narcolo said, almost giggling. "Listen. That's it, okay? No more. Take your money. Go back to Brooklyn if you really want—and put it in a saver or a bank. Pack it in now, okay? Or stay right here—you're welcome, you know. Live well for a while—you've earned it. You could spend quite a while living pretty high with that kind of money, Watly."

In spite of the fact that his uncle looked so cute and vibrant again—full of hope—Watly felt himself getting really furious. He wasn't even certain why. There was a sudden tightness across his chest. He tried to contain it. *Why is the old man fighting against my dreams so?* "That's not the point, Uncle," he said. "Not at all. I need a lot more than that to do what *I* want."

"Why?" The old man's expression was vulnerable and boyish.

He seemed to be begging, pleading for the right answer. For the answer he wanted to hear. "Why do you want this?"

Watly sat up on the couch and looked directly into his uncle's eyes. They were still moist, reflecting the dim light. "Didn't you ever have a dream, Uncle? A passion? A . . . a *reason*?" Narcolo turned and avoided his gaze. "Didn't you ever have something that you wanted so bad it became the focus of your life? Didn't you ever have something that you wanted so bad that the wanting *itself* became the . . . the definition of who you are?" Watly pulled his feet off the table, knocking some of the credits off. "Well, if you didn't then I'm sorry. I'm very sorry. If you didn't, you won't understand. But if you *did*—even for a moment—if you did, you might know what I mean. Maybe getting to Second Level someday is like that for you, I don't know." Watly stood up, ignoring the vicious protests of his leg muscles. "I want my own child, Uncle. I want to be a mother. To raise my own. That's what I want. That's *all* I want. You know better than I that it wasn't too long ago, old friend, when that wouldn't have been much to ask for. But now you have to fight for it. And I'm willing to do it. Call me an egoist if you want to—and maybe that's part of it . . . maybe I want the glory, the little 'me' running around. Or maybe there *is* such a thing as a 'calling.' Maybe there *are* a chosen few. Either way, its my only goal, Uncle—and you're not going to talk me out of it." Watly tried to catch his uncle's gaze. "It's all there is."

"How many mothers do you know, Watly?" Narcolo said softly, his eyes lowered. "How many children? Not counting the CV, when was the last time you saw a mother or a child?"

"It's not an easy thing to be, Uncle—I know that. I know the odds."

"What *are* the odds, kiddo? Do you know? There are kids on the CV. Watly, there are kids all over the CV. But those kids are on Second Level, Watly. They're all on Second. That's where the money is. The antiprophies *alone* must cost fifty thousand."

Watly was getting even more frustrated with Narcolo. He was *tired*, terradamnit! Real tired. "You're not telling me anything I don't already know, old friend. Why do you think I'm hosting? For my health?"

"Fifty thousand, Watly. You'll die before you reach half that amount. Things could happen."

"And a bus or cruiser could run me down tomorrow," Watly snapped.

"I'm not gonna tell you what to do, kiddo." Narcolo sighed and then cleared his throat slowly. It sounded full of gravel. "All I'm saying is to use your head. Why does it cost so much to have a kid, Watly? Why all the expense? Figure it out. Think on it. *Think*. They don't *want* you to have a kid, Watly. Send me to the Subkeeper if I lie. They don't want us to procreate, to . . . to *breed*. They're letting us die off. Second Level can have all the kids they want. The upperfolk. But we're overpopulated, Watly. We're dirty and smelly and we take up space. There are too many of us. And now—to top it off—we're grumbling. We're making them nervous."

Narcolo let out a phlegmy cough. "Do you honestly believe, Watly, that if, by some fluke, some incredible luck, you *got* enough money for the antiprophies, and you *got* a willing female who could pass all the examinations, and you *got* enough money to pay her, and you *got* a chance at the licensing test, and you *got* enough money to take the test, and you *got* enough money for the mothering license—do you honestly think they'd let you pass it? Honestly? They're trying to thin us out, man. It's obvious. Someday . . . someday, when they need more lackeys or cops or servants or . . . paperweights—I don't know —someday, they'll let a few of us have kids. Or maybe they'll just send down a few of their extra ones."

Watly wasn't accepting this conspiracy theory. This was modern talk. California gossip-type talk. He waved his uncle's words away, but the old man continued.

"Let me finish, Watly Caiper. Most of the world is First Level. *Most of the world*. Literally or figuratively, it doesn't matter. Take yourself. Take your hometown. Brooklyn was all First Level, right? You could see the sky above, but you were 'First Levelers'—true? Of course it's true—"

Watly broke in. "We were poor, yes. But there were those who were certainly—"

"You were *First Level*! All of you! They're thinning us down,

Watly. All of us. Too many of us is a threat. That was the whole idea behind prophies. I'm convinced of it. If prophies were just started because of too much of *all* populations, why charge so much for antiprophies? Poor people can't afford them. Why not just have a test or something? Answer me that! I'll tell you why. It's because prophies are not for the rich and the powerful. They can buy antiprophies at the drop of a hat. They can. Second Level is full of babies!"

Watly sat back down, feeling more exhausted than ever. His leg throbbed. Next the old man would be talking revy, at this rate. "I don't buy this stuff, Uncle. It's not my concern."

Uncle Narcolo stepped in closer. His eyes glistened once again. "You have a nice little dream here, kiddo. It's sweet and warm and cozy and I love you for it. I do. But it's just a dream. It's a fantasy. You want fantasies, move to Jesusland. Kiddo, maybe it's time you grew up."

Watly let his head drop backwards. *Who's telling who to grow up?* "What is your *problem*, Uncle?" he asked wearily. "Even if I'm wrong about everything—even if I can't do anything I plan on—the absolute worst thing that could happen is I make a pile of money hosting and have to figure out another way to spend it. Big raping deal."

"No, Watly." The old man sounded sad now. He looked like he'd lost all hope for Watly. "No, the worst thing that could happen is you die. Or worse than die."

Watly didn't have a reply for that. He gazed up at the CV and wished to the subs he'd turned it on long ago. It glistened dully under the single light. Narcolo was staring at him. He looked like he was trying to see clear through Watly's skin to his insides.

"You're going to do it again, aren't you Watly?" Uncle Narcolo said with resignation. "And there's nothing I can say to stop you. Isn't that right?" Narcolo coughed and waited for an answer that didn't come. "Well, you can't blame me. Can't say I didn't try to stop you," he mumbled.

Watly pretended not to hear him. He said nothing. The old man crossed to the armrest and leaned against it. "When's the next hosting, Watly?" he asked.

"Tomorrow night," Watly said curtly, feely edgy and cranky and too tired for all this catshit.

"Night?"

"Seven P.M. Tomorrow night."

There was again a flash of that fear and worry on Narcolo's face that was quickly becoming a major annoyance. The old guy seemed about to say something, but he stopped himself. After a pause, he spoke. "They do it at *night* now, Watly?"

"Apparently." *Go away, old man. I'm too tired to talk anymore*, Watly thought to himself.

"They didn't do that when *I* worked there. I never heard of it. I don't like the sound of it, Watly—"

"I don't care *what* you like, Narcolo!"

Neither of them spoke for a few moments. The only sound was a slight clicking as the stove expanded from its own heat. Watly wanted to apologize for snapping but he couldn't bring himself to do it. He glanced at Narcolo. *I'm sorry. I'm sorry*, he thought. Uncle was just being uncle. Just being family. Caring, and all.

The old guy was dry-eyed now. He was staring blankly in the direction of the kitchen area. Finally, Narcolo wet his lips and spoke. "I've burned the dinner once again," he said quietly.

Watly didn't move. "Uh-huh," he said.

Both of them stayed where they were. "Ah, well," said Narcolo. "Probably would've been a bust anyhow."

Watly gave his uncle a thin smile. He wasn't hungry anyway. All he wanted was sleep. All he wanted was to relax. It had been one mighty long day. And tomorrow probably would be, too. *Ah, well*, he thought, *another day—another ten thousand dollars*.

To himself, he secretly hoped this hosting business got easier as it went along. To himself, he was not looking forward to doing it again. To himself, he was scared. Nighttime hosting did not sound all that pleasant. He was nervous about it. Real hinky. It didn't feel right—though he wasn't sure why. Night was, of course, a dangerous time to be out—but that wasn't all. *He'd* never heard of it either. Watly was worried. Real worried. Perhaps it was just fatigue. Perhaps it was just nerves again. Perhaps it was the fact that his first hosting hadn't exactly been the most comfortable experience. Or, perhaps it was the feeling deep in

Watly's abdomen. Perhaps, it was that that silly, stupid, ticklish tingle in his gut that seemed to say tomorrow night might be the last time Watly Caiper would ever host.

Watly lifted his bruised body and went into the kitchen. Once again he would try to help Narcolo Caiper salvage dinner.

CHAPTER 10

Watly slept very late. There were nightmares, but he couldn't remember them. Something to do with flying. When he finally got up it was more like lunchtime than breakfast and, true to form, Uncle Narcolo was fixing up a meal for them both. It smelled fabulous, spicy and rich. Perhaps *this* food would make it to the table unburned.

Watly went to the bathroom and washed up in the basin. He was still tired and stiff. The water felt good. He moved slowly, luxuriating in the soaking sensation. He splashed the water liberally over his face and let it run down until it dribbled off his elbows. When he was done, he left the tiny bathroom and flicked on the CV. He was not an avid watcher of the cable-vidsatt, but on a day like today it was a good way to kill time. It also helped avoid conversation—and avoid thinking about how he'd be hosting again in a mere six or seven hours.

Narcolo's ancient CV system was in real bad shape. It hummed loudly for a full minute as the receiving mist filled the room, and the image finally appeared it was blurry and lopsided, hovering somewhere near the couch's left armrest. Watly tried another format. Now the image was cleaner but more tilted and closer to the windows. It was livable. He cleared the board and started on the first pleat. Pure static. He went on. The next three pleats were all the same: a special all-day pornathon. Watly went swiftly past pleat five out of embarrassment—it was interactive and he wasn't dressed yet. The next few were comedy and music hall. Then more static. Then old movies in pre-dee format. Then serious sex. Finally he hit on an all-news pleat. He dropped the arm in place to lock it in and sat down.

. . . early today, which our handsome Chancellor called "heinous." It's the third "heinous" this week. The Chancellor likes the word and will probably use it again. It is suspected he may use it while negotiating new trade agreements with the neighboring countries of Jersey, Longeye, Pennyork, and the Noreast Commonwealth.

There is word of continued fighting in the Outerworld. A number of people killed, a number of people not, and a number wounded.

In the local front: Corber Alvedine, president and founder of the world famous Alvedine Industries—the company that brings joy on so many levels—announced today his plans to run for office. "I plan to run for office," he said.

And now, the News Song-Singing Segment:

News, news, news, news,
We're newspeople.
We're newspeople.
Paving a shining way.
We're newspeople.
We're newspeople.
Greeting a brand-new day.
Sing a song of information.
Sing it loud and clear.
Bursting with communication,
Every day this year.
News, news, news, news . . .

And now the local sex news:
The new ratings are in, and experts say low-tech
sex is on the upswing. In the forefront . . .

Watly turned and saw that Narcolo had silently laid out brunch for him on the coffee table. The old man was eating alone in the kitchen area, facing the wall and humming to himself as he chewed. There was some adorable sulking going on there. Watly smiled inwardly. He wanted to break the tension between them—to say *something*—but thought better of it. *Let things cool down a bit more, Caiper. You need a rest.*

The food smelled and looked delicious. It wasn't burned this time. Somewhere in the aroma Watly smelled sunbean, but it was heavily disguised. Narcolo had coated the dish with a high-gloss gel for looks and garnished it with tiny sprigs of some green vegetable. It tasted wonderful from the first bite. Best meal in days. It felt good to fuel the system. Watly could sense his strength coming back with every swallow. His body had been through an ordeal and the long sleep, cool water, and good food helped ease aches and pains. Of course, his mind too had been through an ordeal. But aside from feeling slightly fuzzy around the edges, he was calm and alert. The body was the important thing.

Watly took inventory. He was definitely up for tonight's hosting. Aside from a few cuts and scrapes—and the big, painful bruise on his leg where he'd been kicked—he was in decent shape. Probably the most discomfort came from the sore muscles. That first donor had held Watly's body so very differently that every joint now ached slightly. But it wasn't bad. He'd made it through his initiation hosting in one piece. One bruised, traumatized piece, maybe, but a piece nonetheless.

He watched more CV, jumping the pleats whenever he got bored. The hours passed quickly. Watly said nothing to Narcolo and Narcolo said nothing to Watly—at least nothing directly. There was a lot of mumbling coming from the old guy as he cleaned up the apartment all around Watly. An occasional "Well, don't blame me" could be heard clearly.

Watly finally got ready a short while before his hosting time. The pocket-jacket was still slightly damp, but the veneer pants were completely dry. He'd come to think of them as his hosting clothes. Narcolo had washed the oil and dirt out of both the night before. Scrub, scrub. They were hung on a makeshift wire clothesline in the bathroom. Watly took them down and put them on, butterflies filling his stomach rapidly again. A generalized feeling of hinkiness that he'd been able to control all day suddenly wasn't as easy to repress. The CV probably hadn't helped. He'd had too much of it for one day. Too much news songs, music hall, and porn. And the whole apartment was cloudy with stale CV mist. His mother, of course, would have disapproved. He'd watched for way too long by her standards. "Cable-vidsatts are chains," Pepajer Caiper would say. "They control the people. They poison their dreams." She had not been a fan. But Watly had wanted some mindless entertainment today. He'd thought he'd needed it. But maybe he'd overdone it.

Watly found his shoes near the bathroom door. Narcolo had apparently cleaned them as well. He must have quietly taken a brush to them in the early morning before starting to make Watly's brunch. Scrub, scrub. *Good old Uncle. Why did I have to snap at him so much?*

Narcolo Caiper was sitting reading a leaf in the corner chair. Watly walked over to him and gripped his shoulder.

"I'm going now, Uncle," he said. Narcolo glanced up. He looked pained and nodded solemnly. Watly smiled. "Help yourself to the money, okay, fella? Most of it should be yours anyway."

Narcolo made a sour face. "Peh!" he said. Watly turned to the door but the old man's voice stopped him. "You be damn careful, Watly Caiper. *Damn* careful. Hear me, kiddo?"

"I will, my friend. And . . . I'm sorry about the—"

"Just be *raping careful*!"

Watly closed the door quietly behind him, smiling.

It was a little early to be leaving, but Watly felt like walking. He was also eager to see Dr. Tollnismer again. When he'd returned last evening from his first hosting, she had still been there, looking as radiant as before. Watly himself had been a bit worse for the wear after his sexsentral experience. They'd spoken briefly.

"Here's your cuff back," Watly had said as he dropped the heavy thing on one of the white counters.

She looked at him with surprise and then honest concern. "You look a bit of a mess, Watly Caiper. Are you okay?"

"I'm dandy."

"You're tired, huh?"

"I'm more than tired."

"But you're not hurt?" She looked worried.

"No, not really. I'm a little sore here and there, but nothing too much. I'm still in good shape." He winked broadly. "And I'm still devilishly handsome."

"You're also in the wrong room," she said with a smile. Those incredible teeth again. Her eyes—sensitive and intelligent, shiny.

"Wrong room?"

She nodded. "You're supposed to return the cuff to the cashier downstairs and then pick up your new assignment at the front desk."

"No kidding?"

"No kidding." The doctor turned her head to one side and squinted. "But you knew that, didn't you?"

"Who, *me*?"

"You just brought your 'devilishly handsome' face up here to see me, didn't you?"

"Now that you mention it . . ."

"You go right back downstairs, Watly Caiper, before you get us both in trouble. And don't forget the cuff." She herded him toward the doorway.

He walked backward reluctantly. "When will I see you again?" he asked.

She picked up the cuff and plopped it into Watly's outstretched hand. "You'll see me again when you host again, Mr. Caiper." There was a shy pause before she went on. "Soon—I hope." She gave him her most brilliant smile yet.

Watly stopped at the door. "I'm either suffering from total exhaustion . . . or I'm in love."

"Get out of here, Caiper." She gave him a playful shove. "Oh, and Caiper . . . it's Alysess."

"Huh?"

"Alysess Tollnismer, M.D."

"Glad to know you." Watly had tried to shake her hand but she'd already closed the door on him.

And now, as he headed uptown toward Alvedine for his second hosting, he could hardly wait to see her again. Alysess. As each moment passed he seemed to feel stronger about the woman. He hardly knew her at all but she had somehow become important to him. Very important. Thump-thump heart important. Maybe it was just sex. Just lust. Just those hidden brown breasts he wondered about. Or maybe there was something else. Her vibrancy. Her life. Her . . . name? Alysess. Pretty name for a pretty woman. Poovus material.

There was barely any dripping at all so Watly kept his hat off. He felt good. Aside from an ache or two he was fine. This was going to work out. Things would go his way. The air around him seemed fresher and he was getting almost giddy over the idea of seeing Alysess. Perhaps they could talk awhile before the hosting started. The night hosting.

It was the time of day when most people were going home from work rather than to it. The streets were bustling with activity. Half-filled lowtrucks were being pulled by swiftly, their pullers practically jogging. Bums were accosting all who looked like they had a buck. Watly had taken a little of his money with him and handed a few New York dollars out when the fancy struck him.

The daylites went to half with an abrupt click. Everyone paused for a second to let their eyes adjust and then continued on. It was a pleasant evening. Some of the tenters were cooking meals on the sidewalk with heat-em-ups. Hardly anyone wore a hat. Bicyclists rolled by lazily. Watly allowed himself the luxury of wondering what the weather was like. What the weather was *really* like. He imagined it warm and with a gentle breeze. The sun would be just touching the horizon and everything would be golden. For a moment Watly wanted to run away. He wanted to forget his silly dreams. He wanted to sprint to the Hosting Building, grab Alysess by the wrist, and run off with her. They'd keep on running and running until they saw the sky. The real sky. Then they'd stop and make love under it. And when they were done they'd make love again. And on and on. And then they'd talk. They'd hold each other lazily and talk. Get to know each other. Each other's dreams. As the wind blew and the night grew cool, they'd go to a place where no one had ever heard of Alvedine, or hosting, or money, or Second Level, or being a doctor, or being a mother. . . . Being a mother.

That was the thing.

That was the thing.

Ah, well, sometimes it was nice to dream a different dream, even for a moment.

Watly picked up his pace and bounced along on the balls of his feet. Hosting wasn't all that bad.

It all depended on the donor.

At Alvedine Industries Watly was surprised to find the front doors locked. For a second he thought maybe he'd made a mistake. He searched the pocket-jacket for his assignment slip. It had, unfortunately, gotten washed along with the jacket. Watly found it in a soggy ball in one of the bottom pockets. It was still legible and Watly spread it out against his knee.

Assignment Slip

CONFIDENTIAL TO WATLY CAIPER
FROM ALVEDINE INDUSTRIES
Next Hosting Assignment:
TOMORROW, SEVEN P.M.
(evening)

Report Alvedine Hosting Building

There it was. No mistake about it. Watly turned and tried the doors again. They were all locked. He peered through the glass. The reception area and cashier's station were dark. So were the front hallways. Everything looked closed up for the night. Maybe his assignment had been a typo. Maybe it was supposed to be A.M. But then, it actually had the word *evening* written in. Funny. Night hosting.

Watly walked back down the steps and looked at the building. Maybe for night hosting they had you enter through the cuff-return door. The cuff-return entrance was open twenty-four hours.

Watly rounded the corner and saw the lighted floater indicating CUFF RETURN HERE. What the rape—it was worth a shot. He pushed through the door.

"Watly Caiper?"

There was a tall blond-haired man standing just inside the entrance. He wore the standard all-white doctor's uniform and held a monitor. He was very pale—almost sick-looking.

"I'm him," Watly said, a bit startled.

"You're the night host?" the man asked. He hadn't yet looked at Watly directly. His eyes were focused distractedly over Watly's shoulder.

"That's me, I guess."

The man turned and started down the hall. He was halfway down before Watly realized he was expected to follow the guy. Watly had to trot to catch up.

"Sorry about the front door, Caiper. They closed up early today. Good you figured out how to get in."

"I'm a little confused. . . ." Watly said. He was having trouble keeping up with the other man. "Is the building closed for the day? What's the story with night hosting?"

The tall man stopped abruptly and faced Watly. He seemed suddenly furious. Dangerous. "The world does not revolve around you, Mr. Night Host. Some people have regular hours. Most of the workers go home at five. We only keep a skeleton crew here after that. Any other problems?"

"Take it easy. Take it easy. I was just curious." Watly wondered if there *was* a right side of the bed for this guy to get up on.

He kept his mouth shut as they went to the fifth floor. Watly's tall companion was taking the exit route to fifth, so, since they were entering and not leaving, all the arrows faced them as they walked. Yellow, red, and blue arrows pointed backward. It was strangely ominous. It seemed to Watly like a big sign saying, GO BACK, WATLY CAIPER! GO AWAY!

Nearly comical. Nearly.

The tall blond man was slowing and Watly could now keep up easily. He headed toward the same hosting room Watly was used to. Watly followed, relieved they hadn't changed rooms on him. Relieved it was Dr. Tollnismer's room again.

When the man folded the hosting room's door open, Watly could see there was no one inside. Just the chair, the metallic dinosaur, and the other accoutrements of hosting. No person. No Alysess. No white smile. No smart eyes. No poovus.

"Where's Alys— Where's Dr. Tollnismer?" Watly asked. He was still standing in the doorway, not sure he should enter. The blond man was already at the white counter, fiddling with a cable. He glared up at Watly.

"*What?*" he snapped. He was daring Watly to repeat the question. Daring him to admit to even having *had* a question. *Oh nothing, Mr. Nasty Paleface, I said nothing at all. . . .* That was the proper response.

Watly took the dare instead. "My, uh, usual doctor, Dr. Tollnismer . . . she's not here yet?"

The man sneered. He must have been roughly Watly's age but there was something jaded and dead around his eyes. And that pale, almost cadaverous skin. . . . "I'm your doctor today, Mr. Night Host. Tollnismer doesn't work nights."

Watly felt his stomach grab up on him. No Alysess? *It's okay, Caiper. No big deal. You'll catch her next time. Better to concentrate on the hosting anyway. She'd be a distraction. You're getting obsessed about a beautiful stranger.*

Watly stayed in the doorway. After a while he forced himself into the room and sat in the recliner. He felt a twinge in his leg where the bruise was, so he shifted sideways. Damn, but that Ragman guy had kicked hard.

"Finally decided to join us, huh?" the blond man said, and crossed over to fold the door shut. "Let's get this thing over with." What was all that nastiness covering? Fear? Was the creepo *afraid* of something? He pulled a hosting-cuff off the wall and brought it over to Watly. Everything seemed to be happening very fast. The cuff already?

"Uh . . ." Watly watched the top of the blonde's head as the man secured the cuff on him. "Uh . . . aren't you going to read the Hosting Rights and Regulations thing?"

The man clamped the cuff tightly and looked up. Watly

shuddered. The guy's eyes were totally empty of humanity. Blank. "You heard it last time, mister. There something you forgot?"

Watly swallowed hard. "Where's my euphoric?" The doctor was pulling the hosting device from the corner already. Some of the cables dragged behind.

"Euphorics are not necessary this time, Mr. Night Host."

Watly sat forward. "Wait a minute! Wait just a sec. What about my pains? Aren't you going to ask me about pains? I have pains that need treating."

The man stood over Watly and with one broad hand firmly pushed him back against the chair. "This donor's not picky, mister. You don't need a euphoric and you don't need a pain check."

"What do you mean I don't need a pain check? I have a bruise. A *bad* one. I have scratches. Sore muscles. There's discomfort." Watly felt panic building. Something was wrong here.

"Your donor doesn't care, night host. You want to make trouble? You want to call it off? You can call if off *right now* if you want, but I guarantee you'll never host again. I *guarantee* it." The man's eyes seemed even deader than before. They were like a doll's eyes.

"I just don't understand. This isn't like last time. How can you do it this way? You're supposed to read the rights. You're supposed to give me a raping euphoric. You're supposed to deaden the pains. Am I right?"

The man made a close approximation of a smile with his lips. It looked more like a grimace. The teeth were yellow next to the pale skin. "All depends on the donor. This donor doesn't care about a little discomfort, Mr. Night Host. Now, are we on or not? Yes or no? You doing this?"

Watly felt confused. This was nothing like he'd expected. No rights or regulations. No Alysess. No euphoric. No pain check. It all stank. "I just want some assurances. . . ."

"What assurances, mister?" The doctor turned and released the two cables with end plates. He pulled them chairside.

"Is this guy some kind of pain-freak or something?"

The man was touching the plates behind each of Watly's ears. He returned to the main controls with that eerie stain-toothed smile spreading. "You're safe, mister. I think you'll live through it, if that's what's worrying you."

"What's going on here?"

The man turned and stared straight at Watly with a look of supreme impatience. "What do you mean?"

"There's something wrong here and I don't like it."

"You want out, tell me *now*." The man deftly flipped three ringlets out of their casings and connected two loose cables.

Watly held a hand up. "Can't you just wait a second, Doctor?"

"Yes or no," the man said. His features had returned to their original stony coldness. "I got a job to do. I've got no time for coddling. Yes or no, Mr. Night Host."

Watly couldn't believe the way this was turning out. He was being pushed. He wasn't being given enough time to think. This was all wrong. "Hold on just a second!"

The blond man gripped the final two ringlets and glared. "*Yes or no*! Right *now*, mister! You hosting or not?"

Watly felt he didn't have a choice. There was only one response. If he said no, it was over. No mothering, no nothing. This was the only way. So this doctor was a bolehole, that's all. So the guy was a rapeface. What was Watly going to do—give up all he'd worked for because some underpaid catbreath second-kisser had an attitude problem? This was his only chance to get his dream. But damned if he wasn't going to report this guy's behavior when it was over. This was unacceptable. It warranted a serious complaint.

"Can we just cool down here a second?" Watly said as calmly as he could. "I'll do it. I'll do it. Just take it *easy*, already."

The doctor glared at him and waited for a few seconds without moving. "Calm enough for you?" he said finally, his voice sarcastic.

"Thanks loads," Watly said.

Now the man crossed over and pushed Watly firmly into the chair so that his skin made contact with the two plates. "Here we go. Very calm, very calm, now." With the other hand the tall man released the final ringlets. "Calm, calm, calm," the bolehole muttered.

"Thanks for the reassurance. You've got some bedside manner," Watly said. As his jaws began to tingle, Watly wondered if he might have just made the biggest mistake of his life.

CHAPTER 11

When Watly Caper remembered his youth, he remembered it orange. Every memory of his early days in Brooklyn seemed to take place at sunset. To Watly, those days were always a golden hue.

Sitting on the front steps of his apartment building, playing batball with the neighborhood kids, shin-scrimming off a bus—no matter what—it was always just before dusk. Days began and ended there. In memory, Brooklyn was a perpetual warm sunset. The shadows were long and made you feel tall and grown-up. One could catch a glimpse of the sun between the buildings while walking. Off to the north was Manhattan. Manhattan: the promised land.

Watly remembered standing on the roof of some tall Brooklyn apartment house and gazing at the Manhattan skyline. The Trade Center, the two Empire State Buildings, the Chrysler Building, Citicorp, Alvedine, the Man-With-Hat-On, the Gavy Tower—all shone brightly and a million windows glittered like jewels as the dying light caught them. It was an incredible vision. As he stood there, Watly wondered if it could possibly be as beautiful close up as it was from a distance.

And there were the smells—the smells of Watly's youth. That dirty, gritty, musty smell of the neighborhood. The apartment's spicy, homey, kitcheny smell—as if, no matter what time, a meal had just been prepared moments before. And the smell of Mom. The smell of warmth. The oily, sweaty smell as Watly's mother returned from work. The biting smell of the detergent she used in her job as cleaner of the cleaning machines at the factory.

And then the sponge bath with its scented soaps. The soaps smelled less like Mom than the grease and sweat and industrial detergent. The soaps gave off a soft, wispy, flowery aroma that was nowhere near as tough as the true Pepajer Caiper. She was a strong woman. It was she who had demonstrated against the prophies. It was she who had fought tooth and nail to protect the small local park and its five trees. It was she who had battled to improve keyboard school for the kids, to get more cleaning machines for the filthy streets, to find homes for the Brooklyn homeless, to get nutritious foods—sunbeans and weeders— imported to the stores.

If there had been talk of California back then, she would have been involved. She would have been excited by it all: tracking down every lead she could find, following up on each rumor, investigating, probing. She would have *gone out there*. She would have found a way and gone out to California. She wanted to be a part of things. She wanted to change things. Her eyes were never as fiery and full of hope as when a new cause arose. She lived for it. All this California stuff would have been fuel for her soul. And it would have rubbed off on Watly. There was no way to avoid it. There was power to the woman. Strength. Wisdom.

Pepajer Caiper. Watly's mother.

Pepajer Caiper had cared. It was what she did best. If mothering was Watly's passion in life, then caring was his mother's. As a boy, Watly often wondered what it would be like to live a life without a passion. Without a dream, a driving force. It seemed there were lots out there who had none. No driving force. No bliss. No obsession. It looked like *most* people had none, in fact. How did that feel? How did it feel not to have one

thing—maybe a secret thing, maybe not—that made your life
worth living? How did it feel to wake up in the morning, eat, do
your job if you have one, have sex if it's available, eat some more,
drink, watch CV, play some, sleep . . . and eventually die? And
that's it. That's all. Did it feel empty? Was there a void there? Or
was it okay just to live. Was it okay for some not to be "saddled"
with an all-encompassing, intoxicating, pain-in-the-ass *passionate*
passion all the time. Maybe drinking or drugs or religion were
enough for some. Maybe that filled the void. All that stuff had
certainly been popular at different times. Or maybe *everyone* had
a passion. Maybe most people just didn't see it. They were blind
to it. And only a lucky few could see.

Watly was one of the lucky. He knew his passion from way
back. And his mother was, too. Pepajer cared. She wanted to
make a difference. She wanted the world to be right, to be fair.
She wanted things to be good and beautiful. She wanted her kid to
grow up in a place that was kind and careful and wise. And other
people's kids. And the people themselves. She fought hard for her
causes—one after another. And one of her causes was Watly.

She had always been supportive of him. From the first
days—from the very beginning—she'd been right behind her son.
When Watly had told her of his dream, she'd stayed with him on
it—never discouraging, never cajoling him into a different direction, and never warning him not to get his hopes up.

"If you want something, Little-Watt, you will achieve it," she
had said once. "But if, in the end, you *don't* achieve it, then
the wanting will have been enough. For the wanting is really
all there is anyway." She paused, and then spoke the familiar
sentence young Watly always found cryptic and confusing: "It is
not the place you're headed that's important, nor even the journey
there; it is the road you tread on itself."

Then she ran her fingers through her short black hair, shook her
head vigorously in a characteristic gesture that seemed to signify
the clearing of mental cobwebs, and guided young Watly toward
the kitchen where they prepared dinner together.

As they rolled small balls of dough on the low plasticore
counter, Pepajer spoke again.

"There is one thing, Little-Watt, you must beware of," she

said. "You seek a noble thing, particularly in this day and age. Your purpose is pure and your ambition relatively harmless to others. This is good. However . . ." she paused and faced her son dead-on, "there is a vanity in you. You know it. There is a belief that you are right to the point of violence. No one . . ." Her thin muscular hands rose before Watly and the long fingers spread. Her eyes were serious. *"No one* is right to the point of violence. No one. I see it in you. You feel justified in force. You feel it is available to you as a last resort. You feel it is a viable if unpleasant alternative. I've watched you with your friends. I've seen you strike a playmate. I've seen you threaten when your pride is hurt. You have this in you." Her graceful hands danced for a moment. "But this is not good. This will be your downfall if you can't control it. Remember that, Little-Watt."

Little Watly thought for a moment before speaking. "Isn't anything worth fighting for?"

His mother smiled the smile that always made things all right. A warm smile Watly wished he had seen more of. "There's fighting and then there's fighting. Wait till you have a child, my son," she said. "Wait till you have your child and then answer that yourself. And I will teach you, when you're older. I will teach you the secrets. How to fight without fighting."

Watly didn't understand. Was that a yes or a no? He wasn't sure what her point was. He still felt right. He still felt it was okay to hit back if someone hit him. Watly appreciated the little he understood of his mother's philosophy, and in some ways he wished it could be his. But, even back then, he knew it could never truly be his. There was a thin, permanent streak down his core that would always be ready to fight back. Physically. It was part of his nature. He suspected it came not from his mother, not from his genes, and not from some early trauma. He suspected it came from his life. His short life. It came from his experiences. It came from his neighborhood. It came from his friends and acquaintances. From his days at home on the school interactive keyboard. From his one day a week at social class. From Brooklyn itself. From the gangs. From the toughness of all those golden-orange days.

He fought his way up to adolescence. It was how he had

survived. There was no way else to. Violence was the way of the streets. He hated it, but it was part of life. You had to be tough. Or at least seem tough. Bluff tough. You had to prove yourself. You had to strut and pose and—occasionally, only *occasionally* if you bluffed well enough—you had to punch. And be punched. Watly tried to avoid it whenever possible, but violence did not seem always avoidable. There was a lot of it. But there was a lot of guilt, too. Guilt about his mother. *There was fighting and there was fighting*. Watly did the wrong kind of fighting. Pepajer could fight with no hurt coming to either side. This was the right way. This was the best way. And Watly knew it. But he had never been the most obedient son. Devoted, yes. Obedient, no.

"One thing, Watly," his mother said later. "This is all I ask—all I'll ever *insist* on. Promise me you'll stop shin-scrimming. You'll get yourself killed, and for no good reason." Now she sounded like a typical adult. Scolding. Making rules.

Watly smiled. "I promise," he lied.

Never obedient, was Watly. The very next Sunday, after the promise—after countless promises—he was back on the orange streets with his friends: Tobb Indrel, Herrana (The Flash) Enstich, Basop Pinnegipher, and Chetty Fot. Not fighting this time. Not bluffing. Just playing. Watly was back with them—against his mother's wishes—feeling the rhythm, basking in the danger and excitement. Shin-scrimming. Waiting for the bus. Waiting for the loop to take him. Waiting to be jerked and yanked along, bouncing down the road—maybe skinning a knee or two if the cylinders rode low. Pulled along.

Yes, jerked and yanked and pulled along—laughing and screaming all the way.

CHAPTER 12

Jerked and yanked and pulled along. Wrenched along. Torn violently downward.

Where was he? What was happening? His mind was ripping.

This time the hosting was not gentle. This time it was not smooth. Maybe it was the lack of euphoric, maybe it was the stressful circumstances, maybe it was the speed with which the hosting had started, or maybe it was everything put together. In any case, this time it was different.

The pale-skinned blond man held Watly firmly, pressing him into the plates. There was no feeling in those cold eyes. No empathy, no remorse, no sorrow. Not even hate. Nothing. *I may have made a small error in judgment here,* Watly thought.

Watly felt himself being jerked violently inward. He was being pulled into himself with tremendous force. He was mentally scrambling for balance, for a foothold. Watly was sliding down that same interior hallway as before, only this time it was much steeper and more slippery. He was being dragged, yanked down, kicking and screaming. *I've change my mind,* he thought. *Whoa, hold on here—*

And suddenly the other appeared.

Another "I." This other being was in there with him and approaching rapidly from behind, having no trouble with the slippery steepness. It was scampering toward him like a huge insect, feelers clicking on the invisible interior surface of his mind.

Watly felt much more from this consciousness than he had from the other. Much more. As it neared, there was an impression of power, of size and strength. There was this enormous self-confidence and, at the same time, a tangible sense of winter. Icy cold winter. A blizzard within. The incredible coldness was not just surface. It was solid. Watly felt all this clearly. It was as if the intruder's personality was so strong, so full of winter, that even the mental walls could not contain it all.

Watly experienced a childlike fear enveloping him as this powerful thing neared and passed. *This is a bad. A real bad. A bad thing. There is evil here,* Watly thought. *Cold, wintry evil. A monster. Is this even a human being at all that is climbing into my skull?* He wanted to hide under a blanket and call for Mommy. He wanted to close his eyes and bury his face in his hands. They weren't his eyes anymore, nor his hands. His control was totally gone. That fast. He was a passenger now. It was over.

Watly felt his back arch and his body stretch languorously. The movement felt somehow feline. Graceful but dangerous. Then he felt his mouth move. His tongue explored the upper teeth and gum and then settled back as his lips curled slightly at the edges. Watly felt his lungs expand in preparation for speech.

"Mea culpa, Watly Caiper. Mea culpa. Mea maxima culpa."

Watly felt his fear tighten. It wasn't just that this person knew his name. Somehow that was no surprise. It seemed almost natural. What scared him most was the voice. It was his own voice talking but it was very different. Aside from the expected Second Level accent, there was an oiliness to its tone. There was a sliminess. The voice was dripping with something wet and foul. There was more of that wintry cold quality that had passed him in the dark. An inhumanity . . . a badness.

"That you?" It was the blond doctor talking. He had removed the cables and was shunting the machine back.

"It's me now, yes," Watly's body said.

"I've got your things here." The man was kicking forward a large silver box that had been in the shadows behind the white table. Watly saw it peripherally. His donor did not even glance at it.

"You can leave now, Mitterly. Leave me with Watly. Watly and I would like to be alone. Isn't that correct, Watly?"

The absurdity of the question coming from his own lips just increased its impact. Watly was scared. He didn't ever remember being as scared. He realized with hindsight that his other donor had never addressed him at all. The host had never been acknowledged by that first donor. It had been much more comfortable that way. This directness was powerful in shock value alone.

The tall doctor—Mitterly—set the controls and backed out of the room, almost bowing as he left. He folded the door tightly behind him.

Watly was alone with the donor.

After another slow stretch, the donor guided Watly's body gracefully to its feet. There was none of the tentative awkwardness Watly remembered from his first hosting. This donor was poised and balanced. Confident.

"Well, here we are, Watly Caiper. Just the two of us. We're headed on an adventure, you and me. No time to waste. Let's see what we have here."

The donor knelt next to the silver box and flipped its lid back. Inside was what looked like a pile of clothes and a few small red plastic cases. The donor glanced quickly at each and removed the largest of the cases. It was about the length of Watly's hand and twice as wide. The donor opened it with a deft flip of the wrist. Under the top padding were two small brown wafers and a black metal wand that forked into dual points at one end. The donor removed the wafers and balanced them close together on the hosting-cuff.

"This will just take a brief moment, Watly. Be patient and we'll be done in no time. No time at all."

The donor activated the wand and touched its two points to the wafers—one on each. They glowed slightly at the contact areas.

After trying it at various different points Watly saw contact made as the wafers lit up completely. The hosting-cuff clicked and fell off his wrist. It bounced once before rocking to a full stop at Watly's feet.

"There we are, Watly. We don't need that, do we?"

Watly felt as though he were reeling from some invisible blow. He watched helplessly as his donor hung the cuff back on the wall and put away the tools. He was stunned. He had just witnessed the impossible. The hosting-cuff system was foolproof, or so he'd been led to believe. This was incredible. Impossible. Now, to all the world, he was just Watly. Another severe panic attack, probably the worst ever, started to bubble to the surface. *Control your mind, Caiper. Keep your wits. Think narrowly. Pay attention to what's happening. Come on, Caiper.*

The donor got undressed. This was no surprise to Watly. He was expecting a period of physical inspection like the one he had experienced before. However, this donor didn't seem interested in Watly's body. Not at all. As soon as the clothes came off, new clothes went on—clean black jumpsuit, yellow workervest, and low boots. Watly's few belongings were transferred from the pocket-jacket into the workervest. The old outfit was then stuffed into a corner of the silver box.

Watly could see himself as the donor glanced into the reverse-corrected mirror. He looked good. He looked like one of the lucky few who worked Second and lived below.

"We look wonderful, huh, Watly? What a team, you and me!"

The donor turned back to the box and pulled out the other small red cases. Two of them were placed in the workervest pockets. The third was opened and a long, silver object removed.

"You know what this is, Watly Caiper?" The donor swiveled it in front of Watly's eyes. "This is a fully charged surgical cutting blade with the skin-sealer turned off. In fact, you'll note, the sealer has been removed entirely. It's as sharp as they come, Watly, and it'll go through flesh or bone like they were boiled sunbean."

The donor waved it in front of Watly's nose a few times, then held it away and made Watly's eyes slowly scan the length of it. It was an impressive scalpel. Had Watly not been so terrified of it he might have admired its sleeknees and the simplicity of its design. But it scared him badly. He didn't want to think what it might be for. The oily speech continued.

"Just thought I'd introduce you two. I think you'll know each other better later." There was a pause and the donor pocketed the scalpel in its case. "Let's see what else—oh, yes."

That case also went into the workervest. The donor removed the final red case from the box and opened it. It contained a tiny flask with yellow liquid sloshing about inside. The donor handled it delicately.

"We mustn't forget this, Watly. Oh, no, not this. A little . . ." Watly watched his own fingers pop the cap off the flask, "a little slow-acting poison." The flask was raised to his lips. *Oh rape don't do that please don't do that let me out of here, please I've got to get out . . .*

"Yes, poison. No known antidote. None at all." They swallowed. There was a bitter burning sensation in Watly's throat as the liquid went down. "It shouldn't take full effect until after I've left you, Watly, but when the time comes, it'll come fast." The body gave a shudder as the liquid hit Watly's stomach. There was a brief sense of nausea. "It's a shame you'll not get fade-out pay, Watly. You'll have earned it."

Watly would surely have fainted had it been possible. He was dead. *I'm a raping dead man*, he thought. *It's all over but the dying*.

His donor began to laugh. The laughter started small but increased rapidly. Soon the whole body was shaking with it. Wracked with it. Doubled over. It was a strange sensation. Here was Watly, absolutely terrified, while his body acted overcome with humor. The laughter wound down and broke after a few moments, and the donor—wiping tears—spoke again.

"I got you there, didn't I, Watly Caiper? I had you going for a moment. We had quite a scare, you and I. In truth it's just a harmless liquid, Watly; no effect at all. Not poison. No, no. A small practical joke. Mea culpa, Watly. Mea maxima culpa. Just showing you who's boss. Just getting your attention. Getting acquainted."

The donor threw the empty flask and its case in with the first one containing the wafers. Those two cases and Watly's old clothing were all that was now left in the large silver box. The donor closed the lid and shoved the box down the garbage chute. It would no doubt slide to the building's melting vat. *No evidence,* Watly thought. *No evidence of the cuff-removing equipment—nor of my old clothing. No assignment slip. No evidence of anything. All gone.* Watly found himself strangely mourning the stupid pocket-jacket. It was a trivial thing—but he loved that jacket. It was the nicest damn article of clothing he owned. Now it was gone. He felt he'd lost a friend.

"Well, I hope I haven't traumatized you too much, Watly. It was all in fun. Time for us to hit the road, I think. Time to push off." The donor straightened and smoothed the workervest and brushed Watly's hair downward. In the hosting room there was no evidence anyone had been there. The donor glanced around. All was in order. Tidy. White.

As they exited the building through the cuff-return door, the donor continued a soft running commentary. "It's a beautiful night, isn't it, Watly? A magical night. A night when any number of things might happen. Even down here on the sewer level you can tell it. Even here among the vermin there is magic."

There was a pause as they continued walking. The donor was favoring the left leg slightly. "Ah, Watly, I see we have a soreness here. We have a bit of a bruise on the leg, do we?" The donor stopped walking and slammed a fist directly into the sore area of Watly's thigh. Hard. Watly's peripheral vision blurred for a moment. The pain was incredible.

"Hurts there, doesn't it? I guarantee you, Watly Caiper, that bothered *you* more than it bothered me. You're not dealing with a baby here." Again the donor punched full force into the center of the bruise.

Rape, that hurts! What are you? How can you do that? How can you stand that? Watly's body trembled and his eyes watered. This person was insane. Watly was being controlled by an insane person. For a moment he thought he was losing grip himself. For a moment Watly thought he was drifting away from reality. His mind wanted solace. His mind wanted to think broadly—not narrowly. His mind wanted to float off somewhere. Somewhere

safe and warm. Thinking widely. *At least . . .* Watly thought,
at least let me close my eyes—please just for a while. . . .

> *The me is not the body.*
> *The me is not the body.*
> *The me is neither hand nor face nor sex.*
> *The me is Watly Caiper, I.*
> *(A sense of self.)*
> *The body is an it.*
> *The body is a that.*
> *It could belong to another,*
> *For the me is a movable thing.*
> *The me is a movable thing.*

"Mea culpa, Watly Caiper. You're being a good sport about all
this. It was just another demonstration, Watly. To show which of
us is the stronger. By now I think it should be obvious."

The donor had started walking again and was heading up
Lexington Avenue, ignoring the bums who approached. The walk
was smooth and self-assured. *This person,* Watly thought, *is more
comfortable in my body than I am.* Most of the tenters were inside
with the lights on by now. Watly could see all these warm glows
through the tent fabric on the left and right as they passed. He felt
envy. These people didn't have much, but they were sheltered,
relatively warm, probably decently fed and decently clothed,
and—most important of all—they were *themselves.* They were
who they were. They had no parasitic beasts jumping about in
their brains. Watly would have given everything he had to trade
places with any one of them.

The donor turned on Sixty-third and headed east. Watly could
guess their destination. It was obvious. They were headed for the
nearest tube to Second. There was one on Third Avenue between
Sixty-third and Sixty-fourth streets.

The tube was lit up brightly and the donor approached it
confidently, walking in the precise center of the street. A cruiser
passed by without even slowing. The donor did not falter. They
reached the tube. Watly watched his own hands as they flipped
away the thin metal tube seal and pulled the hatch wide open. He

saw his feet step in and felt the cool air inside. The hatch was closed and resealed behind. There was suddenly no outside sound. There was no echo—just a dead mechanical hum. After a brief pause a pleasant but emotionless female voice spoke.

"Face forward, please," the artificial voice said.

Watly's donor did as told.

The tube interior was shiny black and Watly's face and shoulders were surrounded by a blue-toned circular light. The donor was looking directly into a surveillance lens in the middle of the light. Watly felt naked. He felt so naked he thought for a moment that maybe the lens could see deep into his body. Maybe it could see clear through the high forehead, into the skull, to Watly Caiper himself. Maybe it could see past the donor all the way to Watly—who was, at the moment, well buried. If only it were true. If only Watly could wave a little mental hand and show himself. *I'm here! Don't listen to this bolehole!*

The voice spoke again.

"Place your Second Level travel pass and your identicard in the proper slots before you, please."

The donor brought out Watly's own identicard. This was slipped between a pair of metal lips marked IDENT. Out of one of the previously unopened red cases, the donor produced a card Watly had never seen before. It had Watly's name and image on it, but it was unfamiliar. The donor placed it in a receptor slot marked SECOND LEVEL PASS.

"Please state your name and your business on Manhattan's Second Level."

The donor cleared Watly's throat and proceeded to do a somewhat transparent imitation of a First Level accent. "My name is Watly Caiper and I've been handed the great honor of being hired to work on Second for the night, on a trial basis."

"What is the work, Mr. Caiper?" the disembodied voice asked.

"The cleaning of a toilet, ma'am."

"What particular toilet is to be cleaned?"

The donor fumbled with one of the red cases until it opened abruptly. Inside was nothing. The donor pretended to read from the nothing, shielding the lens's view with a cupped hand.

"At forty-seven East Seventy-second. On the . . . " The

donor squinted, "south side of the street. Second floor. Dirty loo."

"Do you have a temporary working permit?"

"That I do, yes." From the first red case the donor produced yet another card with Watly's face imprinted on it. This one had a ridge-coded section. The donor slipped it into a central unmarked slot. There was a brief humming.

"Is there an explanation," the female voice asked, "as to why said toilet cannot clean itself?"

The donor took a deep breath. "That I don't know, ma'am. Some kind of breakdown, I suppose." The donor brushed a hand clumsily through Watly's hair. The gesture seemed uncharacteristic of both the donor and Watly.

There was another short period of humming and then all three cards popped outward. The donor removed them and carefully placed them in the one red case. The emotionless voice returned.

"Access permitted, Watly Caiper. Standard warning, standard caution, and standard admonition."

"Thank you, ma'am," said the donor, still in character.

"You will be allotted one unmanned copper for escort and surveillance. Have a pleasant evening."

The voice clicked off permanently and the tube began to rise. The donor exhaled slowly.

Watly was going to Second Level.

CHAPTER 13

It was hard for Watly to see much. Most of what he observed was from the edges of his vision. The donor kept their head down and their feet moving. Watly could only get a sense of things—but the sense he got was extraordinary. Fuckable to the extreme.

The first thing that hit him was the air. The air was different—not just fresher, but *richer*. It was fuller somehow. Cleaner even than he remembered Brooklyn air—but then that seemed so long ago. This air smelled like someone had scrubbed it, dried it, and fluffed it before allowing it to enter any nose. Then Watly noticed the unmanned copper. It was nothing like the coppers on First Level or in Brooklyn. Those coppers were all tarnished and old. They always seemed held together with wire and tape and were invariably dragging some part or other along the ground. This Second Level copper was beautiful. It was so well kept and polished it appeared to be some jewel—some ornate pendant for a giant. Watly had never realized that, under the soot, coppers really *were* copper-colored. This one hovered two feet off the ground and stayed a polite three or four yards away. When the donor moved, it followed behind perfectly, like a faithful pet. Its lenses and sensors were always facing its charge. So were its gun turrets.

As the donor walked along Watly was overcome with Second Level. He could see so very little, but he could tell he was in another world. Everything was vertical. Vertical to the extreme. Everything was open and clean. There were trees on the sidewalk. Greenness. Watly's heart felt suddenly full. He couldn't help it. It was like some wonderland. There were no daylites—just a few streetlights every now and then. It was darker than First Level. Even in this darkness (or perhaps *because* of it) Watly could sense open space above. There was no ceiling to reflect the light back down. Something going up could go up forever. Light, air, sound. Up there was nothing but sky. It had been a long time since he'd seen the sky. Seemed like years and years since Brooklyn. Watly wanted to stop for a moment—just a short moment—so he could look around. And look upward. The donor continued walking briskly, head bent forward, focusing only on the creamy white sidewalk.

Watly caught visual snatches of buildings to the left and right. Everything he saw was spotless, well kept, and beautiful. There were no tenters, there was no dirt, there was no dripping. Occasionally a person would pass by on foot but the donor never looked up. Watly could see only shoes. Expensive shoes. Perhaps this was protocol: Never look at the face of the wearer of expensive shoes. Watly didn't know. A sedan passed. With his peripheral vision Watly could see it was a private car. One person owned that car. Incredible.

It was sublimely quiet. Even at this hour First Level was always full of noises—people shouting, buses lumbering past, the hollow echoes following any sound. But here there was serenity. True serenity. Aside from the soft buzz of the copper and the click of the donor's footsteps, there was virtual silence.

Everywhere was space. Space up and space out. Watly felt as though the world had suddenly opened up. The sky felt broader than it ever had back home. It was as if he'd just been let out of a box he hadn't even realized he had been in. He couldn't help feeling good. He couldn't help it. If only the donor would look upward as they walked. Watly desperately wanted to see. He wanted to see everything there was to see. Second Level was intoxicating. *I want to stay here,* Watly thought. *Forget everything else—this is what I want. I want the beauty and the solace. I want the peace and the space. Nothing on the CV ever prepared me for* this. *It's incredible. Shit—there are* trees. *Healthy trees! And the buildings go up forever!*

"Enjoying our little trip so far, Watly Caiper?" It was the whispered voice again from Watly's own mouth. "A few more blocks and we'll be there. Then the fun begins."

Watly felt himself snap back from his Second Level reverie. He remembered he was not in the best of circumstances. This was not some tourist trip. "I'd speak louder, Watly," the donor said, "but I fear our electronic friend has ears as well as eyes."

The donor turned down a different street and then turned once again. Watly had totally lost his sense of direction. He had no idea where they were and nothing he saw was familiar. All he could assume was that they were heading to the address mentioned in the tube. If not, Watly supposed, the copper would have given them trouble. The street they were on now was different from the broad avenue. It seemed more residential, more private. Every few steps the donor would sidestep an ornately decorated flying buttress. No two were alike, each pattern and design unique. Watly wondered if these buttresses had any practical function or were just decorative, fashionable. Either way, they were impressive. Either way the street was a fuck and a half.

The donor stopped in front of a particularly large building, eyes still downward.

"Here we are, Watly. Home at last." There was humor in the cold whispered voice. Watly did not like the sound of it.

The unmanned copper stayed waiting on the sidewalk as the donor mounted the steps to the front door. Watly was amazed to see that the front door was wood. The *entire* door. It was stained a dark color and polished to a shiny finish. He was impressed. The donor touched it and it opened. It was unlocked. Before entering, the donor gave a jolly wave to the copper. "I won't be long," the oily voice said, still with a tinge of irony.

Just inside the door was a tiny wall keyboard. The donor

punched in a series of numbers with one hand and then looked up
for the first time since arriving on Second Level.

There was a small alcove, a short walk down the foyer, and
then . . . wood. Dark brown boards and intricately carved
panels gleamed with polish from every direction. Even the floor
was wood. And the ceiling, segmented in rectangular patterns of
thick wooden beams over crisscrossed light wood. They were now
in a huge sitting room. There was a love seat, a full couch, a table,
and two chairs—all in real wicker. And a bent-wood rocker. The
walls were decorated with portraits of important-looking characters in dark suits. Serious-faced businesswomen and -men. Poli-
ticians. It was definitely a rich person's home. There were heavy,
purple floor-to-ceiling curtains covering what probably were
enormous windows. At the rear was a huge curving wooden
staircase with wooden banisters carved to look like a bird's wings.
Everywhere there was space and more space. Room to run. Room
to dance and twirl endlessly. There was no sound at all in the
building. Not even creaking from all the wood. The donor stood
still for a moment, taking in the room. Or perhaps showing the
room to Watly.

"Not a bad little place, Watly. Don't you think?" The affected
accent was gone and the voice was loud again. Oily loud. Oozing
with oily winter. Badness. The donor crossed the room and
climbed the wide staircase.

"I did a little research, Watly Caiper, and would you believe
what the first five floors of this building are? What the 'sewer
level' of this very building is? A crematorium, Watly! Isn't that
incredible? As we speak, bodies are being melted down below us.
The fire of Hades. It's enough to make one believe in hell and
heaven, huh?" Watly felt his stomach constrict in a brief spasm of
the donor's laughter. "Don't worry, Watly. No one can hear us.
This is a private home. The only recording lenses here are on the
office levels."

At the top of the stairs was a broad carpeted hallway. Every
few feet there was another wood table with another antique on it.
On one was a vase—maybe even from the outerworld, Europe or
somewhere. On another table was an old electronic typewriter,

then a small bronze sculpture, then a carrying case of some kind. It was like a museum.

The donor walked down the hall quickly to the last door on the left. It too was solid wood. There was a brass knocker in its center shaped like an open hand. The donor lifted it and knocked once before entering.

"Here we are, my darling! Honey, we're home!"

It was the largest bed Watly had ever seen. It must have been twelve feet square and the canopy rose a good fifteen feet above it. Everything was draped, lacy and white. The bed was the only furniture in the room. It was up against a clean white wall and across from a single window that had its thick shades drawn tightly.

Lying spread-eagled in the exact center of the bed was a naked form. A woman.

She was stunning. Breathtaking. She was one of the most physically beautiful women Watly had ever seen in his life. Her head was sunk deep into an enormous pile of pillows to the point where it was almost buried, but Watly could make out long, light brown hair. Her face was angelic, yet strong. She had exquisitely light skin that looked pure and unblemished. Almost *too* pale. Maybe even sickly pale, like that blond man's skin had been. . . .

Her body was taut and firm-looking. It was an active body. An athletic body. There was no excess anything. Even her feet were striking, delicate and smooth. Tiny blue veins running across them vulnerably. As for her breasts (the donor's eyes scanned them slowly), they were perfect—full and firm as if she'd just grown them minutes before. As if they'd just swollen out over her ribs ripely. Gravity didn't seem to have affected her. Even as she lay on her back the breasts pointed up strongly. Achingly beautiful.

What is it about breasts, Watly thought, *that's so damn intoxicating? Why do I love them so? Perhaps that is their purpose. To be loved. Perhaps they are plumage. Meant to attract, to cause an ache. No other mammal has them like us. Mammaries needn't stick out like that. It serves no function for them to bulge. Not at all. They each say, Touch me, I am beautiful. Cradle me and fondle me and pinch me, I am beautiful. And they are. And these in particular.*

This whole *body* said, Touch me, I am beautiful. She was strikingly touchable. Strikingly beautiful. Fuckable. Fuckable in the *literal* sense. There was an extreme youthfulness to her entire appearance, though Watly found himself thinking she was older than she looked. *Thirty? Thirty-five? Can't say. . . .* The only physical flaw he could see was that her jawline was just a bit too strong. It overpowered her face—her perfect little flip of a nose, her slightly swollen-looking lips, the long lashes, the high cheekbones. . . . The jaw was just too firm. Tough. It gave her a sharpness—an edge—she did not otherwise have. Aside from that, she was perfection. Watly wondered if perhaps someone like her *needed* one small flaw in order to reach perfection. Perhaps the definition of physical beauty was a person who had perfect little flaws to accentuate the beauty of the rest of the body.

The woman's eyes were closed and her body had not moved at all since the donor had entered.

And then Watly thought she might be dead. The woman looked dead. There was no movement. And that paleness. Deathly paleness. . . . It occurred to Watly that her head was sunken so far back into the mountain of pillows that she could be horribly mutilated without it showing. The back of her head could have been, for all he knew, hacked to bits. It was not a pleasant thought. He did not want to be proven right. Blood and bone and grayish-green pieces of brain. He did not want to see that. The evening had been bad enough already.

"Nice piece of ass, huh, Watly?" The donor chuckled. "Don't you worry, now, Watly Caiper. She's not dead. Not at all. She's just drugged. She's out of it." The donor walked to the bed's edge and focused on the woman's rib cage. Sure enough, Watly could see a very gentle rise and fall as she breathed shallowly. "She is not in any pain, I assure you, Watly. It's all part of the game. You can trust me. The pile of pillows is her throne and she is a queen in respose. Fear not."

The donor began to slowly disrobe, eyes always on the woman. Watly was again taken aback momentarily as his body became aroused without him. His organ filled rapidly, rising with each heartbeat. It was weird, but this time it didn't feel quite as removed as it had with the first donor. The woman *was* attractive. In some other circumstances—another time, another place— Watly could easily see himself being turned on, incredibly turned on, by just such a woman. Yes, indeed. Who was she? Why was she drugged? The drug must have been a powerful one. Aside from the breathing, she was lifeless. What a strange fantasy for the donor to be living out. A beautiful, lifeless woman. *Very* beautiful. The erection felt like it wasn't just the donor's now. Watly shared it, guiltily.

"Now, let's have some fun, shall we, Watly Caiper? After this it's all downhill."

The donor climbed on the bed and—without any fanfare or preparation—began to have intercourse with the motionless woman. To Watly it was a very strange experience. The donor was surprisingly gentle and careful—almost loving—but the woman may as well have been dead. There was moisture down there, something slick and natural-feeling—perhaps a lubricant applied when she'd been drugged in preparation for this bizarre ritual. The wetness made it feel almost normal, as if she too was excited, was aroused. But she was a rag. She was limp, lifeless. There was not a flinch, not a twitch or grunt from her direction. The donor, however, seemed to be enjoying it all immensely. Her inaction did not affect the slow strokes, the loving kisses, or the gentle caresses. There was a tenderness to everything done. The only sound was a moist *slap slap slap* pause *slap slap slap* of the wet joining. It was not at all the way Watly could have expected this donor to have sex. For such a cruel and cold person, this was surprisingly passionate and surprisingly gentle. There was love here, or something close to it. Care.

The slapping sounds grew louder and closer together. The pauses stopped. The donor was pounding hard now with a building lust. Watly felt the rising tickle in his balls and abdomen—the spreading fullness—as he heard an animal groan from the back of his own throat. The huge bed shook violently.

After orgasm, the donor stayed in the woman for a few moments, eyes closed. Watly found it a welcome relief. With his eyes closed, somehow Watly felt more in control. At least he didn't have to look at what someone else wanted him to. He could pretend it was just he, Watly, relaxing. Relaxing after an admittedly incredible orgasm. One of those big colorful ones, where the sweet spasms seem to go on forever.

The period of rest was short-lived. Watly's donor kissed the woman on her beautiful full lips and left the bed. She had not moved more than a fraction of an inch during the whole episode. Aside from the spreading stain on the sheets between her legs and the damp sheen to her body from Watly's sweat, she looked just the way she had when they'd found her. Beautiful and still.

What was this? What had just happened? Rape? Had Watly just been party to the obscenity of a rape? Who had drugged the woman? And why? Just to rape her?

The donor got dressed again.

"A momentary diversion from our main objective, Watly. I'm sure you don't blame me. She is a beautiful specimen. Try not to judge me too harshly for taking advantage of the fair maiden while she dreamt. I suspect her dreams were no less vivid. And Watly, my friend, what man could resist such a treasure?" The donor stopped and looked back at the bed. After a long moment of visual caressing, the donor looked away.

"But now we must hurry, Watly. Time is passing. I wouldn't want to leave your body before our true job is done. No, that wouldn't do at all."

After pulling on the boots and lacing the workervest, the donor left the room without looking back. Watly wondered if the woman would realize what had happened to her when she woke up. If she would feel the trauma of rape. The ultimate abomination. He also wondered, somewhat guiltily, if he'd ever see the woman again. He wondered if he'd ever see *anyone* again.

They did not head downstairs as Watly expected. They continued right past the curved stairway and turned down another hallway. After passing more foreign-looking antiques on more wooden tables they came to a stop at a bank of elevator doors. They were old elevators but looked in perfect condition. The donor summoned up a car. It arrived rapidly and they stepped in. After it climbed three floors, the donor stopped the car and stepped out.

This hallway was virtually identical to the others. The only real difference was in the donor's behavior. Watly sensed a new cautiousness. The walk became slower and more like that of a stalking animal. Occasionally the donor would glance up at the battery of recorder lenses that appeared every few yards on this floor of the building. There was no attempt to hide from them. If anything, Watly almost felt the donor was putting on a show for their benefit. Performing for the recorders.

They turned left at a branch in the hallway and approached the door at the end. The donor slowed as they silently neared. The door looked the same as all the others. It was, of course, made of real wood. The donor pressed an ear against it. Watly could hear nothing.

With great care Watly's donor opened the door a crack. Inside was a spectacular den. The walls were covered with leafcases and old prints and maps. Two wooden desks held brass keyboards and ornate globes. Antique chromells glistened dully from the shadows. Scattered around the room near the ceiling were more recorder lenses staring blankly out. Watching. Listening. Recording everything. A real gas fire burned from a stone fireplace in the corner, casting flickering shadows over the entire room. A heavy leatherlike wingchair faced toward the fire. Watly could see the shadows of two feet under the chair's legs. Someone was sitting in it, feet crossed comfortably.

The donor slipped in and closed the door without even a click. It seemed to Watly that they had stopped breathing. The donor reached into the workervest and slowly removed the surgeon's cutting blade from its case.

The person in the chair shifted and the leatherlike squeaked. The donor froze.

For what seemed to Watly like a full ten minutes the donor remained frozen in position, ignoring any of the body's protests or cramps. Then the scalpel was transferred smoothly to the right hand and gripped there firmly. They took a silent step toward the chair. Then another. The boards creaked.

The occupant of the chair stood and looked over the wing back.

"Who the rape are you?" It was a middle-aged woman. She stepped away from the chair and began backing up. She was thin with short black hair and dressed in an expensive business suit. There was obvious fear in her eyes. She dropped the leaf she had been reading.

Watly felt himself answer. "I'm a friend, my dear. A good friend." The donor moved closer and the scalpel gleamed as it reflected the firelight. Watly felt his whole body tense.

The woman had backed her way into a corner. "What do you want? What the rape do you want? Take it and get the hell out!" Her hands were trembling.

The donor kept advancing. "I want *you*, my dear. You don't know how long I've waited."

The woman's eyes were frantic now. She knew she was trapped. Watly wanted desperately to help her. He'd never seen such terror in another's face. She grabbed the edge of her desk and pulled a brass keyboard up by its cord. "Stay away from me! Stay back!"

The donor kept coming. The woman swung outward with the keyboard and, just as it contacted weakly with the side of Watly's head, he felt his own arm come down violently with the blade. His body was a savage thing, unstoppable. The keyboard bounced to the floor harmlessly as the first stab went into the woman's left shoulder. The charged scalpel went in cleanly and cut clear down the front of the woman, almost removing her arm at the shoulder. And it was Watly who had done it. *Watly*. He had seen his own body do it to her. She screamed horribly and went down, with her right hand up for protection.

The me is not the body, thought Watly.

The donor neatly sliced the woman's hand off at its wrist. Blood splattered all over the prints, the chromells. Her screaming continued and her eyes pleaded.

The me is not the body. . . .

The donor came down again with the blade and it opened a huge hole in the woman's stomach as she kicked out with her feet.

The me is neither hand nor face nor sex. . . .

There were blood and intestines everywhere and still the woman screamed, twitching and spasming.

The me is Watly Caiper, I.

(A sense of self. . . .)

Watly watched his hand come down once more and the blade cut out a huge hole in the woman's chest. Her screaming lessened.

The body is an it.

The body is a that. . . .

The woman squirmed and twisted, but she no longer screamed. A gurgle came from the back of her throat. Blackish blood flowed from her mouth. The donor raised the blade again.

It could belong to another,

For the me is a movable thing. . . .

This time the blade went into the center of her face and cut deeply down, slicing it almost in half. She stopped twitching.

The me is a movable thing.

The me is a movable thing.

The donor slowly stood up beside the mangled corpse, gradually controlling their body's breathing.

"Mea culpa, Watly Caiper. Mea culpa. I'm afraid you've been a bad boy, my friend."

Watly hardly heard. He was somewhere else entirely. He was dancing with Alysess. Dancing in that warm and friendly place where no one ever heard of hosts, or donors, or money, or Alvedine . . . or murder. Most importantly, no one ever heard of murder.

PART TWO

MAXIMUM CULPABILITY

Beware the air

WATLEY CAIPER'S DREAM

CHAPTER 14

"You've been fighting again, Little-Watt," Pepajer said. It was not a question. Watly's small body was a mass of cuts and bruises. His clothes were filthy. He stepped in closer. The orange light of sunset—*Brooklyn* sunset—sliced in sharply through the kitchen window, making it hard to see his mother's sad eyes. She led him to the sink to clean him off. The kitchen table was messy with papers from the neighborhood petition she'd been collecting. She smelled good—musty, dirty good. Hard-work good. The kitchen smelled good too. Spicy and warm.

Young Watt winced as she cleaned the wounds. "For a good reason, Mom," he said.

"Isn't it always a good reason, Watly?" She frowned. "How many times have I told you? Hmm? Never throw your fist, Watly. *Raise* it, yes. And your voice too. And your head. . . ."

"They were calling you *names*—"

"Yes?" Pepajer stopped cleaning the scrapes on Watly's face. She turned his small body toward her. "And?"

Now Watly felt stupid. "That's it," he said, feeling suddenly teary. "But *bad* names."

Pepajer looked honestly bewildered. "So?"

Watly felt sure the tears would come any second now. He tried to fend them off with silence. There was an achy, full feeling behind each eye.

His mother held her hands out to him. "I can fight a word with a wound? A verbal insult with a physical injury? I have the right to hurt someone's *person* for a word?" She gripped his shoulders. "Listen to me, Watly. This is important. *No one* has the right to hurt *anyone*. No matter *what*. Not you, not me. No matter *what*. *That* is the truth no one dares to face. *That* is the frightening reality of life. No one has the right to touch *anyone*."

"What if they touch you first?" Watly said. Now the damn burst and tears flowed freely down his scraped cheeks, stinging. He tried not to sob but that came too.

"Then there are ways. . . . " Pepajer looked off toward the source of the last golden rays touching the tiled floor. "There are ways. . . ."

"*What* ways?" Little Watly cried. "Tell me the ways!"

Pepajer turned and smiled wistfully. "Soon, my baby. Soon. When you're old enough to need them, I will tell you the secrets. For now, you don't need them. You just need to stop fighting."

"I *can't* stop fighting," Watly said, and his mother hugged him hard as he cried. Her strong hands stroked his dusty hair. There was caked blood there, too.

"You can if you want to," she whispered, close to his ear. "That's all it takes."

And Watly pulled back from her arms to look at her. He thought he'd never loved her more, nor understood her less. She smiled at his questioning look. Her hair was caught in the last ray of orange—it burned at the edges with light. The lines in her face were strong lines, forceful *human* lines. The face was loving and kind and oh-so-very wise. Watly felt more tears bubbling up. Through them he saw something sparkle over his mother's shoulder. Off in the far distance out the kitchen window, a building reflected the last of the sun. Watly squinted at the glare. It was a Manhattan building. Way, way off. It was the Alvedine Building. Glowing from on high.

Later, over the rich smells of dinner, Watly's mother raised her hands from across the table, catching Watly's eyes with hers. She wanted his complete attention. Watly stopped eating. He swallowed the weeder he had been chewing.

"You're not selfish enough, Little-Watt," Pepajer said solemnly.

Watly smiled slightly, thinking she was being sarcastic.

"I'm serious, Watly. You're not selfish/good enough. Selfish/good. Good/selfish. That's the answer." Her eyes were unwavering. "The world would be a better place if more people were selfish. Selfish/good. It is the answer, Watly. Everything you do in this life is for yourself, anyway. *Everything*. If you give me a gift, you are giving it because it makes you feel good. You do it for yourself. If you martyr yourself for some cause you do it because the idea pleases you, makes you proud. You do it for yourself. You do *everything* for yourself. It's important to realize that. To remember that."

Pepajer looked down and took another bite of food. Watly kept watching her as she ate, mesmerized. She looked up again and continued. "When you are old enough to have sex, Watly, you will see that the only good sex happens when the participants are selfish. They work for their own pleasure, and the pleasure of giving pleasure. Bad sex happens when they try to please each other at their own expense. That never works. And this is true of the rest of life as well. Fight for yourself, Watly; fight for your own freedom, for your own pleasure, for your own dreams; fight for your own food and shelter, for your environment, and for the satisfaction that doing it for others gives you. Helping others is selfish, Watly. It feels good. It is *profoundly* selfish. Selfish/good."

"Then fighting is good," Watly said. Pepajer wiped her mouth and sighed. "I know, I know," Watly jumped in. "Fighting is *not* good."

"Fighting *selfish*, Watly," she said strongly. "Fight without hurt. Fight so your hands don't get bloody. Fight so they don't shed *your* blood. Fight so you don't feel guilt over injuring another. Protect your fear. Fight so you never have to feel bad about a single move you made. Protect yourself. Fight selfish."

Pepajer leaned forward. "Fight like a coward, Watly. It takes more courage."

Watly stiffened at the thought. The idea confused him. Even offended him.

His mother whispered softly now. "Anyone can be a hero, Watly. That takes no guts at all."

Watly stared into those dark, wise eyes. They seemed so deep, so far away. *I love those eyes,* he thought. *I love them but I don't understand them.*

He tried, as the years went on, to understand her more. But somehow, though there was love and there was caring and connection, he found little understanding. She was a strange woman. A mysterious woman. He needed more time to figure her out.

He never got it.

When Watly Caiper was twenty his mother died. The medicion said it looked like a ruptured appendix, but there was no way to be sure. They couldn't afford a real doctor. They could hardly afford the medicion.

And by the time the medicion came, Pepajer was dead two hours—Watly's tears were dried up on his cheeks and his fingers were cramped from holding a dead woman's cool hands.

The day after it happened, Watly wanted to hit, to hurt. It was a day Watly hungered for violence as never before. Bloody violence. He wanted to lash out and attack the world. Where was a nose to bust? A throat to strangle? Who could he kick? He wanted to kill someone—to kill someone hard—and avenge Pepajer Caiper's death. There was no one to kill. There was no one to hurt. There was no one to kick or strangle. There was only the emptiness—and emptiness that eventually faded. Even his anger passed with time.

But something had changed in him. He didn't want to care anymore. He didn't want to feel for the world as his mother had. Where had it gotten her? What had it done for her? She died in agony, clutching her belly and crying. She died poor. She died with no money for a doctor to heal her. She died with nothing. Crying. "Watly," she'd said between sobs of pain. "You do good, Watly. Do good." And then the hurt got so bad she couldn't talk.

She died with nothing. Just a son named Watly. The pass-along.

He rented out half the apartment and got some odd factory jobs. He, too, cleaned the cleaning machines. Just like Mom. Time passed slowly. He fell in love and he fell out of love. And again. He worked and he didn't work. And again. He dreamed and planned. Babies filled his thoughts. And his ambitions. He got in a few fights. He lost a little hair. He fought less. Then not at all. There was, he discovered, no one to hit. No one to hurt. Mom was right. But Watly revised her. Rewrote her. He decided there was no reason to fight *anything*—whether anyone got hurt or not. The only thing to do was follow your dream. To hell with everything else. To hell with caring. Only care for the self. Selfish/bad, maybe.

Watly focused on his goal. Watly saturated himself with the idea of mothering. He researched it. He read up on it. He tried to find a way around the laws, around the prophies. And finally, on a whim, he wrote to an uncle. He had an uncle who actually *lived* on that almost mythical island. The island that had always dazzled him from afar, the one he always watched on CV, the one where the money was . . . the one where his goals could be realized. A long while later a response came back—return address: Narcolo Caiper, First Level, Manhattan.

And so the process began. Watly Caiper was destined to leave behind the golden-sunset land—the place of his youth, the melting place of his mother's body, and the only place he'd ever known. After applications, forms in duplicate and triplicate, inoculations, interviews and formal requests, visas and travel papers . . . his move was finally granted. He donated the apartment to his local community housing center. This was the same apartment he'd grown up in, the same apartment that smelled like home, that smelled like a meal had just been cooked, that smelled of old scented soaps, and that—yes—still smelled Pepajer Caiper's sweet sweat. He packed one small backpack with spare clothing, looked around a last time, and set off down the road on foot.

It was a two-day walk. The weather was good and Watly's spirits were high. He found it a pleasant journey. As he grew nearer he could make out more and more up ahead. Manhattan looming larger. At one point he even saw the tops of a few trees between buildings. Of course, he knew it was Second Level he was seeing and admiring but First Level he would be going to. It didn't matter. He was still excited.

At the water, Watly was quickly cleared to pass through the gate. To the guard it was nothing—another poor beanhead with dumb dreams and another stamped visa. To Watly it was everything. He stood at the mouth of the tunnel a long while before entering. His mother would be proud, Watly believed. In spite of everything, she would be proud. *I'm in the big time now, Mom. Look at me. I'm finally in the big time. I'm doing good, Mom. Doing good, like you wanted.*

CHAPTER 15

The smell of Mom's kitchen was there again. Watly was sure of it. The sweet smell of hardloaf baking. The spicy aroma of crisp weeders and vegetable scraps. Or maybe it wasn't Mom's kitchen. Maybe it was Narcolo's. Good old Narcolo Caiper. The strong scent of Uncle Narcolo's sunbeans. Something heavy and filling. Or perhaps a mouth-watering dessert. But then, maybe it wasn't the smell of Mom's kitchen or Narcolo's kitchen. Maybe it was the smell of Watly's own kitchen. Maybe it was a kitchen yet to be. Watly Caiper's future kitchen. The aromas were not as practiced— not as sure. There was a primitive quality to them. But it might not be the smell of food at all. It was not really a pleasant smell. It was an overripe smell. If it *was* food it was bad food. Spoiled, rancid food. There was something decaying or rotten. It was a bad smell, after all. What could he have been thinking? It was a terrible smell. It was a horrible stench with an overtone of sticky sweetness. The stench was like feces or urine or vomit . . . or all of them combined. It was the smell of anything bad that could come from a human body. And the sweetness—the sticky sweetness—that was the scent of something worse. That was the scent of fresh blood. It was the smell of death. It was the smell of human death. The nauseating stench of slaughter.

"Mea culpa, Watly Caiper. Mea culpa. I hope I haven't lost you to the jaws of insanity. I suppose that's a very real possibility. But then, you might be better off if it were the case."

Watly saw his own hands slimy with blood. The cutting knife was smoking slightly and had charged down considerably. It too was coated with gore. The donor wiped it on the leatherlike chair. The mangled corpse was just a few feet away.

"You've committed an awful crime, Watly. Just terrible." The bloody hands were raised in a gesture to the lenses. "And the visuals have all been recorded, I'm afraid. Someone should be fast-reviewing the recorders any time now. You're in big trouble, Watly Caiper. I think it's time I gave you a choice. Your first choice of the evening." The donor sat in the armchair and twirled the scalpel playfully on the heavy wooden desk. "We can either opt for suicide—the blade's still got some charge to it so it should be a clean kill—or we could go for the more traditional approach and turn ourselves in for the state to execute. Frankly, the suicide's cleaner and it tidies up all the loose ends. But either way's okay with me. We could go down to the copper and confess. That way you'd get to live at least an extra few days until you were sentenced. You'd get the amusing opportunity to tell your unbelievable side of it to unhearing ears. Perhaps you'd prefer that? I'm open to your suggestions, Watly."

The donor paused as if waiting for a reply.

"But I'm being silly, Watly Caiper. You can't communicate with me. You're stuck. For all I know, you've become a blathering idiot. Let's see. . . . I know—we'll spin for it." The donor flicked the edge of the scalpel again and watched it twirl. "I'll spin this little blade just like that, and if it stops facing away from us, we'll go down and confess to the copper. Unless someone beats us to it and reviews the recording lenses first. In that event the copper would probably just blow our head off as we stepped outside. In any case, if this little sweetheart lands *facing* us, I'll just use the last of its charge and slice our carotid artery. Or maybe you'd prefer it straight in the gut. A deep L-shaped incision. It's more noble, if more painful. Hara-kiri and all. Something from the ancient Outerworld. Yes, that'll do nicely."

Watly watched helplessly as the donor lifted the blade and carefully positioned it in the center of the desk.

"Well, whatever happens, I've had a time, Watly. You've got a fine body and I was proud to use it. I promise to be quick with the suicide if that's what it's going to be. Let's give the old scalpel a twirl and see what's in store for us."

Watly saw that the blood was already drying on his fingers as he watched his right hand reach forward and spin the blade with a firm twist. It spun wildly but remained on the desk. The donor's eyes stayed glued to it as it slowed. It seemed to be moving agonizingly slow—as if intentionally prolonging the torture. First away from Watly, then facing him. Away and facing. Watly thought if he wasn't insane already this would surely push him over the edge. The surgeon's scalpel finally stopped.

"Oh, bad luck, Watly! Mea maxima culpa. I hope you're not too disappointed. Looks like we'll have to let the state kill Watly Caiper. No suicide for Watly. My apologies." The donor rose and straightened the laces on the stained workervest. "Well, shall we go? It's time we bared our soul and confessed to our faithful metal watchdog."

Back outside, they found that the night had grown cooler. Watly was again overwhelmed with the sensation of space above them. The unmanned copper was right where they'd left it, gleaming in the glow of a nearby streetlight. Watly's donor trotted them quickly down the front steps to meet it.

"Do you have vocal?" asked the donor.

The same pleasant unfeeling female voice they'd heard in the tube issued forth from the copper's speaker plate.

"Vocal, yes."

"Oh, good; oh, good." The donor was smiling and Watly could feel his jaws aching from the broadness of the grin. "I guess you haven't yet gotten any special reports regarding this particular building, then."

"Special reports?" the voice said.

"Guess not. Should be any minute now if the surveillance

people are at least *halfway* decent. In any case, I have a confession."

The turrets swiveled to face Watly directly. "You wish to confess a crime?"

"Oh, it's more than just a crime . . . it's . . ." the grin was so broad and strained now that Watly's jaw was tingling, "it's an absolute abomination!"

"What is this crime?" the female voice asked.

And then Watly realized the tingling wasn't from the smile at all. The tingling was from the wafers. The signal was fading. Watly was coming back!

"What is the crime?" the copper repeated.

The donor was not going to give up easily. "The crime is . . ." It was as if Watly and the donor were grappling, struggling for control. They were fighting for the body, wrestling for power. But the cold stranger's grip was weakening.

"What is the crime?" the copper's speaker asked again.

"The crime is . . ."

Watly could feel control coming back to him. He was winning. He was moving forward down the corridor and the donor was sliding back—fighting tooth and nail, but sliding back nonetheless. Watly could move his own eyes. It was over. The donor was receding. As the foreign consciousness passed in the darkness, Watly got the impression that his donor punched a hole through the mental wall that separated them. It seemed a strange act of desperation. Then Watly realized it was not. It was a last attempt at communication—direct communication. Supposedly impossible, but that wasn't going to stop the donor from trying. Mind-to-mind communication. The mental blow was sharp and accurate and left what felt like a small clean hole. A message slipped through just before the hole closed in on itself like a constricting orifice.

Watly Caiper, running will just make it worse. You think you are lucky to have the body back. Well, I gladly abdicate the body to you. This gives you no advantage. You will try to flee. You will try to make others understand. You will try to escape punishment. This will just make your death all the more assured and violent. Take my advice, Watly Caiper. You've killed a very important person. Confess. You have no hope otherwise. If you confess, at least your death will be painless. I have already won, Watly Caiper. I won long ago.

And then the donor was gone. Completely gone. It was almost as if there was a vacuum in Watly's mind. He felt hollow and empty.

"What is the crime you confess?" The copper had neared and its lower bumper was now touching Watly's knee.

"Crime?" Watly said. He felt tongue-tied. His own body was a strange thing. "Not crime. . . . No no no. Did I say crime?" Watly felt lost and trapped, yet he knew he had to keep talking. *Come on, Caiper—think!* "Not a crime at all. Not a real one. No no. It's just that I've raped up the job so badly. Look at me." Watly lifted the edge of the workervest. "First time on the job and I blow it. The whole toilet's a mess. Terradamn thing practically exploded. It was horrible. Whole bathroom's a total wreck. They kicked me out and told me never to come back. Send me to the Subkeeper—I mean it. Look at this—a brand-new vest. Now it's covered with that brownish-red loo cleaner they use. I'll never get it out. Boy, I really blew that one." Watly started walking, uncomfortably aware that the turrets were trained on his back. He heard the copper's engine start as it followed behind.

"There was no crime?" the copper asked.

Watly kept walking. He spoke over his shoulder. "There sure *was* a crime. It's a crime that I've been trying for years to work up here and then the whole thing goes . . . down the toilet, so to speak. It's a damn crime. I'm a sofdick subspawn."

"You said there would be special reports from the surveillance people. What does that mean?"

"Damn right there will be," Watly said. He was picking up the pace, wending around the buttresses. The copper kept up easily. "I imagine it'll take forever to clean all the goop off the lenses. They got all splattered as I left. I didn't mean it. There's that cleaner and then there's the crap from the toilet. It's a real nightmare. If I were them, I *would* file a report. They probably want me arrested or something and I don't blame them. I really don't. I've made such a fool of myself. A once-in-a-lifetime opportunity and I mess it up. A job on Second—can you believe it?"

Watly was navigating on some kind of instinct he didn't quite understand himself. He recognized no landmarks or signs, but somehow managed to keep his sense of direction. Perhaps a subconscious memory of the trip there guided him. The copper had yet to criticize the route, so Watly assumed everything was okay so far. He turned down what seemed to be the original large avenue—this level's version of Third Avenue—and kept up his brisk pace. He walked with his eyes lowered, imitating as best he could the behavior of his donor.

"Must've been the damn Coldy Valve. I didn't even check it. Like a firstfaced bean, I go to clean a toilet and I don't even check the valve first. What a catbreath secondkissing bolehole! Spurted all over the terradamn place. Probably ruined those poor people's rug. Fuckable rug, too. Expensive. I could just scream about the whole thing. We'll just see if I ever get a job on Second again."

Watly glanced up and saw the tubestop ahead. He felt relief. It wasn't far. He became aware for the first time that his heart was pounding wildly. It was out of control. It seemed to Watly his chest would burst at any moment. *Calm down, Caiper. Calm down. You'll make it. Just get to First—that's your element. Get to First Level and you'll be fine.*

"Yeah," Watly said, "I'm lucky if I get a job working for somebody who works for somebody who works on Second. That's the truth. This whole deal was a bust from start to finish." Watly was closing in on the tube. It was only a dozen yards or so away. Watly could see the seal and the hatch handles clearly.

"Just a moment," said the copper. "Just a moment."

Watly kept walking.

The copper slowed and its speaker crackled with static. "Just a moment. Receiving a special bulletin. Receiving a communication from surveillance team zero-five-zero."

Watly kept walking rapidly. The tubestop shone blackly in the streetlight like a huge metallic finger. Watly reached a hand out toward the seal.

"Just a moment. Do not move, sir. Do not move at this time. There is information of a crime. A crime has been committed.

There is . . . acknowledgment of your guilt. Identification: Watly Caiper." Watly could hear the copper approaching slowly. "Cease movement or suffer open fire."

Watly threw his hands out and broke the seal with his left as he simultaneously opened the hatch with his right. He dove into the entrance of the tube and hit the inside floor just as the copper let loose a round. The copper had two standard chip guns and their slugs thudded into the metal of the tubestop. The minute Watly landed he twisted his body sideways so that his position would not be where the copper had estimated it to be. There was the sound of metal being punctured. In the shadows he could see the floor next to him being ripped up as the slugs tore in.

There was a short pause between rounds as the cartridges changed and the copper recalibrated Watly's position to adjust its aim. It would get him for sure this time. Watly lashed upward with his foot and connected with the hatch handle's inner ring. He quickly flipped the hatch closed just as the copper began firing again. The slugs pounded into the outside of the tubestop. Watly jumped up and sealed the hatch. The seal set in fast with a rush of air. Watly stepped to the center of the tube. The blue-toned circular lights stuttered briefly and then went on.

The sound of the copper firing at the tube was incredible. It was like having his head in a bucket while someone kicked it. Fortunately, the slugs were not penetrating to the inside. Not yet.

"Face forward, please."

The voice startled Watly. He turned to the lens.

"Place your identification in the proper slots before you, please," the female voice continued. Watly knew all his cards— and the donor's cards—would be invalid by now. All they'd do was finger him. There was the sound of something shattering and more thumps as the slugs tore deeper into the outside of the tube.

"Is there a disturbance at the exterior of this structure?"

"Listen to me." Watly leaned close to the lens, hardly recognizing his own voice. "Listen very carefully. I have no identicard. I have no travelpass. I am a First Leveler. I don't belong here. Return me to where I belong. It is your duty. I am a danger to this level. I do not belong here. Return me to First Level."

"Just a moment. Just a moment. I am receiving a communication—"

"Forget the raping communication! It's supposed to be hard to get *up* here—not to *leave*!" Watly felt desperation rising in his belly.

"I have a special bulletin and a positive face print. You are Watly Caiper. I have confirmation from unmanned copper Welter-One-One. You are a high-priority death-imperative criminal—"

"You've got the wrong man, ma'am."

"I have orders to hold on Second until you can be removed from this structure."

Watly felt himself trembling. "You have *got* to lower this tube to First!"

The bland female voice did not respond. The lens stared blankly at Watly, waiting with infinite patience.

There was a pause in the pounding from outside. The copper was reloading and repositioning. Watly wondered if it was worth making a run for it. He was about to try it when the chip guns opened up again. At first there was only the loud thud coming from a different side, but then there was a popping sound and Watly felt something whiz by his right cheek. He crouched and rolled back on his rear as sparks flew and the central circular light exploded. A slug must have broken through the tube's skin. Everything sounded louder now. Watly stayed down as the pounding continued. There was a sound like static from the front of the tube and sparks still danced off the ruptured slot board. Watly covered his head. He smelled burning plastic.

"Face forward, please," the female voice said again, only now it sounded distinctly sluggish. A piece of metal dangled and fell off the board.

Watly stayed on the floor. Another slug got in and ricocheted crazily for a second before stopping. "I *am* facing forward," Watly lied, shouting.

"I'm sorry." The female voice sounded almost drunk now. "I'm sorry."

"Are you going to take me down now?" Watly yelled over the din.

"I'll . . . I'll need your cards first."

"You *have* my cards," Watly said. "You've had them for ages!"

"Oh, yes . . . my apologies. And what is . . . what is your reason for leaving Second Level?"

Watly kept both arms crossed over his head for protection and curled himself into an almost fetal ball. "I'm being chased by Watly Caiper! Watly Caiper the criminal! You just confirmed it yourself!" he yelled.

"Oh, yes . . . well, then, we must get you down there rapidly. Yes . . . we must. The man is a murderer."

Watly heard a loud creak and the scrape of metal on metal and then the floor shifted as the tube eased downward. He was going home.

CHAPTER 16

When Watly stepped out of the tube onto Third Avenue between Sixty-third and Sixty-fourth streets he knew he was in deep catshit. One quick look told him that. In either direction he looked—uptown or downtown—he could see cruisers, manned and unmanned coppers, and even foot patrol officers all converging on the tube from the distance. Word was out. First Level police must have just been contacted. The response was extraordinary. *You'd think I killed the Chancellor or something*, Watly thought.

The minute they saw him they began moving in even more rapidly. Watly sprinted across the avenue. He knew they couldn't shoot yet without fear of hitting each other. There wasn't a single pedestrian or tenter in sight on the avenue. Nobody. Watly ran to the corner and dashed down Sixty-third toward Second Avenue, praying there wouldn't be more cops waiting there. He heard the loud buzz as the cruisers and coppers sped after him. Tons of police. Tons of weapons. Tons of vehicles. It wouldn't take them long to catch him at this rate. No contest. None. Watly neared the corner of Second Avenue, running as hard as he could, arms pumping. The crowd of cars and people chasing him began firing. The report of chip pistols echoed loudly. Lots of them. All at once. Watly ran. *A hiding place? A hiding place?* Slugs zinged against the street and Watly could see the bolts from the haver nerve guns out of the corner of his eye.

Damn! Not the nerve guns. Anything but a nerve gun. If I have to die, Watly thought frantically, *I'd rather die from a slug.*

He tried to run in an unpredictable pattern, dodging and weaving, varying his gait. Back and forth. He passed closed gates and sealed windows on either side. No cover. The clicks of a hundred cop shoes behind him—a raping *sea* of cops and coppers. Watly stumbled, almost falling. Another chip volley was fired and the slugs landed dangerously close. Thuds against the pitted road. Watly could feel the rush of air against his body that meant they'd missed by inches. Less than inches. Too close. *Gimme a place. A place to go. Safe place. Where are the raping people?*

The slugs were thudding loudly into the pavement next to him well before the actual sounds of the guns firing those same shots reached him. First, *thud,* then *crack* from the weapons. *Thud . . . crack. Thud . . . crack.*

I'm not going to hear the shot that kills me, Watly thought as he dodged, *until after I'm hit with it. There's something unfair in that.*

Just as he began to round the corner he was confronted by another manned copper coming from the other direction. Face-to-shocked-face. They almost collided with each other. The surprised officer reached off the moving copper and grabbed at Watly's vest. He held a chip pistol in the other hand and Watly struggled to keep it pointed away. They fought for it. The only thing keeping the copper in place was Watly's own body. The machine strained to continue forward but Watly's feet were planted and his body leaned inward. The copper's engine ground loudly in protest as Watly wrestled with the man on top. The machine rocked and whined. Watly could hear the squeal of the other vehicles approaching rapidly from behind him. As if in surrender, he let the officer's gun hand go free, but in the same instant—with a burst of energy—pulled the man right out of the seat by the shirt collar. They both fell clear and Watly heard the gun clatter on the sidewalk somewhere nearby. The newly freed copper bolted forward like an out-of-control rocket. Watly just had time to see the surprised faces on the pursuing officers as the copper plowed into them. There was a loud crash followed by a tremendous explosion of fuel. Watly rose quickly and glanced around for the gun. The officer he'd dethroned was out of it altogether now, groaning like he was having a nightmare. Watly saw the gun behind an upright and grabbed it up quick, running off down Second Avenue.

The confusion and fire would only hold them off a moment. Watly had to make it count. He continued down the avenue, his lungs straining for more air than they could hold, the gun feeling strange and foreign in his hand. Any second and the cops would resume the chase. Backups would be called. Traps would be positioned. There were people on this avenue. *Thank terra for people*. Watly navigated his way around a few tents and practically stepped on a bum.

"Hey, watch it, boss!"

His legs were sore from exertion and on the verge of cramping up. Watly wasn't used to running like this. He was going all-out, running for his life. His calves began to throb painfully. His knees ached. There were a lot of tenters and bums all along the street, mostly asleep—or pretending to be. Watly stumbled again, stepping sideways to keep from falling. He knew he couldn't keep up this pace. He'd drop soon. Everything was weakening. The body was giving up. He slowed down and finally stopped altogether and leaned into a girder, heaving and bent over. It was good to stop. Good to breathe again. Looking back at the avenue from behind the upright, Watly could see the distant lights of the approaching police. They were back in the hunt. Regrouped and recovered.

Watly didn't have many options. He looked down at the pistol in his hand. It was a heavy weapon. The grip was plasticore but the rest was metal. He could try to fight them off, but that would be foolish. The odds were way against him, and anyway, he had no experience with shooting. Even if he had it would be of little use. They'd keep coming. They'd always keep coming. He had no chance with the gun.

Watly could see the police lights reflecting brilliantly off the slick surface of the First Level ceiling. They were not arriving very fast. The cops were moving slowly now. They'd temporarily lost their prey. Watly guessed that since there was no movement up ahead, they were making sure they missed nothing. Odds were that they were rousting every sleeper and searching every tent in their path, while keeping their eyes open for a fleeing Watly Caiper ahead.

Watly looked around him. From a nearby tent there was a soft glow. A few bums lay sleeping next to it. Watly stuck the gun in his back vest loop where it would be hidden. He took a second to make up his mind and then went over to the nearest bum, crouching low. He gripped the man's wrinkled jacket at the shoulder and shook.

"Mister . . . mister. Wake up."

"Uh," the man said. His face was filthy. Underneath the dirt, the features were aged and leathery.

"Mister, do you want to make one hundred New York dollars?"

Suddenly the man was wide awake. "One hundred? One hundred?" His cheeks expanded. "What's the catch?"

"Here's the money." Watly fished in the pocket of the workervest for his money. There was a moment of panic as he thought perhaps the donor never transferred it. But no. It had been with the identicard all along. Watly drew out the bill.

"What's the catch, boss?" The bloodshot eyes narrowed. "This about California? 'Cause if it's about California—"

"Forget California. Nothing to do with it. All you got to do is run. Can you run?"

"I can run like a demon. That it? Just run?"

"When I say so, I want you to run as fast as you can down the avenue. That direction. If I'm right, some cops'll chase you. Stay at the side of the street. Stay near people. No one will hurt you if you stay where it's crowded. You understand? When you get tired, stop and turn around. Let them see your face and you'll be okay." Watly handed the man the bill. "If they catch you before you get tired, turn around anyway. Let them see you. Make sure they see your face and you'll be fine."

"You in trouble, boss?"

"You might say that, yes."

The bum sniffed. "Maybe it's worth more."

Watly snatched the bill back. "Maybe I'll find someone else to do it."

The bum's lips twitched and then he grabbed the money back with a greasy hand. "Just asking, just asking. I'll do your running for you. Wanna swap clothes?"

Watly glanced at the man's outfit. "Let's not go overboard," he said. "There's no time anyway. The running alone will have to do it."

"Sure this ain't about California, boss?"

"I *said* it wasn't, terradammit!" Watly looked up the street. Time was wasting.

"Okay, okay!" The bum stood up. " 'Cause if it had been—" he brushed clouds of dirt off his pants, "if it had been, I'd'a done it for free."

By now the cops were only about twenty yards away. Watly could see their faces clearly. They were angry. The explosion and Watly's subsequent escape had not pleased them. This did not disturb Watly. It encouraged him. He was hoping their anger would make them sloppy. Watly patted the bum on the rump. "You're on, fella!" he said, and then he scrambled back into the shadow of the girder as the bum lumbered down the road.

Watly could hear the cruisers and coppers rev up as they caught sight of the running figure. The old bum was doing his best at running—staggering along at a slow pace near the curb, his tattered smock billowing out behind him. Watly made out the sound of clipped orders being exchanged as the police moved out rapidly. As Watly had suspected, they were drawn to the move- ment. He hoped they would all assume the man was a disguised Watly Caiper fleeing. Watly shrunk down against the damp girder, becoming as small and insignificant as he could.

The parade of police neared and started passing. A few of the cruisers were badly charred and dented from the explosion. Undoubtedly some had been put out of commission entirely. Watly could clearly make out the front-running officers riding their coppers with guns raised. One was even standing up. It was time for Watly to take off now. But he didn't. Not yet. Not yet.

Up ahead the bum was stumbling now, losing his balance and careening back and forth. Every lump and pothole tripped him up. *Okay, enough,* Watly thought. *Time to turn around, old fellow. You've done fine.*

But the bum was still trying valiantly to keep his pace up. His legs looked wobbly and about to give way under him. Watly knew he should take this moment to run the opposite way. The police were misdirected. Their attentions were elsewhere. It was perfect. But he couldn't flee. The bum thing was not working right. Something was wrong. Really wrong. Watly sensed something horrible was about to happen. *Don't push it, friend,* Watly thought. *You've earned your money. Turn around and let them see you're not me.*

The leading coppers had almost caught up with the bum. The old guy stumbled once again and regained his balance by cross-stepping sideways toward the center of the street. He looked ready to drop. *Get to the side,* Watly thought. *Get out of the center. Turn around.*

As if he could read Watly's thoughts, the old bum slowed and began to turn, his face in a broad grin. Watly could see the standing officer in the front copper leveling his weapon. The man never paused. There was a blinding flash as the cop released the bolt from his nerve gun. Its tail streaked down the street and stuck the bum in the center of the chest. There was a shriek. The old man lit up—brightening the whole scene—and in a split second his body was lifted clear off the ground spread-eagled. Watly could see the surprise and agony in the man's face as he landed hard on his back with a loud thud. The charge burned into the man's chest, climbing up his spinal cord toward the brain. Beneath the rags, his torso was glowing. The screaming grew louder. His hands scrabbled uselessly on the pitted street next to him. For another moment his face became a mask of pain—unbelieving, astonished, intolerable pain. Spittle flew from his mouth as his head flopped side to side. The screams grew louder still. Impossibly loud. And then . . . and then he died. No more screams. No more pain. The whole thing had taken hardly ten seconds, but it was an excruciatingly long ten seconds. It was the longest ten seconds there ever was. Watly watched it all in horror. They'd killed the bum. Brutally and violently. Without bothering to see if it was really Watly or not. Watly was responsible. He might as well have fired the gun himself. *I didn't figure they would,* he thought. *I thought they'd see. Just some misdirection. Just some extra time. Oh, rape, maybe I did figure. Maybe . . . maybe I knew. . . .*

The officer who'd shot the old man made the police victory salute and jumped off the copper to inspect the now smoldering body. *They'll see it isn't me,* Watly thought. *They already know.*

People were stirring. Many tenters and bums had been awoken by the noise. Those who had been roused already moved in closer. The whole street woke up. Watly saw lights go on inside tents near him and heard the rustling as people moved about. A few yawning figures emerged from the tents and strained to get a view of the body. A crowd of tenters and bums and even a few apartment people began to gather around the police.

Watly didn't know what to do. He'd lost his chance to flee. The old man's running had, after all, not even served its purpose. The misdirection was lost. Watly had frozen up. The man had died for nothing and now Watly was back where he started. But with a death on his conscience. *I honestly didn't want that,* Watly thought. *I honestly thought they wouldn't hurt him. That they wouldn't take the chance. Oh, shit.*

The gathering crowd was large now and people were whispering questions about what might have happened. "California?" "Is it California?" "Is it starting?"

Watly slowly stood up. A nearby tenter crawled out of her tent to join the excitement. Watly slid in beside her and they walked together toward the circle of people. He knew running would do no good now. He'd stick out like a blue bean and it would just be a matter of time before they caught up to him. He had no running left in him, anyway. He had just killed someone, really.

As Watly surreptitiously joined the crowd, the cops began to try to break it up.

"Okay, folks," one female officer said. "Move along, now. Back to bed. Nothing happened here." She was standing high on a cruiser's roof, motioning everyone away. People mumbled, but few moved. "Move it, folks," she said now, her voice harsher.

Watly could see the officer's trained eyes scanning the crowd carefully as she spoke. The cops were looking for him still. All of them. Staring at each face in the throng of people. Watly squatted down some and looked up between shoulders and heads.

"Come on, people. Just a dead bum. That's all."

She and the others waved the people away with their weapons. It was half gentle wave, half threat. Some of the crowd began to move on. Most just shuffled and mumbled louder. Watly got an idea. He got a crazy idea.

"Back to bed now," the cop said, pointing with her gun toward the nearby tents and apartments. A few voices were raised. "What happened?" "What'd the bum do?" "What's going on?"

Watly watched how the officer was using the weapon to gesticulate with more and more. He kept his eyes focused on her gun as he reached around back and slipped the chip pistol from his vest. It was cold and dry in his hands. He held it close to his body and pointed it upward—toward the First Level ceiling. The damn thing sure was heavy. Heavy and cool. He gritted his teeth and squeezed the trigger. The explosion rocked him backward with its force. His ears rang. The crowd was stunned into silence, looking for the source of the gunshot. Watly held his head down and shouted at the top of his lungs. "They mean to kill us all! It's a massacre!" Watly squeezed the trigger again and the slug struck the daylite overhead. It exploded in a shower of sparks. The crowd was thrown into darkness. *Lucky shot,* Watly thought. There were panicked screams and shouts and the whole group began to run frantically in all directions. Bodies banged into one another. It was a crazy, aimless stampede.

Watly joined in running with the rest, tucking the gun back into place. He was just one more wild-eyed person out of hundreds. One frantic figure among many. There was no way they could single him out.

When he was far enough down the street to feel safe, he glanced backward. Not everyone had run, apparently. In the pandemonium, some had stayed. *Many* had stayed. Some had not been frightened by the shots—they had been angered. Bottles were flying. Shoes. Pieces of concrete. Fists arced. More gun-shots echoed. Screaming rose up high and piercing. Back there in the darkness, the fighting throng became a single living angry being. Someone chanted from the sidelines, "California! California! California!"

Watly Caiper turned and ran on. He was glad to be away from the searchers, glad for the momentary safety of flight. But he was disturbed by the means. Disturbed at the death of the bum, yes. *Rape and double rape, yes. His fault.* But also disturbed by another thing. Disturbed that he, Watly Caiper, had just started . . . a riot. Yes, a riot.

As easy as pie.

CHAPTER 17

Watly made it to Narcolo's apartment. He didn't know how, but he made it. Nowhere else to go. He hoped it would take the police time to call up his records for his residence. Maybe a little time. A little. He had to go home, anyway, at least for a second. And he made it somehow. In hindsight he had very little memory of the trip. There was a vague recollection of stopping to rub the oily slime from a dirty puddle over his workervest to camouflage the bloodstains. There was also the memory of more running, of more hiding in the shadows, and of the gleam of dangerously close coppers in the night daylites. There was a fuzzy recollection involving the sharing of a tent with a bewildered old tenter until hurried footsteps passed by. The old man kept smiling crazily and saying something about how it must be California time. "It must be starting. . . ." There was also some dim memory about a close call near Astor Place where Watly had to pretend to be a drunken bum who kept his face covered.

All this was a fog. All this was like some once-removed story heard long ago. The only vivid part—the only part that really stuck with him—was the thinking. Watly remembered the thinking. If a human brain was a keyboard, then this thinking was input overload. Watly had found his mind buzzing and zipping from one thought to the next.

Why me? What's going on here? What the hell does this mean? I didn't do anything. It was the donor. It was all that crazy donor. But there was no cuff. No hosting cuff. Impossible. Removing the cuff—that's not supposed to be possible. And I've got no proof. As far as the world knows, I did it; I wasn't hosting. Nobody knows I was hosting. Except the donor. And except for . . . except for the doctor. That blond doctor. Mitterly, I think it was. Mitterly. He was in on this. If I could find him . . . and, of course, the donor. Whoever the hell the donor was.

And who else? Who's on my side? No one was there. No witnesses. Narcolo knew I was going hosting but he has no proof. It's just what I told him. He didn't even see the assignment slip. And what about Alysess? Could she help me? Are there records somewhere? This is all crazy. The cops. The guns. They just want to kill me. I've committed murder, to them. And who the subs did I kill, then? The donor killed her—I didn't, dammit! And . . . and why? And who was that other one? The first woman. The drugged one the donor had had sex with—more like raped. Who was she?

What am I a part of? I'll be lucky if I can stay alive, let alone find out! This is insane. What's this all about? If I could just . . . if I could just get proof I was hosting—proof of what really happened—I'd be able to stop all this. But I have to stay alive. I have to stay alive to do that. Alive.

I cannot fight without hurting now, Mom. I'm fighting for my life.

"Oh, hello there, Watly. Sorry . . . I didn't hear you. I guess I was . . . sleeping, I guess. Watly—you look . . . What happened? What are you wearing? You look all . . . What's the story? Kiddo? Come sit down."

The old man was wearing his worn red nightshirt and his face was more creased than ever with sleep lines. He led Watly to the couch.

"Put on the CV, Uncle," Watly said.

"Now, now—we must talk. You look like—"

"Put the damn CV on!" Watly shouted. He was in no mood to argue.

Uncle Narcolo cringed. He set up the machine with practiced hands and found the all-news pleat. Then he stepped back silently to watch along with Watly. The CV mist spread upward rapidly.

> . . . early this morning. Authorities are still putting together the pieces of this tragedy.
> We repeat: Corber Alvedine, founder and head of Alvedine Hosting Industries (the company that brings you joy on so many levels), has been brutally murdered. He was at his home offices at the time. A review of the lenses confirms that the perpetrator was one Watly Caiper. Caiper is still at large and believed to be somewhere on First Level, wearing Second Level worker clothing. He is armed and very dangerous, having already murdered two police officers and an innocent bum during his escape, as well as injuring dozens of street people. Our handsome Chancellor has called these horrible events heinous. "More heinous than many other events," he said, and he has issued a ranking of high-priority, death-imperative to Watly Caiper. This is the top ranking possible. Anyone caught aiding or harboring the criminal is subject to full punishment—up to and including the death penalty. A reward of one million New York dollars has been set for first kill or capture.
> Corber Alvedine is survived by his mate, Sentiva Alvedine. He will long be remembered as a man of foresight, vision, sexual dynamism, immense wealth, and a noble business acumen. His untimely and brutal death may make him eligible for state martyrdom. We mourn his passing. More on this lead story after a brief News Song-Singing Segment. . . .

Narcolo was staring at Watly, his mouth open. Watly began mumbling, "It *wasn't* a man. What's going on? It was a *woman*.

An older woman." He was confused. Everything was upside down. Nothing made sense. *Corber Alvedine?* He was one of the most powerful men in Manhattan.

Narcolo backed up slightly. His voice was hoarse. "What happened, kiddo? Did you do this thing?"

Watly stared into frightened aged eyes. "Give me a break, Uncle! It was a setup. I've been framed. Framed so goddamn beautifully even *I* don't understand it."

"What . . . what happened?"

"It was a setup. Don't you understand? I was hosting. The donor did it. The donor did it all!"

Narcolo sighed with relief. "Then you're okay, kiddo. You're okay. Yes. They'll see the cuff when they review the—"

"The donor took *off* the cuff. The donor had a way to remove the cuff prematurely."

"That's impossible."

"That's what I thought."

The CV was flashing on the image of Watly's own face. It was unsettling to see himself floating fuzzily above them in the living room. He turned away. *Why did they say it was a man? And* Corber Alvedine, *of all men! Why the change? And they say I murdered police and the bum. I didn't kill the bum—at least not directly. And the police they're talking about must've been killed in the copper crash. Why are they lying like this? Bad enough what it looks like I did* do; *why the hell are they distorting it all so much?*

Watly's uncle looked bewildered, frightened. "What're you gonna do, kiddo?"

"First of all," Watly said, trying to pull himself together— trying not to *think*. "First of all, I'm going to change clothes."

The wrinkles in Narcolo's brow deepened. He looked like a wounded animal. "They'll come here, Watly. They'll come here soon. This is the first place they'll look. You live here. It's on record at immigration and at Alvedine. All they gotta do is call it up and they'll know you live here. We've gotta get you out of here."

Watly was thinking narrowly now. Concentrating. "First I need clothes. I won't last another minute in these."

Narcolo ran to the drawers and pulled out some worn clothing—brown shoes, anklepants, and a jersey jacket. He also found a broad-brimmed hat with ear cups.

"Put this stuff on, Watly. Hurry."

Watly threw off the outfit and started dressing. With his back turned he transferred the gun and the other items from the workervest to the jacket. The pockets bulged. Something clattered to the floor but Watly had no time to bother with it. Meanwhile, Narcolo filled a knapsack for him.

"You'll need some food, Watly. For your travels. You may not get to . . . I'm packing a hardloaf and some dried beans. Here's all your money, too. The bills and the untitled credits are fine. Your titled pieces are useless now. They've got your name all over them, kiddo. I'll hold 'em for you. Maybe someday—" Narcolo coughed abruptly. "And here's that booze you bought—the unopened bottle—you might want that. Put your ear cups on, Watly. And pull them tight. Tighter—make them hurt. That pulls the skin and makes your face look a little different. Pull 'em up tighter, Watly—that's it. It stretches the flesh around your throat and makes you look thinner. I know it hurts but it's worth a shot. Keep the brim tilted down." Narcolo closed the bag and handed it to Watly. "If you get out of Manhattan, if you make it—and I'm sure you will—try to let me know. Let me know, kiddo. Try to get a message to me. I want to know you made it."

Watly swung the pack onto his shoulders and turned to his uncle. "I'm not *leaving* Manhattan, my friend. I'm staying."

"You're crazy," Narcolo said. He shook his head vigorously. "I just packed your— But you . . . you can't do that! You *can't*! Don't be crazy!"

"No, no. You're wrong, Uncle. I'd be crazy if I tried to leave."

His uncle almost screamed. "You've *got* to leave! The cops'll kill you! You'll—"

Watly held a firm hand up. "I can't leave, old man. They'll increase security at every exit. I'd have no chance." Watly tightened the knapsack straps. "Even if I *could* make it, I'd have to spend the rest of my life running. This is high priority for them, you understand? They wouldn't rest until they found me. No matter where. Whatever country. They'd track me anywhere in the

UCA. I'd have to go into hiding. I don't want that. No. I have to stay. I have to find out what's going on."

"Outerworld. You'll go to the Outerworld, kiddo. Find a way. There must be some way. They won't follow you there."

"You don't understand, Uncle!" Watly shouted at this little kid, his *son/uncle*. "I'll never make it *out of Manhattan* if I try. I *have* to stay!"

"You'll get killed, Watly. One false step and you're dead. Everybody wants you. No one'll help you."

Watly looked at the little man's face. The eyes were pleading. The mouth trembling. He grabbed his uncle's face roughly and kissed the wrinkled forehead. "Someone already has, Uncle," Watly said.

The old man pulled away.

"I've got no choice, old friend," Watly continued. "I can die running or I can die chasing. I'd rather chase." He paused before going on. "I'd better get going before someone gets here. No time. I'd get rid of those clothes if I were you. I don't want *you* arrested. Or worse."

Narcolo was bunching up the edge of his nightshirt and looked about to cry. "I'm sorry, kiddo. I'm real sorry," he said.

Watly rested a hand on a bony shoulder. "Not your fault," he said.

Before leaving, Watly took a last look back at the CV. The report continued, repeating endlessly. First there was the image of Corber Alvedine, the man Watly was supposed to have killed—a man he'd never seen before. Then the image of Watly himself—a file photo from identicard records. Finally, the frozen image of a beautiful woman with piercing green eyes. She had not appeared before.

> . . . *the grieving mate of Corber, the lovely Sentiva Alvedine, was unavailable for comment at this* . . .

Watly recognized the face. The eyes were not familiar but the features were. The perfect nose, the high cheekbones, full lips, and slightly overpowering jawline. The green eyes were not familiar because they had always been closed. She was the woman in the bed! Sentiva Alvedine was the drugged body the donor had raped! *Okay,* Watly thought. *Okay, so let's get this straight: somebody tricks me into hosting, gets inside my head in order to rape the drugged wife of Corber Alvedine, and then murders a woman who they now say isn't a woman at all. They now say she is Corber herself. Manhattan mogul assassinated by the everpopular Watly Caiper.*

Watly swallowed hard, more confused than ever, and hugged his trembling uncle goodbye.

He peered cautiously in both directions before mounting the steps. As he went quietly up onto the street his mind shifted back into overdrive and his thoughts again raced. Thinking widely. He nibbled absentmindedly on the hardloaf as he walked. *Why? Why? What the hell is going on?*

Soon the daylites would go to full. Morning was coming. And with it, another day in the life of Watly Caiper. But nothing was the same now.

CHAPTER 18

Watly's ears were killing him. It felt like they were being ripped upward off his head. They throbbed with every thump of his heartbeat. Ear cups were out of fashion, yet not so uncommon as to draw attention. They were a good idea, but an excruciating one. Watly didn't know how long he'd last before having to loosen them. He tried not to think about it. It occurred to him he hadn't slept at all. Not even a nap. He was still running on adrenaline. Eventually he'd have to get some sleep somehow. And maybe even a shave. That would be nice. There was the beginning of thick stubble all over his chin and jaw. Maybe that was good. Maybe it helped with the disguise—a broad shadow-casting hat, different clothes, a backpack, the beginnings of a beard, the distorting ear cups. . . . The ear cups. The damn ear cups. *Ow.*

Watly was on Fifty-seventh in front of the Alvedine Building. He'd already finished up the hardloaf. It left his mouth dry but he welcomed the strength nourishment gave him. Better than nothing. The daylites had come on full and the street was filling up with people walking to work. Watly kept moving. He walked up and down the street, his eyes searching. He knew that, dressed as he was, it might draw attention for him to stand still. Everyone but a few bums was on the way somewhere, and Watly wasn't dressed much like a bum. He kept walking back and forth, trying to blend in while scanning the faces around him. He particularly watched those entering Alvedine's front door. Doctors, electricians, hosts, maintenance people—he tried to take them all in. There'd only be one chance.

A cruiser passed slowly and the crowds moved aside. Watly kept moving along with them, involuntarily holding his breath. The cruiser continued onward. Watly glanced back to watch it turn the corner. From the edge of his vision he caught a glimpse of something brown and white going up Alvedine's steps. He turned and walked briskly back toward the building. A woman with dark skin wearing a large birdhat and a white doctor suit was nearing the top step. It looked like it could be her. Watly bounded up the steps. Just before the woman could open the door, Watly grabbed her arm. She turned. It was Alysess. She looked blankly at Watly for a moment. There was no recognition in her expression. Then suddenly her eyes widened.

"*You!*" she said. There was horror in her voice. She looked about to scream. Watly clamped a hand over her mouth and pulled her to the side. They were in the shadow of the door arch on the building's narrow portico. He glanced around. No one seemed to have noticed. Alysess began struggling.

"Listen to me! I didn't *do* anything! Don't believe the reports! I swear to you—it's all a lie."

She still struggled. Her eyes were full of fear.

"I need your help, Alysess. You've got to help me. I've been set up. I swear. You've got to trust me."

Watly sensed Alysess relaxing slightly. She gradually stopped fighting him. She seemed calmer.

"Are you going to scream?" Watly asked.

She looked at him with those perfect brown eyes and shook her head no.

"Promise?"

She nodded her head slowly.

"You're not going to scream?" Again she shook her head. Watly gently removed his hand from her mouth.

Alysess screamed.

Watly clamped his hand back over her face. He cut off her "help" at the "hel—" and swiveled her into the corner up against a cemeld column.

"All right, if that's the way you want it, that's the way you get it. I've got a gun. A chip pistol. You do that again—you do *anything* but what I tell you to—and . . . and you lose your face." He held her against the column with his body and his left hand and pulled out the gun with his right. He let her go, stepped back, and leveled the weapon at her. She stared at it.

Someone walked up behind him.

"Dr. Tollnismer?"

Watly froze. He kept his back to the person and held the gun tightly, close to his belly. Alysess kept her eyes glued to it.

"You okay, Dr. Tollnismer?"

Watly could tell the person was just a few feet behind him. He motioned slightly with the gun. *Come on, Alysess!*

"I'm . . . I'm fine, Jabe." She still kept looking at the pistol, eyes never wavering. She straightened the birdhat. "It's . . . it's a private matter."

"Oh, sorry. Thought something was wrong. Shame of a thing about Corber, huh? See you later at the meeting."

Watly heard the click of the door as the person entered the building. He put the gun in his right jacket pocket but kept his hand on it. "I've still got you covered, Doctor. Let's go for a walk. Where do you live?"

Watly hadn't planned it this way. He'd thought that a couple of words from his honest face and the good doctor would melt. He'd planned on maybe a few brief seconds of fear that could quickly be dispelled. This was not what he'd wanted. Forcing Alysess Tollnismer to help him was not right. Particularly not at gunpoint. In fact it made him feel awful. *If I wasn't a criminal before*, he thought, *I am now. Kidnapping. An old bum dies because of me, according to the report two cops got it in the copper crash, I start a riot, and now I'm kidnapping someone. I'm kidnapping the last person on earth I'd want to kidnap. This is not the way it should*

be. Why couldn't she just believe me? Why couldn't she be like
Narcolo: shock, fear, and finally trust?

Alysess Tollnismer walked along with great dignity, her head
held high. To Watly, it was like walking alongside royalty. How
she could remain so poised and proud under the circumstances was
a mystery to him. Watly felt like shriveling up into a corner. He
felt like stopping and kneeling before her to beg forgiveness. He
didn't. He continued onward with his hand on the grip of the chip
pistol and his eyes on the doctor. Her birdhat was splendid. Its
back had gotten slightly crushed against the beam, but otherwise
it was perfect. The opalescent sudofeathers reflected each daylite
they traveled beneath. Its wingspan was broad enough to protect
her white outfit from drips. She wore it well. Watly wanted to
compliment it.

"Nice hat," he said.

They kept walking. Watly felt like an idiot.

After a while they reached Alysess's apartment building. She
lived on West Eighty-fourth Street in a decently kept brownstone.
There was no guard or other apparent security system. Dr.
Tollnismer calmly led the way.

Her apartment was very nice. It was larger than Narcolo's and
better furnished. The window looked out on the street below and
daylite streamed in brightly. There were many well-worn books
and leafs lying about and a relatively new CV in one corner. The
window was open a few inches and, since the building was close
to the Eighty-Second Street exhaust, there was a slight breeze. It
was a pleasant sensation to feel air circulating freely. Alysess
walked straight to the one armchair and sat down. Watly saw
anger in her eyes.

"Nice place you've got here," Watly said weakly.

She glared at him. "Am I next?" she asked. She was barely
containing her fury. "Am I your next victim?"

Watly collapsed into the love seat opposite her. He had to make
her understand. He had to make her believe. "I didn't do anything.
I swear to you."

Alysess took her hat off and carefully placed it on the table
beside her. "You're lying," she said.

"I'm *not* lying. I'm *not*. Somebody did this to me. Somebody set me up. How can I prove it to you? How can I make you believe?"

"You can't," she said flatly. There was an extra redness to her dark skin. Her jaw was set. Her eyes were full of hatred.

Watly Caiper started to cry.

At first his eyes just watered and then it was like a dam had burst. Soon he could hardly catch his breath between sobs. The tears poured down. His nose began to run. He'd been framed, shot at, chased, traumatized, abused, witness to a horrible murder done with his own hands, deprived of sleep for hours, forced to watch a bum die in his place, lied about on the CV, and now . . . now he was not being believed. He wanted it all to stop. All of it. He wanted a bath and a shave and a warm bed. He wanted a time out. And he wanted—maybe most of all—to take off those damn ear cups!

He unsnapped them and felt the blood rush back to his ears as he threw the hat off.

"Watly—" Alysess started speaking.

Watly pulled the gun out of his jacket and pointed it straight at the doctor's pretty face. His vision was blurry from the tears. "*What? What?*" he yelled. "You want something?"

"Watly, listen to me. . . ." she said as she leaned toward him.

"No, *you* listen to *me!*" Watly screamed. He almost choked on all the wetness. His face felt liquid—part of the river of tears. He was melting. "You listen to me! I'm going to tell you what happened! I'm going to tell you from the beginning, dammit! And you're going to believe me! Because . . . because you've *got* to. Because it's gotta be that way."

"Watly—"

"Shut up! You hear me?" He waved the pistol at her. "I've got a gun! You *have* to listen! Now shut up and *listen!*"

Alysess shut up. And Watly talked. The whole while the tears kept coming. Watly could feel the collar of his jersey jacket getting damp as the tears fell. And still he continued. He told his tale. He told her about the blond doctor and the evil donor. He told her about the removal of the cuff. He told her about the trip up to Second Level. He told her about the strange tryst with the drugged woman, Sentiva Alvedine. He told her of the murder, and of his horror. He told her of his escape and of the poor old bum who had died. He told her of the riot. He told her how the news report said it was a *man* who was killed, and how they'd said the man was Corber Alvedine. He told her everything. And still the tears came. And the jacket grew wetter. And Alysess's face came closer. And the gun pointed lower.

"Say that you believe me now, Alysess," Watly said finally. "Say that you do." He dropped the gun to the floor. The doctor looked at it a moment before speaking.

"It's a crazy story, Watly."

Watly looked at her. "I know," he said. "I know. But I'm not stupid enough to make it up."

Alysess took a deep breath. Her bright eyes looked uncertain, confused. "I realize that, Watly." She picked up the gun, held it a moment, and then gingerly handed it back to him. "I believe you, Watly Caiper. I do." She smiled just a little. Again the pistol fell to the floor.

Watly kissed her. The kiss was not a kiss of love or a kiss of passion. It was a kiss of thanks. It was a kiss of supreme gratitude. She responded slowly, but soon their tongues met and continued the conversation—understanding, thanking, listening, relating. Watly was still crying and then it seemed as if they both were and neither could tell whose tears were whose. They rolled to the floor together. Maybe she liked him after all.

Things happened slowly. It wasn't clear how. It was blurry and teary and cloudlike. After a time they were both naked somehow, though their lips never parted. Their sexes met briefly—touching tentatively—and then intimately. It was impossible to tell if Watly entered her or if Alysess enveloped him. Either way it was fluid and graceful. They joined together. Merged. Neither moved. There was a great wonderful wetness there. A meeting of slipperiness. Strong smells. They just held each other—he inside her and she around him. They were pressed as tightly as two people could be—arms hugging strongly around backs, breasts to breasts, tongue to tongue, thigh to thigh. They were frozen that way. No rocking, no thrusting, no grinding. Just *being*. Existing in almost the same space. Connected. They exchanged subtle signals by clenching secret muscles. It was a coded conversation. And still neither moved. *This is my harbor,* Watly thought. *This is my home. I have found my protection. I have found a warm, empty cave and crawled inside. I am finally safe in this stranger.* Their signals continued and their tongues still danced.

And that was all the motion.

Eventually, after a great passage of time, a very gentle rocking began. It started with their chests and worked downward. The movement was perfectly in sync, and still so subtle it was almost nonexistent. An end arrived for Alysess and her tongue searched for more as her secret clenching increased. It was a fiery, colorful end. Watly helped her. The movement quickened. Another end came and Watly helped her again. Then his own appeared and she, in turn, helped him, kissing and clasping him through it. It was smooth and beautiful, full of secrets and full of hope. Watly stayed in her and she around him. This was where he wanted to be. Home.

Before long he was in a warm bed with clean sheets. Someone dark and soft and beautiful was there beside him. She was a part of him. He searched and found smooth pink among all the brown, and she found hard among his soft. . . .

And again there was no motion for a while.

When sleep finally came to Watly, it came fast. It came with visions of a perfect set of brilliant alabaster teeth smiling from a mahogany face.

CHAPTER 19

You can tell a lot about a person by the apartment she keeps. Nice neighborhood, nice height (third floor), and pretty well kept building. Street view, too. Watly wandered around Alysess's place, snooping unashamedly. Now that he was alone he could investigate openly. It was his way of getting to know her better. Getting to know this stranger. Getting to know these strong feelings he had about her. To Watly, each drawer he opened and every cabinet he rummaged through brought him closer to the woman.

The doctor's large placene wardrobe held little clothing: a dress suit, a few pairs of shoes, some sweaters, another white uniform, a jacket or two, a few buzbelts, a couple pairs of anklepants, an overcoat, and not much else. On the leafcase she had an extensive erotica collection. Watly flipped through it casually. She collected all types, some quite obscure and high-brow. Watly was impressed with her taste in porn. Near the CV were her music tubes and the player. She had a diverse range of these as well. From contemporary (Engin and Croadly, the Keze) to classical (Beatles,

Mozart, Manilow . . .). Next to the player was a bowl with a few uncashed work tokens and some extra keys. In the kitchen area, Watly could gather that Alysess was a loner. It was a barren kitchen, not one for hearty meals. It seemed hardly used. Obviously the good doctor threw her food together carelessly and without much regard to taste. Watly made a mental note to remember he must cook her a decent meal one day. It was the least he could do. Right now she was most probably risking her life for him. She was certainly risking her career.

She had woken him, after a few short hours of sleep, with a kiss to his forehead.

"Wake up, little Watly."

Watly didn't want to.

"Wake up, now—sleepyhead. I've gotta go."

Watly opened one tired eye and saw Alysess in the process of dressing again in her white uniform.

"What's going on?" he asked, feeling disoriented.

"I've got to get back to Alvedine—for both our sakes." She was pulling on her white boots now. She was wearing only her pants and a belt. Her bare breasts swung pleasingly as she secured the bootclamps.

"You're going back?" Watly opened the other eye as well. He felt groggy. Emotionally hungover.

"I've already missed half the day. If I don't show up at all it will raise suspicion. Someone might come looking. I'd better go in. I'll make up some excuse why I'm late." She lifted her head and gazed at Watly with those clear brown eyes. She smiled. "Watly, didn't anybody ever teach you it's not polite to stare at someone's tits while they're talking to you?"

Watly grinned sleepily. "But they're such nice tits. They're extraordinary tits, actually. Best tits I ever saw. World class."

Alysess leaned over and kissed Watly's forehead again. "They like you too, Mr. Caiper. But right now . . ." She pulled on her top, "right now they're going undercover."

The bed felt warm and comfortable. Watly pulled the covers up to his neck and lifted his knees. He wanted to stay in it forever.

"Do you have to leave?" he asked.

Alysess let her face go serious. Very serious. "If you want to stay alive, I have to leave," she said. "Besides, maybe I can find out something for you. I'll see what I can learn. I've got to be cautious, but maybe I can get some new pieces to this puzzle."

Watly scooted forward on the bed and touched her arm. "You be very careful, Doctor. I don't want anything to happen to you. You realize you could get death for helping me."

"Watly, as far as they're concerned, the fact that you're here in my apartment at *all* is helping you. When I let you in the door with me I became a harborer of a high-priority, death-imperative criminal. It can't get worse than that"

"Yes, it can," Watly said softly. "You could get caught."

"I won't get caught," Alysess replied. She smiled once again. "I'll go to work, I'll apologize for my lateness. I'll do my job. I'll ask a few questions. I'll voice my natural curiosity, glance at a few files, chat with a few peers, pick up my work tokens, and come quietly home. That's it. That's all. It won't take long. You can go back to sleep while I'm gone. You look like you still need it."

Watly made his best cherub face. "I couldn't sleep without you," he said coyly.

"You'll do just fine." Alysess seemed to be getting tense. She put her birdhat back on and went to the door. Her back looked tight and arched.

"Alysess." Watly rose from the covers. He felt suddenly frightened to be left alone. "Before you go—"

"Don't say it, Watly," she interrupted.

"Don't say what?" he asked.

She looked annoyed. "Don't say 'I love you, Alysess,' or 'Be mine, my dear,' or ' Let's live together forever,' or 'Will you be my poovus," or *whatever* it was you were going to say. Just don't say it. It doesn't mean anything." She looked really pissed now. Her hands were clenched. "You're in a bad fix and I'm helping you. I believe you. I like you. You like me. We screwed a few times and that was real nice. Real nice. But Watly, you don't really know me and I don't really know you. We don't love each other. You have no idea who I am. And vice-versa. We're strangers. Let's realize that. You're a nice guy, Watly Caiper. A fuck. And I'm a nice woman. A fuck, too. And we make good sex together. It's a nice collaboration. And I was there when you were afraid of hosting and now I'm here when you're afraid of dying. You've got a lot of emotions wrapped up in me. But don't project onto me something that isn't there. I'll help you because you're in an unfair mess and I feel bad for you. I'll help you because it's the right thing to do. But I won't have you thinking of us as mates. I won't have it. I'm not your poovus."

Watly was stunned by the speech. It was totally unexpected. She must have been chewing on that one for a while. *This woman's been burned*, Watly thought. *Burned badly*. "I wasn't going to say that at all," he said calmly. "I was just going to say how nice you looked."

Alysess had straightened the birdhat and smoothed her blouse. "Oh," she had said, and looked off uncomfortably. "Well, thanks,"

And then she was gone.

And Watly was happy. He was happy because he was convinced that, in her own convoluted way, Dr. Alysess Tollnismer had just revealed something important. She'd revealed that she loved Watly Caiper. Just as he loved her. Or maybe not. Terradamn, he was confused.

After snooping a second time around the whole apartment, Watly rolled up the bed and went into the bathroom. For a wanted man, he felt pretty good. He washed rigorously and shaved with a borrowed razor. He hoped Alysess wouldn't mind. He left a burgeoning mustache alone on the hopes that its presence would change his appearance some. Actually, he kind of liked it. It gave him a rakish, devil-may-care look. *After all this is over*, he thought, *I might just keep it*.

He dressed in the same old clothes Narcolo had supplied, and found some soljuice and a piece of hardloaf in the kitchen to nibble on. After flipping on Alysess's CV he settled into the love seat to watch.

> . . . *because we love to learn,*
> *and love your viewership to earn,*
> *We'll keep it up through thick or thin,*
> *No matter what, we'll fill you in!*
> *News, news, news, news . . .*

"And now an update on the Corber Alvedine trag-
edy: The investigation continues and all available
police have been mobilized on this case. The chief
investigator on this massive personhunt is Sergeant
Ogiv Fenlocki. Here is his report:

"We've sealed off Manhattan. This Watly Caiper has
no way to leave the island without being caught.
Our people are moving in on him. Anyone he
knew—any of his acquaintances, friends, or anyone
he came in touch with—they're all being systemati-
cally sought out, contacted, and watched carefully.
When he turns up—and he will—we'll get him. He
can't hide forever."

"Sergeant, do you have any theories about a motive?"

"It seems pretty obvious to us. This Watly Caiper
was a one-time host. Apparently he couldn't hack it.
It pushed him over the edge. His first and only donor went to sexsentral and had a run-in with some
lowlifes. This donor has already been tracked
down, and he has confidentially testified to us.
Watly was probably traumatized by the hosting experience. It happens. He wanted to lash out at the
head of the whole hosting system. So he killed
Corber. But don't underestimate this guy. This
Caiper had the intelligence and wherewithal to
forge a number of travel documents to get to Second
and the cunning to escape the police a first time.
This man's shrewd. But he won't get away again.
We'll catch him and we'll kill him. The people have
spoken."

Watly watched this Sergeant Fenlocki closely as he talked. *This
is my executioner*, he thought. *This is the man responsible for my
own death. It's his job to see that I die.*

The sergeant was an older man with a liberal spattering if gray
hair around the temples and a face full of character lines. He spoke
clearly but very softly. His eyes seemed gentle and compassion-
ate. First Level cop eyes. *This is a reasonable man*, Watly
thought. *If I could just talk to him* . . .

Sergeant Fenlocki was still speaking.

". . . if we have to go on a door-to-door search, but
we'll find him. And if we discover anyone is helping
him in any way, we'll prosecute that person to the
full extent of the law. That's a promise."

"Thank you, Sergeant Ogiv Fenlocki, and good luck
with the case. Here again is the image of Watly
Caiper, the murderer. Remember, there is a reward
of one million for first kill or capture.

"And now a report on sex newsmakers. . . .

Watly turned the sound down. Suddenly he felt awful. What
was he going to do? How was he going to get out of this? Wasn'
there some way to clear his name? Turning himself in would do no
good. The Crimcourts would just be a formality. He was already
convicted and sentenced by the "people." What raping "people?"
The raping government is what raping people. Shit. He was
drowning and he was dragging good people down with him
Narcolo Caiper and Alysess Tollnismer—both could be given
death for what they'd done. Alysess had sheltered him and was
now looking for answers at Alvedine. Narcolo had clothed him
and packed a bag. . . . The *bag*. Narcolo had packed some
booze, hadn't he? Now was just the time. Drinking was a sub of
a lot more comforting than trying to figure out a solution to all
this.

Watly found the bag under the armchair and fished out the
booze. He poured himself a tall one in his juice glass and took a
sip. It hit the spot. *Funny*, Watly thought, *with my reward money
I could get anything I want*. He laughed. *One million New York
dollars. Wonder if they pay off if you kill yourself*. . . .

He took another swallow of the booze and closed his eyes as he
felt the warmth work its way down. *This is all a crazy nightmare
I have half a mind to walk into a police station and tell them off
"You're* all *wrong!" I'd say. "Not only didn't I kill Corber
Alvedine, but the person I didn't kill was a woman!"* Watly
laughed again.

He must have dozed off because when he opened his eyes i
was darker. The daylites had gone to evening outside. Watly rose
stiffly and shut the CV. He was still tired. His back ached from

sleeping in the love seat. He walked over to the window and peered out. The street was slick and wet-looking. A few bums wandered by. A lonely bicyclist. Watly could feel the breeze from the window's crack as he moved closer to it. It looked like a nice night.

Then, bobbing in the distance down Eighty-fourth Street, Watly saw the birdhat. The colorful birdhat. It was Alysess! She was coming home! Watly pressed his face to the glass. She looked calm and dignified as before. Ever poised, Watly thought. But there was something wrong. She was not alone. Two men walked with her, one on either side. Watly squinted to see better. One of the faces was familiar. Watly tried to place the man. He was a tall man wearing a brown hat and a long brown pocket-coat. Then Watly felt his stomach rise up into his throat. He recognized the man's face now. He'd just seen it a while ago on the CV. It was the Sergeant. It was Ogiv Fenlocki. His executioner.

CHAPTER 20

Watly backed away from the window into the shadows. What was going on? Had Alysess betrayed him? Had she turned? Was all that a lie? He couldn't believe it. That couldn't be true. Something must have gone wrong. She'd been caught or something. *Rape on stale weeders!*

Watly looked around frantically. He was a dead man—he had to hide somewhere. The bedroll was too small. The wardrobe was too obvious. The only place in the whole apartment to hide was in the bathroom. That was ridiculous. There had to be someplace. Someplace else.

Watly heard the downstairs door open and bang shut. They had entered the building. It would just be a few seconds before they arrived at the apartment. Two short flights of stairs. Watly spun around. Where was the gun? Where the subs was the gun? He heard their footsteps as they climbed the stairs. It sounded like they'd already reached the second floor. One more flight.

The gun was under the love seat, half hidden by the front leg. Watly snatched it up and gripped it tightly. Again he looked around for a place to hide or for a way out. There was the window—but there'd be nothing to stand on out there. It was a long way down to the street.

He could hear voices as they reached the third floor. They got louder as they started down the hall to the apartment door. Watly looked at the window once again. Maybe there was something to hold on to out there. Maybe—

"I still don't see why this is necessary." It was Alysess's voice. She sounded strained and agitated. There was the clink of keys fumbling. They were right outside the door.

Watly stuffed the gun in his pants and pulled the window open. He heard the keys drop.

"Oops. I'm sorry. I seem to be all thumbs today," came the voice. She sounded overly loud—like she wanted Watly to hear.

He pulled his body up into the window frame and swung out sideways. There was nothing to hold on to. Nothing. He swung the other way. Still nothing. Not even a pipe to stand on. Watly leaned out backwards—almost falling—and looked up. Four feet above the window running lengthwise was the CV cable. It carried the building's signal. It looked weak and flimsy.

Watly heard the key entering the lock. It was a very specific sound—a final, distinct click as metal met metal in perfect fit. He looked again at the cable. It would have to do. He pulled the window half closed and braced himself against its ledge. *Please— let that thin little cable be stronger than it looks*, Watly thought as he hung there.

The door to the apartment opened. Watly pushed off hard with his feet and sprang up into empty space. His aim was good and he hit the cable with both hands, grasping it instantly. It bowed downward under the strain. He pulled his legs inward and tried to find a foothold on the top of the window frame. There was a thin lip—just enough for the toes of his shoes to balance precariously. The cable bowed still more. It was secured to the building with a series of flimsy-looking metal clamps every few feet. Two of these snapped in half and Watly sagged still lower. His right foot slipped from the lip. Watly fumbled but brought it back in place. He was clinging with all his strength. He felt like a spider—a spider defying gravity and climbing a sheer wall. *That's it, Caiper. Keep that image. You're a spider, Caiper. A spider.*

Another clamp snapped. Watly looked at the cable itself. It was a bit frayed but it looked like it was holding up. The clamps were the problem. They were the weak point. Watly felt himself sagging lower. His rear end must have been in line with his feet by now. Voices came from the apartment.

"I'm sorry, but I just don't understand." Alysess's voice still sounded tense.

"Look, Tollnismer—"

"*Doctor* Tollnismer," she interrupted.

"I'm sorry, *Doctor* Tollnismer," the man's voice said.

"That's okay, Fenlocki."

"*Sergeant* Fenlocki," he snapped.

"Of course."

There was a moment of silence.

"Look, Doctor . . . look, we're not accusing you of anything. It's just a precaution. We're covering all the possibilities. We're dealing with a very dangerous man. Mind if I look around?"

"What has this man got to do with me? And yes, I *do* mind."

"This is the bathroom? Nice bathroom. Doctor, listen . . . we're doing this with anyone, *anyone* who had any contact at all with the murderer. You had contact. It's as simple as that. You doctored his hosting. What's in here? Ah, clothes. *Nice* clothes. This your bedroll?"

"I only met him briefly. . . ."

"That's all that matters. We're sorry about the inconvenience. I'm sure it's only for a short while. What we'd like to do, if you don't mind—and we're asking this of all Watly Caiper's acquaintances—is put up a direct surveillance lens right over there by the ceiling. You won't even notice it. It's a fish-eye and can take in the whole apartment. We'd also like to put a plainsclothes officer—my partner, here, to start with—down at your front door for twenty-four hours. That way if this Mr. Caiper *does* try to contact you or any of the others, we'll know right away. It's really just a formality. Mind if I open up the window more? You get such a nice breeze here."

Watly pulled himself upward as far as he could. His arm muscles screamed in protest.

"Sergeant, I don't think any of this is necessary," Alysess said abruptly.

"Nice view you have here, Doctor," the sergeant said.

The voice was very near to Watly—almost directly below him. Another clamp snapped. Watly felt himself sag downward slightly. He pulled in with his arms even harder. Any lower and he'd be mooning an officer of the law.

"Do I have any say in all this, Sergeant?" Alysess asked angrily.

"Frankly, no. You haven't any choice. But I hate phrasing it that way." His voice faded some as he left the window. "Truth is you're stuck with it until we catch the guy."

"What about my privacy?"

"There's no lens in the bathroom, Doctor. Nothing to fear. If you want to masturbate or fuck or something without an audience, you'll have to do it in there. This is just temporary, you understand."

Watly thought his arms would fall off. He tried not to think about it. *I'm a spider. I'm a terradamn spider.*

"Is that *all*, Sergeant?" The doctor's voice sounded angry and rebellious.

"Why, isn't that enough?" The sergeant laughed and another male voice—his partner—joined in. "Are you all set with the lens, Akral?"

"All through, Sergeant," the other officer said.

"This is Akral, Dr. Tollnismer. He'll be on your front door stoop if you need him."

"I'd like to be alone now, if you're done," Alysess said bitterly.

"Oh, we're done, Doctor. One question, though, before I leave. You've just come back from work now, have you?"

"You know I have, Sergeant. You came with me."

"And you were there all day?"

"Pretty much. What's this got to do with—"

"Do you normally leave an open bottle of booze, a half-filled glass, and some bread lying around all day?"

There was a pause. Watly held his breath.

"Sometimes I get lazy, Sergeant Fenlocki. I leave things out," Alysess said calmly. "I leave things open."

"Ah, so this was your breakfast?"

There was another pause.

"On occasion I have a nip in the morning." Her voice droned lazily as if she were bored with the questions. "I happen to like it. Maybe I like it a little too much."

"Do I detect a little CV mist in the air?"

"The machine happens to leak."

"What about this hat?"

"I wear *hats,* Sergeant."

"And this knapsack?"

"Is it a crime to have a knapsack now?"

"Not at all, Doctor. But understand my concern. I'm on a very important case. The people want results and they want them fast. We have enough concerns nowadays without worrying about a loose murderer. Believe me. If you see anything of possible interest to this investigation, you must contact me immediately. Or if you remember something. Something you may have overlooked."

"I'm very tired, Sergeant."

"My apologies, Doctor. You've had a long day. I'm sure you'd like to return to your . . . breakfast."

"Thank you, *yes,*" she said strongly.

"Don't forget, Doctor. Don't forget the penalty for helping this particular man." The sergeant's voice was cold.

"That does not concern me, sir," Alysess said.

"I thought not, Doctor." There was the sound of footsteps. "We'll be in touch—or, I should say, we'll be watching." He laughed heartily and the other man joined in the laughter once again. Then there was the click of the door closing, followed by hollow silence.

Watly let his arms relax some and he slumped down even lower. Rape, he was sore. He heard Alysess moving around in the apartment. Was she looking for him? After a few seconds, he heard the window open all the way directly below him. There was a soft gasp. Alysess must have seen him hanging there. She couldn't say anything or the lens would pick it up. He heard her quickly close the window all the way with a loud thump. Then there was the sound of a shade being pulled. Now Watly assumed he couldn't be seen by the lens if he lowered himself some. He let his feet slip off the edge of the lip and hang below him. They swung freely for a moment and then touched the bottom window-sill. He stepped on it firmly, taking some of the stress off his arm muscles. *I thank you, Alysess. And my arms thank you.*

Watly could see she had pulled down a flimsy brown window shade so he was protected from the lens. He tried to stretch and twist his back without losing his grip. His body felt full of kinks and knotted muscles.

Watly heard voices on the street below. The sound traveled.

"All right, Akral. Just stay right here and keep your eyes peeled. You'll be relieved in four hours by another officer. Good luck."

"Thank you, sir."

There were footsteps as the sergeant walked off. Watly closed his eyes. *Please don't turn back. Please don't glance up at the apartment window, Ogiv.*

The footsteps continued without faltering and faded into the distance.

Now what? Watly thought. *I'm hanging from the outside of a window like a monkey. I can't go in 'cause the lens will see me. I can't talk 'cause the lens will hear me. I can't climb down 'cause there's no way to. I couldn't climb down if there was a way 'cause there's a man standing guard below. This is wonderful. And Alysess can't help me 'cause she's got to act natural for the lens. This is just terrific. Not to mention that my arms are going to give out soon. Rape or toast. There's got to be an answer. I can't get trapped here. Not like this. If I get caught anywhere near here they'll put two and two together and arrest Alysess for complicity. Kill her, too.*

Watly heard singing coming from inside the apartment. It started as humming but quickly became full-fledged singing. Alysess had a pleasant voice and she used it in a relaxed, unself-conscious manner. It sounded as if she were just passing

the time. She was singing an oldie—one of the popular tunes from
a few years back.

> *"When I'm down I write to my poovus,*
> *I write to my poovus every day.*
> *When I'm low I write to my poovus,*
> *I write to my poovus and I feel okay. . . ."*

All right, Watly thought. *I get it. You're going to write
something down and give it to me. You have a plan. Good thing
someone has a plan.*

The singing stopped. Watly heard nothing from inside the
apartment. He held on. Still nothing. He kept holding on. It felt
like he'd been holding on for ages. Watly tried to redistribute his
weight. He let his arms go looser and his feet take more of the
burden. Another cable clamp broke and the cable swayed lower.
It was actually better that way. Watly could now hold on with one
hand at a time, giving the other one a rest. He kept alternating.
Come on, Alysess. What are you writing, a novel? Watly assumed
she had secretly slipped a pen and some paper into the bathroom
and was writing in there. *Damn the lens. Damn the stupid
sergeant and damn his little helper and damn the whole damn
super-efficient police force! Send them all to the Subkeeper!*

Come on, Alysess! I don't have all day. Watly felt the arches of
his feet cramping up. He tried to wiggle his toes and alternate
bending his ankles slightly. This was torture. *If you have a plan,
then tell me,* Watly thought, *because my body ain't gonna hold out
much longer.*

He held on with his right, leaned a little, and glanced down the
left side of his body. There was Akral, three stories below, sitting
on Alysess's front steps. He was lighting up an illegal cigel and
gazing off down the street. *Just don't glance upward, you big
sofdick subspawn,* Watly thought. Akral looked like a real
beanhead, but he was probably smart enough to figure something
was afoot if he happened to see a man clinging to the outside of
a window frame. Watly had to give him credit for *that* much.
Come on, Alysess!

After what seemed like a full ten or fifteen minutes Watly heard noise coming from the apartment again. Alysess had come out of the bathroom and was moving around once more. *It's about time.*

A thin dark hand reached around the brown fabric and pulled the window open, leaving the shade drawn. Watly waited without moving. There were more shuffling sounds from within. He heard Alysess begin to hum again. She was making a good show of acting calm and natural.

Watly could see light streaming out around the edge of the window shade. Alysess must have turned on every single light in the apartment. *This was a smart woman.* The more light inside, the harder for the lens to see *outside* should the shade billow for a moment. She had increased the contrast as much as possible. Her gentle humming continued.

Suddenly the shade flipped up and Watly tried to sidestep as a heavy blanket was thrust directly at him. Alysess was pushing her comforter out the window. Watly lost his footing completely and swung from the cable. Alysess held the edge of the blanket and shook it violently out the window. She continued humming. Watly twisted his body and tried to get his left foot back on the edge of the sill. The first time he slipped but the next try it held. Alysess was still shaking the blanket as if trying to remove any dust or dirt. Watly glanced down at its bottom. Clipped to the lower edge of the comforter with a surgical clip was Watly's own knapsack. Alysess was trying to pass it to him. She kept humming and Watly noticed she was consciously avoiding looking anywhere near his direction. Watly let go of the cable with his right hand. This made his body swing out some. Another cable clamp snapped and the cable lurched lower. Almost all Watly's weight was on the toes of his right foot now. He leaned as far as he could. Alysess started pulling the blanket back in slowly. Watly watched the knapsack come nearer. He'd only have one chance. Just as the edge of its strap reached the windowsill, Watly bent his right knee and stretched out his right hand. He did not aim for the bag; he aimed for the surgical clip. His thumb nicked it and fumbled for the handle. Alysess continued pulling the blanket. Another cable clamp snapped and the jolt almost made Watly lose his grip. He swung out lower and released the clip with a twist. The knapsack fell freely and Watly lashed his hand out frantically. It dropped.

The bag's strap just barely caught against Watly's wrist and he lifted it upward clumsily. Alysess pulled the blanket all the way in and slid the shade down once more.

Watly caught his breath and raised his left foot back up on the sill, centering himself again. Every muscle in his body was killing him. His nose burned with each raw inhale of air. He stretched up his arm and let the knapsack slide down so it was slung over his right shoulder. There was a small sheet of paper stuck to the outside of the sack. Watly leaned forward to try to read it. The lighting was horrible but Alysess had written in large block letters.

> READ LONG NOTE LATER.
> THERE IS A CHARGED PIPE CUTTER
> AND STRONG BELT INSIDE BAG
> HOPE THESE ARE OF USE.
> IN 5 MIN. I WILL TRY TO
> DISTRACT AKRAL.
> IF YOU CAN'T GO DOWN, GO UP.

Watly flipped open the bag with the one hand. Sure enough, right on top there was a pipe cutter and the pink belt from Alysess's bathrobe. Both things had been in the bathroom. They were obviously the best she could do as far as tools went. A plumbing device and a clothing accessory. *Fabulous*, thought Watly. *Raping fabulous. If I need to fix a broken sink or add a splash of color to my wardrobe, this stuff'll really come in handy. Some plan this is. Hardly worth the wait.*

Watly leaned back slightly and looked upward.

If you can't go down, go up, she had written. Up? Up where?

CHAPTER 21

Well, ain't life grand, and all, Watly thought. *This is really something to tell the kids about someday. Make a delightful after-dinner anecdote.*

Watly kept hanging there outside Alysess's apartment window for quite some time. He stared at his primitive tools—the pipe cutter and the belt. What good were they? His arms and legs were ready to give out. He was convinced the only reason he wasn't at that very moment sprawled on the street below was that his hands had locked and frozen in a closed position on the cable. Another clamp snapped. Watly tried to raise himself up to the same level as before and he got a horrible cramp on the arch of each foot. The pain was excruciating. He pointed and flexed his toes as far as possible to ease the stabbing sensations. The only thing stopping Watly from giving up entirely was the thought of Alysess. Unless he could get away from her apartment he'd be burying her with him when he was caught. He couldn't live with that. *Go up,* she'd written. Watly leaned out and looked upward. He couldn't very well scale up the sheer side of the building. There was nothing to hold on to—no hand- or footholds. The cable ran sideways—not up and down. He couldn't very well climb sideways.

Watly looked to the left. About fifteen feet from him was the corner of the building. Its edge was decorated with heavy inlaid quoins all the way up the side, one above the other. From a distance they looked like they stuck out a good two inches from the surface. *That* looked climbable. Unfortunately it also looked impossible to get to. Even if Watly had the strength to climb the cable hand over hand across the side of the building and even if the cable could hold his weight through all that without snapping any more clamps—even then he'd fall short. The cable stopped a good five feet from the rusticated edge of the building. Its left end went into a small hole in the facing. He was at an impasse. Total dead end.

"Hello there. Is your name . . . Akral?"

It was Alysess's voice rising up from the street below him. Good old Alysess. She was creating a diversion. A diversion for what? What good is a diversion if you can think of nothing to *do* with it?

"I thought you might be thirsty so I brought down some water," she said.

"That's very kind of you, Ma'am."

Watly looked at the pipe cutter again. It was a strong one. Heavy-duty. It looked like it could cut through a thick pipe with hardly a squeeze. Or a cable. A cable. Watly looked up. A cable. Cut the cable. Hold on to the left cut piece. Yes. Cut the cable and swing. This was an idea. It was awful, but it was an idea. Finally a plan.

"This really hits the spot. I appreciate it." Akral's thick voice was loud and unrefined. Watly liked the sound of it. It was like a voice from his past life. A Brooklyn voice.

"Here's another glass."

Watly tied one end of the belt to the pipe cutter's handle. The knot was loose but was the best he could do with one aching hand. The other end he looped around his neck and clipped to his collar with the surgical clip. This way if he let go of the cutter it wouldn't fall. He repositioned the knapsack higher on his right shoulder. It would have to do. He couldn't very well pull it up over both arms.

Looking up at the cable, he carefully slid his left hand as far over as it would go. He found a thin notch in the cable there. It was the indentation where a clamp had been. Watly gripped it firmly. He took a few slow deep breaths and raised up the cutter with his right hand. The hand was trembling slightly. Watly steadied it. He slipped the cutter's mouth over the cable directly in front of him. *Here goes nothing*.

"Not many folks would be this considerate, ma'am," Akral said down below.

Watly squeezed the handle and cut the cable. It made a soft popping sound and a few sparks flew out but that was all. There was a long moment in which nothing happened. Watly stood there, suspended by inertia. Both feet were still on the sill and his left hand gripped the now severed cable. Nothing moved. Gradually everything began to tilt outward and to the left, as if in slow motion. Watly let go of the cutter and reached to grab the end of the cable with his right hand. His whole body was swinging out and around now. Finally his feet slipped off the sill and Watly was in midair. He grabbed the cable with all his strength and felt his full weight come down on it. There was a tremendous jolt and Watly could feel and hear all the remaining cable clamps breaking one after another—*ping-ping-ping-ping-ping*. He was swinging wildly and getting lower and lower. He felt his grip weaken with each snap.

Akral's voice was even clearer than before.

"Did you hear—"

"—I almost forgot," Alysess interrupted. "I came down to offer you a sexual release as well, if you like."

Watly's shoulder and hip slammed into the side of the building. His left hand slipped out of its groove on the cable but found another lower one. He used his feet to push away from the building. Now he was swinging like a pendulum, left and right. With each left swing Watly tried to hook a foot around the edge of the building. The cable was slippery and its clamp grooves were shallow. Watly felt himself slipping lower and lower. He was losing his grip.

"You're offering me some sex, ma'am?"

Well, not really," Alysess replied. "I'm not up for it myself—

trying to cut down, and all—but I've brought down some really primo porno with me. I thought you might like a release."

"On my own?"

"You bet. I'll hold the porno, if you like."

Watly finally got a leg wrapped around the edge of one cemeld quoin and the crazy swinging stopped. The pipe cutter still dangled from the belt and clanked against hard cemeld.

"What was that—"

"Take those pants down and enjoy yourself, Akral. This neighborhood isn't a public sex zone but no one bothers over that anymore. Let me show you the porno. Come on, Akral—take it out."

"This is most considerate of you, ma'am."

Watly gripped the edge of the building with both legs, trying to steady himself with the cable. The stones had thinner footholds than he'd thought. It wasn't going to be easy. He pressed his body flat into the cold rock and let go of the cable with his right hand. He grabbed the thin edge. Then he let the cable go entirely and held on to the quoins with both hands. The freed cable swung away. Watly hugged the corner of Alysess's building with both arms and legs.

"That's a lovely organ, Akral. If I wasn't trying to ease off contact sex a bit, I'd join you."

"Thank you, ma'am."

Watly tried to catch his breath. It wasn't easy. With every inhale he felt the butt of the chip pistol digging painfully into his ribs. *Should've put that back in the knapsack*, he thought.

No more subshitting around, Caiper. It's time to start climbing.

"Don't hurt yourself, now, Akral. Make it last."

The climbing was slow work. First Watly would slide his right hand up a little until his fingers found the edge of the next stone. Then he'd do the same for his left. After that he would slowly lift a tentative right foot until it found an edge to rest on. And the same for the left. The chip pistol, the belt with the cutter hanging from it, and the swinging knapsack all conspired to make life difficult. If *one* wasn't in the way, then another was. Watly wished he'd left them all behind.

"That's a great one, ma'am." Akral's voice sounded strained.

"Shall I go back to that one?" Alysess asked.

"Yes, please!" came the reply. Akral's heavy breathing could be heard from way above.

Watly kept climbing. *Go up*, Alysess had written. And so he did. He went up. One inch at a time. It was amazing to him that he didn't fall. It was as though he was defying gravity. The best thing he had going for him was the clinging. He was literally hugging his way up the edge of the building.

"I believe I'll be finishing soon, ma'am."

"Try to make it last, now. That's the way."

Watly wondered how far he'd gone. Looking around wasn't easy, so he had no idea where he was. How far up was he? Akral and Alysess did sound fainter now. Perhaps Watly was already nearing the ceiling. But then what? One could only go so far up. Maybe there'd be a way around the building. Or there might even be some space between the roof of the building and the First Level ceiling. Some roofers and stuff. Room to run. That was possible. Watly wasn't sure how tall the structure was. He hadn't noticed. In any case, he'd cross that bridge when it collapsed on him.

"There you go! There you go! Excellent. Just excellent, Akral! Let me help you wipe that up."

"Thank you very much, ma'am. This was most kind of you. Not many people would be this considerate. I greatly appreciate it."

"No trouble at all. Hope you enjoyed it."

"Oh, I *did*, ma'am. What was that last one? It was a real doozy!"

"That was a sensory M-drawing by Schlent and Ro. It's one of my favorites too."

Watly banged his head on a rusty horizontal pipe. He had reached the ceiling without even knowing it.

There was no space above Alysess's building. No room for roofers, not even a narrow channel. In fact, it looked like the building went a good deal higher up on Second. Ah, well. Watly reached up and held the pipe. It was wet and slimy, but strong enough to take his weight. It came out of the building at "roof" point and ran across the First Level ceiling toward the center of the street. Watly turned himself some and grabbed the pipe with both hands. That's when he saw a place to go. Safe haven. There was his answer. Finally an answer. Finally some good news.

"Care to try again, Akral?" Alysess's faint voice asked from way below.

"Oh, no, ma'am. One's my limit. Anyway, I'm really supposed to be on duty, and all."

Watly started hand-over-handing it across the pipe. His feet dangled limply below him. His goal was only a couple of yards away, but the trip was not easy. More than a few times Watly thought it was all over. He would fall. He would come crashing down five stories onto poor old Akral before the man could even get his pants back up. Gripping the slippery pipe was next to impossible. Watly kept on. He somehow got a steady momentum going and that constant motion seemed to be the only thing preventing him from falling. As he neared the edge of his destination, Watly lifted his legs and swung to get them up high. This was the hardest thing of all. His stomach muscles had given out almost entirely. They'd been through enough. Lifting his legs was agony. He let them hang for a minute before trying again.

"Anything else I can do for you, Akral?" Alysess asked.

"No, thank you."

Watly lifted his legs and painfully swung them up again. This time they made it.

"If you need a bathroom before you go off duty, I've got a wonderful W.C. upstairs," Watly heard Alysess say. He felt a ball of air catch in his throat. He smiled to himself.

"Thank you, ma'am," said Akral.

"Best W.C. there is."

"Thank you, I'm fine, ma'am."

Watly slid himself onto the hot platform—legs first—using the pipe as a guide.

"Well, good night, then, Akral."

"Goodnight, ma'am."

Goodnight, Alysess, thought Watly.

It was damp up there. The wind whipped around Watly Caiper and he felt his hair blowing in all directions. He didn't care. He stretched out flat and rested his cheek against his sleeve. It felt wonderful. The metal he lay on was hot. It was almost painful, but that didn't matter. Finally his muscles could rest. Finally his screaming arms could relax. The relief was most welcome. After lying motionless for quite some time, Watly slid the knapsack up closer and opened it. There was the long note from Alysess, the credit pieces and bills, Narcolo's care package of dried sunbean, and—thank you, *Doctor*—the booze. She had returned the booze.

Watly took the bottle out and turned on his back. He had about a foot and a half of vertical leeway. It was cramped but it was livable. He slid over and leaned his neck into a center post. He didn't have room to sit all the way up but he managed to scrunch his way up so that his head was against the ceiling. It wasn't too uncomfortable. The strong smell of mildew was somehow comforting. He tilted the bottle and took a swig. Nothing had ever tasted better. He felt the liquid expand and work its warm way deep inside him. Girl, that felt good. *Without much effort*, he thought, *I could seriously enjoy developing a drinking problem*. He closed his eyes. His palms were a painful mass of broken blisters and every muscle in his body seemed to have been ripped and torn. The important thing, though, was that he was alive. He was still alive. He rummaged for some of the dried sunbeans and ate a few. They were salty and bitter, but Watly wasn't complaining. He was glad they were there. He shifted so that his rear end didn't get too hot against the metal. After a few more sips of booze he opened his eyes and tried to get his bearings. It was very dark. Watly had plenty of room side to side, but almost no room up and down. That was fine with him. As long as he could rest. About twelve feet in either direction were the four end posts—one at each corner.

Suddenly everything shook briefly and there was a loud *click* sound. It got even darker. The daylites had gone to night.

Including the one he was sitting on.

It had never occurred to Watly that someone could actually fit above a daylite. From the street they had always looked flush with the ceiling. It would have been hard to imagine a crawlspace above each one. Yet here he was, Watly Caiper, sprawled out on top of a daylite having a picnic. There was very little space between the daylite and the ceiling, but it suited Watly fine. And now, at a night setting, even the heat was no problem. Already the metal felt cooler. And the strong wind was invigorating. *The small space must create a vacuum or something to increase the breeze like this*, Watly thought. *Most pleasant.*

He flexed and relaxed his legs to ease the tension from them. Rape, what a climb. What a climb indeed.

As he sat chewing bitter sunbeans and sipping the booze, slipping slowly into a comfortable haze, Watly pondered over the doctor. The wonderful doctor. *Perhaps . . .* he thought, *perhaps when all this is over and I've cleared my name and everything's back to normal, perhaps Alysess would be my poovus. Perhaps, even, she would consider carrying my child. That would truly be wonderful. I can't think of better genes. Yeah, right. Keep dreaming, Caiper. You're slipping into a Jesusland-style fairy tale. When this is all over, you'll be lucky to be alive.*

Watly took another big swallow of booze and closed his eyes, falling asleep. Falling asleep way up above everything he knew.

CHAPTER 22

"Akral?"

"That you, Littwore?"

"Take off, now. I'm your relief. Any action?"

"It's dead out here."

"Sounds like another boring-to-extreme deal."

"The doctor pornoed me off a while back, though. Maybe she'll do the same for you."

"That'd be nice. See you."

"So long."

The changing of the guard. Watly glanced over the edge of the daylite to get a look at his new baby-sitter. He couldn't see much. Just the dark top of a head and a set of broad shoulders. A female, it looked like. The figure sat on the stoop and glanced upward. Watly slithered back over to the center of the daylite. He couldn't stay here forever. There would always be a cop down there. Sooner or later Watly would have to start moving on. He had noticed a thick beam ran from daylite to daylite. It should be possible to crawl from one to another without too much trouble.

That way he could leave the area. But not now. Now he needed to rest. His body couldn't go on.

Watly took out the note Alysess had stuffed in his bag. It was too dark to read it. He moved closer to the edge of the platform but still couldn't read it. He fumbled around in the dark for the pipe cutter. There it was. Still hanging from his neck. Watly found the readout switch by feel. He flicked it on. A tiny red light glowed on the cutter's handle to show it was still well charged. Watly held the cutter up against Alysess's note. There was just enough light from the readout to make out one or two words at a time. Fortunately the doctor's handwriting was clear and neat. Watly began reading, moving the cutter across the page for each line.

Watly:

Sorry about all this. Important—I will go every evening to a bar in Sexsentral from 7:00 to 8:00 P.M. Meet me there when you can. Should be safe. It is on 46th and 6th and is called the "Vagina Oblongata." We'll talk there.

Meanwhile, I found some things out today:

1. There was never any such thing as "night hosting." I checked records and the only people in the building that night—or on any night—were the cuff-return cashier and his guard. According to the records, NO ONE was in any of the donor rooms. And those rooms are very secure. There is no indication of a break-in. Don't know what this means but it doesn't help your case.

2. Everyone says removing a cuff is impossible. If it WERE possible, word is the only one who could do it is—get this—a doctor named Aug MITTERLY. He's apparently a real scientific wiz—invented the newest design of hosting machine. I couldn't get an address on him or anything else. He may live on Second. This part checks out with your story, though.

3. As far as the world is concerned, the murdered person is Corber Alvedine. Everyone at work was

mourning his loss, though no one knew him personally. There's no mention of a woman at all. I even
saw pictures of the victim—mutilated just as you
described—but definitely a man. No explanation.
This is weird. Is it possible you were mistaken as to
the victim's sex?

4. Everyone is sure you did it. Your file shows a reputation for fighting when you were young. Your first
donor says the hosting was pretty traumatic. He
thinks it pushed you over the edge—something
about being threatened and kicked. Your final interviewer, Mr. Oldyer, says you seemed unstable. As
for the forged I.D.s and the scalpel, people are saying you probably bought them from the black market with money from your first hosting. It doesn't
look good, Watly. I'll try to find out more, but I have
to go slow. I've already snooped a little too much.
People will suspect. Good luck, Watly.
See you at the bar ASAP.

Love, A.T.

Watly kissed the paper and clicked off the cutter's readout. She
was remarkable. A major fuckface. Truly remarkable. Poovus
material. Someday Watly would have to find a way to repay her.
He folded the paper and stuffed it back in the bag. After fumbling
some more, he found the bottle again and took one more sideways
sip before closing it. What a day. It was all incredible. *I've got to
put the pieces together*, he thought. *I've got to find the answers.*

*Why me? Why was I picked for this role? I'm not a murderer.
Is it that streak of violence they wanted? And why not just kill
whoever it was and escape? If you're that smart you could
certainly get away with murder without the help of a host. Maybe
they wanted a scapegoat just to be sure? I don't know. It's crazy.
I've got to find proof I'm innocent. No setup can be that perfect.
If I never find proof I'll never get out of it. If I don't solve this, I'm
dead.*

Watly rolled onto his side and closed his eyes. It was so dark
he could hardly tell the difference. His brain hurt. He was thinking

in circles. *Stop thinking, Caiper,* he thought. *If it's not productive, turn it off.*

Watly turned it off.

He stretched out with his legs across the warm metal surface. His right foot brushed against something. Something small. Watly recoiled, suddenly frightened in the blackness. He brought his foot out tentatively once again. There was definitely something there. A small object near the edge of the daylite. Watly turned the cutter on once again and swiveled his body around toward the object. In the dim red light of the cutter's readout, he could see what looked like a ragged bowl. It was made of garbage—scraps of cloth and paper, metal spokes, and small broken pieces of placene. It had been painstakingly made to the rough shape of a small bowl. He brought the cutter closer to the object's side. *No,* thought Watly, *it's not a bowl at all. It's a nest. It's a bird's nest. Subs—it's a real bird's nest up here on top of this daylite. Imagine that.*

Watly was amazed. He could hardly remember the last time he'd seen a bird. And yet, against all odds some diehard First Level bird had determinedly continued to exist and defiantly built a little home for its family. A testament to survival. Watly felt it was almost a sign. It seemed like a good omen, a small ray of hope. He raised the cutter and, scooting a little closer, pointed the red light down inside the nest to see better.

Inside the nest was death. Three little skeletal remains of newborn birds curled together, all beak and bone, their empty eye sockets blank and accusing. The naked skeletons clung to one another, as if shrinking away from death itself. Watly clicked off the cutter swiftly and pulled himself across the daylite, as far away from the little tomb as possible. This was *not* a sign. This was not a sign at all.

CHAPTER 23

Watly Caiper was flying.

His arms were flapping gracefully and he was soaring gently over Brooklyn. Yes, that was Brooklyn below. And there was his old street—the old brownstones. Watly banked and swooped down between the buildings for a closer look. On the street below, a few young boys were shin-scrimming off a passing bus. It was a dangerous but exhilarating pastime—exciting to watch even from above. The boys were soon gone and Watly soared to the south. There was his apartment house. The place of Watly's youth. On the front steps two women waved up at him, smiling broadly. They were proud. Proud of Little-Watt. One of the women was his mother, Pepajer Caiper, looking young and vibrant. Next to her was Alysess—thin, strong, and dark. She was wearing her all-white outfit and smiling with those perfect teeth. The two held each other and beckoned to Watly. They no longer seemed as joyful. Watly circled them, diving lower. They were calling now, waving more frantically.

Come down, Watly. Come down. Beware the air. Beware the air.

Watly circled once again and prepared to land. The sky was clouding over rapidly. The wind rose. Dark thunderclouds moved in. Watly looked up. Heavy black clouds rolled over above him like a solid blanket.

Pepajer Caiper yelled from below, *Beware the air, Watly!*

He was suddenly frightened. The sun was being covered—completely covered. He looked back down but there was no one there anymore. The street was empty. Pepajer and Alysess were gone. His building was gone. The streets were unfamiliar. The wind grew stronger, as if trying to blow Watly to the ground. He tried to climb, to gain altitude. The clouds covered now like a solid ceiling. The wind drove him down harder, whipping at him with a frenzy. He couldn't rise. Watly felt himself lose control; he could no longer flap his arms. He couldn't fight anymore.

Beware the air!

Watly was driven hard toward the ground. Only it wasn't the ground. It had changed. It had transformed. It was now fire. Solid fire. The ground had turned to fire and he was plummeting into it. A reverse Icarus.

He landed brutally on the flames. And he began to burn. Every part of him began to burn. Now there was a baby with him and the baby was burning as well. The baby's flesh was on fire. It was a naked girl baby and as its skin seared off and the muscle beneath began to bubble, it gazed up at Watly. There was no fear or pain in its eyes. Its clear dark pupils were cold and calm. Watly stopped breathing and his heart stopped pumping blood.

"Mea culpa," the baby said, smiling an oily smile. "Mea culpa, Mommy."

Watly *was* on fire. This was no dream. He was burning. Shit! Burning up! He tried to jump but slammed his back into the ceiling. It was morning. The daylites had gone to full. The whole platform was heating up to an unbearable temperature. Steam rose from the evaporating moisture. The surface was scorchingly hot. His nightmare was nothing compared to this reality. Watly scrambled to stuff all his things back in the bag. His knees and elbows felt like they were being seared off. *Rape, rape, rape,*

rape! He gathered everything and pulled the knapsack over his shoulders. As quickly as he was capable, he slithered to the far edge of the daylite and started out over the plasticore beam that connected the two platforms. That was better. The beam was cool to the touch. What a relief.

The sweat and fear and claustrophobia left him gradually, easing out of him with each breath. Soon he was calm. Soon he was himself again. The dream was gone; the heat was gone.

Watly stayed on the center of the beam. His eyes adjusted slowly to the bright morning. He could see down easily now. The street was full of people going off to work. He glanced backward. There was a new surveillance cop sitting on the steps, looking bored. All was as it had been. Alysess's shade was drawn. Watly wondered if she'd left for work already. *Ah, well. Have a good day, my love.*

In the full daylite, Watly could see everything below him. It was amazing how far up he was. Five stories didn't sound like much, but looking straight down from it on a one-foot-wide beam made it seem pretty damn far indeed. At least he didn't have to worry much about being seen. Being up there where the daylites were was perfect cover. Watly figured it was like standing behind a searchlight; the brightness of the light would make it impossible to see things around and behind it. He felt invisible. If it wasn't for the heat problem everything would be fine. Traveling from daylite to beam to daylite was going to be painful. Hot and cold, Hot and cold. Ah, well. Such is life. Either hot or cold. *You can't have everything, right, Caiper?*

Watly started to crawl across the beam. When he reached the next daylite he found himself making little grunting and squealing noises as he scrambled across the burning platform. This would never do. On the next beam Watly stopped and spent some time ripping off both of the cuffs on his anklepants. He wrapped the fabric around each palm to protect his hands. That should help. And on he crawled. The farther he traveled, the stronger the wind grew. Hot and cold. Hot and cold. Watly stopped on one of the beams to have a dried sunbean breakfast. He finished the packet but passed on the booze this time. No drinking now. *Not a good time to get dizzy . . . or throw up,* he thought to himself.

By taking one perpendicular crossbeam, Watly changed direction and headed down the avenue. The wind picked up even stronger and he could make out the roaring sound of an exhaust fan up ahead. On he went. Hot and cold. Hot and cold. The places it got him most were the knees, elbows, and palms. At one daylite, Watly tried to turn over and slide across on his rear end—but that was even worse and it took twice as long. So he continued on his front—painfully but steadily.

The crowds below thickened. Tents with their cloth tops pointed toward him were scattered on sidewalks and curbs. Lowtruck pullers, bicyclers, and pedestrians filled the street. Manned and unmanned coppers as well as a few cruisers whizzed by, totally oblivious to Watly's plodding journey up above. They looked small and insignificant from that height—harmless little toys. *Looking for me?* Watly thought. He smiled to himself. On he went. Elbow, palm, knee. Elbow, palm, knee. Hot and cold. Hot and cold.

After a while he actually found himself humming. This surprised even Watly. It was a strange place to hum. But he had Alysess's letter-writing tune in his head, he had the breeze at his back, and he had the rhythm of his own movements to give him a beat. It seemed fitting. He hummed on. The volume of the fan he was approaching became so loud he could barely hear himself. *Perhaps I should sing*, Watly thought. *Then I could hear myself better.*

Watly crawled onward and let loose his raw and scratchy singing voice.

> *"When I'm down I write to my poo—*hoo-*vus,*
> *I write to my poovus every day.*
> *When I'm low I—"*

Suddenly the fan stopped. Watly cut off his singing midword. There was silence. The huge roar of the exhaust had clicked off abruptly, leaving only a hollow echo. Watly's ears rang. The wind died to nothing. He strained to see ahead. What had happened? Had he been spotted?

Watly cautiously climbed along another daylite and its beam.

Up ahead he could make out a man near his own level. Watly froze. The man was sitting in a wire basket way up on the end of a long jointed metal neck. He was covered with dirt and dust. It looked like he was reaching up and taking the bars off the front of the exhaust fan. *He must be cleaning it out,* Watly thought, *cleaning all the garbage the fan sucks up.* The man got the bars unlocked. He swung them down and lowered the basket back to the street. Watly crept closer. He was only a few yards from all this now. The fan cleaner was back on the ground, surrounded by paper and garbage, readying an enormous hose and strapping it to the side of his basket. He was probably going to use the hose to snake into the opening and empty out all the garbage. Watly had never seen this procedure before. He wondered how often it had to be done. He leaned closer. The fan's huge gray blades were clearly visible behind the open bars. Up behind the blades was darkness. Up. Up there. Second Level. The air *had* to let out on Second Level. Somehow. It had to. Maybe there was a way to Second. Maybe this was the chink in Second Level's armor. And Second Level was where it happened. Second Level held the clues—possibly the answers. Sentiva—the house—the scene of the crime. . . . It was an open invitation. *You got a better idea, Caiper?*

Watly looked down. The fan cleaner was preoccupied with attaching the hose. He was leaning over, concentrating on his actions. Watly scrambled forward as fast as he could. *I can't believe I'm doing this,* he thought. *I can't believe I'm going back there. Back there where I don't belong. I'm a beanheaded, first-faced catfucker.*

He reached the edge of the last daylite, took off his makeshift hand pads, and shoved them in the bag. They'd just get in the way. The cleaner was still busy. Watly gauged the distance carefully and braced himself. He pushed hard with his feet and caught hold of one of the door's bars. Immediately he swung his legs up and—despite his tortured stomach muscles and the broken blisters on his hands—pulled himself up into the hole below the blades. He landed hard, sprawled across the metal bars. One quick glance told him that the man below was almost done and about to rise back up in his basket. Watly rolled to the side and saw there was a ledge all around the inside "cage." He flipped himself up on it and pressed into the wall.

The place smelled. It smelled like everything mixed together. Eau de First Level. The wall next to Watly was moist and greasy. There was a thin screen right above him and, beyond that, the enormous blades. They looked like some huge propeller from an ancient upended boat. Watly touched the screen. He had to get to the other side. Fast. Next to him the cleaner's hose stuck through the hole and began snaking all around, sucking down the remaining garbage. Watly kept himself pressed firmly into the wall. He remained motionless, allowing the filthy hose's mouth to suck at him up and down before moving on. It was not a pleasant sensation—like having a mindless worm pull at his body.

So far the cleaner hadn't seen him. The hose worked its way around the other side. Watly saw it sucking up wrappers, paper, hats, scarves, money, and all kinds of assorted clothing and garbage. He glanced up again. If he couldn't get up to the other side of the fan before it was turned on again, all would be lost. *This was a great idea, Caiper. A great idea.*

The damn screen. Watly tried to rip at it with his right hand. No good. It wasn't very strong but it was strong enough to stop him. Maybe the pipe cutter? There was nothing for its mouth to grip on to. The hose receded from the opening. The cleaner began lowering his basket. Watly turned onto his back and lifted his knees up to his chest. One, two, three, *kick*! He slammed both feet violently into the screen. It gave some. Watly noticed it had buckled near the edge. He glanced down. The cleaner was returning without the hose. He rose up in his basket and swung the bars back up, locking the door with a loud clink. *No going back now,* Watly thought. *I'm locked in. Even the pipe cutter won't go through bars that thick.*

The cleaner guided his little basket back to the street.

Watly kicked up at the screen again. *Please, don't turn the fan on yet!* Again he kicked. Now the screen was bent and beginning to rip at the edge. That's the way. One more violent kick and he was through. The hole was just big enough. Watly rose to his knees and pushed his way through the screen. It was a tight fit.

The knapsack got caught but Watly wrenched it through angrily. *Don't activate that fan, mister! Not yet!*

He was in the fan chamber now. It smelled dark and burnt. It smelled of machinery and oil. He rose up to grip the edge of one of the huge horizontal blades. There was some space between each one—just enough for a person to climb through. Watly heard a rumbling sound.

"Don't do this to me!" he said aloud. He didn't say it out of fear—it was a threat. "*Don't you do this to me!*"

The solid gray metal was slippery. Watly pulled himself halfway up onto the huge fan blade just as there was a loud clank and the sound of heavy machinery revving up. Watly slipped off and fell back into the screen. There was the grinding of gears. The walls vibrated. Watly jumped up and grabbed the blade again. It started to move.

Oh, shit. The fan was on. It moved slowly. Just slowly at first. He pulled himself up waist high onto the blade as it began to spin. *Give me a second, please,* he thought. *Just one second. . . .*

And then he was up, sitting balanced on the thick, slanted metal as the chamber seemed to move by around him. The speed picked up. Everything was rotating. The chamber was becoming a blur around him. *I'll be shredded,* he thought. *I'll fall and be shredded. Cat food.* He slid to the edge and dove off just as the blades began to twirl faster. For a moment he was in the air and then one leg landed on the rim around the outside. The other hit nothing but empty space. There was a thin ledge just like the one in the cage below. Watly wavered on its edge, one leg out, his arms seesawing for balance. Then he was okay. He found his center. Both legs were planted firmly and he was leaning forward. He was fine.

The fan's scream increased. Louder and louder. Watly's clothes flapped and danced madly around him. Billows of air struck his back harder and harder, pressed him into the wall. *My ears,* he thought. *My ears are going to explode!* Watly reached into the bag to find anything—*anything* for his ears. The fan's roar increased. The sound was intolerable.

The bottle, the cutter, the note, the belt, the money, the chip pistol, the pants cuffs. . . . Watly grabbed up the pants cuffs.

He stuffed the edge of one into each ear as far in as it would go. The rest he mashed against the outside. Then he whipped out the belt from Alysess's bathrobe and tied it around his head and under his neck, pressed the balled-up-fabric into his ears. It was better. It helped. He made the knot as tight as possible, trying not to choke himself with the coarse material. The sound was okay now. He could survive it this way.

Watly turned slightly—still pressed up against the metal—and looked around. The noise was still so loud it was almost impossible to think. A wall of wind shoved Watly back into the hard metal. The chamber was of cylindrical shape with the fan centered at the bottom. Watly looked upward to the top of the cylinder. The room was tall. Very tall. There was another fine screen way up there about twenty feet above. Watly looked around him. There were no ridges in the wall. It was all solid, curved steel. There was nothing to hold on to and nothing to climb. Below him was a vast roaring fan waiting to puree him and above him was nothing but twenty feet of air. The one exit in the place—the screen—was way above and there was no way to climb to it.

Great, Watly thought. *Just great. I wonder when the next cleaning day is—two days? three? a week? I'll never make it. They'll open the place up and find diced Watly. Whose idea was this anyway?*

Watly leaned heavily into the metal wall and watched his clothes flap and flutter as if they were trying to jump off his body. *I should've listened to the dream,* he thought with irony. *"Beware the air,"* they'd said. *Beware the air.*

CHAPTER 24

It was a beautiful day on the Second Level. The municipal building on Eighty-first and Koch Avenue had been freshly painted recently—a bright powder blue that intensely reflected the sun's rays. The most dazzling part of the whole building was the polished tube that gleamed like a silver chimney up on the roof's rear left corner. Ringed with golden sound mufflers, the tube disappeared into the white gravel on the roof's surface and reappeared on the west side of the building a story below. It was held in place by delicate brass lion's-head clamps—and angled all the way down the side of the building until it entered the pristine road surface below.

It passed through four thick layers of road surface—whitetop, plasticore fibers, cemeld, and iron gratings—and a middle layer of sewage pipes, water pipes, cables, and assorted wires. It opened out into the anterior fan chamber, which was surrounded by the layers of First Level ceiling, more pipes and cables, iron, steel, cemeld, and the fan motor. Inside the chamber itself was a tall man with the beginnings of a mustache and the beginnings of a

bad headache. His name was Watly Caiper and he was a bit on the
hinky side at the moment. Below him was the fan, model 307,
recently cleaned, currently in operation. Below that was *First*
Level's Koch Avenue.

It was dripping lightly there, daylites on full. The street
sweepers had yet to arrive to tidy up the unsightly mess left by the
fan cleaner. A half-full bus passed by slowly, listing to the right,
one of its cylinders malfunctioning and in need of repair. Two
bicyclists raced up the street toward the long line forming on the
corner. The line was for Level Lottery tickets. Although tickets
didn't go on sale until later in the week, people were already
camping out on the line. It was a very popular, semi-annual
contest. Once a year, one winning Firster was promised the prize
of life on Second Level. The event was always broadcast live on
all CV pleats. Lottery tickets sold for five hundred New York
dollars each, and most people bought more than one. By the end
of the week, when the tickets went on sale, the lines would be two
blocks long.

At the hopeful lottery players' feet, the First Level sidewalk
was lumpy and pitted, slick from the drips that fell. Below it was
more piping, old, rusty sewage pipes, the melted-garbage reinforced tubes, CV cables, electrical cables, keyboard wires, and a
concrete foundation. Below that was a layer of crisscrossed steel
beams. Then there was thick plasticore. Under that: clean red
tiles.

Perfect, rectangular tiles, blood red and highly reflective.

The tiles curved downward to form the ceiling and walls of a
large, unfurnished room. It was one of many rooms. On the floor
of the room were more tiles, also red, but these were scuffed and
scratched.

In this particular room there were thirty-seven people. Fighting
each other. There below the street of the First Level, a war raged.
Combat training. Hand-to-hand, unarmed fighting. A combination of karate, jujitsu, and street fighting. The thirty-seven were
learning how to kill with their bare hands.

Ten of them—ten of the thirty seven—had once called themselves the Skyfinders. They had gathered and talked with each

other about California. One morning, like many had before them, they disappeared. Missing and presumed dead, as planned.

That day of their disappearance, the Skyfinders had woken up disoriented in a red-tiled room much like this one. They were naked and had been blindfolded and bound together with thin cord.

"Do you mean what you say?" a deep voice boomed at them.

"About what?" one of them squeaked out timidly.

"About California, about Revy, about freedom," the voice answered.

"Who *are* you? *Where are we?*" another Skyfinder asked.

There was a long pause. The tile was hard and cold against their bare bodies. They were hungry and scared. They were all sure they were about to be executed.

"I am the Ragman," the resonant voice finally said. "And you, dear comrades, are in the subs. Welcome to the revolution."

CHAPTER 25

The strangest thing happened to Watly. He lost his knapsack. There in the fan chamber he lost it. But only temporarily. Just for a moment. It went on a little trip and came right back.

It happened when he took the thing off. He was going to go carefully through its contents to see if anything inspired him. If nothing inspired him, he planned to get as drunk as possible with what was left of the booze. Watly pulled the bag off his shoulder and started to open it. He lost his grip. As the bag fell Watly lashed out with his right hand to grab it. He couldn't grip it so all he ended up doing was knocking it into the middle of the room. Watly grimaced, prepared to watch all his belongings fall into the fan and be pulverized. They didn't. The bag hit the central air current and flew straight up the middle of the room toward the ceiling. Then Watly saw the bag sort of slip sideways off the powerful blast of air and fall outward into the wall, sliding back downward into Watly's hand. All this took place in a split second. Fascinating. It had ridden the air upward—balanced on it like a pail on a jet of water. It had done a full loop-de-loop.

Watly looked down at the blades. They were a complete blur. He could see through them to the bars below. Beyond that was the light of the street. The shadowy forms of a few rushing people could be seen clutching their hats and bustling along. Life went on down there, below the smear of whizzing blades.

Watly looked upward. The upper screen seemed miles away. He put the knapsack back on, tightening its straps. *If I can fly in a dream,* Watly thought, *who says I can't fly in reality?*

Watly let his body lean forward slightly. Instantly he felt an increase in wind. It almost shoved him back against the wall. He kept his back arched and his hands at his side. With his legs straight and locked he let himself lean even farther. The wind held him. His body was pointed in at an almost forty-five-degree angle. He didn't fall. Watly lifted his arms outward—palms in—and let the increased wind resistance push him back up. Incredible. This just might work. The air was not just air in here. It was a palpable thing. You could touch it—feel it—ride it. Use it like a tool. It was alive.

Watly leaned inward again. This time he tried to gauge the air current. It was like some invisible rushing rapids buffeting skyward—a reverse waterfall. Watly tried to relax his body, bending at the knees and elbows. *Now or never, Caiper. Now or never.* He took a deep breath and jumped forward. His body plowed into the center of the chamber and the breath was knocked back out of his lungs. He'd landed on an almost solid ball of air. He was out of control, careening wildly in empty space. His clothes tore at his body and dust blinded him. He was in a void, held aloft by a screaming jet of wind. Invisible hands shoved him about. Watly felt his body rising. He tried to balance. More clouds of dust flew into his eyes. He brought both hands in to cover his face. He pulled his limbs inward for protection. Suddenly he was tumbling end over end, heading straight down into the center of the fan.

Spread your body out, Caiper! Open up. Make your body a sail.

He tried bringing his hands back, but he did it too swiftly. He was off center now, spinning down toward the side of the air channel. The fan's blades were closer still. Watly vaguely made out the edge lip as it neared. He twisted and flipped himself toward it, landing on his hip with a thud. All this had taken just a few seconds.

Okay, Caiper. Not bad. Live and learn. We'll try again.

He stood up, rubbed the painful hip, and prepared to jump again. This time he leapt off too forcefully. He dove into the middle of the airstream, flipped over in a perfect unintentional somersault, and landed feet first on the far side, almost falling back into the blades. It took a moment for him to realize what happened.

It was nearly comical. *Dazzling,* Watly thought to himself. *Just dazzling. I should be on the CV variety or music-hall pleat.*

Once more, Mister Caiper. Watly turned and pushed off— using less force this time—and aimed for the very center. He kept his arms and legs spread wide but slightly curved. Body facing toward the fan. The skin of his face fluttered like cloth. Again the dust blinded him. He closed his eyes but kept himself in position. The air held him. He was rising higher and higher. Any tiny movement changed his resistance and altered his position. A bending of the wrist sent him sideways. A flexing of the ankle leaned him forward. Bringing his arms and legs in a little made him go back down. Keeping them spread out made him rise. It was a very delicate balancing act. He kept his arms and legs spread and his hands cupped and relaxed. He was in free fall, wind whipping all around him. He was flying like in the dream. *Look, Ma, no hands.*

Beware the air, Watly thought. *Beware the air.*

He was riding the air. *Riding* it. Straight up to the ceiling. It felt like he was clinging to the top of an enormous sphere that might roll and tip him off at the slightest wrong movement. He was weightless, going up and up. Within seconds his back hit something—something that gave a little. It was the screen. Watly was plastered against it, twenty feet above the fan, his body held in place by the force of wind. The knapsack dug into his back. He could feel the booze bottle against his spine.

Now what? he thought. *Here we have a young blind man stuck to a ceiling. Very good. Take a bow, Caiper. For my next trick . . .*

Watly opened his eyes. They were painfully irritated and full of dust. More flew in. Through the blur he could see very little. He slowly tilted his head back. There was a metal frame around the edge of the screen holding it in place. Watly moved his hands slightly toward it. It had a very thin ridge around the edge—just enough to stick the tips of his blistered fingers under. He turned his hands palms up and gripped it.

Already he felt his body losing balance on the invisible sphere. He'd changed the resistance. Watly held tight with his fingers. His legs swayed lower, no longer being pushed as strongly into the screen. Soon he was hanging by the frame, his body totally vertical. The wind flew past and over his now streamlined position. But it still helped him. His fingers alone could never have held him in place.

Watly kicked back and forth with his feet and then let them dangle. Occasionally he would swing them back up and the intense wind would catch his torso and hold him until he moved them back down. His body weight was loosening the screen's frame. He could feel it slipping out. Now his fingers fit easily under the ridge. He tried to sway and bounce without losing grip. His side of the frame pulled lower. It was coming all the way out. After one particularly hearty bounce, the frame's edge popped out completely, swung downward, and hung open. Watly clung to the edge of it as it dangled from one corner. Above was darkness. His body swayed against the unstable metal. Slowly and gingerly he climbed up the side of the screen, hand over hand, using the wind's help. The air seemed to push and guide him onward, keeping him from falling or sliding backward. Soon he was at the opening, pulling himself through with his hands. Up into the darkness.

Above the fan chamber there was a right-angle bend and then a horizontal tube. It was almost pitch black inside. The only light came from behind, through the opening where the screen had been. Watly had to stoop to fit. In a way the wind seemed stronger here, more concentrated and channeled. Watly followed it along, letting it continue to push him and goad him forward. It made a hollow groaning sound as it echoed down the pipe.

If he held his arms out, his fingers trailed along the curved walls. The metal was cold, dry, and seamless. Watly walked onward, crouched like some strange simian. The farther he went the darker it became. As he continued, Watly realized the roar of the fan was now more bearable. He was putting some distance between them. That was good.

Now it was pitch black. Watly walked on steadily, his back aching. *How far have I walked?* The tube began to tilt upward slightly, angling into a gentle slope. Watly found himself slipping backward every now and then. With no point of reference, it was impossible to tell just how steep the slope was. But it was definitely getting harder to continue. He began to use his hands, pressing outward against the sides. This helped him gain some control back.

Then Watly walked into a wall. It was a soft and malleable wall but it still surprised him. He reached forward to touch it again. It wasn't really a wall at all. It was a fibrous, netlike skin that the air easily passed through—some kind of filter. Watly found that it ripped and shredded quite easily. He tore an opening in it, stepped through, and passed beyond it. He figured it must be something workers replaced every so often—after it had trapped enough of whatever small particles made it through the first two screens.

After traveling awhile longer Watly squatted down in the darkness and leaned into the curved walls. He needed to rest. As he sat, his body wanted to slide back down the tilted tube, but Watly pressed his feet into the side opposite him and wedged himself in position. His body was beyond fatigue. It was actually at the strange point where aches and pains turn into mere sensations. Discomfort became an awareness of one's limitations and little else. He almost felt good. Martyrish, long-suffering, endurance-testing good.

Watly did not rest long. After a short while the surrounding darkness seemed unsettling. He would rather be moving, concentrating. Sitting still, the mind wandered too much. The darkness was too total. If he let them, amoeba-shaped objects began to float vividly before him. Smiling monsters started to appear and dance. Then burning children. Mutilated women. . . . Watly rose and climbed on.

He passed through three more of the soft filters before he saw light up ahead. It was very faint and very far ahead but it was real. And something else: It was not daylite. It was not man-made. Somewhere at the end of the wind-filled howling tunnel was sunlight. Up ahead. Real, honest-to-terra sunlight.

CHAPTER 26

It was out under the real sun that Watly Caiper killed someone new. This was arguably his fourth murder. If one counted the poor bum (which Watly did), and if one believed the news report about the two police officers in the copper crash (which Watly wasn't all that sure about), then he had already killed three people. Or, at least, had been responsible for their deaths. One could even stretch the point and count the big one—the donor's murder of that woman. It *had* been, after all, Watly's own hands that had done that job. But Watly refused to count that. No, four was enough. Four murders in three days was plenty. This was escalating way out of control. Everything had been blown out of proportion. Watly Caiper. Misunderstood Watly Caiper. Watly Caiper: potential mother. No. Not at all. Watly Caiper: serial killer. *Blood on your hands, Watly. Knock 'em down one at a time, do you, Caiper?* And this was the worst. This death. It couldn't really be called an accident. And no one was in charge of Watly's mind but Watly. "There's fighting and then there's fighting," Watly's mother had always said. "No one, *no one* has the right to hurt another person. If there's anything sacred in this world, it is a person's physical integrity. A person's life."

Watly felt sick. He burped and tasted stomach acid. *Killer.*

Everything had been going along so well. The light up ahead in the tube had gotten brighter and brighter as he continued forward. Watly saw the glow reflected all along the shiny curved walls. The hollow groan of the wind seemed to echo less and become a loud, breathy whistle sound. Watly used more and more effort to climb as the angle increased. Pretty soon he seemed to be going almost straight up, pushing out with his arms and legs for leverage. Inching up the smooth surface, the only thing keeping him in place the constant outward pressure of his limbs. Two times he slid back downward and lost a lot of ground before stopping completely. On he went. He wasn't going to get discouraged.

The light was almost painful now. It seemed too bright, too fast. Watly found himself squinting, his eyes tearing up. Eventually he was right below it. The tube angled in a sharp curve and pointed directly up. Watly wedged himself in position—feet spread—and leaned into the tube's bend. Right above him, divided and sectioned into geometric shapes by thin metal bars, was blue. Crystal clear blue. The most brilliant blue ever. And a touch of puffy whiteness scattered here and there. But the blue—that light, pure color—was the thing. It alone was worth the climb. Sky.

Watly blinked. His eyes felt virginal, never used before. He reached up and tested the metal bars. They were thin and square-shaped. The pipe cutter clipped them neatly with no problem—*pwonk, pwonk, pwonk*—and they bent back easily. Soon Watly had an opening big enough to pull himself through. He did just that—squirming a bit and shifting the bag to make it—and he was out under a dazzling sun. A real sun.

Watly jumped off the rim and sat down heavily. He leaned back into the shiny surface of the tube, feeling the ridges of the golden sound mufflers, and ripped off his makeshift ear protectors. What a relief to have them off. He massaged his lobes and rubbed the line under his chin where the belt had been tied. He was on a roof—sitting in white gravel on a Second Level roof. His unbound ears throbbed and Watly winced at the loud moaning whistle that still came from the mouth of the air channel behind him. He crawled a few feet away from it and sat again, hugging his knees. All around him was sky. Beautiful sky. Watly could see forever. He breathed deeply. The air was charged. It was full and rich and felt like medicine to his overworked lungs. *What's the season?* Watly wondered. *It's late spring, isn't it? I've lost track. What was it back in Brooklyn? That was my last sun. Yes, it must be late spring by now. May, maybe.*

Skyscrapers gleamed all around. In the distance the really tall ones towered like giants over the city. Watly was awestruck. To the left, the Gavy Tower seemed to tilt west and touch the edge of the sun. Its golden exterior burned with reflections. Watly felt the warmth of real sunlight—daylight, not daylite—hit him on the nose, cheeks, and forehead. And there was Alvedine—that chunky, broad-shouldered building that seemed to rise forever. And the two Empire State Buildings with their shiny connecting bridges. The Man-With-Hat-One. And the Chrysler. All of them. Vertical space. Air. Sky. Sun.

Watly drew little circles in the gravel with the pipe cutter. The sights were incredible. His mind felt numb. He leaned back into the knapsack and continued looking upward, breathing slowly and deliberately, relishing every inhale as if it were a gourmet meal.

Suddenly there was a crunching sound from directly behind him. It was the noise of heavy footsteps on gravel. Watly spun around.

"You're a pretty craft one, huh?" the cop said. He stood just a few yards away and held the double-bolted haver nerve rifle with both hands. "I told my partner, Neper Balden, I said—I said, 'Neper, this Sergeant Fenlocki fella's crazy. Posting a cop at every single exhaust tube is just insane,' I says." The officer hocked loudly and spat a thick wad of mucus onto the gravel. "'Waste of police,' I says. 'Who the hell's gonna climb up one? Huh? Who's got the eggs? An air tube? No one could. And what for?' But the sergeant's a stubborn man. He seems to think it's a likely escape route. 'Second Level's weakest point,' and all. Well, wouldn't you know he was raping right. And I was wrong. How about that?" The officer grinned and showed a missing front tooth. "It's Watly Caiper hisself and I've got him."

The man's feet were spread and planted firmly. He was bracing his stocky form against the inevitable recoil of the nerve gun. "Yes-sir-ee. Yes-sir-ee. It's the *man*. Watly Caiper." He laughed and spat again. Watly rose forward up on his knees.

"I'm gonna kill you now, Caiper." The cop chuckled. "It'll be the easiest million a body ever earned."

"Just a second, officer." Watly felt sweat trickle down his forehead. He got nearer the man by walking slowly forward on his knees. "One last favor . . ."

"Nuh-uh, Caiper. This is it." The office sprang the bolt.

Watly crawled closer still. He had to get near. "Just one favor. Do it in the head. I want it fast."

"And why should I, Mr. Mutilator? Why should I? Why not just get you in a hand or foot? You know how long that'd take? Maybe a full minute or two. The longest raping minute of your life. I could just stand here and watch it climb up the nerves of your arm as you screamed and rolled around. It'd serve you."

"In the head, please," Watly said quietly. His face was now only a foot and a half from the barrel of the gun. Close. Real close.

"No way. I got no reason to. And since you asked for it special, I'm *definitely* not doing it in the head. Too good for you." The man spat again—this time at Watly. He missed and the spit hit gravel.

Watly pleaded with his eyes. The officer turned the gun down and over slightly so it was pointing at Watly's left hand. This was good. This was a chance.

"Kiss this world goodbye, Watly Caiper."

Watly moved even farther forward. He found himself suddenly aware of the weight of the pipe cutter in his hand. He lifted it slightly. His senses seemed heightened. Everything slowed. It was as if the outside world was suddenly shifted into extreme slow motion. He saw the officer's finger as it began to gently squeeze the trigger. He saw the gleam in the man's beady eyes—the smile and the growing look of pleasure. He saw his own left hand rush forward—as if no longer a part of him—and grip the cold barrel.

Watly then saw the world tilt as he sprang forward and the perspective changed. There was a blast from the rifle and a bolt flashed out harmlessly toward that clear blue above. A struggle began—a fight for control of the rifle. They were rolling around on the gravel, the gun pointing away from both. And again Watly became aware of the pipe cutter. He was thinking—even while fighting furiously—that someone had once told him something about the human skull. He tried to remember. A street tough in Brooklyn had said it. "Hit a person on the side of the head," the guy had said, "if you want to *kill* them. Right in the temple. But if you only want to knock them out, hit them on the top. The top of the head."

On the top. Okay. The top. And so, somehow, Watly got room to swing and came down with the pipe cutter. Hard. The handle hit directly in the top center of the officer's head with a cracking thud. That did it. *Bonk.* The battle was over. The man went limp on the white gravel and the rifle clattered down. Over. Over.

Watly knelt again. He was heaving for air. *That should keep the cop out for a while,* he was thinking. *That should hold him. Out cold, he is.* Watly leaned in to the officer. *Yup, out cold.* Only it was more than that. Much more. The man was dead. Stone cold dead. No breathing, no heartbeat, and a stream of spittle dripping from the gap between his front teeth. Watly had killed the cop with a blow that was only supposed to make him unconscious.

Shit. Not another one. What about the rule? What about the old saying. Hitting someone on the top of the head wasn't supposed to kill them. It was a proven rule of thumb, wasn't it? A fact? A law of nature or something? Why didn't anyone say it depended on how hard you hit? Why didn't anyone say these rules weren't always true when it came to the fragility of the human skull? Of human life?"

After a few moments Watly threw up. He had had enough.

"Welter-five-nie. Welter-five-nie. Where's your call-in?"

The cop's speaker was squawking.

"I feel sick," Watly groaned from a few feet away.

"Do we read you? You feel sick?"

"I feel really sick," Watly said, hardly aware he was speaking to someone.

"We copy. Take a personal-time, officer. We have authorization."

"That's great," Watly said as he held his stomach tightly.

"Hope you feel better. We'll send a replacement. Signing off."

There was a click. Watly felt chilled and weak. He shuddered all over. Did they send a replacement? Oh, rape on dried catshit. Watly looked around. The only thing he could do—the only plan he had—was distinctly unpleasant. *Distinctly* unpleasant. He shuddered again. Is there no limit to what one will do to save one's own neck? Does it never end? Selfish/bad, this is. Selfish/bad.

Fifteen more minutes passed before Watly threw up again. This time it was more like the dry heaves. Painful spasms with no results. Things had changed. Things were different now. Lots of things. He was now dressed as a police officer. He had on the snappy blue jacket and pants and the rakish cap—all slightly large. Over one shoulder was his knapsack and over the other was the haver nerve rifle. Back behind him was the air tube, and somewhere way down inside it—perhaps still sliding lower, down and down—was the body of a stocky dead man wearing only underwear. Somewhere near *him*, near this dead guy, was a pile of filthy old clothes—a jersey jacket and anklepants. Above all this, the bars over the tube's opening had been neatly bent back to look as natural as possible. The disturbed gravel of the roof had been smoothed. Everything was calm and serene. Untouched.

Watly walked across the roof stiffly—toward the raised door that let into the building below. He felt empty inside, both literally and figuratively. He felt he had thrown up not just food. He had thrown up part of himself. He had vomited out some intrinsic part of Watly Caiper. A little piece of his humanity, his morality—or something. The other murders *had* been different. Watly had not pulled the trigger on the gun that shot the bum. He had not carefully aimed the unpiloted copper at the two officers. He had not planned the riot. (Had anyone died in that? It could be.) And he certainly had no intentional part in the donor's killing of that poor woman. He had been powerless in that.

But this was not the same. This Watly did on his own. Self-defense—yes. But still, a man was dead. And he was to blame. Directly. He had killed him with a blow to the head and coldly shoved him down an exhaust tube. Undressing a dead man, pulling off all his clothes, dragging a half-naked corpse across a

roof, scraping skin off on the rough gravel, hoisting the heavy
body and squeezing it down past metal bars . . . had Watly
really done all that? Had he been capable? Oh, rape. This was a
sickness. All of it. This was a cancer that grew more and more.
Worse and worse.

Numbly, and without trying to hide himself at all, Watly took
the roof elevator down to street level. He stepped out onto the
sidewalk and began to walk south. No one paid any attention to
him. A foot-patrol officer was apparently no rarity. He saw quite
a number of pedestrians strolling up and down the avenue. All
were exquisitely dressed. Their clothing was really fuckable—and
probably unbelievably expensive. Wild shocking colors and opalescent fabrics. Everything looked shiny and brand-new. No
patches, no stains, no rips. And those fancy shoes again. Leather?
There was something different about the people themselves, as
well. The skin on their faces looked exaggerated—too light or too
dark. One extreme or the other. *Caricatures* of people, instead of
just people. And some of them seemed surprisingly young to
Watly. Impossibly young. Younger than Watly himself.

Watly let himself become submerged once again within the
sights and sounds around him. It was the only way he could
continue. *Look and smell and listen and breath, Caiper. Don't
think. No more thinking. Never think again. Life is too short to
think. Thinking just gets in the way. Thinking slows you down.
Just look around you. See the beauty. Smell the cleanness. Hear
the peace.*

It struck Watly suddenly—almost physically—that the most
wondrous thing about Second Level compared to First was a very
simple thing. A basic thing: People had only one shadow here.
Just one. Like Brooklyn. The solitary sun cast only one elegant
shadow for each object. On First Level there was *never* only one
shadow. Down below, as one walked from beneath one daylite to
another, a fan of shadows danced about, fused and separated,
faded and grew—always in motion and never alone. Here it was
different. Here a person could have a sense of solidity. One
person: one shadow. Elegant.

A sedan went by, one woman driving. It was an antique
car—in perfect condition—retrofitted with a new engine at the

back but without compromising the original lines. Watly's stride faltered and he stared at it. Beautiful. Fuckable. It was a bright red Chevy from the nineties or maybe turn-of-the-century, in incredible shape. Following it a more modern vehicle zipped past—again a private sedan, clean and polished, only one driver, cylinders blazing beautifully.

Watly looked down at the smooth, unbroken surface of the white streets. Unblemished whitetop. No potholes, no lumps, no primitive makeshift repair jobs—none of the patchwork, almost archaeological quality of down below. The streets and sidewalks up here looked virginal—boring in their lack of character. But they were beautiful. Everything was beautiful.

Watly tried not to show his awe. More people passed by and he almost bumped into one. A few First Levelers in workervests and black jumpsuits trotted along with eyes lowered. Watly picked up the pace and turned east. Structures were set apart up here on Second. Watly had never realized how many buildings must have been five stories or lower down below. It seemed most of them never made it up this high. Those that did make it to this level bore little resemblance to their lower counterparts. There were beautiful slate roofs, tile walls and shingles, and golden and wooden entranceways. Sprawling private homes with gingerbread-carved flying buttresses, ornate cupolas, brightly colored shutters, and striped awnings. Tall house-offices made from old high rises. Even the skyscrapers looked personalized. Some had crenellated parapets at the top and others were painted in vast bold graphics and abstract designs. Space and more space.

Watly saw something up ahead, coming toward him. Something incredible. On his side of the sidewalk, nearing with every step, two people approached him. One was a thin, middle-aged man wearing a colorful cape. The other was clutching the man's hand and running alongside him, trying to keep up. It was a child. A lovely little child. Four or five years old at the most. It had wide and curious eyes and perfect pale skin. Watly felt his throat constrict.

The two neared and passed by, brushing close. A child. A baby, really. Hardly more.

Up ahead was another—another child. This one with a woman.

He was a little boy and had a shock of bright orange-red hair. Freckles. He was younger still, and seemed wobbly on his legs. Awkward. Watly felt dizzy. He felt an achy love kind of feeling for the *smallness*. For the youngness. For the beauty. This was a kid. A real live *kid*. A boy, talking with great animation and energy.

Watly got closer and could make out a few words. The child's voice was high and breathy and full of giggles. His little cheeks were red with exertion and he gestured broadly and unself-consciously with the one free hand as he spoke. As they brushed past, ignoring him totally, Watly made out one word in particular. He heard it clearly, as if it were meant for him. Again his throat grew tight and Watly thought for a brief moment that he might cry. He might break down right there on the street—right there in a police uniform on the Second Level—and cry hysterically. He didn't. He swallowed and controlled the urge, pressing it inward. He kept walking. But still that one word echoed over and over in his head. It wouldn't stop. The word had been said casually by the child. It had been plunked down in the middle of a sentence with little thought. But Watly had still heard it.

The word was *mommy*.

CHAPTER 27

Watly hadn't remembered the bay windows. Of course, the first time he stood here at the foot of these steps, he'd not been himself. Not himself at all. And now as *just* himself looking up at the front of the large building, he could take it all in. To either side of the front steps were deep bay windows made of a weathered wood. The building was imposing and powerful-looking and seemed—from Watly's perspective, at least—just tall enough to graze the sky. There was no movement from behind any of the windows. The place was lifeless. It was waiting, daring him to take a step.

Watly knew that even a man dressed as a policeman would draw attention if he stood gaping up at a private home for too long. It was time to move again. Time to get going. Time to trot up those same front steps he had climbed what seemed like years ago. Time to pay another call at the Alvedine residence. Watly shifted the heavy rifle's strap and started forward.

There was an eerie sense of déjà vu as Watly touched the front door and saw it was completely unsecured. A trap? The wooden door swung inward easily without a creak. Just like it had before.

To the right Watly saw the plate with numbered keyboard. A security device, no doubt. *Let's hope it's off,* Watly thought.

He took a step into the foyer, closing the door behind him. Ahead was the sitting room, illuminated by all the natural sunlight streaming in. Watly took another step down the short foyer. There was no one around and no lenses visible. It seemed safe enough. If it was a trap it sure didn't look like it yet. He edged forward slowly. As he advanced, hinkyness overcame him. His chest felt tighter and his pulse quickened. Maybe this was a bad idea. Maybe he should never have come up here. Never have come back to Second and *certainly* never have come back to this house. Not *this* house.

He took a step forward.

This *was* an awful idea. He was going to die. He was going to die any second now. It was inevitable. It *was* a trap.

Watly was having trouble breathing. His chest felt tight and constrained and his skin was crawling. It was a horrible panic attack, or something.

He took one more step forward, almost in the sitting room now. He was sweating in what felt like great sheets of liquid all down his face.

Rape, I'm going to die, he thought. *I'm going to die and it's gonna hurt real bad. It's the pain I don't want—the pain!*

Watly couldn't move forward anymore. He'd gone as far as possible. His legs were trembling.

Maybe I'm dying right now! Maybe this is it! Maybe I'll die right here all by myself. All alone. The worst kind of death you can have. A lonely death.

He took a step backward and suddenly felt better. Another step and the fear subsided even more. He backed up all the way to the door. Now he felt okay. His confidence was back. He felt himself again.

This was strange. What was the story here? Watly took another tentative, experimental step down the front hallway. Sure enough, his fear increased. The sense of dread and fright was an almost tangible thing coming on stronger with each step down the hall. This was not just Watly. No, something more was at play here.

Watly retreated again and looked back at the wall keyboard.

Etched in the lower right-hand corner of the metal plate was some small writing:

ANXIETY FIELD CONTROLS

An anxiety field. *That* was the security device. No wonder the door had been unlocked both times—the house was protected by an anxiety field in the front hallway. An old but effective method of stopping intruders. Supposedly illegal now. Watly glanced around. This entrance was the only way in—as far as he knew. The outer windows had looked solid and impenetrable. Anyway, he would attract attention trying to climb to one in broad daylight. No, this was the only way.

Maybe he could push his way through an anxiety field with sheer willpower. It might be possible. Watly backed up against the door and gritted his teeth. *I can do this*, he thought. *All I need is strength*. He pushed off from the door and plowed forward toward the sitting room.

Again his breathing quickened and his skin broke out in sweat. *This won't work*, he thought. *It can't. Something terrible will go wrong. Maybe I'll burst a blood vessel in my head. Or maybe I'll have a heart attack.*

Watly continued onward.

Or maybe someone has already come in behind me and is about to shoot me in the back of the head—or in that little valley just between the shoulder blades. Or maybe they're aiming for my neck. Right where my skull meets my spine. The slug will bite bone and shatter my brain. I'll feel it busting my head open. I'll feel every moment.

He was moving slower now, each step torture. He was overcome with the same kind of powerless horror he'd experienced when his mother had died. Only worse. His vision blurred as he approached the area he had been stopped at before.

My whole life has been a disaster. My whole life I've never gotten anything I want. My dreams are all dead. I'll never be a mother. No child for me. None. I'll be caught and killed. And . . . and . . .

Watly thought he might wet himself. The feelings of impending doom and inevitable death were intolerable. He couldn't move forward anymore.

And if I ever do have a child, it will be deformed and insane and it will kill me when it's strong enough. And . . .

It was no good. He was frozen in place—just at the end of the hall.

And the next woman I have sex with will grow teeth down below and bite me off midstroke. . . . *And any minute now someone will stab me in the eyes.* . . . *And then bugs and small animals will envelope me.* . . .

Watly backed up. It was useless. The fear grew so intense down near the end of the anxiety field that it was impossible to pass. He kept retreating until he was leaning back into the door, relieved the terror was abated. Now he was okay. But he was still not inside. He was still at square one.

Watly wiped the sweat off his face with the sleeve of his "borrowed" blue uniform. He turned toward the wall and stared at the small bank of numbers. Nine little buttons, set up in rows of three. One row on top of the other. If only he could remember the combination. If only he could remember the numbers. But he'd never really *known* the numbers. The donor had known them. The donor had punched them in quickly as if well practiced. Naturally, Watly's eyes had been on the board at the time—he'd had no choice—but the actual combination had gone by too fast. And there had been other things on Watly's mind.

Da, da, de-da—the donor had hit the buttons. *Da, da, de-da. One, two, three-four.* Four of them. Four numbers and the field would be deactivated. Watly could hear the rhythm in his head—*da, da, de-da.* If only he could remember the digits. The donor had done it all in such an offhanded manner—barely looking at the board. It seemed like months ago now. Years.

Watly looked at his right hand and tried to hold it the same way the donor had—index finger pointed, the others curled slightly, thumb relaxed. He brought his hand near the keyboard, trying to replay the foggy memory of that evening. *Da, da, de-da.* Watly gave up on remembering the actual numbers—he just concentrated and tried to envision the movements his own hand had taken back then.

What had the sensations been like? How stretched was his arm? How much of the board was visible between his fingers when they'd hit the first number? What had the negative space between his hand and the doorjamb been shaped like? Had the wrist twisted from one number to the next? Watly tried to digest all this, put it together in his mind, and come up with some viable answer. *Da, da, de-da. Remember the rhythm.* . . .

It was time to give it a try. Watly punched in four numbers on the keyboard, trying to mimic the same rhythm and sensation as in his memory. *Da, da, de-da.*

There was a mechanical hum. A small green light flashed on the board. *Yes.*

He'd done it. Watly strode forward rapidly down the hallway—he didn't know how long he had before the field came up again, but he wasn't about to get caught in the middle. This time any anxiety he felt as he passed down to the all-wood sitting room was *real* anxiety. None of this stimulation-to-the-fear-centers-of-the-brain business—just some honest-to-goodness straightforward shit-willies. Shit-willies that came from being on Second, from breaking and entering, from being in the house where it all had occurred . . . and from everything else that had happened and that might happen yet. It still could be a trap. This anxiety was surprisingly comfortable compared to the all-encompassing synthetic fear the field had induced. It was almost pleasant. Almost.

Watly had crossed through the sitting room and was halfway up the large curved staircase before he noticed someone was coming down it. Straight at him.

He almost bumped into the graceful form before him. Like a dancer she moved, and like a dancer she stopped in her tracks.

In the split second that he became aware of her presence—even before she became aware of his—Watly surprised himself. There was a flicker of something within him—less than love but more than lust. Not like Alysess. Alysess was something else entirely. With Alysess, in spite of their short acquaintance, he felt something strong—something important. If what he felt for Alysess wasn't love, it was certainly a close second. But this . . .

But this was different. A look at the vision before him brought out a hint of something disturbing—something primitive. *Why is it*, Watly wondered, *that we are all so pulled toward the aesthetic—for its own sake? Why do we have this drive to be with, to touch, to make love to that which pleases the eye? Do we think that the beauty will somehow rub off on us? Why is our libido, our lust, our passion so intertwined with our concept of beauty? Why do I, Watly Caiper, want so much to poke myself into loveliness? To enter it, to affect it, to be wanted by it, to be a part of it? Beauty. Beauty like this person before me. I can almost understand why one would kill for such a one as this.*

There she was. Sentiva Alvedine in all her glory. The incredible face, those intense green eyes that had been hidden from Watly's view, the strong—almost overpowering—jawline, the flowing dark hair, that statuesque body. . . . She was wearing a dark business suit—not unlike the one worn by the murder victim that night that seemed so long ago. Even under the sexless outfit, her physical beauty was not hidden. The rise of the breasts, the slender waist, the hips. . . . *This is a goddess*, Watly thought. He was overcome with the desire to apologize for the actions of his donor. His first instinct was to say: *I'm sorry my body took advantage of yours. Yours is not a body to be taken advantage of. No body, of course, is a body to take advantage of. But somehow, the rape of your body is a perfect example of why rape is a curse, but fuck is not. Fuck is a beautiful thing, rape is an obscenity. The ultimate obscenity. And, incidentally, Sentiva, about that murder . . .* But Watly said nothing. He gazed blankly up at her.

Sentiva looked stunned for a moment. "Officer?" she said. "How did you get—"

Then Watly saw recognition pass over her face. *She must know me from my news-file photos*, he thought. *She recognizes me. She sees before her the man who murdered her mate. Her mate? Whoever the hell it was.*

"You're . . ." She drew back up a step and Watly—with some reluctance—shouldered the haver nerve rifle.

"Yes, I am," he said quietly.

"Yes, I see that," Sentiva said, rapidly composed again, no hinkyness in her expression at all now. "Yes, you are."

She had a beautiful voice. Like Alysess's but less youthful, more mature. Her Second Level accent was thick and obvious but somehow sounded softened, no harshness in its tone. Watly gestured with the rifle for her to continue down the steps. "I'd like to talk to you."

"What makes you think that I'd like to talk to the man who murdered my poovus?" she said, stepping slowly down past Watly with her hands in front of her, palms out and fingers spread. The gesture was not so much one of supplication as it was of temporary truce. *I will refrain from hurting you at the moment,* her hands seemed to say—even though it was he who held the weapon. There was no fear in her face, only anger. Watly wondered if maybe she knew some advanced form of self-defense or if there was additional security he hadn't caught. Or maybe this is just what it meant to be a Second Leveler: brave, tough, and fearless.

He kept the rifle trained on her as she stepped to the sitting room. She still moved like a dancer, gliding effortlessly and gracefully around the furniture. She was a class act.

"Because I didn't do it," he said with as much conviction as he could muster.

She sat on the wicker couch. "I see."

She's putting me on stage, Watly thought. *She knows that if I had come here to kill her I would've done it already. No wonder she's not afraid. She knows I've come here to talk—or else she'd be dead—and she's saying, "So? Go ahead. Talk."*

Watly shifted his weight nervously from one leg to another. "I'm innocent. This whole thing is a frame-up."

Sentiva reached slowly to the table before her and opened the small wooden box on it. Watly raised the rifle in warning. She pulled out a cigel and snap-ignited its end with one fluid movement.

"Cigel?" she asked.

Watly shook his head. He was about to comment on their illegality, but then—considering the situation—he thought better of it.

Sentiva took a long, sensuous drag off the cigel and glanced up at Watly, her delicate eyelashes obscuring the tops of those intense emerald irises. "What do you want from me?" she asked calmly. "Haven't you done enough?"

"I want . . ." Watly leaned on the arm of the chair opposite her, gun still raised, "I want some answers. I didn't do this and I need help figuring out who did."

Sentiva smiled slightly. Two little dimples appeared beside her full lips, and her already beautiful face became more beautiful still. But the smile was full of irony. "You want *me* to help *you*? Why? Why should I believe you?"

Watly stood again. "You tell me why I would be here if I *did* do it."

"Because you're scared," Sentiva answered.

"Then you tell me *how* I did it. You explain it to me. Tell me where I learned the combination to your anxiety field. Tell me how—how I drugged you before I even *got* here. Tell me how I forged passes so good I got to Second Level with no problem. And last of all—last of all, you tell me, if I *was* smart enough to do all that—if I was this incredible criminal mastermind—how come I was stupid enough to get caught? How come I murdered someone in full view of the office recorder lenses?"

"Some criminals *want* to get caught," Sentiva said coldly.

"That's catshit."

"Then you tell me," she countered, punctuating each word with a jerk of the cigel, "how come it's *you* we see on the recorders? You tell me how come I've watched a certain recording over and over and it's *your* face that I've memorized. It's *your* hands on the scalpel. Why is that, Mister Caiper?" Her voice was raised for the first time. A brighter spark of anger glowed within each eye.

Watly paused before speaking. "I was hosting," he said finally. "Hosting against my will." Even to him it sounded like a lie.

"Then where was the—"

"I know," Watly interrupted. "Where was the cuff? The cuff was removed—and no, I don't know how. But it was."

Sentiva puffed out a perfect pink smoke ring. She was calm again. "Why should I believe you?"

Watly shrugged. "You don't have to. It would be nice, but you don't have to. I still want some answers anyway."

"Answers to what?"

Watly sat down fully on the chair's cushion. "Why do they say it was Corber Alvedine who was killed?"

"Because it was."

"It was a woman."

There was silence for a moment. "Yes, that's right. It was," Sentiva said dispassionately.

Watly was confused. "You can't have it both ways, Sentiva. Why do they say it was Corber who was killed instead of the woman?"

Sentiva pushed out the cigel and exhaled the last of its pink smoke. "Corber *was* a woman."

CHAPTER 28

"You are an incredibly naive man, Watly Caiper. Incredibly. In fact, I'm tempted to accept your insane story as truth on that ground alone. Do you believe every image you see on the CV? Do you think that every person on it *exists*? Or that they always exist in the form that you see them? You don't understand that a person can be *keyboard-manufactured* for vidsatt?" Sentiva was staring at Watly as if he'd just told her that he'd always thought the world was flat. She had ignited another cigel and was dragging heavily on it between sentences.

Watly was pacing now, back and forth across the carpet in front of her. "Are you telling me the murdered woman *was* Corber Alvedine? But I've *seen* Corber Alvedine," he said loudly. "I've seen him all the time on—"

"—on the CV?" she interrupted. "Is that where you've seen him? Ever seen him in person? Do you *know* of anyone who's ever seen him in person? No? The woman you killed *was* Corber. Corb*ell*, actually. She had always *been* Corber Alvedine. From the beginning. The founder and president of Alvedine Industries."

Watly stopped pacing and faced Sentiva squarely. "But why? Why the pretense?" he asked.

Sentiva exhaled impatiently. "Because we decided on it. One of us had to be a man, Mr. Caiper. Corbell and I are mated. Poovuses. We have been for ten years. Up here things are different. Things are not like on First Level. Up here people want a certain image and it must be maintained. People want high-profile couples to be male-female. One must keep up appearances. We drew lots and Corbell became . . . Corber. Open same-sex relationships are not acceptable. So—for the past five years, every time you saw Corber on the CV, the image you saw was keyboard-created. It's quite simple."

"But how . . ." Watly still didn't feel he had the story straight, "how can you *keep* a secret like that?"

Sentiva smiled again. "Oh, you needn't, really," she said. "It's quite a common practice up here. Many do it."

"Why?"

"For appearances, Caiper. For appearances."

The pink smoke from her continuous cigel smoking was getting thick. Watly waived some of it away.

"Okay," he said slowly, "so this woman, Corber—Corbell, or whatever—this poovus of yours—who would want to kill her?"

"*You,* apparently," Sentiva said abruptly, her smile gone.

"I already told you—"

"All right," she jumped in. "You plead your innocence. If we accept that—and I must say you've almost convinced me with your stupidity alone—if we accept for the sake of argument that you didn't do it, then *everyone's* a suspect."

"Everyone?" Watly stepped closer. By now the swinging rifle was just a nuisance. It banged into his arm.

"One makes a lot of enemies building an empire as big as she did within only a few years. And she was headed for politics. *Big-time* politics. Corbell was not always well liked," Sentiva said carefully.

"Did she have a specific political opponent?" Watly asked.

Sentiva looked mildly embarrassed. "*No one* liked her politics, Mr. Caiper."

"No one specific?"

Sentiva shrugged.

"What about jealousy?" Watly asked. "Romantic jealousy?"

Sentiva smiled and crossed her legs. "Again," she said, "it could have been . . . anyone."

"Yes?"

"I *am* . . . well liked," she said, raising her eyebrows to punctuate the double entendre. Her Second Level accent seemed to be getting thicker by the moment.

Watly took a deep breath and tried to clear his mind. There had to be an answer here. "Who knows the combination to the anxiety field?" he asked.

"Corbell, me, and, apparently, you," Sentiva replied smugly.

"Nobody else?"

"If you're telling the truth, then yes, somebody else does know it—the murderer."

Watly frowned. So far, all this wasn't very productive. "Tell me what you remember from that day—the day of the murder."

Sentiva rolled her eyes and pushed out her latest cigel. She started speaking with boredom in her voice—as if she had recited the same litany of events over and over for the cops. "I had my usual exciting and glamorous Second Level day. I spent most of the afternoon working upstairs in Corbell's office, helping her with some correspondence. We had dinner out. When we came back, Corbell went back up to her office and I went to my bedroom. All I remember was going to the window to look out. I felt a stabbing pain in my neck and that was all." Sentiva shifted on the couch. "Next thing I know, I'm waking up stark naked on the bed and the police are pounding on the door." Her cheeks seemed to be getting flushed with anger—no, with genuine rage. "Apparently, I had been raped."

Sentiva paused, sat up stiffly, and Watly watched the redness drain from her face. "And then the body upstairs . . . " she said, "the body of Corbell . . . it was . . ." She lifted her strong jaw up defiantly, as if to stave off tears. Her cheeks reddened again, but not from anger. She was making a strong attempt not to cry, it seemed. Not to grieve in front of the possible murderer of her poovus.

Watly stepped toward Sentiva, searching her eyes. "Do you

remember anything—a sound, a smell—from right before you were drugged?"

She paused and seemed to be seriously pondering the question. She took a long moment. "Nothing," she said finally, shaking her head.

Watly pushed the cap back and rubbed his forehead roughly. "Did Corbell have a *real* rival? Is there anyone who had really expressed a strong interest in you lately? Someone who might want to get Corbell out of the way?"

Sentiva looked irritated. "As I said before, Mr. Caiper. I have many friends. And admirers. Sex partners, even. But I have no lovers. Quite honestly, I know of no one who would kill for me."

"What about the politics? What was she going to run for?"

"Maybe nothing," Sentiva said. "Maybe Chancellor."

Watly swallowed. "Chancellor? Of Manhattan? Wow. Now, who wouldn't want her to—"

"You want a list of everyone in Manhattan politics, Mr. Caiper?" Sentiva interrupted harshly.

"Well . . . what about Alvedine Industries? Who's next in line for the job? Who's running the business now that 'Corber' Alvedine is dead? Could it be that an ambitious—"

"I don't think that's the motive, Mr. Caiper."

"Why not?"

"Because—at least for the time being—*I'm* running Alvedine Industries."

"Oh," Watly said, feeling somewhat foolish. "Well, what about Corbell—did *she* have a lover? Could there have been some kind of lover's quarrel?"

Sentiva looked at Watly coolly. "We were both faithful to each other, Mr. Caiper. In our way. That was our arrangement. That was our life."

"Isn't it possible—"

"No," she snapped harshly. "It's not possible at all."

Watly felt frustration rising. He wanted to pace again but he stopped himself. "Can't you think of *anyone* who might have done it? What you're telling me is: 'Nobody and everybody did it'! This doesn't *help* me!"

"Is it my job to help you?" Sentiva yelled suddenly. "As far as the world is concerned, *you did it*. Is it my job to give the scapegoat a scapegoat?"

Watly realized this entire trip to Second Level might have been worthless. He pushed the police cap back down on his scalp. It felt itchy. "All I want is a clue," he said softly. "Just a clue."

Sentiva said nothing for a while. After some time, she snap-ignited another cigel and pink smoke filled the room once more. "I would help you, Mr. Caiper, if I could," she said. Her eyes were focused at some middle distance between them. "I would. Honestly. But if you didn't kill my poovus, I don't know who did. No one specifically *gains* by her death. Many people gain, I suppose. I don't *know* who killed her." She looked at him quizzically. Her gaze traveled down to his feet and back. "I think perhaps you didn't."

Watly smiled weakly. "Thank you for that," he said softly.

"Don't thank me, Mr. Caiper. It's not that much of a compliment," Sentiva said, pushing a strand of her long hair away from her face. "I've only been convinced because your simple-mindedness rules you out. You are a prime example of the sheltered, First Level, CV-born-and-bred mentality. You're a tried and true *plurite*."

"What's that?" Watly asked, not sure he wanted the answer. She had said it like the strongest curse.

"A plurite?" Sentiva laughed. "You mean to tell me you don't know what a *plurite* is? This just gets better and better. Your stupidity is astounding!"

Watly felt himself flush. He tried not to get angry. "What is it?" he asked again, his voice controlled.

Sentiva stared at him, smiling. "What race are you, Watly Caiper?"

"Huh?"

"What race? What kind of person? What breed? What's your genetic ancestry?" Sentiva seemed to be getting a kick out of Watly's bewilderment.

"Race? I'm . . . " Watly faltered. "I'm just a human being. . . . "

Sentiva glared. "I'm not asking for your *species*, I'm asking for your race. I'm asking about your ancestors."

Watly was totally confused. "I . . . I'm whatever everyone else is."

Sentiva laughed again, sounding even more aloof this time. "Ah—there's where you're wrong, Mr. Caiper. You're a plurite. You're a Fist Leveler. You're a mix, Caiper—you're a mongrel like everyone else down there. A blend. A combo. A . . . stew. The only purity left in the world is on Second Level." She stood and turned around slowly. "Look at me, Caiper. What's the difference between us? Do you see the difference? Did you see a difference in the people in the street up here? Have you even noticed?"

"We're *all* mixes. . . . " Watly said quietly.

"Wrong again, Mr. Caiper. You're just proving your ignorance. We on Second are *not* mixes. Not like you." She looked at him with disgust. "You're all a little bit of one thing and a little bit of another. A little bit of *everything*. You're all mutts. Look at yourself. Your skin is darker than mine, your nose is broader, your eyes more slanted. You've got every damn thing in you. Touch of this, touch of that. All squished together. It's subtle with some, but you're all the same. You bred together, Mr. Caiper. For generations races mingled and mingled and now you're all plurites. Oh, there are variations—some are darker, redder, some are curly-haired, tall, short, eyes more or less almond-shaped—all varieties. But you're all mutts. We up here are pure."

Watly stepped back a few feet. He was speechless for a moment. "What about the First Levelers who've made it to Second?" he said angrily. "Doesn't that disprove all this? All those First Levelers who've made it up here must corrupt your 'purity.' "

Sentiva sighed and crossed toward Watly. "What makes you think," she asked softly, her eyes dark, "that any First Leveler ever *made* it to Second?"

Watly shook his head. He felt slightly dizzy again. This was too much. "It happens. You hear about it all the time. People sometimes get enough money. And—hey—people win the Level Lottery, you know. I see it all the time on the—"

"On the *CV*?" she interrupted. "You see them win on the *CV*?"

There was something almost like pity in her eyes. She nearly whispered it now: "The 'Cee-Vee'?"

Watly stepped back another few feet. He felt disoriented. This was all like some Narcolo Caiper conspiracy theory. This was crazy. Everything he'd ever heard . . . "I don't believe this." He swallowed dryly. "You don't look that different from me. Nobody I saw up here looks that different from me."

"But we are. You are a plurite, and we are all just people. Pure caucasoid ancestry. Pure mongoloid. Pure Negroid. Pure everything. We are all of a kind. Not a single blend among us. Within *your* ranks there are variations, yes. But still you are all mixtures. Look at your history, Caiper. Your past is a legacy of genetic corruption. You are all the products of miscegenation."

He coughed. "What's that?"

Sentiva laughed coldly again. "Never mind, Caiper. It's an old term you wouldn't understand. In fact, you understand so little it's remarkable you've survived at all. Your whole concept of reality, Mr. Caiper, is based on the CV. Your entire existence is based on a fabrication. Your truths are based on a lie. You've bought the line just like everyone else. It's incredible. I almost feel sorry for you."

Watly felt his anger rising. He couldn't control it now. "I don't need your damn pity!" he yelled. "And I don't need your condescending attitude either. I may be naive about Second Level—or a lot of things, for that matter—but you're no better. You may have more information available to you, but you're no smarter. I doubt you'd last five minutes back where *I'm* from— back with us 'composite' people." Watly was shaking. He tried to regain control of his emotions.

"Touché, Watly Caiper. Touché." Sentiva sat back down. She still seemed totally relaxed—no fear, no worries. A tough Second Level Woman. Sublimely civilized. "You may be right. Living on Second Level does tend to give one a distorted view as well, I'm sure. Personally I've never been down there."

"You should try it," Watly said coldly. "It might open your eyes." He looked down to the plush carpet, mad at himself for letting go like that. This was not the time. This woman could be a much-needed ally if he played it right. In spite of her hot-and-cold attitude, underneath was something that almost read like warmth. Under the elitist snobbery was—what?—affection? She might help him.

Sentiva turned from Watly and looked across to the large windows. Sunlight glared off their surface, obscuring the outside world. "Well, Mr. Caiper, unless you have more questions—or you want to haver me with the rifle, or take me hostage—barring all that, I'd appreciate being left alone now."

That was it. It was over. Watly realized the uselessness of their conversation. All it had done was mess up his sense of reality. All it did was confuse him. It had gone nowhere. He had no new clues—no leads. The whole damn trip was for nothing. And now he could look forward to trying to get back down the way he got up—or some other way entirely if inspiration struck. In any case, it was a hell of a lot of wasted energy for naught. He wasn't even positive if he had another ally or not. Her conversion to his side, if it had happened at all, had not been obvious. At least it seemed she understood his innocence, whatever good *that* did.

Watly started toward the door. "Can you turn off the anxiety field for me?" he asked, sounding—to his own ears—too much like a sheepish little boy.

She rose and crossed to the near end of the foyer. There was another numbered plate on this end. She punched in the code and the light went green. Watly turned to her once more. "There's nothing you remember? There's no one you suspect? No one in particular? Friend? Politician? Sex partner? No one with the code?" he pleaded one last time.

Sentiva inhaled and Watly got a brief sense of the shape of her perfect body under the dark clothing. The memory of those delicious, firm breasts. . . .

"No, Mr. Caiper. Unless . . ." she squinted, "unless Corbell gave the combination to her private doctor—which I doubt. It's highly unlikely."

Watly perked up. "Her doctor? Who was her doctor?"

"Mitterly. Dr. Aug Mitterly."

Watly smiled. "Well, it's something. I already knew he was involved, but at least this confirms it. Maybe he's the mastermind. Maybe he *hired* the donor as a hit man—"

"You'd better hurry or the field will come up again," Sentiva said quickly.

Watly walked down the foyer toward the front door. "An address? An address on the doctor?" he asked over his shoulder.

"Four-oh-one Park Avenue south. Second Level," Sentiva said after him. "Perhaps, then, Watly . . . perhaps I was of some help after all."

He turned and saw she was smiling a genuine smile. No sarcasm, no condescension, just a genuine warm smile. She was spectacular. A fuck. Yes. And perhaps she was on his side now as well. If nothing else, *that* might come in handy.

"Goodbye, Sentiva," he said.

"Goodbye, Watly."

Watly turned and opened the door.

On the top step, right before him, was Sergeant Fenlocki, flanked on either side by two officers with guns drawn. A few steps down four backup officers squatted with rifles poised. On the street below were three spotless unmanned coppers with each shiny gun turret trained on Watly. Around those were various cruisers and more police—all with guns aimed at Watly. The amount of dark barrels facing Watly seemed almost infinite.

"Hello, Mr. Watly Caiper," Sergeant Fenlocki said with a smile. His nasolabial folds deepened. "We discovered your . . . calling card . . . in a certain air tube and thought we might find you here." His grin grew. "The jig—as they say—is up."

PART THREE

UNDERNEATH IT ALL

For the pull is a killer
and my day has just begun.

PULL SONG

CHAPTER 29

Walking through the tunnel from Brooklyn to Manhattan was not as easy as it sounded. From end to end the tunnel was well over two kilometers long. The air was stale and stagnant. At times it seemed almost impossible to breath. But Watly was in good shape back then. He'd just had that two-day walk from his childhood home and he was ready to take on Manhattan for the first time. One long, empty claustrophobic tunnel was not about to slow him down. No. He was in the big time now. Doing good. Besides, he'd only have to do it once. He was on a one-way trip, headed toward his glorious future. Yeah.

At the end of the tunnel, his papers were double-checked carefully by a Manhattan customs officers. The officer accepted his immigration reluctantly. She looked vaguely disgusted that yet another person was being added to this already crowded place. The questions were routine.

"Is this your first time in Manhattan?"

"Yes, ma'am."

"How much money do you bring with you?"

"One hundred forty-five New York dollars."

"Are you diseased in any way?"

"No ma'am."

"Got any drugs?"

"No, ma'am." (*Like the scanners wouldn't have picked it up if I did.*)

"Are you carrying any wood on you?"

"No, ma'am." (*And if I was and had declared it*, Watly thought to himself, *you'd take it from me and sell it, right?*)

"Any friends or relatives live in California?"

"No, ma'am."

On the officer went, one question after another. When she was done, Watly's visa was branded and he was on his own. All alone in First Level Manhattan. Free to tackle the glamorous life.

The first thing he noticed was the dripping. The air was thick with moisture and large drops dribbled from the daylites and the ceiling above. The whole place reeked of mold and mildew. The streets were slick and greasy-looking. Watly's hair was getting damp. It was sort of like rain but oilier and it descended unevenly in big pendulous drops. *I must get a hat first thing*, Watly thought.

"Hat, boss?" A voice came from behind. "Hat for your wet head? I've a cheap one for you. You got anything other'n New York money, boss? You got foreign money? Penn money or maybe Jersey? *Great* drip hat for Jersey dollars. . . ."

Watly walked by rapidly, ignoring the sales pitch. He was smart enough to realize he wasn't very smart. He was just out of the tunnel and an easy mark. It would be wise to go straight to Uncle Narcolo's without delay. People down by the tunnel probably waited there just to take advantage of those like him. The "new ones."

Two workers pulling a heavily loaded lowtruck crossed in front of him. They were concentrating on their labors but still singing a jolly pull song. The song was energizing—a work song, a "let's get the job done" song. Watly listened and picked up the tune as they passed. It was an easy tune, the melody strong and motivational to get your heart going. He sang it while he walked the long blocks toward his uncle's place, checking his direction sheet every now and then.

I've got aaaarms for the pull.
I've got aaaarms to do my work.
For the pull is a long one
and the way is dark.

I've got llllegs for the pull.
I've got llllegs to keep me firm.
For the pull is a killer
and my day has just begun.

More workers pulling lowtrucks passed. This area was full of them. Goods needed transporting, and this was the way. Pull songs overlapped and mingled and soon Watly had lost his entirely.

"You're fresh, aren't you, Jacko?"

Watly was startled by the voice so close by.

"Don't be frightened. Just noticing your freshness. You new today?" The short woman was walking right alongside Watly. She was in her eighties easily—maybe nineties but had no trouble keeping up. Her face was heavily shadowed by the wide brim of her hat.

"I'm just in, yes," Watly said reluctantly. He picked up his speed a little, trying to leave the old woman behind.

"You think I want to rob you, huh? You think you're gonna get taken 'cause you're just in?"

Watly kept silent, walking faster still.

"Jacko! Jacko, not all here is evil. There's such a thing as good here. . . ."

She touched his jacket but Watly tore it out of her grasp. "Whatever you want, I'm not interested," he said loudly.

"I want you to make a right, that's what I want."

"What?"

"Take my advice. One more block straight and you'll be robbed and beat up bad enough to be dead. That's all, Jacko. That's my help. I had to do it. We all ain't bad."

Watly slowed and squinted. "And this is true?"

"Every fresh one who goes up there gets ripped an' rolled bad. They see you comin'."

The old woman started walking away.

"Why the warning?" Watly asked.

She turned. "We aren't all bad, Jacko. Like I said, there's good here if you look for it. Look around you, fresh one, no one else is afraid like you. Your fear makes you stick out—makes things happen to you. Bad things happen to the afraid. You got no eggs showing. It's a deep and drippy drip-day and you have no hat. This is also funny."

"Where should I get a hat?"

The old woman tilted her head and stared at Watly with her shadowy eyes. "I'll give you mine as a lesson, Jacko. Not all is bad here."

"I can't take it."

"Take it." She undid the strap.

"How much?"

"A gift to the fresh one." A toothless smile opened up and her eyes glimmered.

"I'll give you five New York dollars for it," Watly said, and he took out his money sack from the satchel.

"No, no," the old woman said, and she thrust out a withered hand. Before Watly had even realized it, that same hand snatched up his money sack and the tiny woman zipped down the street and disappeared around a corner with amazing speed. Watly was left standing there. Open-mouthed and broke. This was the country of Manhattan. The island country.

Welcome to the new world, Jacko.

Watly walked on toward Narcolo's place, stunned. Totally stunned. He avoided the direction the old woman had warned him about, on the off chance that it might actually be the truth. This was all quite an education.

Another lowtruck rolled past. The tarp over its cargo flicked up briefly as it hit a bump. If Watly had not been so distracted, he would have looked. But he was preoccupied. He had just been robbed—expertly and cleanly. By an old pro. A *very* old pro.

If he *had* looked—glanced over to see what the truck contained—he would have been killed instantly. Right then and there.

Killed by the pullers. For the truck contained weapons. Hundreds of stolen weapons headed for a secret place. Headed for the subs. Grenades, pistols, rifles. And the two singing pullers wouldn't have chanced that the bewildered-looking man with no hat on could keep a secret. They would have blown his head off. Some secrets were that important to keep. Secrets about Revy.

CHAPTER 30

Watly looked closely at the wrinkles in Ogiv Fenlocki's face. The ridges and valleys were long and etched well into his features. Behind each nasolabial fold an echoing furrow mimicked the deepening that occurred with every mouth movement. The thick eyebrows were flecked with gray. The hair—not unlike Watly's—was receding a bit. Just enough to make the face seem bigger—enlarged upward. The eyes were sharp and observant but filled with a humor—a philosophical smile. *It is indeed a kind face,* Watly thought. *A good and thoughtful face. The sergeant is a good man. In point of fact, the sergeant is one of the "good guys." They all are. Good guys. They are not the enemy. Not a true enemy anyway.* Even that cop on the rooftop whose clothes Watly still tried to fill out—even he had been a good guy. He was a fat, ugly spitter and a cruel—even sadistic—man, but he was on the right side. He died a hero. He'd spent his days risking life and limb battling the "bad guys" for the sake of his community. And he died doing just that: fighting someone who, as far as he knew, was a bad guy. And those two police who'd died in the copper crash:

both "good guys" sacrificing their lives while trying to kill a dangerous fugitive. All these were not bad people. Those chasing Watly all this time, tracking him down, they were not the enemy. These were people who were—if it weren't for the small matter of Watly's innocence—on the side one should root for. These people slept at night with clean consciences. Good guys. First Level fucks.

"Caiper, Caiper, Caiper. You're a hard man to catch," the sergeant said with a smile of admiration. "For a while there I thought we'd never get you. But here you are"—the man looked almost disappointed—"returning to the scene of the crime. Tut, tut, tut. I'm surprised. I thought you'd make it a little tougher."

Watly took a step back but Sentiva's door had closed behind him. The police moved in closer.

"Maybe you'd better give me your weapons, Watly." The sergeant gestured to his entourage. "These guys'll kill you for breathing funny. It's over, kid. The only reason no one here has taken you out yet is that the share of reward is a little bigger if we let the state kill you. A few dollars difference. So, unless you want to die a couple days early, let's keep it all smooth and easy. You'll live a few more days and my cops'll get a week's bus fare."

Watly handed over the nerve rifle limply. Then he gave Fenlocki the chip pistol.

"The bag too. Please."

Watly handed the bag over, and it wasn't until it was out of his grip—just beyond his fingertips—that he remembered the note inside. Alysess's note. "Love, A.T.," it said at the bottom. And the name of the bar. And the times she'd be there.

He had just killed his love. With the transfer of a knapsack he had doomed her. Why hadn't he destroyed the note? Why? It would be easy for the sergeant to tell it was from her. Now Watly hadn't just been captured. Now the worst had happened. He had dragged Alysess down with him. Out of stupidity. The note. He should have ripped it up long ago. Raping damn!

Sergeant Fenlocki slung the rifle and the bag over his shoulder. "Let's all go for a walk, Watly Caiper. Let's go below where we both belong—where we both feel more comfortable." They started slowly down the steps, all of them together. All eyes and guns trained on the unarmed man in the oversized cop's outfit.

Watly was desperately trying to come up with a way to get the note back. Or to destroy it. But this sergeant was smart. Any attempt to retrieve it—or even a small indication of discomfort over it—would surely be picked up on. No, the sergeant would see the note no matter what. Sooner or later it would happen. Grabbing it back at this point would do no good. A quick movement like that and they'd all open fire. He'd be dead on the spot . . . and they'd *still* have the note. If Watly was convinced he could destroy the note in some way by sacrificing his life then and there, he might have done it. But there is no way. Ogiv Fenlocki would read it and he'd get her.

They reached the middle of the street and started down it, surrounded on all sides by weapons, cops, and machinery. The officers in front walked backward to keep their captive in view. Fenlocki walked slowly, almost casually, beside Watly. When he spoke he spoke softly, so only Watly could hear.

"You've done remarkably well, Mr. Caiper. Remarkably—"

"There's a note," Watly said abruptly. "In the bag there's a note. It incriminates another for aiding me." He searched the sergeant's eyes for a glint of sympathy. There was none. "When you read it, pay attention to what it says. It is not the note of an accomplice. It is a note of a friend trying to clear an innocent man. I am, sergeant . . . I *am* innocent."

Fenlocki smiled. "I'm not a judge, Mr. Caiper. I'm a police officer."

"You're a good guy," Watly said. "And your job is to get the bad ones."

"True."

"I'm not a bad one. I'm not. But that's okay. That's okay. I wouldn't believe me either. Let the state kill me, if that's what has to happen. But don't let the state make two mistakes. When you read the note, remember what I said and destroy it."

The sergeant smiled.

"Please," Watly said, his eyes lowered.

"I will do my job, Mr. Caiper. And if the note incriminates

someone, I'll get him and I'll take him in. The state will handle it from there."

A tubestop gleamed up ahead. It was the same one, in fact, where Watly had had his run-in with the copper. None of the damage showed. Now it was newly repaired and sparkling in the rapidly setting sun. Its long shadow stretched across the avenue and touched a nearby doorway. Things were getting orange now. Orange all around. All the coppers' turrets and bumpers glowed as if lit from within. Fenlocki's hair was rim-lit from behind, bringing out silvery highlights and the hint of his scalp underneath. Sunset. The sad, simple color of sunset. It was almost the same golden-orange that Watly always thought of when he recalled his youth. Brooklyn orange.

"Now, Watly, there's a certain awkwardness approaching here. Obviously we can't all go down the tube together. Only you, myself, and two other officers can fit. In case you were thinking this would be a good time to try to escape, I must warn you—I've taken precautions. Another vast . . . *herd* of police awaits us down below."

Watly shrugged, feeling weary and lost. He was almost glad no opportunity for resistance showed itself. The sunset calmed him. It made everything seem unreal. Unreal and unimportant.

"My running days are over, Sergeant," he said quietly.

"Good, good. Shall we?" Fenlocki motioned toward the tube's open hatch. "Hands clasped over your head please, Watly."

Watly did as he was told. They left the golden-orange behind. Watly, Ogiv Fenlocki, and two officers rode the tube to First Level. All the while the barrel of the sergeant's pistol was gently touching the base of Watly's skull. *This man takes no chances,* Watly thought. *He needn't worry.*

As promised, the street below had as many—if not more—cops as on Second Level. The uniforms were perhaps not as well kept and the coppers were a bit more tarnished and dented, but their weapons were just as lethal and all pointed steadily and confidently at Watly. He was well covered. The daylites had already gone to evening, so the lighting was soft and subtle—not exactly a sunset, but moody nonetheless. It is almost romantic in a dim, wet, reflective way.

"Now we walk downtown." Fenlocki lowered his own weapon. "A nice easy stroll, Mr. Caiper, and then I will leave you in the capable hands of our Crimcourts. Let's make this as easy as possible."

Again they started a slow walk surrounded by police, cruisers, and coppers—only this time it was First Level. Better. At least it felt like home. Dirty, smelly, ugly, wet—yes. But home. Better to die at home. One's home was always a fuckable place, no matter how ugly.

The streets cleared in their path. Tenters quickly dragged their tents aside. Watly felt a part of some surreal parade. People gathered on the sidewalks to watch the group pass. *I am famous and these are my fans,* Watly thought, looking at the faces. *Maybe Sentiva was right. Plurites, huh?* People *did* look different down here. They didn't look as extreme, they didn't have that caricature quality those above had. There was no extreme paleness, no inklike darkness, no harshly slanted eyes, no tiny noses, no flat, broad noses. . . . Everyone here was soft-looking. A mix. Everyone here looked a little like everyone else, while still being different—still having individuality. Variations on a theme. Could she have been right about this "race" business?

Up ahead, the avenue was almost empty except for a few bums and a far-off bus. Somewhere a meal was being cooked and the smell of sunbean wafted over Watly. Girl, he was hungry. When had he eaten last? Morning? *Food would be most welcome right now, thank you.*

The cops up front directed bums off to the sides. Some seemed reluctant but they all went eventually. That distant bus neared, picked up speed. Watly caught a snatch of conversation coming from off to the left.

"That him?" "That the guy?" "He the one did the big kill?"

The circle of police around Watly and the sergeant continued steadily down the avenue as if connected together by invisible ropes. *We are a comical group,* Watly thought. *All this fuss for me?*

"I'm almost sorry the chase has ended, Watly," the sergeant said with a smile.

Watly gazed off ahead, feeling numb inside. The oncoming bus was moving faster and swerving slightly from side to side.

"What the—" Fenlocki stopped walking and stared.

The bus was barreling into them—into them all—at top speed. Watly froze. He tried to see into the swerving windshield as it approached. The driver was hunched over the controls, eyes determined.

The bus plowed into the front coppers, sending them flying to the sides with an enormous *crack*. They crashed into a nearby building—one of them exploding on impact. An officer flew across the street, flung aside by the bus like some scrap of cloth. Then another. And another. Through the now cracked windshield the driver winced but continued staring straight outward. The bus was aimed directly at Watly. At Watly and the sergeant.

And as the huge machine bore down on him, Watly finally recognized the squinting face at its controls. It was a familiar face. It was Uncle Narcolo. Narcolo Caiper.

Their eyes met.

CHAPTER 31

A lot of things can go through a person's mind in a fraction of a second. When the pressure's on, a fraction of a second is an enormous length of time, mentally speaking. Life slows down under stress, and the brain goes into overdrive.

Watly's brain shifted into just that mental high gear as the enormous vehicle approached with Narcolo's face up behind its windshield. He thought at first his uncle had gone crazy. Stark raving mad. The old man wanted to kill Watly for some reason. Wanted to kill him before the state could—smash into him and crush his body with the huge machine. *Why, uncle? Why?* But there was no insanity in the determined eyes. There was complicity. The eyes said: *Here I am, my friend. Here I am, kiddo!* It was obvious Narcolo saw himself as the cavalry, coming dramatically to the rescue in the nick of time. But how? By mowing down the one he intended to rescue?

And then, a split second before the bus reached him, just as Ogiv Fenlocki dove to safety, Watly felt a familiar rhythm. A rhythm from his youth. A long-forgotten ritual. Narcolo had a plan after all. Narcolo knew Watly—the old man knew the young one's past. Well enough, at least. He'd thought the problem through. Yes, the angle was wrong. And yes, the bus was going much too fast, and yes, the street was too crowded—but *still* . . . it could be done.

Uncle Narcolo had plans. Watly was expected to go shin-scrimming. Shin-scrimming like he was a daredevil kid again.

Shin-scrimming for his life.

The movement came back to him. Watly sidestepped the bus at the last minute, twirling out on one foot, and reached up a hand, waiting for the cylinder loop to take him. It did—incredibly quickly—one tremendous jerk and Watly thought his arm was being wrenched out of the socket. The bus had him—he was flying along, pinned to the side, one arm on the loop of the blazing cylinder and the other flailing. His legs were bent, toes pointed, as his knees and calves bounced and scraped along the rough road surface. *I'm taller now,* he thought to himself absurdly. *My legs are long, so this is harder.*

There was a loud burst of gunfire from behind. The bus swerved evasively but the sound of slugs rupturing metal still reached Watly's ears. He could do nothing to hide his body. He felt naked and vulnerable. The bus was racing up the avenue, turning from side to side. Another round of *tunk tunk tunk* as the slugs hit nearby. And then a bad pain came to Watly. Not from the shin-scrimming. No—that would be scraped knees and shins. It was a slicing pain in his left arm—the loose one. A slug had got him, gone clear through his upper arm. His vision blurred. The pain echoed outward from his arm and rippled over his whole body. Burning pain. Ripping pain. More slugs clanked into the bus. Someone was in hot pursuit, probably racing along just yards behind. *Tunk tunk tunk thud.* Another pain. This one in his side. A slug in the side. *How bad was it?* Pain now and lots of it. The arm, the side, the shin-scrimming knees . . . his body was going. *How bad? How bad was it?* Maybe just a flesh wound in the side. Just surface. Could be just that. But the arm was bad.

The bus turned wildly and headed down another street. As Watly was jostled and bounced through the turn he caught a glimpse of what was following. No cops—just two unmanned coppers. Apparently it had all happened too fast for the police—they'd been left in the dust. But the coppers were right behind—right behind all the way, putting holes in the bus. And in Watly.

This side street was narrower so the coppers couldn't come up alongside. They continued firing, though, and the slugs landed real close. *You can't lose these guys, Uncle,* Watly thought. *They'll stick with us till we're both dead.*

Something wet was dripping down his arm and his side. He wanted to believe it was fuel from the cylinder. Or maybe drips from above. That's all he let himself think. He felt dizzy and a little sick.

The coppers fired again and Watly could feel Narcolo strain the old bus's frame by bringing the speed up even more. The shin-bouncing was almost too much to fight against.

I'm too old for this shit, Watly thought. *This is ridiculous. I've had just about enough. After all the crap I've been through, and now they've got me shin-scrimming like some pre-pubescent with a death wish. Shot, no less. Arm and side. I'm a real mess. And the raping machines keep on shooting. Shoot shoot shoot. Give me a break.*

Tunk tunk tunk—the metal ruptured with ragged slug holes near Watly's head. *Oh, good,* he thought. *Get me in the brain where it won't do any damage. A fine idea. And Uncle, how about slowing down to the speed of sound? What do you think?*

Uncle Narcolo *did* slow down. He did more than that. He slammed on the brakes. Slammed them so hard Watly's body flew up totally horizontal, his arm still hooked in the ring. His side smashed painfully into the top of the cylinder and then he was jerked back the other way—this time by a tremendous double crash as the coppers plowed into the back of the bus. They both exploded on impact and pieces of metal went flying in all directions. Flames lashed out angrily from the rear of the bus.

Watly hung from the one arm, totally limp. The bus wasn't moving anymore—it had thumped down to the road surface, dead. The nearby fire was warm, so very warm. Comfortable, really. Just close enough to toast the skin. Watly felt himself slipping into a pleasant daze.

His mother's voice was there. "Caring for others," she was

saying, "is caring for yourself. If you don't care for yourself, you can't fight for others. That's the trick, Watly. Be selfish. Be selfish and the love of self will spread to the love of others."

Had she really said that? Watly didn't know. *It's all catshit. All damn catshit.* Watly was tired and warm. So warm. Burning and burning like in that baby-dream. . . .

And then there were arms around him, helping him out of the loop. He was loose again. The same arms guided him away from the burning bus. *Leave me. I like it here.*

It was Narcolo. Weak little old Narcolo Caiper, practically carrying his nephew to safety. Uncle Narcolo: the strong one. And then there was a loud boom and an increased billow of warm air at their backs. *A summer breeze.* Narcolo led Watly to the side of the street and up on the sidewalk. Their shadows flickered from the fire behind them.

A nearby building—three or four limps away—had basement steps. As was customary, the basement was sealed but, crouching low, they could climb into the space under the front stairs and hide in the trash there. They did that, and Watly let himself collapse on a pile of smelly clothes there in the shadows. A few cats scampered off fearfully. *Hey, kitties!*

Narcolo knelt over him and ripped at Watly's bloody jacket to see how bad he was hit.

"It looks here . . ." the old man whispered, "looks here like they got you. Shot at you, kiddo. Got you good. Side's not too bad. Looks to me—to my eye—like it's just on the edge. Slug skimmed right along by you, really. Gave you a kiss and went away. But that arm. That's nasty, kiddo. A nasty wound there."

Watly looked up as his uncle worked over him. The wrinkled face was expressive, the eyes alive. There was nothing but concern and love showing on the old features. Watly felt a wave of warmth and gratefulness wash over him. A giggle erupted from Narcolo's throat.

"Your knees and shins aren't in great shape either, kiddo. Gettin' a little on in years for shin-scrimming, huh? These pants of yours've been ventilated from the thigh down."

"It was sort of a spur-of-the-moment thing," Watly said with a weak smile.

"That it was. That it was."

Narcolo tied up Watly's arm with a piece of his shirt and used the rest of the fabric to throw together a pressure bandage for the injured side. Watly felt really awful. The pain from both his arm and side was intense now—a continuous burn that gained a little kick with each heartbeat. Worse than that, though, worse than all the slug holes in the world, were his knees. His calves. Everything down there. The skin had been scraped off real bad. It wasn't serious—not at all like the other wounds—but it hurt even more. Too much skin surface scraped—scraped like when you were a kid and kept falling down on a rough sidewalk. Times ten. Times a hundred.

"You're gonna be fine, kiddo." Narcolo winced in sympathy as he applied the makeshift dressings. "Just fine."

"How'd you get the bus? Where'd you get the bus?" Watly asked, trying not to look at all the blood he'd just noticed—*his* blood. It had spread in a dark stain over almost all his clothes.

"The bus? The bus? I commandeered the sucker. Took it over. It had no passengers on it anyway. I flagged it down and threatened the driver. Yes I did."

"Threatened? Threatened with what?"

Narcolo grinned mischievously. "Ho, ho—threatened with . . . *this*." The old man reached into his wrinkled jacket and pulled out the scalpel—Watly's scalpel. The donor's scalpel. *The* scalpel. It was still coated with dried blood from the Alvedine murder. "Found this little gem on my apartment floor after you left me. Right before the cops came looking and put that damn *surveyor's* lens in, or whatever you call it. Guess *somebody* must've dropped this little knife while changing." He laughed quietly and passed it on to Watly as he spoke. "It came in handy, though. You'd be surprised how quickly people leave you alone if you wave a bloody scalpel at them. Bus driver only needed one wave."

"You're crazy," Watly said weakly, turning the blade in his hand. "Why? Why'd you do it?"

Narcolo turned toward the light from the street above. "Heard on the CV. They said they'd got you. Captured you. Bringing you down for execution. I couldn't have that. No, I couldn't let that be. Not at all."

"How could you take a chance like that with your *own* life? Do you know what you've done? You've pulled yourself into it. You've—"

"Shhh! Traffic coming."

There was a *whish* sound from the street above. Coppers and cruisers. Lots of them. Then footsteps and loud voices. The police had finally caught up. Watly and his uncle held perfectly still. After a moment Narcolo whispered very quietly, "Don't worry, kiddo. We're too near the bus. They'll never expect that. They'll think we ran away. No one'll bother looking right next door. We're safe here."

"They couldn't have gotten very far." Sergeant Fenlocki's voice carried well above the others. "You and the unmanneds go west. Melltez and her group are going north and east. You go south with the others. And you, trace me all the routes to sexsentral—it's the easiest place to hide. Akral, stay here with me."

There was the sound of more footsteps, cruisers moving, and then the sergeant's voice again, loud. Almost too loud.

"Akral, let me give you a little lesson in police work. . . ."

"Yes, sir."

"Some things are very easy, Akral," Ogiv continued, his voice echoing. "Like this stuff on the sidewalk. What's that look like to you? Quickly now!"

Watly gripped the scalpel tightly.

"It looks like blood, sir."

Their voices seemed to be getting much closer. Watly felt himself go cold. He couldn't tell whether it was fear or the loss of blood or both, but he was suddenly freezing. He held the scalpel as if it would magically protect him from everything.

"Excellent, Akral. Excellent. That's exactly what it is. Exactly. A trail of blood. Looks brown to the untrained eye, but actually it's red. Excellent. A perfect trail of blood. Where does it go?"

"It goes . . ." Akral's simple voice was much softer than the sergeant's, "it goes from the bus all the way—"

"All the way down those steps there, right, Akral?"

"Yes, sir."

Now Watly could see the sergeant's boots and the bottoms of his pants. Behind him, Akral's thick legs were also visible.

"Good work, my friend. Good, simple police work. Let's have a seat on these steps, shall we?" The feet disappeared to the right. "There we are. Quite comfy, actually."

The sergeant's voice was coming from directly above Watly and Narcolo now. He was right on top of them. Watly could even hear the slow breaths Fenlocki took between sentences.

"*Rape!*" Watly whispered to himself.

"Sergeant, a question. . . ." Akral sounded bewildered.

"Not just yet, Akral. Not just yet. Another quick lesson for you. Things are not always what they appear to be. The drops . . . they could be some kind of sauce—or soup, even. Yes, soup. Perhaps someone went down below us for dinner but spilled on the way."

The daylites abruptly cycled down to night setting. *It's that late?* Watly could no longer see Narcolo's features clearly there in the shadows. All was dark. Only a faint shaft of light made its way down to their cavelike hiding place.

"But sir, it's obviously—"

"Quiet, Akral. Suppose you're right. Suppose below us right now—trapped like wounded animals in a cave—are Watly Caiper and his escape mate, Narcolo Caiper. I'm sure I recognized the old man as our eggy bus driver. So there they are, hypothetically. Cornered and helpless down a little hole. Any hunter will tell you the most dangerous animal is one that is cornered and wounded. You back off a little when that happens. Just a little, but you *do* back off.

"If they are down there, Akral, they have a weapon. Deduction. Narcolo didn't get hold of that bus just by asking nice. They may be *well* armed, for all we know. Trapped, wounded animals with long teeth. Nothing worse than that. They can't win, but they can bite you damn hard before you pull them out of their cave. I send anyone down there now and we're going to suffer some losses. I don't want any more losses. The people don't either.

"Who knows what kind of weapons the hypothetical Watly

Caiper and the hypothetical Narcolo Caiper might have if they're hypothetically down there."

Ogiv Fenlocki paused briefly and then spoke again. Watly pictured him smiling conspiratorially. " 'Course, they might not have much at all—a club or a knife, maybe. We might just be able to go down there and excise them quite cleanly. Boom, boom. But there's no sport in that, Akral. Time and again Caiper has proved to be . . . *inventive*. I'd hate to saunter casually down those little stairs and plug them both after all that. Boom, boom. Two dead things. No, the chase is too important. He's done incredibly well till now. If they were down there, *if* they were, I'd clear the street for, say, half an hour—a running start—and *then* come after them. That way they'll die like they ought: like people. Not like some trapped beasts. There is more honor in that death, Akral . . . and more honor to the executioner."

"Yes, sir."

"But, of course, they're not down there at all, are they, Akral? No, of course not."

"Of course not, sir."

"Then let's take the rest of the officers and look elsewhere." His voice grew soft. "For a while, at least. For a while. Perhaps we'll try back here after a moment or two. . . ." The voices faded to nothing as they walked away. At least it *sounded* like they were walking away.

In the darkness, Watly listened to the sound of his uncle's breathing. He could hear the fear in each of the old man's breaths. Apparently, Narcolo had his doubts about the catshit performance they'd just heard and its implied promise. Watly hadn't bought it at all. If he'd ever thought he'd known what it felt like to be trapped before, he'd been wrong. *This* was trapped. Fenlocki was trying to lure them out.

They were raped.

CHAPTER 32

Tears would be good.

Tears would be nice right now. A long, childlike crying jag—full of sobs and shudders and chokes and wails and trembling shoulders—that would be welcome. There would be a release in that. The tears would bring freedom from the knot of steel cables tightening Watly's chest. Tears might relieve that throbbing ache that began behind his eyeballs and spread throughout his head. Tears just might allow him to feel like a human being again.

But Watly Caiper had no tears now. He had anger—a narrow constrained rage in his belly. Anger at life itself. And he had emptiness, helplessness. A sense of abandonment, of loss. A sense of being all alone in the world. Of unfairness. A sense that he had lost his net below and his security blanket above.

He wanted to feel betrayed, but he couldn't. He wanted to hate Narcolo, but he still loved the old man. It would be easier if he could despise his uncle. It would be easier if he thought Narcolo Caiper was a bad, evil man with no morals. He didn't. He understood. And that just made it worse.

"Ain't hardly such thing as family anymore, kiddo," Narcolo had said once. And he'd been right.

In spite of his wounds Watly squatted lower behind the dead floater. The floater was one of the explicit ones that had lost its lift entirely and was resting on the sidewalk next to an overturned lowtruck. From his hiding place behind it, Watly could see across the crowded street to the front of the Vagina Oblongata Bar. If Alysess hadn't been caught yet, Watly might get to her before the police did. Maybe, just maybe, he could prevent Alysess Tollnismer from suffering the same fate Uncle Narcolo had. Unless she was already captured. Or dead.

Watly and Narcolo had waited silently in the darkness under the steps for a good five minutes. They stared at the dim shaft of light coming down the steps. They inhaled the stench of garbage, of dirty rags, of the nearby smoldering bus, of Watly's own blood. They breathed. Gradually Watly's eyes grew accustomed to the darkness. He could now see Narcolo's haggard features and the shine of his moist eyes. He could see the dirty white of the two mismatched pieces of cheap placene sheeting that sealed off the basement door near his feet. He could see a small pile of what looked like catshit in the far corner near the sealed door, and another lump of rags and garbage. Catshit. Or maybe it was people shit, unless it was the biggest raping cat ever.

Watly listened. No sounds came from the street above except for what seemed like normal First Level noises: footsteps, a bicycle, the rumble of a lowtruck being pulled along, snatches of passing conversation, some arguments and small tussles.

The fire had probably gone out by now, though Watly could still smell the acrid smoke. No doubt people were gathering around the wrecked bus and coppers, taking whatever parts they could for black market salvage. Hands would be grabbing for any piece of burned metal or charred wiring that would come loose. Fights and pulling matches were probably breaking out every few seconds.

It seemed the police had actually left. It appeared Fenlocki really *was* giving them a head start—counting to ten, as it were.

The man did have a liking for the chase. Maybe he enjoyed playing awhile with his prey before going in for the kill. Just like a cat.

"You think it's safe?" Narcolo's voice filled the small dark space, cracking like an adolescent on the last word. "You think they really left?" This was the same man who stole a bus? This timid eggless creature?

Watly thought for a second before speaking. "No," he said simply. "No, I don't. We're dead, Uncle. They just want to lure us back out so they can kill us safely. Fenlocki's no fool." He tried to move. He tried to sit up. Not for any particular reason. He just wanted to sit up. Maybe it's better to die sitting up. Everything throbbed. His body was one enormous heartbeat, pounding viciously into his wounds. "Oh, rape. . . ."

"Easy, Watly. Move slowly, now, kiddo. Let me help you. We'll take some of these old clothes here, dude ourselves up like bums. That'll help cover the blood and stuff." Narcolo draped the smelly rags over Watly's shoulders and around his waist.

Neither of them could stand in the cramped quarters. Watly stayed on his butt, knees up, and halfheartedly resisted his uncle's attempts to dress him. "What's the point, Uncle? We're dead."

Narcolo continued to wrap Watly's stained police uniform in dirty cloth.

"Don't you get it, Narcolo?" Watly said intensely. "We're raping *dead*! There's no way out!"

Narcolo was still squatting over Watly, messing with the rags, his hands fumbling in the dim light. "There has to be, kiddo. There has to be. This can't be. You can't die."

"Don't kid yourself, Uncle. You're gonna die too." The pain was bad. Right now the idea of it ending permanently didn't seem all that horrible. No more pain. No more running. "If we don't go out soon and let them mow us down," Watly said, "Fenlocki'll finally get impatient and send down someone to kill us right here in our 'cave' . . . in *spite* of our 'long teeth.'" Watly held up the small scalpel. It was probably almost out of charge by now. "Some teeth," he mumbled.

Narcolo was breathing really heavy, trying to drape some rags over himself. Watly could see the tears flowing down the old man's cheeks. "You can't die from all this, Watly Caiper. I can't let that happen. It's okay if I die. I deserve it. I deserve it. All my fault."

Watly saw the beginnings of panic in his uncle's shadowy face, desperation. "Okay, Narcolo. It's okay. We'll . . . uh . . . find a way. Just let me think here." There was no way. Watly knew it. What way could there be? Die here or die out there—that was the choice. But Watly couldn't stand seeing his uncle like this. His surrogate child.

"I did it, Watly," Narcolo sobbed out. "It's all my raping fault."

"Shhhh. Shhhh. Nobody's fault. We'll be okay."

"No, no," Narcolo gasped, his words slurred by the tears. "They asked me—'cause I used to work there—asked me if I knew someone. This was right after you wrote to me."

"Uncle—"

"They wanted someone specific. A person with a temper. A person who wanted to be a mother. . . ."

Watly stared at his uncle's pale face. The eyes seemed to be sinking deeper and deeper. "Who wanted this? What are you saying?"

"The doctor—Aug Mitterly. But he's just an underling." Narcolo coughed and a stream of spit dribbled from the side of his mouth. "They promised you wouldn't be hurt, Watly. They said they needed a host for a special assignment—secret, and all. Something criminal—but they promised not to hurt you."

Watly could hardly believe what Narcolo was saying. The old man—his beloved uncle—had helped to set him up? Watly could see the guilt, torturous guilt, etched in his uncle's features. The guy was falling apart with it, almost hysterical with it.

"They promised me things. If I waited. I had to be silent. They promised me things. Promised. I couldn't resist."

Promised him things, yes. Watly smiled sadly to himself and spoke very quietly, pulling his uncle's face close to him with his one good arm. "They said they'd get you to Second Level if you'd help them, didn't they? That's what they promised you?"

Narcolo gasped again and sobbed loudly, nodding his head. "And that you wouldn't be hurt," he said. "They told me that.

And then things just got worse and worse. And I couldn't tell you. It was all my fault. I just couldn't. I wish I'd never—" Narcolo choked and coughed into his shirtsleeve.

Watly saw his uncle's tears glide down deep wrinkles and join with the stuff running from his nose. There was love in those eyes. And such sadness. Such regret. Pain. "Not your fault, Uncle." Watly said. "You didn't know what it was going to be like. You were a pawn, just like me. We were both just pawns here."

The old man's eyes glazed over as if a light were dimming inside him. "A bad pawn."

There was a sound at the top of the steps and Watly turned to look. Footsteps? A shadow of movement was coming down toward them.

"Who was it, Uncle?" Watly whispered. "Who was the donor? Do you know? Who's the *real* person behind all this?"

It was a cat coming down the steps, sniffing out their hiding place. It stared at them with curiosity and then scampered right across their bodies, leaping into the shit corner and disappearing.

Narcolo's feeble voice echoed. "You've got to live, Watly. Run, kiddo. Run. And get away. Just get away. Try to get out of the country. Try to get to the Outerworld, even, if that's possible—"

"Who was the donor, Uncle? Please. Who is Mitterly's boss?"

"Bad. Very bad."

Now there *were* footsteps coming down. Footsteps for sure, this time. Human ones. A large shadow descended slowly toward them.

"Narcolo—" Watly whispered vehemently.

"Use me, Watly. Let me be your shield. Use me as a shield, kiddo. Let me do that for you."

"No, Narcolo!"

"You've got to let me do that for you!" the old man cried. "It's my fault, don't you understand?"

The shadow came closer, tilting and weaving as if the person casting it was drunk. It loomed in the angled entrance to their hiding place, a dark cloud in the night sky.

"I will not use you, Uncle!"

Watly looked behind him. Where had the cat gone? How had the cat disappeared? *Kitty?*

Now there were boots and the bottom of a cape visible. The approaching legs were unsure, wobbly.

"Who's in there?" a slurred female voice called out.

If the cat disappeared . . . How can a cat disappear?

"Who is it?" the person asked, stepping closer.

She's a cop, Watly thought to himself, grasping the scalpel tightly with a sweaty left hand. *Got to be.* But the clothes were not cop clothes. The boots were beat up bad, left sole flopping down like a gaping mouth with each step nearer. The bottom of the cape was in shreds and filthy, and she smelled like rancid sweat and booze. *She's dressed like a bum and acting drunk to throw us off. They've had time to fix her up like that. I should try to kill her now.*

"Go away! We're busy!" Uncle Narcolo croaked out.

Fenlocki's a smart bean, Watly thought. *I'd do the same thing. Force us into a judgment call. Make us take an extra second to figure out if she's just an innocent bum. That way she has time to—*

"This is my raping *home* you're in!" the cloaked figure blurted out loudly, leaning down to look at the crouching creatures inside.

Makes sense, dammit, Watly thought. *A bum's home. Human shit in the corner, rags to sleep on. . . . Makes too much raping sense. Damn you, Fenlocki!*

"Leave us *alone*, okay?" Narcolo shouted, sounding seriously hysterical now.

Rags. . . . Where the rape did the cat go in those rags?

The woman reached into her cloak and fumbled inside as she leaned closer. "You wanna drink? I got some sharing booze here somewhere. . . ."

Narcolo slid quickly sideways so that he was directly in front of Watly. Watly's view of the woman was blocked now.

"*Narcolo!*" Watly shouted.

There was a loud boom and Narcolo's whole body was thrown up against Watly's knees.

"Ow," Narcolo said with no emotion.

Watly looked over his uncle's shoulder to see the woman's chip pistol. She fired again. Narcolo's body lurched back violently once more, the force knocking the wind out of Watly. The woman cop walked closer, squinting to see.

"Oh, no. I'm dead, kiddo. She killed me," Narcolo said, sounding quite calm now. His body went limp against Watly's legs. The chip pistol went off again and Watly could hear the thud and feel the lurch as another slug pounded into his uncle's body, shoving him back again.

Watly screamed. He leaned over sideways and threw the scalpel—no, *shot* the scalpel—overhead—up and out. *Hard*. It flew the few feet invisibly—not even a blur in the dark. The female cop was probably dead even before she fell forward and hit the rags, never knowing that the blade had passed right through her left eye and was lodged in her brain.

Watly leaned down over Narcolo's shoulder and looked at the old man's chest. There was a large stain all over his chest and stomach that looked black and oily in the darkness.

"You'll be okay, Uncle," Watly whispered. "Slugs just kissed you and went away. Like with me." It wasn't true. There were things wrong under Narcolo's bloody shirt Watly didn't want to know about. Serious things. Everything was all messed up and wrong down there.

"Officer?" It was Fenlocki calling out. "How'd we do, officer?"

"No, I'm dead. I'm killed," Uncle Narcolo said to Watly, sounding like he was whispering underwater. His words seemed half obstructed with liquid.

"You'll be *okay*, dammit!" Watly moved from behind Narcolo's body and turned to hold his uncle's face in his hands. Narcolo's head went totally limp and the body went slack below it. In the dim light, it seemed as though this surrogate child's wrinkles were filling in, his features relaxing, his cheeks swelling with long-lost youth. He looked young. Peaceful. Finally calm.

"Officer?" It was Fenlocki's voice again.

"Wait," Watly said to his uncle, holding the old man's face tighter, squeezing the jaw. "Please wait." But Narcolo Caiper was quiet. Finally calm and quiet.

"Are we done, officer?"

"We're coming out! Hold it a second! Don't shoot!" Watly shouted.

Where had the cat gone? Watly scrambled to the corner, throwing the endless piles of rags aside. At the lowermost edge of the sealed doorway there was a six- or seven-inch-tall gap where the placene seal did not reach the bottom. A hole. A cat hole.

"Vaidid?" Fenlocki's voice was near. "Take two others and go down there. Use the nerve guns."

"Hold it!" Watly shouted. "We're coming out with our hands up!" He reached back and pulled his uncle's lifeless body toward him. *My shield*, he thought. *My shield*. He propped Narcolo's body up next to the hole and started pushing his way through. He let the body lean into him as he shoved. The cheap placene bent inward some, giving a little, widening just enough for his torso as he went in head first. There were footsteps coming down the stairs now.

I hope there's a back exit to this building, Watly was thinking as he tried to get his rear end past the narrow opening. He tried not to notice how his dead uncle was slowly falling to cover the cat hole. *My shield*. He tried to concentrate on the pain caused by scraping his wounded body through the tight hole. *Think of the pain, Watly. Nothing else.*

Just as he pulled his feet in beyond the lip, there was a blinding flash of light behind him as his Uncle's corpse lit up from the nerve gun blast.

My shield, Watly thought again. *My raping human shield*.

CHAPTER 33

Watly was making up a story in his head. It was the story of an old man, the story of a sweet old man. A man who had lived a pretty empty life. A life of day-to-day nothingness. But a life full of dreams. Dreams of good things. Dreams of comfort. Dreams of beauty. Dreams of Second Level. And someday, someone—maybe someone impressive—came along and told him he could have those dreams . . . for a price. "Find us the man we want and we will let you have your dreams," the someone said. And so the old man was torn. "Will this man I find be hurt? What do you seek him for?" "No harm will come of him by our hands," the someone could have said. "It's merely a little bit of shady business we need him for—don't you worry."

The old man thought it over—perhaps for a few moments, perhaps overnight, perhaps a week—and finally said yes. Yes to his dream. Yes to the good life. Yes to what he'd always wanted, always watched with envy on the CV, always tried to win in the Level Lottery. Yes to a dream that, it now seemed, was a lie all along. Yes to an impossibility. And for that yes he was punished.

Punished as far as one can be punished. Punished to the point where the punishment ends.

Watly still had no tears for Narcolo. He crouched behind the floater, staring across the street to the front of the Vagina Oblongata Bar, and thought of his *own* death. *When they get me,* he thought, *and they will . . . when they get me I want it quick. I want it so I don't even know it happened. I want to be me right to the end—living and being—and then: snap. Nothing. That's what I want. No pain. No realization. No sense that the end approaches. Someone should sneak up behind me and shoot me directly in the brain.*

Watly shivered. The fine hairs in the back of his neck tingled and he sensed that someone was indeed sneaking up behind him. He turned but there was nothing. No one. He looked back to the street. It was still crowded with people. Nobody noticed him. If there *were* cops around, they were well hidden. *There must be police somewhere.* They'd read the note. They had to be near the bar, in the bar, or watching the bar. Again Watly's hair pricked up. Someone behind him. A very soft whisper—almost inaudible— reached his ears.

"W.C."

"Huh?" Watly turned slowly. A shadowy form on all fours scuttled around the overturned lowtruck behind Watly.

"W.C.?" the voice asked.

"That's me," Watly said weakly, afraid to smile until he was certain.

She was wearing a long, dark brown hooded cloak that left her face in shadows but her voice—lilting and singsong—gave her away. "Watly Caiper, you look like shit!"

She was alive. Alive and beautiful as ever. She was not dead. Not riddled with slug holes. Not breathing last breaths through blood-filled lungs. And now . . . now there were tears. Alysess was alive. They held each other tightly for a moment. There was a wonderful brief kiss that seemed like medicine to his wounds, and then Alysess's long arms were around him and his were around her. Watly felt as if he were holding on to her for dear life.

Please please please. Hugging and hugging and hugging. He thought that this was the end. This was the end of everything. This was all there would ever be. The holding would last forever—just like this. On and on. But no. The clinging ended after a time. They touched foreheads and leaned into one another. Now they were two. Now they were two separate people. Now Watly felt shame. Horrible shame for bringing Alysess into it all in the first place. He'd done everything wrong. From the beginning. *God, but I blew this whole thing*.

"You really do look like shit, Watly," she said as she pulled away.

"We have to—we have to get out of here," Watly said. "They know to look around here." He glanced back at the busy street.

"They're inside the bar, Watly. Waiting for us. I saw them go in. Eight cops. I've been casing the area longer than you have."

Watly looked at her with respect. Then he tried to stand. "There'll be others looking for us. They must have some patrolling, looking. We have to go."

"Can you walk?" She winced in sympathy at Watly's pain. The light from the dead floater made her skin glow from under the shadows of her hood.

"Not well but well enough," he said with as much confidence as he could scrape together.

Watly could see Alysess look down at the bloodstains that showed through the rags. Some of it was his, and some of it was Narcolo's. Her medically trained eyes took in his injuries, judging, assessing. "How the hell did you get here in the first place?" she asked.

"I don't know. I don't remember. Lots of things have happened." He thought for a second, steadying himself on the edge of the floater. "I think . . . I think I may have run."

"Shit on cemeld," she said quietly. She didn't speak for a few seconds, scanning her surroundings. She was looking for something—maybe a specific object, maybe just an idea. Her eyes brightened after a while. "Help me turn the lowtruck over, Watly. We'll put the floater in it and pretend to be shipping it. You can use the yoke as a crutch and just make like you're pulling. Let me do all the work."

Watly smiled. And did as he was told. He liked not having to think, not having to decide anything.

Soon they were pulling. Or, at least, Alysess was pulling. Watly let her bear the weight of the cart as well as most of his own weight. He leaned on the placene yoke and tried to look like he was helping. They went slowly down the middle of the street. Straight down the center. Hiding from no one: two pullers pulling a lowtruck. Loudly singing a pull song. Watly even tried to do some harmonizing.

> I've got aaaaaarms for the pull.
> I've got aaaaaarms to do my work.
> For the pull is a long one
> And the way is dark.
>
> I've got llllllegs for the pull.
> I've got llllllegs to keep me firm.
> For the pull is a killer
> And my day has just begun.

Everyone ignored them: a couple of workers pulling a lowtruck, bellowing a pull song. One in rags, one in a cloak. Another lowtruck passed and friendly nods were exchanged. They were invisible. A cruiser neared and politely drove around them. Hosts prowling around sexsentral, their cuffs shining obviously in the dim light, walked around Watly and Alysess without a glance. Cats scurried away. Those having various kinds of sex on the street itself tried to move aside without uncoupling. It was a warm evening—a big night in the middle of sexsentral—and a lot of people were naked or almost naked. Some danced down the street as their different body parts bounced a beat or two behind. Watly and Alysess kept onward, singing their way west—to the rougher districts.

The streets got darker in this area where daylites hadn't seen repair in years. The dripping from above was light but constant. They had to duck to avoid low floaters—many with only the starwet sign on them, the universal symbol for orgasm. Others were normally explicit floaters, their images endlessly repeating the same movements over and over. It was hypnotic. Watly's eyes drifted lazily from one to the other as he dragged his feet along. Everything ached so bad. He was tired. *Stay alert*, he admonished himself. *Stay awake. Look at the signs. Look at the people.*

In and out, up and down, push and pull. Wetness, smoothness, softness, hardness. The rocking, the thrusting, the sucking, the nibbling, the rubbing. Real, on the signs, and on the floaters. All around him. He felt sleepy. Tired and dizzy. *Sex, sex, and sex. All this sex—it's not very sexy.*

"Sexsentral is not about sex," Pepajer Caiper had said to a curious little Watly once. "It is a shrine to the phallus, to the vagina. That is not sex. There is no lust in sexsentral. No passion. Lust is a good thing, Watly. When you grow older you will see. Lust is the most wholesome part of life. You were born of lust. You were born of a sweet animal rutting passion. I hope your life is full of that. Everyone, after all, is the product of a fuck. Never forget that, Watly. We are all products of fucks. It is nice to think that the better the fuck, the better the product. It is nice to think that babies born of wild uninhibited lust are happier people. Sex is life, Watly. Fucking is the most pure and wonderful thing a human being can do. But there is fucking and there is fucking, Little-Watt. Sexsentral is a fine but sad place. People do not get what they seek there. There is no savage lechery, no wildness. No passion. It is a place inhibited by genitals."

Watly was drifting off. He forgot to pretend to be pulling. He forgot to sing the pull song. His lids wanted to close badly. His legs wanted to slip out from under him. *It's very festive here, though, Mom*, he thought. *Very festive. And the folks seem happy and having fun.*

His eyelids were closing all on their own now, and he felt himself starting to slip into sleep, or into a faint, or into shock or something. He would have gone down, he would have dropped right there on the street, if he hadn't heard—with his last vestige of consciousness—the sound of a bolt from a haver nerve gun firing.

The electric crackle of the bolt was followed by the ting of metal as it struck just behind them. Watly forced his eyes open and turned to face the floater in the lowtruck. Its edge glowed yellow as the bolt looked for a nerve before dying out. *More shooting. More chasing. I haven't the energy. I'm tired of running. Okay, okay. So kill me. Big deal.*

"Get in the truck, Watly." Alysess was shoving Watly, her eyes wide.

Watly froze. His vision blurred. "What the subs good . . ." *More fleeing, more chasing . . .*

"Just get in the raping truck, you bolehole!" she yelled, and nearly threw him in on top of the floater. Watly landed hard on his bad side and heard another bolt being fired even before he saw the flash as it zipped toward them. It hit the tail end of the truck and died out just as Alysess started pulling.

She pulled with a vengeance. She ran. With the weight of a heavy lowtruck, the dead floater, and Watly himself—she *ran*. Pulling it all behind her down the center of the street, feet splashing in the puddles. To Watly it was like being in a powered vehicle, bouncing along the road, trying to stay inside. He held on to the edge of the truck and pulled his sore legs in. Alysess was screaming now at the top of her lungs.

"Get out of the way! Get out of the waaaaaaaay!"

Behind him, Watly could see the cop who had fired trying to catch up. He was running along toward them with his haver nerve gun held out in front, braced with both hands. Watly kicked out at the floater, pushing it, shoving it with his feet. Finally it fell off the end of the truck. It bounced straight down the road a bit, but the cop easily sidestepped it. He stumbled slightly afterward but it hardly slowed him.

All Watly could think was: *Not the nerve gun. Why a nerve gun? Anything but a nerve gun, terradammit!*

The crowds on the street tried desperately to get out of the way. They were more afraid of the nerve gun than of the speeding lowtruck. Another bolt streaked across to them. People nearby screamed. Naked bodies scattered in all directions. Everyone scrambled for safety as the bolt went dully into the road surface just to the side of the truck. All around was panic, although the cop seemed pretty careful about bystanders. He wasn't firing wildly. He wanted to kill only a specific two.

"Get out of the raping way!" Alysess was screaming. She abruptly shifted direction—turning the truck strongly—and it almost flipped over as they banked. Watly had to lean sideways to keep from falling out. They righted themselves and headed down a narrow alley, Alysess never faltering, never missing a step. Rape, she was strong.

Thank, you, Alysess. Thank you for being the strong one.

"Move, move, move!" she was screaming. Couples and groups stopped what they were doing and fled to the sides of the alley. Painted faces peered out from the shadows. A scrawny little man with nothing on but a hosting cuff—his chest was covered with blood—stared at them with excitement. He looked like a bloody ghost, grinning madly in the dark as they passed. The cop fired again. This time he aimed high. The bolt just missed the side of Alysess's face and flew up the alley, illuminating what lay ahead for a split second before dying out. What lay ahead was a dead end. A wall. The alley did not exit back to the street.

Alysess kept pulling "Move move move!" Behind them, the cop slowed down, probably realizing he had the two trapped. There was no way out. He used his speaker, apparently calling for backup. Alysess finally slowed. She brought them to a full stop just short of the dead end. Watly could hear her panting. He sat up stiffly and climbed out of the truck, rolling off the edge, legs throbbing.

The dead end was piled high with garbage, mostly placene and lumps of powdery cemeld. A few coils of dented cable leaned into the dark walls. *No cat hole here,* Watly thought. There were no working daylites in the alley. What light there was crisscrossed in long beams from windows way up above, reflecting dimly in surrounding puddles. Watly saw Alysess pull back her hood. Her eyes shone in the darkness, rising and lowering with each breath. She was still at the front of the truck, holding on to the pole as if it would protect them.

The cop was casually approaching, walking as if he were out for a stroll, his right arm extended straight out with the gun. He stopped about five yards away. A long shaft of light sliced across the officer's face, showing it clearly.

It was Akral. Watly could see that now. Good old Akral.

"Mr. Caiper. Doctor." Akral nodded to each of them. He too was short of breath. "Hoo-girl. Okay, now. I'm going to have to kill you now. Regulations. At this point I've got to. Sorry, sir. Sorry, ma'am." He aimed the gun at Watly.

"Akral—remember when I pornoed you off?" Alysess jumped in, desperation in her voice, her heavy breathing getting in the way of her words.

"Yes, ma'am, and thank you again. I'm afraid it has no bearing on all this, though. The community's in danger with you folks running around like this, and capturing you-all hasn't exactly worked. So it has to be this way." Akral aimed the gun again.

Watly realized he wasn't kidding. Akral wasn't going to be talked out of this. He was a good cop and he was going to do his job. And his job right now was to kill them. No more running, no more chasing. Just a quick kill. "Does it have to be a nerve gun, Akral?" Watly asked. "Do you have a chip pistol or something—anything?" There was no ulterior motive to the question—no tricks. It was an honest question. Motivated by an honest fear of pain. *I am going to die now,* he thought, *but at least let's not have any more pain.* "A knife? Do you have a knife?"

"I'm sorry, sir. The haver's all I've got. I'll go for your head, so it should be pretty instant."

"What about Alysess, Akral? Please, Akral—can't you at least let—"

"No more talking now, sir," Akral interrupted. "Sorry. It has to be this way."

Watly could see the gun was now pointed directly at a place between his eyes. The barrel was no longer visible to him—just the hole at its end.

This is not fair, Watly thought. *This death is not fair. None of this is fair. This whole life is not fair. Second Level is not fair. Hosting is not fair. Purebreds over plurites is not fair. Not letting anyone get to Second is not fair. The C-raping-V is not fair. The lie of the Level Lottery. Antiprophies are not fair. Making motherhood so difficult is not fair. Pepajer was right. Caring is selfish/good. Caring is good/selfish. This world is not fair to me. It's not fair to my friends—to children I might have. Things are wrong, and I've done nothing. And now I'm dying. And death is the greatest unfairness of all.*

Akral made a slight gentle expression of apology with his eyebrows—just between the executioner and his victim—and then Watly knew it was about to happen. Death.

CHAPTER 34

The reason for having children, Watly thought, *the reason for wanting a child is that then it's okay to die. It is all right to die if you have a child. The child grows. You've left something. A part of you remains.* Dying now—in this way, without being a mother yet—was wrong. A mother can die. A mother has left a mark on the world. There is someone, however different from you, someone left to carry on. The pass-along.

With children one would not be immortal, but death would be so much easier to bear. For eventually, all we finally become is a memory, and the memory of mother is strongest. So, in your offspring, your memory would live well. Memory of mommy.

"Is he a nerve gun?" The naked old man had stepped into the light. He stopped between Akral and Watly—just off to the side. Some of the blood on his chest had dried and caked but there were still fresh shiny rivers of dark red running down his stomach and dripping off the end of his penis. Hundreds of small cuts and lacerations crisscrossed his torso as if he'd been sliced at over and over. He was smiling. The only thing on his small wrinkled body was the hosting cuff—big letters *F* and *O* on its side. He pointed. "That gun there—is he a nerve gun? He looks like a nerve gun."

Akral glanced briefly at the old man over his extended arm. "Please go away, sir. This is official business."

"He's a nerve gun, isn't he?" the old man said, laughing. Watly noticed the old guy—or at least the donor—was getting physically excited by all this. The bloody penis started to rise. It was reflected blurrily in the shiny metal of the hosting cuff. The cuff on the wrinkled arm looked funny. Odd. Not at all like Watly's had been. The huge *FO* . . . big yellow letters: *FO*. Fade-out. This was a fade-out host.

A final host.

"Stand back, please," Akral said quietly. He was going ahead, interruption or not. On with the kill.

Again his eyebrows formed a look of apology. He sprang the bolt and—as Watly looked down the barrel—the officer pulled the trigger.

This was it.

Time slowed to a crawl.

A burst of blinding light exploded from the gun and flashed straight toward Watly's head. Simultaneously, the bloodied old man shrieked gleefully and—like some young child playing— dove out with hand extended to grab for the flying bolt as if it were a ball in a game. He snatched at its tail and made contact just as it zipped by him.

Watly closed his eyes. *Now I die.*

But the bolt never reached his face. It had found nerves already in the fade-out host's fingers.

The old man was on the ground now, shrieking at an ear-shattering volume with what seemed both agony and laughter. His right hand was glowing—on fire from within—as the bolt climbed up his nerves toward the spine. His left hand pulled frantically at the bloody erection. "I die! I die now! Yes. Yes. Pain so bad!"

The screams got louder. Akral stood frozen in place, his jaw slack.

Watly was walking to the prone figure. He found himself speaking rapidly—loudly—without thought beforehand. "I am thinking of the host. I am thinking of the one inside. I share your pain, old man. You do not die invisible. I know you're in there. You are mourned. Your pain—your pain is not secret."

"I die! I die! Yes. Yes! The hurt so good!" the donor yelled, splashing from side to side in a muddy puddle.

"Akral!" Watly shouted to the dazed officer. "Akral—shoot him in the head!"

Akral did not move. The bolt's glow was now at the old man's elbow, eating its way slowly up the nerves of the arm.

"Dammit! Shoot him in the head, Akral!"

Akral blinked twice and lowered the gun to the old man's face.

"Yes! Yes!" the donor groaned.

Alysess had come up beside Watly. "Do it, Akral. Quickly," she said with a doctor's quiet authority. Her features were clenched in horror at the scene.

Akral inhaled sharply and let loose the bolt. The old man's penis erupted in a white fountain of orgasm just as the fire enveloped his head. A final "Yes!" and he was gone. Just an empty body, the head glowing from within. No donor, no host.

Watly closed his eyes, his empty stomach spasming. "I hope the bolehole donor had a good time."

Akral still held the gun downward, his body trembling. He made a feeble attempt at the required police victory salute but stopped halfway. He too looked nauseous. *Have you never killed someone before, Mr. Policeperson?* Watly was thinking. *Oh, it's not such a big deal. Happens all the time.*

Watly looked around him. A crowd had gathered. A familiar crowd. A crowd like the one he had run into once before—what seemed like long ago. They were of indeterminate gender, their faces painted ornately with bright designs, the eyes dark. Their costumes shreds of torn rags. Alysess and Watly stepped closer together and stood side by side, shoulders touching. Akral was still staring down at the body.

"You killed our cuffer!" one of the painted creatures said angrily to the officer. "You killed our fade-out cuffer!"

"I . . ." Akral couldn't stop looking at the withered bloody flesh still glowing below him. "I . . ."

"You've taken the kill from us. This is not nice. You've stolen the evening."

Watly noticed lights approaching from the end of the alleyway. Akral's backup was here at last. More cops.

"Fair is fair, peace man. Fair is fair." The one speaking stepped in closer. "Gonna kill these two, were you? Let us have 'em and we'll be even." A dozen or so knives were drawn and held up in a gesture of both salutation and threat.

Akral glanced around, looking dazed. "What?" he said groggily.

The talkative one began pushing Akral out of the circle. The officer tripped on a piece of placene as he was shoved backwards. "You go with your buddies at the end of the alley. All you cops there. You hold them there. Give us an hour with these two. Then we'll be even. Fair is fair. Dice 'em up nicely and then, when they're real dead, they'll be yours. You took our fade-out."

Akral tried to resist briefly but the creature pushing him was firm. "It's the way of the streets, you know. Take our kill and we take yours. Both of 'em. Fair is fair. You can have the bodies after. We want no credit." The creature took a breath. "We want an *evening.*"

Akral went. He walked toward the mouth of the alley, waving back the other officers. Fair was fair, and Akral was one of the fairest.

"You have one hour," he yelled over his shoulder. There was relief in his voice. He seemed happy enough to relinquish the kill. One bad kill had shaken him up enough. This way the cops could still share all the reward—without having to deal with the dirty stuff. Leave the dirty stuff to the ones who like it. Fair is fair.

Watly looked to Alysess and then at the circle of vivid, wild faces that surrounded them. *Out of the fire into a bigger fire,* he thought to himself. *How many times must I die? How many times must we die?* He turned to her again. There was fear in Alysess's face but there was strength as well. There was that pride—that look of poise and nobility that never left her. It gave Watly courage. It told him she hadn't given up, so he shouldn't either. Watly lifted the corner of his lips in a tiny smile. Alysess returned it. *That woman has eggs.*

The talkative one—he or she—returned to the center of the

circle. "Well, well, well. Let's all take a little piece of these ones, shall we, boys and girls? Just one little slice each to start."

There was laughter. The circle drew in closer. Watly stared at the dark brown eyes of the one who spoke and saw something familiar in them. Something he'd seen before.

The leader circled Watly and Alysess, slowly pulling a knife from beneath tattered rags. The knife too was familiar to Watly. The shape of its handle and the delicate arch of its tarnished blade. *I know that blade*, he thought. *I've seen it. The plastic handle* . . .

"You can't cut me, Tavis." Watly said quietly.

The leader faltered. "What did you say?"

"If you cut me the Ragman will be angry, Tavis."

Suddenly a hush swept the group. No one moved. The brown eyes before Watly opened wide. "How do you know the Ragman?"

Watly smiled with false confidence. "The Ragman is my friend. The Ragman does not want us hurt."

The brown eyes looked bewildered and turned to Alysess. "And this is true?"

"Oh, yes, absolutely. Very true," Alysess chimed in—perhaps a bit to quickly.

"How do you know him? How do you know Ragman?"

Watly smiled again. "Oh, we go way back, Ragman and I. He'd be most pleased if you'd take us to him, safely and unhurt, and all."

"You lie," the leader said, turning.

"Do not."

There was a pause. The painted faces whispered among themselves. The central creature seemed confused, consulting the others. Faces frowned and heads shook. The whispering continued, finally ending in laughter.

"I'll take you, and if you're lying, Ragman himself will kill you."

Watly swallowed dryly. "Hey, that's fair."

"We'll take you now."

"What about the cops?" Alysess asked.

Watly looked off to the lights and the crowd of police officers waiting down at the end of the alley.

The leader slipped the blade back beneath the tattered rags. "We're not leaving that way."

Watly glanced around. "What other way is there?" he asked. *Another raping cat hole?*

"If you know the Ragman as you say, then you can know of the way. If you don't, then the secret will die with you."

Watly tried to smile again but it wasn't easy now. "Okay by me. You have a secret passage?"

The brown eyes glanced around the circle of faces as if looking for approval from each one before speaking. Each head nodded once before the leader spoke again.

"We go down, Friend-you-say-of-Ragman. We go down to the subs. Down to the subway."

CHAPTER 35

The journey to meet the Ragman was a long one, starting at the end of that dark alley.

The painted, sexless creature led the group to the far left corner of the dead end and, with the bodies of the other painted creatures blocking the view of the distant police officers, Tavis knelt there in the oil and puddles. There below was a pile of powdery cemeld with a tangle of rusty cable sticking out of it. At least, that's what it appeared to be. Tavis touched a few of the cable strands in quick succession—"Yes, boys and girls, yes"—and the whole mound of cemeld slid silently and smoothly to the side to reveal a dark hole.

It was pitch black down there.

"You first, Friend-you-say-of-Ragman."

Watly looked down in the darkness. All his life he had heard stories about the subs—horrible stories. "Be good or the Sub-keeper will get you!" The part of Watly that was still ten years old, that still believed, didn't want to move. This was wrong. This was a bad place. "My arm—my arm is hurt and I can't use it. I can't climb," he said firmly. It was true. The arm felt dead, hanging limply from his shoulder. The only indication that it still belonged to Watly at all was the constant throbbing that radiated outward from the slug hole.

"Two legs is all you need for steps, Friend-you-say-of-Ragman."

Watly squinted, trying to see the steps. There were stairs down there? Watly stepped forward and dangled a sore right leg into the hole, feeling around for a step. There. He looked at Alysess. She gave a little shrug and touched his shoulder.

And so, slowly—slowly and gingerly—Watly Caiper and Alysess Tollnsmer descended into the darkness. Down and down a steep metal stairway, the clanking sound of the others right behind them. After a few moments the opening way above slid shut and all was dark. Dead dark. Dark enough so Watly wasn't sure if his eyes were closed or not. Dark enough so that things began to dance before him like they had in that air tube what felt like years ago. First hairy amoebas, then toothy monsters, then real things. Real things. A young cop with a scalpel deep in her eyesocket. A gentle old dreamer with his stomach blown apart. A naked fade-out host dying in agony during his donor's orgasm. A fat police officer whose skull is crushed with a pipe cutter. A business-woman who is sliced to pieces as she screams for help. Death and more death. Death all around. Death and darkness.

No more death. Let's have life instead. Think life, Watly. New life to replace deaths. Life. Birth. Babies. Little babies. The beauty of babies. The soft hair. The plump cheeks. Babies that smile so wide they make you feel all soft inside. Babies with hands and feet that can't be real—that seem some joke of nature. "You see? Little fingers just like real ones! With nails and everything!" And little minds. Starting from scratch. Little minds waiting to be filled. Clean slates. Children. Children growing every day. Children left to carry on. . . .

There were no more steps. Watly's foot touched a flat surface of some kind—a floor or a platform—and he stood fully on it, waiting for Alysess. She came down and they held each other in the blackness. The touch was comforting. More bodies joined them from above. Tavis's voice echoed.

"Sure is dark down here. Why don't somebody hit the lights?"

Somebody hit the lights.

Searing white exploded all around. Watly was blinded. Blinded by a tiny pinlight a few feet over his head. After a moment his eyes adjusted some. They were in a small square chamber, the walls rusty black and the floor wet and sticky. Watly reached for Alysess's hand and held it tight. She gave him a sympathetic look that seemed to say, *Everything will be okay, W.C.*

Aside from Tavis, only five of the others had come along. Their painted faces glowed under the one pin. They looked inhuman—almost monstrous. Splashes of color with eyes and lips and teeth. Just across from the foot of the stairs was a small doorway, sealed tight. Tavis approached it and pulled out the curved blade again. The tip of the blade fit neatly into a tiny slot beside the door. There was a mechanical hum. Tavis turned the blade twice like it was a key, and the door seals suddenly popped.

"Here we are, Friends-you-say-of-Ragman. Welcome to the subs."

And Watly was pushed through the now open door. Into the subs.

It wasn't until he became aware of Alysess beside him—gripping his elbow a little too near the wound—that he realized he'd just been standing with his mouth half open. Staring at the subs. Staring at the world *below* First Level.

Bright and clean and beautiful. Fuckable to the *Nth* degree. Watly and Alysess stood on a pure white platform. The walls around them were plated with deep red placene tiles that curved inward near the ceiling. Clear pinlights hung low from above, clustered into little constellations and nebulas. Below the plat-form, running off into the distance in either direction, were two gleaming metal tracks, brightly lit, running on and on into infinity, curving off along the center of the shiny red tunnels. There was not a speck of dirt or dust or dampness anywhere. Watly could even see himself and Alysess reflected in the red-tiled wall across the tracks.

And yes, he did indeed look like shit.

Tavis had resealed the door behind them all and was now, with the help of two of the others, pushing a large one-wheeled vehicle from the side of the platform over to the nearest rail. With a few hearty shoves the vehicle merged with the track and snapped into position. The one large yellow wheel was locked onto the rail with its flexible teeth and now the whole thing rolled easily back and forth. Tavis motioned for Watly and Alysess to climb up into the raised cab.

"All aboard this here unicarriage now. Don't you worry, the cab is self-balancing. Go on—step up."

They climbed up into the padded seats as the cab swayed and dipped slightly, adjusting for their weight. Tavis and the silent others followed. And then—with the touch of a cable and the release of one ringlet—they were off.

The unicarriage zipped along quietly through the gleaming tunnels. Alysess held Watly's hand. Her fingers were warm and strong. Watly faced straight forward on the cushion, wondering what might come next. Every few minutes they passed another broad platform where more one-wheeled vehicles sat in neat rows off to the side. On some of the platforms Watly caught glimpses of shiny doorways, one after the other along the outer edges. A few were open and he could see red hallways stretching into the distance beyond.

On the rail beside them, another unicarriage neared and passed, the painted figure in its cab nodding. Watly saw Tavis nod back. They passed more platforms, more doorways. Fleeting images of people could be seen down the long hallways. After a while they came up to the largest platform yet and Tavis slowed the unicarriage to a full stop. The ceiling seemed higher above this platform. Pinlights filled the air above their heads.

"Here we are, boys and girls. Out we go."

They all stepped down, one at a time, with Tavis leading the way. Alysess and Watly walked side by side across the pure white platform.

"Through here, Friends-you-say-of-Ragman," Tavis said. One of the side doors stood invitingly open. They all walked through it and down a tiled corridor. There seemed to be an endless maze of hallways turning this way and that, but Tavis and the others knew just where to go and they walked swiftly, sometimes pushing Watly and Alysess when they had trouble keeping to the rapid pace. The group began to pass people as they walked on—some with painted faces like the others, some looking more normal, like people out for an evening constitution. Some in jumpsuits, some in workervests, some in rags, some in stylish pocket-jackets. Just when Watly thought his legs would give out for real, they all stopped before a large, blood-red doorway and Tavis knocked on it once. There was a pause.

"Come," a voice said softly from the other side.

Tavis, Watly, Alysess, and two others walked through the door, leaving the rest of the alley creatures behind. They entered a small dining chamber. Like the hallways and tunnels, the walls were tiled in red and the floor was white. A CV set low on the news pleat was playing its crisp images near one corner. In the center of the room was a brown placene table full of various dishes, each brimming with food. A small bearded man sat hunched over the table, concentrating on eating some kind of greasy bird meat. *Real* bird meat. He was chewing loudly and smacking his lips after each swallow. Watly recognized the man's clothing: Though raglike, it sparkled richly at the creases. And the eyes too were familiar. Wise eyes. It was the Ragman.

"Ragman," Tavis said as the bearded one chewed. "Ragman, sorry for the interruption—"

"Ragman is the Subkeeper," Watly said quietly to no one in particular. He turned to Alysess as if to ask her, *Could this thing I've just said be? Could I be right?* She looked confused and her gaze moved from Watly to the seated man before them.

The Ragman stopped eating. He looked first at Watly and then to Tavis. Tavis looked stunned. *I didn't tell them,* the painted face seemed to plead.

The Ragman pushed his bird meat away. "You children," he said, his composure regained, "have come very close to giving me indigestion."

Watly smiled.

The Ragman rose and rounded the table, looking even shorter than Watly remembered him. "This is the Caiper fellow?"

"He says he's a friend of Ragman." Tavis laughed nervously and began to tell the story of their capture. Watly wasn't listening. He was looking at the food. There were some spiced weeders. There was a healthy mound of sunbeans. There was . . . who knows what, but it looked tasty. And the bird meat. A whole wing, it looked like. . . .

He felt himself salivating. Food! To break the trance he tore his gaze from the table and looked at the CV image. They were reporting about his most recent escape—from a dead-end alley. Apparently, the police were baffled. A few sexsentral denizens were being questioned but there were still no clues as to how "Caiper and his cohort" had disappeared.

And then Watly realized something bad was happening. Again. The Ragman had listened quietly to Tavis's story and had even nodded a few times. Then he had leaned back and mentioned remembering Watly's face from the earlier hosting, and also from the recent CV reports. And now . . . now he was giving Tavis permission to kill them. Quickly.

"Kill them both, my children," the Ragman said, "and collect the reward on the male. The money will be a help. It is our right."

Tavis drew the familiar blade once again. This time he/she was smiling proudly. This time he/she had permission from the boss. The Ragman stepped back and averted his eyes. "Let blood flow, my children. With regret, but for the good of the cause, let blood flow."

Tavis drew close with the blade as the other painted ones came up behind Watly and Alysess.

Well, this is swell, thought Watly.

The Ragman stared off at the CV image.

And death comes again. I am killed again. And Alysess.

"We can *help* the cause," Watly said. He was surprised how desperate his voice sounded.

The Ragman did not turn. "You don't even know what the cause *is,* my child."

"I know the cause, Subkeeper." Watly's mind was racing. "I know what all this—" he gestured around him, "is for."

"Yes?" The Ragman did not turn.

"You're . . . you're preparing. Getting ready."

"For what?" The bearded face was expressionless. Tavis touched the tip of the knife to Watly's throat. Someone held his arms from behind, squeezing his wound roughly.

"For the revolution," Alysess's voice jumped in.

The Ragman squinted. She had spoken of Revy aloud.

"Yes," Watly said quickly. "The revolution. You want to take back Second Level. The subs are your base, your headquarters. You've been making ready. We know this. We can help." The words that came out—came from nowhere—sounded right. "And we know about California," Watly added.

The Ragman's smile was condescending. "Just what do you know about California?" he asked.

Watly swallowed what felt like an eyeball-sized lump of air. It rolled right past the tarnished blade as Alysess spoke. "We know . . . we know . . . the *truth*," she said.

"And what," the Ragman asked, "is the truth about California?"

Watly searched the bearded man's knowing face for an answer. The guy was smug. Cocky. *There's no way you could know or even guess what happened in California*, his expression said. *No way*. The Ragman raised his eyebrows. *Care to hazard a pathetic one before you die?* Watly scanned the room—the red walls, the food, the CV, Tavis's cold eyes, the Subkeeper/Ragman—and tried to let his mind empty. The point of the knife was turned inward to his neck.

What is the answer? What is something I would never guess, would never suspect? What makes this man so confident I know nothing? Nothing . . . nothing . . .

"Nothing," Watly finally said.

The Ragman visibly stiffened.

"Nothing at all happened in California." Watly smiled. "Not anything. Nothing."

The Ragman's face grew pinkish as Watly continued. "It was all rumors. All designed to get the people going here—create hope; set the stage. You all made it up. Sent some people out to the western countries to start the stories. It's all catshit. Planted seeds."

"How do you know this?" The Ragman seemed honestly disturbed.

Watly smiled even broader. He was right. Rape on a crosstown copper, he was right. No California. Just rumors. It was all just the *idea* of revolution. The *idea* of success.

Watly felt the beginnings of a sting from the blade's point. "We can *help*," he said loudly, the smile gone now.

"They lie, Ragman," said Tavis. "All lies. And guesses."

"How can you help?" the Ragman asked. Watly could see his guess had struck home deeply. The Ragman's hands trembled slightly. *Amazing. Simply amazing.*

"I'm a doctor." Alysess's voice sounded strained. "I can help you."

From the corner of his eyes, Watly could see her trying to pull away from the hands that held her. She was not successful.

The Ragman smiled slightly. He was composed again. "A doctor. We can always use another doctor." He paused for a moment and Watly felt Tavis gently trace across the skin of his throat with the blade—just on the surface. "Kill only Caiper. Spare the doctor," the Ragman said, and with that he sat back down to noisily continue his meal, looking satisfied with himself. His hands were steady now.

"I can help too!" Watly said as the blade broke skin. He squirmed but the hands that held him were too strong.

"What can you do, my child, that we can't do better with your reward money?" The Ragman took a large mouthful of weeders.

"He . . . he . . ." Alysess seemed at a loss.

Watly scrambled for an idea—a lie—anything. A reason to be kept alive. "I know secrets, Subkeeper," he said.

The Ragman laughed, almost choking on his food.

Tavis joined in with the laughter and used its rhythm to prod gently at Watly's neck. "He knows no secrets, Ragman."

"I can make your revolution have no death," Watly said.

"No death?" the Ragman asked, still laughing, as he poked at his sunbeans with a bird bone.

"No violence—no hurt—no blood. I know the way."

"Who taught you this 'way'?" the Ragman asked, chewing on a sunbean he had speared.

Watly squirmed again uselessly. His wounds throbbed. "My mother. My mother taught me—Pepajer Caiper."

Ragman swallowed the sunbean. "Pepajer? A good woman, she. Much potential. We were just in the process of recruiting her when they poisoned her. A sad case."

Watly felt his legs go weak. *Poisoned?* His eyes blurred. *Poisoned?* His legs gave out entirely. The person restraining him was now supporting him. Rape. Could this be true? Poisoned? *No.* "Yes," Watly said. His voice caught. "Yes. But before she died . . . before they . . . killed her, poisoned her . . . she *taught* me things." Watly felt drunk suddenly. His mother had been murdered. It made sense. It made a perverse kind of sense. Not the appendix, after all. Poison. She was a troublemaker.

"What things?" Ragman asked. "Taught you *what* things?"

"Gentle things." Watly answered, his mother's face vividly floating before him. "Selfish things. Secrets. Tricks. Ways to revolt without killing."

The Ragman wiped his beard on a sparkling sleeve and held up his right hand. Tavis froze at this signal. The knife was withdrawn. "*You* have killed," the Ragman said solemnly.

Watly went totally limp. "Yes," he said quietly. "And I was wrong to."

The Ragman tilted his head and gazed at Watly sideways, his eyes narrow. "Tell me these secrets."

Watly felt tired all over. All he wanted was to rest. Rest and turn his brain off. His mother had been murdered. Poisoned. Incredible. "Help us and we'll help you," he said softly. "That's the deal."

The Ragman picked what meat was left on the bird bones and nibbled on them loudly. Some crumbs lodged in his beard. He spoke slowly, still looking for more meat. "Tavis, my sincerest apologies. No evening for you tonight, my child. Perhaps I'll find you a fade-out tomorrow. Meantime, show these two to a room and get them some food and a bedroll." He looked up, first to Alysess and then to Watly. "*Two* bedrolls, my children?"

Watly smiled weakly. "One."

CHAPTER 36

The room was all red. Red-tiled floor, red-tiled walls, and red-tiled ceiling. A few pinlights hung from one corner and they reflected over and over on the shiny surfaces. Watly almost slipped on the tiles but caught himself and leaned into the wall, wishing his battered cop boots had more traction. Alysess turned at the doorway to face Tavis, who had just led them through the maze of hallways to leave them off at the room.

"Do you have medipaks here?" she asked.

"Medipaks, you want." Tavis glowered. "If it's not one thing it's another—food, a room, medipaks, life . . ."

"I'll need a medipak equipped for slug wound in the left arm and right side—"

"*Left* side," Watly said, sliding down the wall to sit on the floor.

"*Left* side," she continued, "bad scrapes and lacerations to the knees and shins, shallow knife cuts across the throat . . . oh . . ." She thought a moment. "And a bruise to the left side of the jaw. Got that?"

Tavis stuck a swollen-looking tongue out and walked off. "*Got*-it-got-it-got-it."

Alysess folded the tiled door shut and squatted down next to Watly. "How do you feel?"

"I've been better but I'm okay," Watly answered. He shook his head groggily. "What was that about a bruise on my jaw? I don't have a bruise on my jaw."

That's when she did it. That's when Alysess hauled off and socked Watly solidly in the mouth, sending him sliding clear to the other side of the room.

"You do now," she said, massaging her knuckles.

Watly let himself stay there in the corner without righting himself. Not moving at all. His shoulder was touching one wall and the top of his head another, his face pressed firmly into the cold floor. Aside from the shock of the blow, the pain itself wasn't too bad, and his position was pretty comfortable. Violence, violence, violence. Well, it could have been worse. Compared to his other wounds, the jaw was nothing. "What the rape was that for?" he asked into the tile.

"That's for the fact that you ruined my life, is what that's for!" Watly heard the squeak of her shoes as Alysess stood and began to pace back and forth across the small chamber. "I don't give a damn if you've saved my life X amount of times and I've saved yours X amount of times and we've been through this and we've been through that and survived all sorts of stuff and smiled and nodded and touched hands—the fact *is*—" The squeaking stopped and Watly turned his head slightly to see her standing directly over him, looking for all the world like she was about to sock him once more. "The fact *is* that now *I'm* in this catshit up to my ears. My career is out the *window* because of this thing of yours, and now they want to kill *me* as well—all because I tried to help you out of this insane *stupid* situation you're in. You've buried me right along with you!"

Watly started to speak but realized he had no response.

"Don't you understand? *I have no life left*. I can't go back. I have nothing. And here we are in this underground city—hanging out with the legendary Subkeeper himself—now involved, on top of everything else, with some crazy revolutionary eggless crap that hinges of your 'magical' ability to overthrow an enemy without violence. How the rape do you overthrow an enemy without violence?"

"I don't know," Watly said weakly.

"You *what*?"

"I don't know."

"Oh, great!. That's even better! Now we're really home free!"

The door folded open suddenly and Tavis appeared with the bedroll, a medipak, and a tray of food.

"Can I watch?" the painted creature asked sweetly. "Can I watch you having sets?"

Alysess grabbed the tray. "No, you can't watch and no, we're not *having* sex—or 'sets' either. Now leave the stuff and get the hell out of here!" she yelled, dropping the tray before Watly. "And bring us another bedroll!"

As she threw the door closed Tavis's voice came through with: "A servant I'm not!"

Watly sat up, ignoring the food. "I never had any intention—"

"I don't give a *damn* what your intentions were—or are. The fact is, unless some kind of miracle happens and you convince the whole damn *island* that you're innocent—and me along with you—I'm stuck here." She turned and began pacing again. It struck Watly that there were no windows or openings at all in the pure red room. Just a door and, in the far corner, a small toilet/sink combination. Alysess walked from one wall to another—four long strides in each direction. "Even if you *do* prove your side of it—prove it to everyone—I might still be stuck here. Probably would. I helped a priority-one criminal and they know it. Whether you're innocent or not I'm still through. Over. If I don't get killed for helping you I can always get killed while being 'doctor to a revolution.' What fun."

"I—" Watly coughed. "There must be a way to—"

"There is no damn way to *anything*. I never should have gotten involved. I never should have helped. First this person wants to kill me, then that person, then another—and when I finally can stop to catch my breath—think for a minute—I realize my life is over. It's over." She leaned forward, picked up a piece of food, and popped it into her mouth.

Watly held out a hand toward her. "I'm sorry" was all he could think to say.

"So am I," Alysess said bitterly, with no acknowledgment of his hand. She chewed and swallowed loudly.

"Well . . . so am I. So am *I* sorry." Watly dropped the hand and grabbed something brown from the tray. It tasted salty but good. "I didn't *plan* it this way, you know. I didn't say: 'Let's see who I can rope into this thing and mess up real bad.' *I'm* not the one chasing us. *I'm* not the raping cops. I'm not whoever the hell it is who started all this crap! I never wanted this to happen." He swallowed and took another piece. "You think I want this? You think I like that now you're in this as much as I? You think that makes me happy?"

Alysess reached for more of the food and snatched up a handful angrily. "You want to know what I think? You really want to know?" She shoved more of it into her mouth and chewed until she could speak again. "I think you're *glad*. I think you're glad you have *company* in all this melted garbage. I think you're happy you're not alone!" Her eyes lowered to the bloodstains on Watly's clothing.

Watly sat up taller and leaned into the wall. "*That's* catshit." He ate one of the small green things.

"It is not catshit," Alysess said as she pulled over the medipak. "Misery loves—"

"Oh, come on! I didn't intentionally—"

"You can't tell me—" she started, carefully removing Watly's clothes to get at his injuries. By now Narcolo's makeshift bandages underneath were caked with dried blood. "You can't tell me it isn't nicer going through all this *with* someone than without."

Watly reached around Alysess to get at more of the small green things. They were quite tasty. "That's not the point. I never intended to get you caught up in all this. You're acting like I—"

"That is *exactly* the point," she snapped, and began treating his wounds with the salves and dressings from the medipak. Watly flinched at the sting. "It shouldn't hurt," she said as she spread more ointment over the slug wound in his arm.

"Well, it *does*."

"Well . . . *good*!"

Tavis threw the door open and dumped another bedroll beside them. "A servant I'm *not*." The androgynous voice was bitter and the painted features tightened up in anger.

"Fine!" Watly yelled. "Then leave and we won't treat you like one!"

Tavis turned back in the doorway, colorful face suddenly calm and angelic. "Are you going to have sets now?"

"No, we are *not* going to have 'sets' now," Watly said, trying to get up. Alysess held him down and continued treating his wounds. "But if and when we ever *do* decide to have 'sets,' we will stick our heads into the hallway and quietly call out your name—'Tavis? *Taaaay*-vis?' we'll say—so that you can, if you're nearby, hear our gentle call and come to watch us. How's *that*?"

"That'll be fine," Tavis said, and left the room.

"Jeez!"

"Stop wiggling, Watly—or I'll never finish this raping stuff."

"Well . . . finish the raping stuff." He scooped up more of the green things and gulped them down.

Alysess worked on his arm, his side, both legs, his neck, and—finally—his jaw. Doing the jaw seemed to bother her more than the rest. She avoided looking at Watly's eyes as she worked on it and kept her head lowered toward the medipak.

When she was done treating him they both finished what was left on the tray, eating silently, neither looking at the other. After the food, they unrolled their respective bedrolls—one on each side of the room. Watly was by the door and Alysess by the far wall.

Watly used the toilet and then lay down on his bedroll and stared at the ceiling, looking at the geometric patterns the tiles made. His own dim reflection was sectioned into hundreds of tiny Watly-bits.

"This whole thing's a mess," he said quietly.

There was a long pause.

"Yes, it is," came the reply.

Watly turned to see Alysess was also lying down, staring at the ceiling. The pinlights near her bedroll put her face in silhouette. Her features were hidden, but the outline of her nose, forehead, lips, and jaw was clear and sharp.

"I'm sorry," Watly said. "Really."

Something sparkled on her cheek, just below the eye.

"I know you are," she said. "I am too."

Soon the bedrolls were brought together, the pinlights lowered, and after a while—after a long while—Tavis was called in.

As Watly and Alysess made love, Watly would occasionally look over to the corner, where Tavis—watching quietly, intently—fiddled beneath his/her raglike clothing with whatever genitalia she/he had down there. It still was impossible to tell. Whatever the creature was, it enjoyed the show politely through to the end.

"Are you a he or a she?" Watly finally asked softly after the pleasure faded to memory.

"Yes," was Tavis's answer.

CHAPTER 37

The wounds healed slowly. As the next few days passed Watly was sore and uncomfortable. Alysess told him that, though it would improve, he had permanently lost some mobility and strength in his left arm. Permanently. This was not pleasant news.

His side still ached but was getting less sensitive daily and his knees and shins were all scabbed up and itching like crazy. Other than that—other than *all* that—he was fine. His body was pulling together, knitting, closing . . . regrouping. Gaining what strength there was to be had.

And there they were. He and Alysess. In the subs.

In this elaborate and strange complex of tunnels and platforms and hallways and rooms. It was virtually a whole city under Manhattan. A *Third* Level. With CV, water, food, electricity, ventilation, everything—obviously tapping into the First Level supplies somehow. Stealing a little here, a little there, plugging into this or that source. Raiding the cables, the pipes. A new world—beautiful in its own way. Clean and dry and closed off. How long had it been here? And how long had its denizens been building, expanding, planning, plotting, preparing . . . making ready the "revolution"? Creating, no doubt, the painted-face style for the express purpose of anonymity. Manufacturing a First Level underworld for its own uses. Maybe even molding sexsentral itself into one large hiding place. And all—all led by the Subkeeper. *The* Subkeeper, late of fairy tales and bedtime cautions. A real, live person.

"Corbell Alvedine was one of us, you know," the Subkeeper said. "She was on our side. She would have helped our cause." He stared at Watly. "If I thought you had actually killed her, I'd have turned you in myself. Or killed you. For revenge. She was a good woman. Was going into politics. Trying to change the world from the top down. *That* is why she was killed. She was killed by the same kinds of people who killed your mother. People who saw someone active, strong—someone who could make a difference, cause problems. This was a political murder, my children, make no mistake. An antirevolutionary murder. Mark my words."

Watly and Alysess marked his words. They marked his words often. He was a powerful man. The more time they spent with him and saw what he controlled—what he had, in face, *created*—the more respect they had for him.

The disappearances Watly had heard vague stories about suddenly made more sense. People who had vanished—people who had organized or spoken out against the way things were—hadn't necessarily been taken off and killed. No. Many were down here now. The Ragman had recruited them. His people had quietly captured the outspoken ones to join in the revolution. And if friends and relatives of those who had vanished chose to believe they'd been murdered for their views, so be it. All the better for the revolution.

On their second day in the subs, the Subkeeper had taken Watly and Alysess on a tour—not of the entire sub level, that would have taken too long—just of their immediate area. They'd visited conference rooms, libraries, research laboratories, metal ___s, dining halls, sleeping quarters, wardrobe and disguise ro__ astonishingly well stocked armories. Weapons of ever___ there, lined up one after the other on racks along___ walls. Nerve rifles, chip pistols, grenades, sonic disrupters, scrambler rifles, I-cutters, and I-bazookas, gas guns and blast canisters . . . everything. All clean and shiny, well kept. Perhaps each one stolen or bought one or two at a time, little by little, so as not to draw attention. Maybe some were smuggled in from Jersey or the Noreast Commonwealth. Maybe even from the Outerworld. Or perhaps most of them were manufactured right here in the workrooms. Either way, it must have taken years to gradually build up these tools of revolution.

"I suppose we won't need all these when you teach us the secrets," the Subkeeper said as they walked down row after row of weapons. His tone was cynical, almost teasing.

"I never said that," Watly answered defensively. "Don't put words in my mouth. You'll see when the time comes." Watly couldn't help but cringe at all the death equipment around him. How many lives could this room take?

"The time will come sooner than you think, my children," the Ragman said. "We're almost ready. We have the firepower now. And we're well staffed. We have a trained army." The Subkeeper spoke proudly. Watly thought of the painted creatures of sexsentral, hungry for blood. This was an army? Was this an organized revolutionary force? He turned to Alysess. She rolled her eyes.

"And the *people*, my children," the Ragman continued. "Most importantly, the people. They're ripe now. They are ready to help us. The seeds are planted. 'California' worked. 'California' was a success. All people needed to hear was that others had done it, that others had succeeded. The rumors did it. The plan succeeded beyond even *my* expectations. Hope inspires, my children. Hope works wonders." The Ragman stopped at the door and all three of them stood and looked back at the room full of deadly contraptions. "We will begin soon, my children. It is our time. Life is unfair, yes. But it need not be as unfair as it is now. We can change it."

Watly agreed. Life is unfair. But was this the way to fairness? Killing? Guns?

"You may fail," Alysess said quietly.

Watly shot her a sharp glance. *Don't anger him on this subject, lysess!*

"With you two to help us," Ragman said with a smile that seemed full of sarcasm, "how could we do anything but succeed?"

And on they walked, down one hallway after another, through one room after another. Watly found himself amazed at his own thoughts as they traveled. He was actually caring. He was actually worrying about the revolution. Worrying *for* the revolution. He was thinking they were right to rebel, right to seek change, yes. They were justified. *We all are justified,* he thought. *But this is not the way. No. This is not the answer.* He was—subs help him—thinking like his mother.

The three of them continued walking in silence down the blood-red corridors. Those in their path stepped aside as they passed, some almost bowing to the Ragman. It was obvious he was the leader. He held real power down here.

Watly wondered, as the days in the subs passed, what would happen if he couldn't come up with "secrets" to tell them when the time came. What would happen if he couldn't think of ways to revolution without death? He'd have to come up with something. His mother would have had the answers. She would have known. Watly hadn't a clue. What *were* the secrets of fighting without fighting? Selfish/good warfare?

But that was all another problem. He'd probably never live long enough to worry about it. He was still wanted for murder. He still had to solve the crime. Revolution or not, Watly was a high-priority, death-imperative criminal. And Alysess had conspired to help him. He had to resolve those problems above all others. Fast. Time was growing short. It was evident that the subs would not be hospitable forever. A week or two maybe, at the most. Watly and Alysess were not expected to relax and hide out there. This was not a reprieve. This was not a new home, secure and protected. They were temporary guests. As soon as Watly was well enough, they were expected to get on with their business, clear their names, and then earn their keep as revolutionaries. Watly thought he already detected impatience in the Ragman. If they did nothing, soon he'd toss them to Tavis for his/her slicing-and-dicing pleasure.

During their sub stay, Alysess was put to work right away. There were plenty of wounded Revies—hurt in combat training or up in sexsentral—who needed doctoring. Watly himself, injuries and all, was made to earn his food down there in the subs soon after. When Watly was well enough for light labor, the Subkeeper gave him duties as a sub tile cleaner. It seemed fitting to clean. Just like Pepajer had. Just like he had in Brooklyn. Just like Narcolo had around the apartment. It was nice to be mindlessly busy in the family tradition.

Watly would dress in the protective jumpsuit and helmet, help move out the furniture from the room to be cleaned, and blast off the dirt from the tiles with a high-powered sprayer. Each day he did a different room or hallway. Each day he had a new co-worker.

He always tried to find out more about his surroundings as he worked, snooping around and prodding his co-workers for information. "Where did the subs get funds? How did they tap into the CV, keyboard cables, water, and other supplies? Who were they stealing from? Where did the money come from to build such a place?"

What answers he did get were usually vague and evasive. Watly got the feeling the subs had not been created and maintained using the most moral means. "The end justifies . . ." and all. Watly's questions usually did little more than make his partners distinctly hinky.

One particular co-worker, a tall, broad-shouldered man, said nothing at all to Watly's queries. He worked silently next to him almost to the end. Watly gave up on him and hummed the poovus song. The hours passed slowly that day.

When they were almost done cleaning, Watly was finishing up the corners and edges with his needle nozzle. His partner was putting away some of the equipment.

"You the Caiper guy?" the man asked, finally breaking the silence.

Watly nodded.

"I knew your mother. Years ago. We worked together in Brooklyn before I came here to join the Revy preparations."

Watly stopped spraying and looked at the guy, trying to see his face behind the protective helmet. The glass was too dark.

"There are others down here who knew her, too," the man said softly. "Others who were 'disappeared' to the Manhattan subs.

We should talk sometime. We could talk about your mother. She was a fuck. It was a long time ago, but I remember her. She had eggs."

"I'd like that," Watly said.

The man nodded and picked up his cleaning machine. He pulled off his helmet as he left the room. "See you around."

Watly caught a glimpse of the man's face as the guy walked out. Darkish skin, a high forehead, and a distinctly crooked nose. A very familiar-looking face. Similar to—

"Hey, mister!" Watly called after him. "Hey! Were you my mother's poovus?"

But the man had already vanished down the maze of red corridors.

And Watly had to go back to the matters at hand. Healing, cleaning, learning, and trying to figure out the puzzle he was enmeshed in. He'd find the man later. Later.

Now he was pressed for time. He had to solve all this murder catshit. At least he had equipment at his disposal now: keyboards, files . . . and the Ragman's expertise. The Ragman's expertise was most important of all. Watly did not waste it. Each day he fed more bits and pieces of the story to the Ragman and each day he was astounded at the tiny revelations that came back. It seemed as though his world—everything he had taken for granted—was being pulled apart and blown away one astonishing section at a time.

"The removal of a cuff," the Ragman was saying as he chewed, "is child's play, Watly. Technological child's play. I could do it tomorrow if I needed to. All you need is money, a lab, and a few intelligent scientists." He drank some soljuice and wiped at his beard with the back of his hand. They were all in a large dining hall, seated at one of the long placene tables. The Ragman sat on one side with Tavis to his right, and Watly and Alysess sat on the bench opposite. The crowd had thinned and only a few people were left, scattered about the room in small groups, talking quietly and finishing their lunches.

"What about the cards—the forged travelpasses?" Watly asked.

"I could make you a new set in half an hour, my child. It's

quite a primitive method of tricking a travel tube, actually. It proves nothing. This surprises you?"

Watly got the feeling the Ragman enjoyed playing teacher. He even seemed, perhaps, to be growing fond of them as time passed. Impatient, but fond. Here were two new pupils he could mold. Two new faces to amaze. Tavis, on the other hand, sat silently through these talks, eating everything in sight—often from other people's plates—dark eyes darting about anxiously.

"Why does it drip so much, my children? Do you know?" the Ragman asked as if following a lesson plan. The question was posed as though he expected—*wanted*—the wrong answer.

"The rain," Watly replied softly.

"What rain?"

"When it rains on Second it leaks down here," Alysess said.

The Ragman smiled. He had gotten his incorrect answer. "And when it *doesn't* rain? It can't rain forever. When it is sunny above? Why does it still drip on First level?"

Watly thought a moment. He looked at the Subkeeper's expression. The answer was not apparent in the bearded one's eyes. "I always thought it just got so wet from the rain that the drips continued."

"Did you?" The Subkeeper looked pleased. "And you?" Alysess nodded. "You are both typical, my children," he said. "You take things for granted. You don't question, look for answers. 'Why is it always so wet down here? Why is everything soaked?' You don't ask. You don't think to ask." He stopped to drink more juice before continuing. "Let me ask *you*. What's the deal with wood? You tell me: Why is there no wood? Why is it so expensive? Huh? Is it rare? Is it impossible to grow a tree nowadays?"

Watly shrugged. "It must be very difficult to—"

"Nonsense!" the Ragman snapped, but he didn't look honestly upset. He was enjoying himself—teaching, surprising his students, challenging them. "There are trees all over the world, my children. Trees growing all over the UCA. We've yet to kill *them* off. Surely you've seen the images of forests on the CV. Well, I've seen them in *person*. The only reason there are few trees in Brooklyn is there's no raping *room*. No raping dirt for them to grow in." There was a pause in the conversation as the Subkeeper looked down to see Tavis stealing bits of weeders from his plate. He ignored the behavior as if he were used to it.

"Perhaps . . ." Alysess spoke hesitantly, "perhaps the cost of importing them—importing wood—into Manhattan, Brooklyn, and so forth, brings the cost up to—"

"Then why was it all pulled out, my children?" The Ragman grinned again, looking as if he knew the secrets of the universe. "Why was it all removed from First Level years and years ago? Every scrap of it. Beams inside of walls were torn out and replaced by steel, cemeld, or whatever. Floorboards were ripped up and placene layed down. Why? Is wood a jewel? Is it unreplenished? No. Trees *still* grow in this world: forest reserves out west, the protected zones in Jesusland—We couldn't raping *breathe* if there weren't trees out there. The keepers of the rain forests still get paid off by all the UCA countries . . . and importing wood is no big deal—I know this for fact. Then why? Why is a simple wooden pencil something so rare and precious down here?"

"I don't know," Watly answered.

"Because you don't *think*, my children. Nobody thinks anymore. The answer is right in front of you. Why is First Level soaking wet—*saturated*—and why is there no wood down here? Why? Put it together in your head. Put the two things together. It's not an accident. It's intentional. It's all Second Level's doing. It's on purpose. They *make* it leak down here—there's water running through the First Level ceiling. All through it. It was *designed* that way. *Designed*. And the wood business—it's all the same thing."

"Why?" Alysess asked—but the answer seemed to be coming into her eyes already. She looked disturbed.

"Fear," the Ragman answered.

Watly was still confused. "Of what? Fear of what?"

"Fire. The fear of fire."

Watly took a long drink of his own soljuice—it tasted freshly made—and put his glass on the table very slowly. "All that—the drips, the scarcity of wood—all that is to prevent fire?" Watly had trouble digesting the thought.

"That's it. Fire. Bad fire on First and up goes Second. Couldn't have that, now, could they? So they keep us wet—they soak us—and take away what's flammable. Then it's safe."

Alysess seemed to accept the idea more readily. "It all makes sense," she said, looking upward at the lights floating over them.

"How do you know this?" Watly snapped at the Ragman, suddenly angry.

"I know this."

"Is it because you have the sight? Is *that* it?" Watly remembered their first meeting—he and the Ragman—and the words spoken back then: *I have the sight—it is how I have survived this long*. And Watly remembered the warm palm on his forehead and the warning of death, death all around.

"I have the sight," the Ragman said now, finishing his juice with one gulp. "But that is not how I know this." Tavis suddenly stilled, eyes down, listening intently. "The sight does not give me a picture. The sight does not tell me a story. It is a flash—a pinpoint—a tiny fragment I am left to interpret as I will."

Watly leaned closer over the table toward the Subkeeper. "Can you use it now? Can you use it to help me? Help *us*?"

The Ragman looked annoyed at Watly. Tavis began eating again, noisily cleaning everyone's plate but his own. "First of all," Ragman said, "you don't understand it. It is not a fortune. It is not a warning. It is not a *possible* future. It is a flash of what *will* happen. No matter what. It will not tell me something that can be used as a guide to avoid a personal badness. It will only tell me the inevitable. It tells me nothing that can be avoided. In fact, the avoiding may be what causes the thing to pass."

"But the knowledge is useful, isn't it?" Watly demanded.

"All knowledge is useful, my children." The Subkeeper smiled wryly. "Such as how to revolt without death."

"Why don't you use the sight to find out?" Watly snapped. Alysess gave him a warning look. *Don't push your luck, Watly,* her expression said.

"I cannot pick and choose what I see, my child, any more than you can reach into unfamiliar darkness and decide what you will touch." The Ragman pushed Tavis's hand away from his plate. The feeding frenzy seemed to have finally become annoying to him.

"Help me. Help *us,* " Watly said.

"That is *exactly,* in case you've forgotten, our deal. I help you and you help us. I will not, however, put my people in jeopardy. Any of them. But I will use my resources to assist you two in clearing your names—" he laughed an abrupt little laugh, "if that's possible. And you, in turn, will help *us.* The doctor will doctor . . . and the Watly will . . . what? Tell us some secrets, yes?"

Watly looked down at his now empty plate. "Yes," he said. He suddenly felt foolish—caught in a lie. *How can you revolution without death?*

The Subkeeper rubbed his beard gently from side to side. "My only problem is . . . once your name is cleared—if it *is* cleared—once your name is cleared, why should you still help us? Why should you keep your half of the bargain?"

Alysess pushed her plate of food toward Tavis, giving up on eating from it herself. "You have our word," she said.

"The word of two hunted people is not a word, my children. No, I have to make it impossible for you to change your minds." The Ragman thought for a moment. "Ah. I have it. The police want to kill you both now, isn't that the case?"

"Yes," Watly answered.

"Well, if you successfully, with my help, change *their* minds about that—but then don't help us—*we* will hunt you down and kill you. And we, my children, will be a lot more successful. You can't hide from the subs. We *are* Manhattan now."

Watly's throat felt dry. He was out of juice. "We will help you. Just help us. Use the sight."

"There are other ways to help you, my children. The sight won't—"

"I want you to use it." Watly felt anger welling up.

"Watly." Alysess touched his arm. "Maybe this isn't the best idea—"

"The *sight,*" Watly demanded.

The Ragman smiled. "Very well."

Again Tavis froze in position, listening. The Ragman reached his arm across the table and touched Watly's forehead with his palm. The palm was warm and dry, relaxing. Above his beardline, the Subkeeper's cheeks went pale. Very pale. Tavis seemed to have stopped breathing. All conversation in the dining hall ceased. Finally the Subkeeper removed his hand from Watly's head and placed it down slowly on the table before him. He looked shaken. Troubled.

"What?" Watly asked.

"Watly—" Alysess tried to break the mood.

"*What?*" He yelled it this time.

The Ragman closed his eyes. "I see a fat man—big—enormous . . . and dead. And, and . . . I see, I see a baby."

Watly shivered. "What baby?"

"That's all." The Ragman's eyes were still closed.

"That's *not* all. You see more!" Watly was half standing now, leaning over the table.

"Watly—" Alysess tried to pull him back to his seat.

"That's all you need to know, my child." The Ragman's voice was soft and motherly. There was sadness in his expression. His cheeks were still pale—almost pure white. Almost Second Level white.

"What else do you see?" Watly grabbed at the Ragman's collar.

Tavis, eyes still on the lunch plates, began to laugh.

"Watly, let's drop it—okay?" Alysess pulled on Watly's arm.

Watly just held the collar tightly, shaking it from side to side. Some of the golden flecks came off on his hands. Tavis's laughter rang wildly.

"All right, Mr. Caiper." The Ragman's eyes sprang open angrily. "I'll tell you what I see. And remember, this is not a guess. It is a *fact*. It is the *truth*. It is inevitable." Red showed through beneath the pale cheeks now. Deeper and deeper red. "I see . . . violence and pain. I see agony." The wise eyes closed for a moment. "I see your *death*, my child. I see the death of Watly Caiper."

The hall echoed with Tavis's laughter, loud and gleeful.

CHAPTER 38

To be back on First Level was nerve-wracking enough for Watly, let alone to be half naked to top it off. But the Ragman's dressing advice had been firm: "When people dress they always dress for one of two reasons, my child," he had said. "Either to *reveal* or to *conceal*. All clothing accomplishes one or the other. A wanted man will be expected to hide—to conceal himself. That's why you must do the opposite. No one expects a criminal to dress to reveal."

And so the Ragman had sent Tavis off to bring special clothing: heavy boots, a blue short-sleeved pocket-jacket, and, finally, thin black pants with a large clear plastic bubble at the crotch. Everything from Watly's belly button to his upper thigh was completely exposed.

"Nice cock, Caiper," Alysess had quipped after he'd dressed.

"Thank you for your delicacy," Watly had answered.

And he'd waddled off, the stiff bubble chafing unpleasantly. Should he find himself in an emergency that required still *more* misdirection, the pants were equipped with a ringlet which, when pulled, engaged a vacuum that should produce a reasonably healthy erection for all to see. If nothing else, the outfit was certainly absurd enough to distract those around from wondering if the wearer was a priority-one criminal.

"When one wants to hide from searchers," the Subkeeper had said earlier, "one must become an annoying thing the searchers shove aside so they can see better. This is an important secret of survival."

And so in this outlandish outfit—along with a touch of bright makeup across the forehead and cheeks and a small hairpiece— Watly walked down the middle of First Level's Park Avenue in the broad daylite of afternoon. He was headed for Oldyer's apartment.

Mr. Oldyer: the "big man" of Alvedine, the one who—if one went by Narcolo's confession—must have known at least *something* when Watly first walked in. He must have been instructed to pass Watly—to accept him as a host. He was a part of the conspiracy. A part that was one of the first steps toward roping Watly Caiper in. And now Oldyer was either dead or going to die soon, according to the Ragman's sight. *I see a fat man . . . big—enormous . . . and dead*.

As he walked, Watly wondered, not for the first time, if *he* was going to kill Oldyer. Did the Ragman's sight mean Watly would commit yet another murder? In self-defense perhaps? It was this kind of questioning that had made Watly insist on the Ragman providing him with a weapon. "If I am to kill Oldyer then I am to kill Oldyer," Watly had said.

"We don't know that," the Ragman said. "You-who-would-revolution-without-death need a weapon?"

Watly thought fast. "Remember, I never said revolution without *weapons* or the *threat* of weapons. I just said revolution without *death*. Anyway, this is not the revolution I'm doing here. This is my personal investigation, you see."

This feeble argument was enough to do it, and now, as he walked, Watly could feel the butt of a small chip pistol in his pocket-jacket, brushing reassuringly against his ribs. In the other pockets were various items the Ragman thought might come in handy. Money, credit pieces, food, and a variety of Subkeeper's "override" documents and cards. Watly felt well prepared. And he was back in his element. Back with his people. Back on the First Level. Smells, drips, and all.

The traffic was thin and Watly pressed steadily on. Most people he passed looked at his crotch and not his face. The outfit was working well. Occasionally Watly would glance down at himself and catch sight of his limp penis dancing back and forth with each stride he took, wagging like a tail. *I wouldn't look at my face either,* he thought.

Walking rapidly, it didn't take him long to get from the secret sub exit near Thirty-forth Street to Oldyer's apartment building on Twenty-third off First Avenue. Watly walked in through the front hallway without hesitating and bounced up a flight of stairs. The stairways and landings were well lit and freshly swept. Oldyer's place was on the second floor, a back apartment. Watly neared the door, but stopped when he heard voices from inside. Two males talking. They sounded angry.

He crouched, touching the pistol through the jacket, making sure it was still there, and crept toward the door. As he got closer the words gained definition.

". . . no more than we decided. That's it. You've already been paid all you're going to get. We're not interested in blackmail. You don't frighten us, Oldyer."

Watly recognized the flat, emotionless tone. It was Mitterly. Dr. Aug Mitterly.

"You fail to understand, Mr. Mitterly"—it was Oldyer's voice now—"I'm not asking. I'm *telling*."

There was the sound of movement behind the door now—rustling and scraping. A struggle, perhaps. Watly turned and swiftly climbed another flight. He knelt near the landing and leaned under the plasticore railing to look down at the door. After a moment the door opened and a tall blond-haired figure appeared, dusting off his jacket. It was Mitterly. He left the door open behind him and calmly walked down the stairs. Watly heard the footsteps fade as Mitterly exited the building. Then no sound. Nothing. Watly waited a beat or two and climbed down to look in Oldyer's apartment.

It was dark in there and it took a second for all the shapes to become specific. The place was a mess—just what you'd expect from a man like Oldyer. It was small and filthy, cluttered with crap. Piles of clothes and garbage loomed in every corner. Ancient porn chromells hung cockeyed from the walls. There was no movement. Then Watly realized the big man was sitting near the door—right in front of him. Still. Perfectly still. Oldyer was dead, yes. Throat slit ear to ear, eyes wide and bulging. Blood had run down the front of his enormous white-shirted belly and onto the floor. His whole body was just a huge pile of lifeless blubber now. Another pile just like all the others in the cramped room. Nose hair and all. Blubber. Dead bloody blubber. Watly turned away.

The familiar sense of rising nausea overcame him. *Does death ever get easy to look at? Even the death of a crass, disgusting, awful man? Thump thump thump. The man with the placene pencil. I still owe you five New York dollars for that thing,* he thought absurdly. A wave of dizziness washed over Watly. *Why was there so much death?*

Mitterly. Suddenly Watly felt he had to catch up to Mitterly. Where had the doctor gone? Watly closed the door on the body of Oldyer and rushed down the stairs. Back on the street, Watly ran west to the avenue and, once at the corner, spun around, looking for the blond. Off in the distance toward the north, Mitterly's light hair could be seen bobbing up and down as he slowly, confidently walked up the street. Watly jogged toward him. A few people smiled as he passed, enjoying the bouncy view within the pants' bubble. After a bit more than a block Watly had caught up and needed to slow down in order to remain safely behind the doctor.

For a man who had just slit another's throat, Aug Mitterly was certainly relaxed. He strolled along easily, arms swinging loosely by his sides. Watly stayed a few yards back and to the left. Where was the doctor headed? Home? To his "boss"? Or off to murder someone else? Maybe this was "cleaning day." Maybe he was wiping out all the loose ends. Everyone connected with this mess.

No more death, cold man. Please. No more.

Watly looked at the pale skin above the back of Mitterly's white shirt collar as they walked. Purebred skin. *How old are you, Aug? How old? Older than me? Old enough to have known my mother? Old enough? Maybe it was you, Aug Mitterly. Maybe it was you who poisoned her. Maybe it was one of your first jobs.*

She was murdered, Aug. The Subkeeper told me so. She who wouldn't hurt anyone. She who said there was fighting and then there was fighting. She who cared. Selfish/good. Subkeeper and his people had their eyes on her, yes they did. Going to recruit her for the revolution; Subkeeper said that. But somebody found out—or maybe she was just too much trouble. She knew how to fight. How to make noise. How to point and say, "Hey, this isn't right." So they killed her. Dead. No. Not her appendix at all. Poison in the gut.

Suddenly Watly wanted to kill Mitterly right there. He wanted to pull out the chip pistol and shoot him in the back. He wanted to punish him for everything—whether he'd been responsible or not. He wanted to kill him for Narcolo: an old man who had died because he was unhappy. And for Pepajer: a woman who had tried to make things better. And for Alysess and her ruined career. And for the fat man, Oldyer, who had died of greed. And for all the people Watly had hurt or killed while trying to live—just raping live. And for Corber—Corbell—Alvedine: the first victim in the whole mess. And for the unfairness of it—the unfairness of it all. Of the hosting. Of hosting *period*. Of Second Level. Of plurites vs. pure-ites, of the drips. Of wood. Of the CV and its lies. Of life, dammit. But mostly . . . mostly Watly wanted to kill Aug Mitterly for himself, for Watly Caiper. Selfishly. Selfish/bad.

The Ragman had seen death. Death for Watly. And Watly did not want to die. He did not. And Mitterly had no right to live if someone like Watly could die. None at all. Well, Watly wasn't *going* to die. *He* was going to break the rules. He was going to live in *spite* of the sight. He would prevail. He and Alysess.

Dr. Mitterly stepped into the tube back on Third between Sixty-third and Sixty-fourth and sealed the hatch behind him. Watly waited a moment outside it, giving Mitterly time to get to Second. Then he stepped in the tube himself, wondering how much of his makeup had run from the tears. Tears that were gone now. They had hardly been noticed.

"Face forward, please."

Watly fished for the override cards. No sweet talking, no bluffing. Just a quiet ride. Easy as pie. And soon he was on Second Level himself. Walking a block or so behind Mitterly.

Walking in the rain.

The doctor had pulled out a birdhat and Watly could guess that the unusually wide wingspan probably kept him perfectly dry. As for Watly, he was soaked. But the rain helped. It helped his spirits. Real rain felt cleansing. The water was pure and cool and regular. Real rain like before Manhattan. Brooklyn rain. The drops were small and close together—not like the drips below. Watly tilted his head back as he walked and let the water bounce off his face and run down his jacket. The Second Level streets were empty. Aside from the occasional private vehicle streaking by, it was just him and Mitterly. Mitterly kept steadily on, not looking back once. The wings of the birdhat flapped slightly with each step. Watly kept his distance.

After a few turns, Watly realized where they were going. They were almost there, in fact. Mitterly was going to the Alvedine residence. To the home of Sentiva Alvedine.

You're going to murder her, just like Oldyer, aren't you, doctor? Watly thought to himself. *If you kill her just because I spoke with her once—just to tie up that loose end—then I've lost my one Second Level connection. I've lost the one person in power who might become an ally. I won't let you. I won't let you kill again.*

Watly suddenly felt very calm. He was calmed by the decision he had made. The decision to stop Mitterly before Mitterly could kill Sentiva. In whatever way necessary.

The doctor was climbing the front steps to the Alvedine house now. Watly stayed behind one of the flying buttresses of the building next door and watched. The blond man slowly reached to the top of the steps, glanced around behind him, and then knocked sharply on the wooden front door.

On instinct—*now, Watly, now*—Watly started out from behind the buttress and climbed quietly up the steps behind Aug Mitterly. His boots squeaked slightly in the rain, but not loud enough for the sound to travel. Just as Watly was almost behind the doctor, Sentiva opened the door.

"Yes?" She was wearing something long and white that made her look angelic and vulnerable. She stared blankly at the doctor for a moment until her eyes shifted to the side as she saw Watly coming up behind. "Wha—?"

This must have tipped Mitterly off. He whirled around, a large scalpel ready, those empty doll's eyes of his gleaming. The birdhat flapped wildly, splashing water everywhere.

"Watly Caiper! Mr. Night Host!" He smiled and lunged out with the knife. He knew how to handle a weapon. He didn't wield it like a doctor, he wielded it like a trained assassin—like a man who was used to killing, who took pleasure in it. The blade was thrust out expertly toward Watly's heart. It would have gone in cleanly and killed instantly. It never got there. Watly Caiper let his reflexes take over. Savage reflexes. Angry reflexes. He pointed the pistol and squeezed the trigger. There was the shock of recoil; Watly's elbow was jammed hard into his own belly. *Pow*. Caiper shot Mitterly in the neck. One slug. *Pow*. That's it. Blackish blood from a new hole.

The hat vibrated for a moment and then flapped gently as Aug Mitterly gave Watly a look of serious startlement and concern, and then collapsed backward into the doorway. The blond-topped head twitched and spasmed. There were some choking sounds before he was dead. As dead as Oldyer had been. And Narcolo. And Pepajer. . . .

Watly dragged the body into the foyer and closed the door on the rain as Sentiva watched.

"I'm sorry. I'm sorry, Sentiva. I think he came here to kill you. I'm sorry." There was a lot of blood soaking into the hall rug. Watly was dripping wet. His nose was running badly. Sentiva stared at it all briefly and then straightened, composed herself, and snap-ignited a cigel. She was beautiful as ever. Pale and strong in her flowing robe. From two small frosted windows beside the door, shadows of rain streaks rolled down the front of her face. It almost gave the illusion of tears.

"Leave him, Watly. You've got to get out of here."

In the dim light Watly looked down at the chip pistol he held, then to the body. "Here we go again," he said aloud to himself. Death. Murder. Selfish/bad.

"You've got to leave if you don't want them to blame *this* on you too, Caiper." She exhaled a cloud of pink smoke.

"What're you going to do with him?" he asked.

"I'll take care of it," she said with her Second Level superior voice. "But someone may have heard the shot. You'd better leave."

"How will you explain it?"

"*I'll* take the blame, Watly. I'll claim self-defense. They won't do anything to me. I'm Second Level."

Watly tried to see what was going on inside her head—what she was about. She was expressionless. Blank. "You're helping me," he said.

"I'm helping you because you deserve it." She turned toward the door. There was a pause. "I *do* believe in you."

Watly stepped over the body and nearer to Sentiva. He touched her shoulder. She tensed. "Leave while you have time, Watly."

It struck him that she was a tragically lonely figure. Lonely and sad. He felt bad that she had lost her poovus. Bad that she looked so alone. Rich, privileged, pampered, but very sad. There was something hidden about her. Hidden and distant. "Thank you for your help," he said, not knowing any better way to put it.

"*Go*, Watly."

Watly turned to the door.

"Thank you," he said again as he opened it.

"I will . . ." she started, the words hard for her, "I will help you again if I can. If it wasn't for my people, you wouldn't be in this mess. Hosting wouldn't exist."

"You're not to blame," Watly said as he stepped back into the rain. It seemed like he'd been saying that a lot lately. The rain was coming down harder now. It was difficult to see any distance. The street was a soaked blur.

"I am part of the problem," her voice came from behind. Watly started down the steps. He had to be careful not to slip. "Mea culpa, Watly Caiper. Mea maxima culpa."

Watly stopped in his tracks. His cheeks felt cold. The rain beat down on his head, running off his shoulders and splashing to the ground. Some of it got under his jacket and trickled its way lower, following the line of his spinal column. His drenched hairpiece itched. He turned back toward Sentiva to see her standing in the doorway. She exhaled more pink smoke. Her head was held high.

"What did you say?" he asked softly. The downpour almost obscured Sentiva from him. She seemed transparent, cloudlike. The stairs and front of the building appeared to telescope in, squashing together and becoming flat as a chromell. Everything was on an angle now—the stairs, the door, the windows—all tilted. And the woman herself. Watly felt vertigo almost overpower him. He was sick. His legs wanted to give out suddenly. Cold. So cold. He held himself up by willpower alone. *"What did you just say?"* Watly's hands were trembling.

Sentiva smiled slightly. "Oh, dear, Watly Caiper. Have I blown my cover?" she asked. Her voice was oily now. Very oily. Wintery. It had a cruel and powerful undercurrent. If anything, to Watly's ear her voice was evil. Pure, unadulterated evil.

And deadly.

CHAPTER 39

A plan was trying to form in Watly's head. It wasn't succeeding. But he kept at it. Thinking. His mind was buzzing as he slipped his rain-soaked override cards into the tube's slots. *Holy rape on sunbean toast!* Again, with no arguments the tube lowered easily down to First. Watly stepped out, barely aware of his surroundings now. He was concentrating. Somewhere in the equation, somewhere in all the complex *stuff* he was deeply embroiled in, there was a solution. Or, if not a solution, at least an idea. A chance. Some convoluted long shot would do, if necessary. And now the stakes were higher. Oh, rape, were they higher. Veils had been lifted—lifted from unexpected directions—and nothing was as he'd thought. It was a new game now. A whole new game.

Watly headed—hardly realizing it—to the camouflaged sub entrance near Forty-fifth and Vanderbilt. As he walked, an unmanned copper buzzed by and slowed for a look at him, but Watly ignored it and it soon left. He was alone in the alley now. There was no one in sight nearby. Watly leaned over a pile of garbage. It was strikingly familiar, crowned with seemingly random strands of cable. He manipulated the pieces in the sequence Ragman had told him, and the hidden door slid aside. A quick glance around and down he went. Back to his new home. The subs.

He set up the unicarriage himself, rolling it along beside the platform and locking its teeth into place on the rail. The cab bobbed forward and back as he climbed in, but quickly stabilized. Watly pulled the driving ringlet from its casing and the unicarriage slid forward. The tunnel walls streaked by. He wiped what was left of the makeup streaks from his cheeks and pulled off the soggy hairpiece. He would have no problem finding the way now. The Ragman's directions had been clear. Watly could sit back and ride the unicarriage to the main platform. There he would meet the Ragman and Alysess.

Watly hoped the Ragman would not be too upset about the chip pistol. He had not expected to return without it. Perhaps the Subkeeper would just be happy to see Watly alive. That would be nice. Alysess certainly would. And they would both be anxious to find out what had happened. Well, Watly certainly had quite a tale for them. They would be, he was sure, as shocked as he had been. As he still was. *Rape on toast.*

It had taken a long while for the truth to sink in. About Sentiva. Back there in the rain, standing in front of the majestic Alvedine residence, Watly had felt nothing but bewilderment at first. *Sentiva the donor?* But he had not been so bewildered that he forgot about his gun. He raised the pistol up and slowly climbed the steps toward the strikingly beautiful woman. She was leaning in the doorway and puffing out casual pink smoke rings that vanished when they drifted out into the rain. One of her legs was crossed in front of the other. She exuded confidence.

"I *have,* haven't I?" she continued calmly. Those dimples came back into view. "I've given myself away. What a shame. Not to worry, Watly Caiper. Everything works out all right in the end."

She seemed totally oblivious to Watly's weapon. Her strong jaw was relaxed. She stepped aside and let Watly back into the foyer. He kept the gun trained on her chest.

"*You,*" he said. It wasn't a question.

"That it is, my little friend." She smiled. "Me."

"You are the donor."

Sentiva took a last long drag off the cigel and then dropped it on Mitterly's drenched back, stamping it out with her heel. The dead body vibrated from the impact. "Love your pants, Watly."

"How could you be the donor?" he asked.

"Gee, I don't know." Sentiva stepped over the body and crossed lazily into the sitting room. Watly followed, gun raised.

"You were here! In the bedroom! You weren't even in the Hosting Building."

Sentiva turned and her face went as cold as her voice. The eyes looked almost inhuman—like something mechanical. "Ever hear of cables, Caiper? Ever hear of wiring? What are you—stupid? I'm loaded, you fungus. I can pay for anything I want."

"You ran cables from the Hosting Building to here?"

"Over months, yes. Little by little. Bit by bit. Different worker for each stage. Right to my bedroom. Right to the forked donor plates in my pillows." She looked disgusted. "*Now* do you get it?"

"You can be a donor from your bed," Watly said softly.

"Brilliant deduction."

"But why?" Watly tried to read something other than blank coldness in her eyes. "Why did you do it?"

"To kill Corbell. Is that so complicated?" She looked at Watly as if he were a bug. "Is it beyond your comprehension?" she asked. "*To kill Corber Alvedine*. To stop her dangerous thinking and to gain control of the most powerful company in the country of Manhattan—possibly the world. Is that motive enough for you? That's what I wanted from the beginning. And I've got it."

Watly stepped closer to her. She leaned back on the great wooden banister carved into the shape of a wing. She seemed taller than he remembered her before. He almost felt as if she loomed over him.

"The perfect murder, Mr. Watly Caiper, is one in which the one who committed it *would* be the prime suspect—the *only* suspect—but isn't . . . because she simply could *not have committed it*. Not to mention that someone else—" she nodded toward Watly, "seems to have been caught in the act. Airtight alibis and plenty of insurance, that is what I have created.

Oh—and I always make sure anyone who knowingly helps me has more to lose than I do. A simple rule."

"Why didn't you just hire someone else to kill her?"

Sentiva ran a hand through her hair and shook her head slightly. It was almost the same gesture Watly's mother used to make so often. "Oh, but you miss the point, Watly Caiper. You miss it entirely. I've been looking forward to killing Corbell for years. This was my reward. This was the prize I got for putting up with her—for pretending affection, gaining her confidence, listening to her spout garbage—crazy garbage. I even took her *name*, for rape's sake. The company name. The name of an insane person. Corbell was a sick woman. A sick and very dangerous woman. She was going to run for Chancellor next election. She might've won, too. This was simply not acceptable. Not at all. She had a secret agenda. A revolutionary agenda. She would've turned the world upside down. Everything we hold dear up here would have been destroyed. She had ideas, Caiper, diseased ideas, about *fairness, justice, freedom*—all the old catchwords. If she had her way, diseased plurites like you would be swarming up here. Or maybe she'd've just ripped up the Second Level—torn out the roads so this island country was one level again—she spoke of that often. 'I've got to help those poor folks down below,' she'd whine. And I listened, Caiper. Day after day. Nodding politely and smiling. 'Yes, my darling poovus, you will change the world.'

"No, Watly Caiper. To actually kill her myself was always my aim. I would not have had it otherwise."

Watly shivered. He remembered what it was like having this heartless *thing* inside of him. This murderer. This *badness*. She was not just unfeeling, she was evil. She scared him. Where did she come from? How did someone *get* like this? Watly had to strain to remember that *he* was the one with the weapon. *He* was the one with the upper hand. But she didn't seem to think so. Her well-toned body was relaxed, her expression one of utter confidence. She wet her lips carefully. Watly couldn't help but remember her body naked. Funny how his mind worked.

"The hosting . . . you had sex with yourself?" Watly asked. He remembered the strange, almost loving fuck; the donor's comments—*I suspect her dreams were no less vivid;* the lifeless body, head half buried in pillows. . . .

She smiled and fingered her white lacy collar. "I'm the best. Why not? Anyway, you might say I took onanism to its logical extreme, yes?" She let out a burst of cold laughter.

Watly felt weak and confused. "Well, it's all over now. Everything," he said slowly. Sentiva reached out to Watly's waist and he flinched—almost shooting her right then and there, blowing her chest open—but she wasn't attacking. She popped the ringlet on his belt with a flick and then backed off to the banister again.

"Mea culpa, Watly. Mea maxima culpa. Just thought I'd pull your little rip cord to see what developed."

Watly suddenly felt incredibly embarrassed and small. He wanted to hide. The pant bubble's vacuum engaged and he could feel an involuntary erection developing. "Hey."

"Nice to see you still like me, after all we've been through," Sentiva said. Again she laughed.

"All right, now." Watly tried to stand tall and dignified. He held the chip pistol lower, trying to block her view of his rising organ. He reinserted the ringlet, knowing it would take a while for the vacuum to shut off and his penis to empty and relax. *Great. How To Make Watly Look Foolish: Lesson Number Eighty-seven.* Shit, she knew how to keep you off balance. "All right, now. I've got you. Cut the crap. I know the story now. All of it. I'm going to turn you in."

"No, you're not."

She said it so matter-of-factly Watly took a step backward and had to stop and regain confidence before speaking again. "I have a gun," he said. "And I have you. You lose. It's over."

"No, Watly, it's not over." She still stared at the bubble, her eyes amused, condescending.

Watly took a deep breath. "I have *won,* don't you see? I know the truth!"

Sentiva closed her eyes and looked impatient. "Where's your proof, Watly? You've got no proof, catbreath. And if you try to make trouble for me now that you know it was indeed *moi* . . . if you try to make noise and raise some questions, I have you covered. You'll keep quiet." She smiled wide now and the deep dimples flashed. Her eyes were still closed, as if Watly weren't worth looking at. "Poor Watly Caiper—do you think I'm a fool like you? Do you think I could come up with a plan as elegant as this—a murder this perfect—without safeguards?"

"*I* have the gun!" Watly felt sweat on his forehead running into his eyebrows. "I could just kill you. I just *might* kill you."

Sentiva's eyes popped back open, flashing. "Who *cares* what you 'might' do, you little fool. You *can't*. I have insurance." She started walking toward him. "I'm not stupid. I cover all my bases. *All*."

Watly took a step back. She kept advancing, pressing forward. "I am the one calling the shots now, Sentiva," Watly said. In truth, he didn't feel so sure.

"Every step of the way I have covered myself. I think ahead. I was prepared for any eventuality." Sentiva slowly reached a hand out toward the gun. Watly backed away farther, keeping it trained squarely on her chest. "You can't kill me, Watly." She was crowding him.

"I can and I will!" Watly yelled. He was almost back at the foyer now.

"Do you remember that liquid we drank, Watly Caiper? Back at the hosting? Do you remember? I teased you about it being poison?"

"It *wasn't* poison! You said!" Watly was having trouble keeping the pistol steady.

"No, it wasn't poison." Sentiva's hand brushed the end of the pistol. "Not at all." She gripped the barrel firmly, but she didn't try to turn it away from herself. "Mea culpa, Watly Caiper. Mea maxima culpa."

Watly felt himself back into a wall. He couldn't move farther. He was trapped. "What was it?" he asked. He still held the pistol grip, finger leaning on the trigger. Sentiva held the barrel of the chip pistol with both hands but she still didn't try to turn it away. She guided it toward herself as she stepped even closer to Watly. She clasped the point of the gun—aiming it down at her own belly—and smiled. The dimples deepened but the smile was empty. It did not extend into her eyes.

"Antiprophies," she said quietly.

Watly trembled. "What?" His hand relaxed on the gun grip.

"Antiprophies, Watly." She held the gun right to her abdomen, pressing it into her flesh, daring him to fire. "I bear your child, Watly Caiper."

CHAPTER 40

Watly was flying again. Soaring way above the buildings, diving in and out of clouds, feeling the white moistness of them on his face as he passed through. His arms angled gracefully, guiding his body in a slow turn. Down below . . . the brownstones of Brooklyn. All was golden down there, as it should be. The sun was sinking. Brooklyn-orange spread out below him. But up here in the clouds there was still sun. Yellow sun. No shadows in the sky. Watly squinted when he turned westward. The glare burned his eyes. And down on the steps: two small figures. Pepajer Caiper and Alysess Tollnismer, looking up. They were motioning to him. Trying to indicate something. Near them: two more figures, smaller still. Watly entered a cloud suddenly, feeling the wet cold brush by, and came out lower than before. The other figures were the Ragman and Tavis. They were motioning just like Alysess and Pepajer. Motioning to him. What did they want? What were they saying? Now there was another figure. A tall man, unspecific and fuzzy around the edges. The man he had cleaned with. The man with the high forehead and the crooked nose. He was motioning as well. It looked to Watly like they were all shaking their heads. "No," they were saying. "No." No what? What were they warning him from? They waved at him with broad arm motions. "No."

Another cloud, not visible before, loomed up and enveloped Watly. He was flying blind now. All around him was white. Brooklyn was gone. The sun was gone. Alysess and Pepajer and Tavis and the Ragman were gone. The air was thick with white. Even his own arms before him blurred out into whiteness at the fingers. He kept going forward—the cloud had to end eventually, the air would break through soon.

And then there was a shadow. Something dark nearby. Watly swerved. His body rolled briefly, but control came back fast. And the something dark was still there. Just to his side. A shadow beneath the white, pacing him, tracking him, keeping up.

Watly tried to dodge left. The darkness followed him. He dove lower. The shadow was there with him. Watly called out. "Who are you?" The shadow neared his side. "*What* are you?" he asked.

The darkness deepened as it neared. And now there was a human hand, reaching out toward Watly's side as he flew. A female hand.

"Are you a friend?" Watly asked.

The hand held Watly's. And he felt comfort, warmth. This shadow was a good shadow. This darkness was the darkness of a friend. The hand released and slipped back to whiteness for a short time. When it returned something gleamed in its palm— something golden like the sunset below. And the hand reached to Watly again, this time holding the object to Watly's arm. The female hand drove the object in just below Watly's shoulder, slicing deeply into the flesh, and Watly could feel it pass through muscle to reach bone—snagging on it a moment—and then carving through the bone with a pop, and out to the other side. There was no pain. Watly's arm dangled, held there only by the thick fabric of his shirt, and then it fell off into the whiteness below. Watly had no control now and he tumbled wildly. He kept trying to balance using the arm that wasn't there. A face appeared near him in the cloud—the shadow's face revealed—smiling. It was the face of a child. A baby. Pure and angelic: totally guileless.

"It's all right," Watly tried to say as he fell. "It's not your fault." But he couldn't say anything. The fall left him breathless. His mouth formed the words but no sound reached his own ears. The next real sound he heard—and heard very clearly—was a cracking, a loud crunching sound from his skull and spine smashing into the sidewalk right below the old brownstone he had once lived in. The sound of his own death.

Watly woke with a start, sweaty and nauseous. He had slept through the unicarriage's trip to the main sub platform. Had in fact passed it entirely. Now he would have to turn and backtrack. He fiddled with the machine's controls, unsettled but with no memory of his dream at all. What *did* flash through his mind—and it was a comforting thought at a time when comforting thoughts were hard to find—was that the Subkeeper's sight had seen the *event* of his death, yes . . . but not the *when*. Nothing about *when*. It could be a long time away. Watly might still have a lifetime ahead of him.

After all, he thought, *we all have to die sometime*.

CHAPTER 41

"She's holding her unborn child hostage, don't you see?" Watly was getting exasperated. They were all still in one of the sub's libraries, where Watly had found them on returning.

His throat was dry from all the talking. The nervous energy he'd been running on was fading now. He realized with surprise that he had actually just recapped the whole story. Over the last few hours he'd gone back almost to the very beginning. Although he'd already relayed bits and pieces of it to Alysess and the Ragman, this was the first he'd tied it all together for them. Rehashing it was exhausting—almost like reliving it. From Narcolo to the first hosting and everything in between. From Oldyer to meeting Alysess to the air shaft to Sentiva Alvedine to right now. Right up to the concept of conception. Conception: the start of a life, the start of a brand-new person. There, buried in the sexual reproduction equipment of a beautiful and deeply evil human being, one small thing clung to life—and gradually formed, gradually differentiated. Right now it was there. A future person. Not quite even a human yet. Just a living thing, clutching to existence. Fighting to be.

The Ragman was looking a Watly with a puzzled expression. "This hostage thing is part of her plan?" he asked, and sat down next to a stack of leafs.

"This was her insurance," Watly answered. "She probably planned the timing of the murder around her most fertile moments. Hell—" Watly ran his hand up the middle of his brow, "It's why she picked *me* to start with. She knows I won't touch her now. I know the whole story but I still won't touch her. I make a move against her and she can threaten to abort. She *will* abort. This woman—you don't know her—she could stab herself in the womb just for spite."

"And if you don't make a move?" Alysess asked quietly. She was seated at a keyboard station, looking somewhat daunted by Watly's long and complicated tale. She also looked distinctly pissed at him.

"If I don't finger her, and if, within the term of her pregnancy, I turn myself in and confess . . . she promises to raise the child and let the child live."

The Ragman laughed.

"And you believe her?" Alysess said, looking pained for him, but at the same time gritting her teeth with anger.

Watly inhaled deeply "No. I don't believe her." He took a few steps toward a display of antique chromells. "But I don't know what to do. She has me. I was chosen for this reason. She *knows* me. She took the chip pistol right out of my hand. Just like that. But first she kept it pointed at her belly, saying, 'Shoot me, Watly. Shoot me in the baby.' That's how she kept saying it: 'Go ahead—shoot me in the baby. In the baby. Do it.' But I couldn't. I couldn't and she took the gun from me. She just took it and told me to leave. I don't know why she didn't kill me right there. I guess she didn't want the attention. Rather leave me for the cops. 'Mea culpa, Watly Caiper,' she kept saying. And I couldn't touch her. I couldn't. She planned it that way. She hand picked me for this insurance. Because of who I am." Watly felt his shoulders slump involuntarily. "There is a fetus growing inside her that is . . . part mine. Part my genes. And I—I want to be a mother. All my life I want to be a mother." Watly looked down at his feet.

The Ragman shook his head. "Being a mother means raising a

child. Being a mother means *mothering*. Being a mother has nothing to do with genes. Being a mother has nothing to do with conception or whose chromosomes create the—"

"I *know* that. Don't you think I know that? But Sentiva knew it would still be enough to snare me. She knew it would trap me. It's my weak point." Watly felt his eyes watering. "There is a future *baby* in her. From *my* sperm. A baby growing. Part *mine*. Don't you understand? A baby!"

"It's not a baby, Watly. It's a terradamn *embryo*," Alysess said. "You're going to let something that's not even a raping *fetus* yet control you?" She looked off disgustedly. "And if you turn yourself in and you are then happily executed and she raises this child . . . who will be the mother then? Sentiva! Is that okay with you? Is that what you want? And what kind of person would that child grow into with that *thing* to raise it?"

"I know, I know! But what am I supposed to do? I don't want her to abort." Watly turned to face Alysess squarely. She turned toward him and he looked into her eyes. "At this point, it's as close as I'll ever come to getting my dream, and she knows it. It's all I've got now. I know it's silly, but it's all I've got. My only shot at pass-along. *She knows it*. She always knew it. She's dangling it over my head."

Alysess looked furious but she spoke very softly. "So you're giving up. One raping embryo inside the rotting womb of a monster stops Watly cold."

The Ragman leaned back and folded his arms. Tavis was nowhere around. Watly thought the short-bearded man looked naked without his painted sidekick. Perhaps the Ragman had located a fade-out earlier and Tavis was out "having an evening." Anyway, it was a welcome absence. The androgynous one made Watly nervous. "I'm not giving up," Watly said. "Did I *say* I was giving up?"

"You sure as rape *sound* like you're giving up," Alysess answered heatedly.

"Aren't I allowed to express the fact that I'm upset without you saying I'm giving up? I'm just upset, okay? I'm not having a very good day. I haven't had a very good *month*, for that matter. I'm *upset*. I am *not* giving up. What I'm doing—" Watly sniffed, "is trying to come up with a plan. I would *welcome* any suggestions instead of criticism." He turned toward the door. From the corner of his eye he could see Alysess glaring at him.

The Ragman raised his hand, his face serious. Behind his intense eyes, Watly could almost see the thoughts brewing. "Sentiva cannot be blackmailed by you—made to . . . do something . . . to do something in our favor—now that you know she was the donor?"

"How can I blackmail her? She has *me*. First of all, the world thinks I did it—I have no proof—and second of all, she's holding the embryo as a hostage."

"Calm down a second, my child. Let's think, now." The Ragman looked down the banks of keyboards and long rows of CVs that filled the room. Watly followed his gaze. In the distant corners a few people were quietly sitting at their stations doing research. The low pinlights over their heads shone brighter than the others. CV mist made the room look soft and foggy. Watly wondered if the guy with the high forehead and crooked nose was anywhere around. It would be nice to talk to him now. To talk about Pepajer.

"What if someone else blackmailed her?" the Subkeeper asked, his eyes still focused at the far end of the room.

"Who the hell—this is pointless." Watly spun back toward the door and started to walk out.

"Does she know Oldyer is dead, my child?" the Ragman asked, bending forward slightly and bringing his gaze back to those near him.

Watly stopped. "Huh?" He turned back toward the other two.

"Does Sentiva know Dr. Mitterly killed Oldyer?"

Watly thought about it. His brain felt sluggish. "I assume," he said finally, "that Mitterly was on his way to tell Sentiva about it when . . . when I killed him." The words didn't want to come out. Particularly not in front of Alysess. *All right, so I'm a raping murderer. So?*

"Then Sentiva doesn't know the fat man is dead." The Subkeeper smiled. He seemed to be enjoying himself. This was a game to him.

Watly shrugged. "No, I guess not."

"But she may know he was becoming a troublemaker—asking for more money, and all?" The Subkeeper's eyes were starting to sparkle almost as much as his clothing.

Watly squinted at him. "She may."

"There you have it, my children."

Watly and Alysess looked at each other. The tension between them had lessened. The anger had passed, replaced by curiosity.

"There we have *what*?" Alysess asked.

"Think, my children. You never use your heads. A plan. A *plan*."

Watly stepped closer to the Subkeeper. "What's the plan?"

The Ragman took a deep breath. "A few days from now, Sentiva walks into a police station and confesses—in detail—to everything. Just like that. The hosting, the murder, the conspiracy, the conception of the fetal hostage—*everything*. She turns herself in. You surface shortly thereafter and tell the rest of the story. You are off the hook. The charges are dropped. Meanwhile, Sentiva has already changed her mind about the confession—tried to retract it, deny it—but by now it's too late for her to take it all back. Nobody buys her suddenly reneging. And now she's under constant protective restraint—originally her *own* suggestion. Originally from her *own* mouth. This physical restraint and monitoring lasts right up to the birth of her child. After some legal shenanigans, the state awards the infant to you—partly out of your qualifications and partly out of something I like to call 'official guilt.' Sound good?"

"It sounds—" Watly sat down on a stool across from the small bearded man, "with all due respect, Subkeeper, it sounds like a raping Jesusland fantasy."

"No, no. A *plan*, not a fantasy, my child." The Ragman's eyes showed amusement.

"I don't see it," Alysess said.

"*Now* I understand," the Ragman said broadly, "why you two needed our help so badly. You're both a bit beanheaded."

Watly tried not to get defensive. He realized how much the Ragman liked to play teacher. "Why would Sentiva confess? Your scenario still makes no sense to me."

Alysess joined in: "Yes, it's a wonderful story, and all —"

"Because, my little slow-thinking fugitives, you turn the tables on her. Take the ball. Give our delightful donor friend a taste of her own medicine."

Watly flopped both hands in his lap, frustrated. "I still don't see how—"

"It's time, don't you see," the Subkeeper interrupted with a wink, "for Sentiva Alvedine to do a little involuntary hosting herself."

CHAPTER 42

Watly sat in front of the keyboard for a good fifteen minutes before beginning. He stared at the colored light-keys and tried to organize his thoughts. This wasn't going to be easy. Or at least, it wasn't going to be easy on his nerves, that much was sure.

Watly stretched his arms back over his head to loosen all the tight muscles. Then he primed the board's main ringlet and started to type. CV mist filled the air before him.

> COMMUNICATION ACCESS CODE:
> SUSPENDED
> TRACER CODE: SUSPENDED
> SENDER CODE: NONE
> BILLING CODE: NONE
> VISUAL: DENIED
> AUDIO: DENIED
> POINT OF ORIGIN: DENIED
> OVERRIDE SYSTEM ON SUB-115
> AUTHORITY

Watly paused and glanced up at the Ragman. The bearded face nodded approval, sympathetic stress showing in the lines of his forehead. Alysess nodded also, her eyes on the CV image above the board. Watly continued.

```
SENDING TO TRIPLE WELTER ONE,
SECOND LEVEL BLUE
FOR: SENTIVA ALVEDINE
#        #        #
SENTIVA ALVEDINE.
#        #        #
```

Watly waited, looking at the CV image, his fingers poised over the light-keys. Even now, while waiting, he was trying to think like Oldyer. He was trying to *be* Oldyer. He typed the name again.

```
SENTIVA ALVEDINE.
```

Still no response.

```
SENTIVA ALV
YES?
```

Watly held his breath. He felt Alysess and the Ragman stiffen next to him.

```
SENTIVA ALVEDINE?
WHO IS THIS?
IS THIS SENTIVA ALVEDINE?
WHY IS THERE NO SENDER CODE? WHO
IS THIS? WHERE IS THE VISUAL? THE AU-
DIO?
THIS IS NOT A TRACEABLE BOARD, SEN-
TIVA. YOU CANNOT TRACK THIS COMMU-
NICATION.
WHO ARE YOU?
```

Watly waited a second before typing.

```
A FRIEND. A DEAR FRIEND.
```

There was a pause before the written response came through.

WATLY CAIPER?

Watly choked on a ball of air, coughing violently. The mist shimmered. Thank terra there was no audio. A shiver ran up his spine as the coughing subsided. He almost believed Sentiva could somehow see him—see right through the cables, and right through his masquerade. Her typed question floated a few inches from his face in the CV mist, taunting him. Did she really know? Maybe she was just guessing. She *must* just be guessing.

Watly steadied his fingers and placed them carefully back on the proper light-keys. He typed.

WATLY CAIPER? YOU'RE JOKING? IS
MISTER CAIPER STILL ALIVE?
REMARKABLE. IMAGINE MY SURPRISE.
*WHO THE HELL IS THIS? I'M SIGNING OFF
NOW IF*
IT'S ME, MY DEAR. OLDYER.

Again there was a pause.

IS IT.

Watly had to play this very carefully. He didn't even know if Oldyer and Sentiva had ever actually met. She hadn't typed a question mark. Why hadn't she typed a question mark? Maybe a question mark—such a vulnerable little indication of ignorance—would not be her style.

HOW NICE TO COMMUNICATE WITH YOU.
WHAT DO YOU WANT, OLDYER.
HAD A LITTLE VISIT FROM THAT BLOND
DOCTOR FRIEND OF YOURS TODAY. FEL-
LOW TRIED TO KILL ME. NOT A NICE
MAN AT ALL.

There was no response for what must have been a full ten seconds.

A PITY HE FAILED.
I BEG TO DIFFER. BUT, WHATEVER THE
CASE, MY LITTLE FRIEND, I WISH TO
STRIKE AN AGREEMENT.
I DON'T MAKE DEALS.
YOU WILL WITH ME.
WHAT DO YOU HAVE TO BARGAIN WITH?
YOU KNOW WHAT I HAVE TO BARGAIN
WITH, YOU SOFDICK SUBSPAWN. YOUR
FREEDOM, YOUR LIFE. I COULD TURN
YOU IN. I'VE GOT THE GOODS ON YOU.
ADMIT IT, LITTLE FRIEND, I SCARE YOU.
NO ONE EVER SCARES ME, MR. OLDYER.
EVER.
OH? WHY WOULD YOU TRY TO KILL ME
IF I DIDN'T FRIGHTEN YOU? I MUST BE
PRETTY IMPORTANT. I'M THE ONLY ONE
LEFT WHO CAN LINK YOU TO THE MUR-
DER.
THERE IS NO CONNECTION BETWEEN YOU
AND ME. YOU ARE NO MORE THAN A
LOOSE END.
WELL, THIS LOOSE END WILL START
FLAPPING IF WE DON'T COME TO AN
AGREEMENT.
YOU HAVE ALREADY BEEN PAID HAND-
SOMELY FOR YOUR SERVICES, MR.
OLDYER. WE HAVE NO FURTHER BUSI-
NESS.
I HAVEN'T BEEN PAID ENOUGH. I
HAVEN'T BEEN PAID ENOUGH TO KEEP ME
QUIET. AND I CERTAINLY HAVEN'T BEEN
PAID ENOUGH TO BE POKED AT WITH
YOUR DOCTOR'S SCALPEL.

The CV image stayed blank for a while. Watly waited for
Sentiva to continue the conversation. Had he pushed too far? Did
she buy any of this? He glanced at the Ragman and Alysess. They
both nodded encouragement. *You're doing fine*, their faces said. A
message from Sentiva finally appeared.

HOW MUCH.
AN ADDITIONAL ONE MILLION NEW YORK
DOLLARS.
YOU'RE INSANE, MR. OLDYER.
I ALSO HAVE HIGH EXPENSES. I HAVE
SOME UNEXPECTED MEDICAL BILLS NOW,
AS WELL AS THE EXPENSE OF TRAVELING
FAR FAR AWAY—THE OUTERWORLD,
PERHAPS—WHERE I COULD LIVE QUIETLY
FOR THE REST OF MY VERY LONG LIFE.

There was another break before Sentiva responded.

HALF.
HALF WHAT?
I'LL GIVE YOU HALF A MILLION.
AND I'LL STAY HALF QUIET.

During the next pause both Alysess and the Subkeeper gave
Watly a cautionary look, warning him to be careful, not to go
overboard. But Watly thought it had been a nice touch. Oldyer
wasn't a compromiser.

*VERY WELL, MY FRIEND. WHEN IS THIS
MILLION-DOLLAR BLACKMAIL DROP OF
OURS TAKING PLACE. WHEN WILL YOU
PICK IT UP.*

Watly look a deep breath. This was it. This was the make-or-
break point.

I'M NOT PICKING IT UP AT ALL, MY
LITTLE FRIEND. I'VE BEEN LESS MOBILE
SINCE MY LITTLE RUN-IN WITH YOUR
DOCTOR'S BEDSIDE MANNER. MY HEALTH
IS NOT IDEAL. NO, YOU'LL DELIVER IT,
DEARIE.
*WHERE SHALL I SEND IT, MY OBESE EX-
TORTIONIST.*
NOT SEND, SENTIVA. DELIVER. IN PER-

SON. ALONE. UNARMED OR THE DEAL'S
OFF. AND I GO TO THE COPS.
HOW SHREWD OF YOU.
TONIGHT. ON THE FIRST LEVEL.

Watly held his breath as he waited for her reply.

I DON'T TRAVEL TO THE FIRST LEVEL.
THEN I DON'T KEEP MY MOUTH SHUT.

No words appeared for a while. Watly thought he might have
lost her. And then—

WHERE.
YOU'LL LIKE THIS. IT'S A FITTING LOCA-
TION.
WHERE.
ALVEDINE. HOSTING ROOM NIE WELTER
ONE. MIDNIGHT.
CUTE.
NO WEAPONS. NO FRIENDS. OR YOU'LL
NOT FIND ME.
FAIR ENOUGH.
COMMUNICATION ENDED.
*OH, OLDYER, BEFORE YOU GO, ABOUT
YOUR INJURIES—MEA* . . .

Watly slipped the main ringlet back in its casing and the
keyboard dimmed. The connection was severed. It was over. He
pushed his chair from the keyboard. He was exhausted. Alysess
moved closer and put a hand on his shoulder. "Good job, Watly."

"Yes, my child," the Ragman said with affection. "Good job."

"Was it? Was it really?" Watly leaned back in the chair and
stretched. "I don't know. She's very smart. She could've known
from the beginning it was me. She could've been playing along."

"I don't think so, Watly," Alysess said. "I think you fooled
her."

"Remember—" Watly turned and looked at them both, "she is
not to be taken lightly. She is incredible. I know for a fact. Even

if I *did* fool her just now, she's still dangerous. Very, very dangerous. I could feel her anger even in the typed words. I could tell she's not going to keep her end of the bargain. I could feel it. She has no intention of paying Oldyer off. He *is* a loose end. She wants to kill him. Probably planned to kill him all along. Was just waiting for things to die down. I've got to be ready for that. She could just as easily kill me."

Watly stood up and started for the door. It was time to change clothes. Tonight he had a heavy date. Tonight he would be meeting Sentiva Alvedine again and—much as he'd grown accustomed to them—the penis-bubble pants simply wouldn't do.

CHAPTER 43

What if the sight were a lie?

What if the Subkeeper's visions were just so much fancy footwork? Hocus-pocus? Suppose a person combined common sense with educated guessing and mixed in a little old-time theatricality and a pile of catshit—wouldn't they get the same thing? Couldn't the Subkeeper be doing with his sight the very same thing Watly had done in saying he knew how to revolution without death? Couldn't he be *faking* it? Why not? It was a great way to impress people. The bearded fortune-teller might just be using it to keep his position of authority. And if so, then the whole "violent death of Watly Caiper" thing might not only happen far in the future . . . it might never happen at all. Watly might live a long and full life—well into old old age. And then die softly, pleasantly—years and years from now. Wasn't that just as likely as not?

Or, okay, Watly thought. *what if there is such a thing as sight? It's possible. What if there is a way for some people to catch snippets of the future? Okay. Well, who's to say it can't be misinterpreted? Who's to say the Subkeeper can "read" it correctly? He's got no credentials. There's no such thing as "sight licensing." Who's to say the man didn't make a mistake?* And more: what's to prevent the interpreter from *lying?* How was Watly to know if the Ragman was telling the truth about what he saw? Suppose he had wanted to scare Watly, shake him up a little, put him in his place? It was possible. Watly didn't know the guy that well. Why trust him?

Some goofy little scruffy guy lives underground, lords over a bunch of beanheads who like slicing people up, spends his time planning an impossible overthrow . . . then comes along, touches my forehead, and says I'm going to die. Why the rape should I believe that?

Watly *needed* this kind of thinking. It was the only way to calm himself down. His own mortality was hanging heavily over him and he needed to feel more comfortable. It was particularly hard now. The hosting room was very dark. It seemed like images of Watly's own death were lurking in every corner. The only light came from the open doorway. It sliced across the white floor and then faded out before reaching Watly's position behind the hosting chair. Everything else in the room was shadowy and dark. The huge hosting machine with its many dangling cables was just a vague gray shape in the corner. Behind Watly, the reverse-corrected mirror reflected nothing but the doorway half blocked by the chair's silhouette. If Watly moved to the side, he could see the dark edge of his head in the mirror. He avoided moving. The sight of motion in the reflection—even his own—disturbed him. Everything was so still. Everything so quiet.

Watly reached down to see that he still had the blast canister Alysess had prepared. It was there, next to his foot. He picked it up and held it tightly in his left hand. All he had to do when the time came was compress its top. One push and the gas would shoot out in the direction the thing was aimed, knocking Sentiva out cold. An hour's worth of sedation in one blast. That should do it. All he needed to do was point it in the general direction of her face, get close enough, and press. Bingo. That was the plan. He hoped he could catch her before she fell so she didn't get hurt. The pregnancy, and all . . . the future baby.

The canister was curved in a moon shape to fit in his hip pocket but Watly wanted it handy. He placed it back down next to his left foot again. Then he thought better of it. It should be even handier. *Hold on to the thing. Stay ready. Keep your finger poised over the top*.

Watly reached to pick the canister up again. As he bent low something moved. Something in the corner of his eye—not the reflection of his head in the mirror, but something from the direction of the door. Like a cloud obstructing the sun for a split second, a shadow had flickered past. A person? A late-night worker? Or was it Sentiva? Had she passed by the door? Had she actually entered the room? Or had it just been the edge of Watly's eye—an eyelash he'd seen and thought—

Watly gripped the concave canister tightly, remembering what a cold-blooded killer Sentiva Alvedine was. *But she's expecting Oldyer,* he reassured himself. A slow-moving, enormous, supposedly wounded man who couldn't possibly squat down behind a chair. A loud, impatient man who wouldn't be able to sit silently in the dark for more than ten seconds.

What time was it now? His buzbelt's timekeeper was on mute. It must be late. Surely it must be midnight by now.

Watly slowly transferred the canister into his right hand, holding it in the firing position. He inched his head up cautiously to take another peek at the doorway. It was empty. And nothing in the darkness moved.

There was a slight sound—very slight—that came from directly behind Watly. It was very soft and very brief. It sounded to him at first like it must be his own shoe moving ever so slightly in the tile. Or perhaps the fold of his pants cuff slipping from where it had snagged on the back of his heel. It was that kind of very subtle, almost imperceptible sound. But Watly heard it. And he knew, after a moment, that it wasn't his shoe or his cuff. Someone was there.

"That's funny"—the voice whispered right behind Watly's head—"it doesn't *look* like a Mr. Oldyer. It looks like a Watly Caiper. I'm not surprised."

It was Sentiva. Next to him. Right there—smelling warm and slightly sweaty. Watly turned. He came up high with his right hand, clutching the canister, ready to fire. She was on him—over him—before he could even twist to face her. And there was something in her hands stretched taut. Something threadlike that caught the dim light and sparkled. It was a charged sawcord. Deadly.

"This time you've overstepped your bounds, my friend. This time you've gone too far. Instead of a dead Oldyer there will be a dead Caiper." He heard anger in her voice—fury at Watly's trick. Or perhaps fury at having her suspicions proven right.

The thread was up and over his head. Watly threw his hand up and turned to flee, his face stopping smack against the back of the chair's headrest. The canister slipped and was out of his hand. It had fallen, trapped between his raised arm and the chair.

Sentiva was on his back now, her arms pulling the thread in from behind. Watly saw dimly she had overshot some. The glimmering cord was not just around his neck as she'd intended. It went all the way over the back of the headrest, the blast canister, and his right arm. He struggled but there was no leverage. His arm was twisted all the way to the left, pressing on his neck. Sentiva tightened the cord. There was a burning odor as it bit into the metal of the headrest.

Watly kicked backward with his feet but she moved too fast for him. He hit nothing, his feet wild. He was choking against the pressure of his own arm angled across his throat. There was no air at all getting to him.

And now a loud pop as the cord cut through one of the two steel posts on the headrest. She pulled tighter, whispering, "mea culpa." The voice was dead winter.

Watly tried to grab backward at something with his free hand. He found a handful of her hair and pulled hard—as hard as he could. Her tightening of the sawcord never faltered.

More burning smell and the second post popped. The headrest flew off. Watly fell backward onto Sentiva, losing grip of her hair. She grunted but kept the cord taut. It was now digging into the canister, cutting right through it. Watly could hear the hiss as the gas escaped uselessly. It was expelled outward—into the darkness.

Another three seconds and the cord would finish cutting the canister neatly in two. Then it would slice through his arm, severing it completely in a moment, just a moment, and then, finally, it would dig into his neck, decapitating him in one quick pull. Was this the violent death Ragman had foreseen? Was this the way it had to be? Watly felt himself grow weaker from the lack of air.

Somewhere hanging low down by his right side was a new Ragman-issued chip pistol—but he was nowhere near it now. Now that he *would* use it—use it quickly—he couldn't get to it. He tried reaching across his own body, feeling for the butt of the gun. He stretched farther, his body contorted. His fingers brushed it. *There.* He wrenched his body sideways and pulled at it. The pistol was free now, but he had no grip. Where was the grip? His fingers fumbled with the weapon. It slipped out sideways and clattered to the floor beside them. He twisted violently again, reaching for it once more. Now it was close. Almost in reach. A few more inches. . . . Sentiva kicked it with her right knee. The gun slid far away. Watly felt consciousness slipping from him.

He reached back again to get her hair but she didn't even seem to feel the pain. *Pain is nothing to her,* Watly thought.

"Mea culpa," she grunted, pulling harder still.

In the dim corner of the room the hosting machine lurched. It seemed to be moving toward them, leaning in closer.

The sawcord now popped the canister in half and the two parts rolled from Watly to the floor. They made a sharp clattering sound. He felt new pain as the thread dug through his jumpsuit and into his arm. With all his strength he pulled hard with his left hand and ripped out a whole tangled clump of Sentiva's hair. She continued pulling the cord in. "Mea maxima culpa," her strained voice came. He tried twisting his body side to side, rocking, flailing his legs about—but the cord held him.

The vague form of the monsterlike hosting machine slid all the way out from the wall and a dark figure climbed from behind it.

Now the sawcord was digging deeper in Watly's arm and he felt blood spurt out.

The dark figure neared and knelt next to them, and Watly saw a canister in the shadowy hand aimed just behind his head—aimed at Sentiva's face.

"No fair, Watly," came Sentiva's voice next to his ear. "I see you've brought company—"

Then there was a sharp percussive sound from the canister—*cagoon*—and Sentiva's arms finally went limp. Totally limp. She was lifeless behind him. Harmless. Out of commission.

Watly coughed and choked and gasped for air as he sat forward. The sawcord fell to the floor. He struggled to breathe again. His Adam's apple felt mashed and battered. After a long bout of coughing, he tried to speak.

"What the rape"—Watly's voice sounded hoarse to his own ears—"*took* you so long, Alysess?"

Her eyes shone in the darkness. "I couldn't see a damn thing from back there in this light. Why didn't you call for help? I would've come out sooner."

"My throat—" he coughed again, "was otherwise occupied."

Alysess closed the door and put the lights on, blinding them both with the brightness. When their eyes adjusted, she began cleaning Watly up. She was quick but gentle. The doctor was back in her element now. After dressing Watly's injured arm—fortunately the cut had not gone too deep—Alysess had him help her lift Sentiva into the hosting chair. The unconscious woman's limp head lolled all the way backward. Watly was reminded of how she'd looked the first time he'd seen her. Naked and vulnerable.

"She'll have to do without a headrest," Watly said hurriedly. "It's her own fault."

"You'd better get going, Watly. You've got less than an hour to get up there and get set. With Sentiva's pregnancy I don't dare give her more sedatives. And sometime soon the guard will be by. . . ." Alysess looked worried.

Watly kissed her and smiled grimly. "Just don't let her wake up. She'll kill you in a second. Be careful."

"It's *you* I'm worried about," she said. She opened her

medipak and began pulling equipment out. "Hurry. I'm going to set up to turn this stuff on at one-fifteen exactly."

Watly kissed her again and left.

He was on his way up. Taking a little "vacation," as it were. It was Watly Caiper's turn at the controls.

Watly Caiper's turn to be the donor.

CHAPTER 44

It would have been nice to go right back to the subs. It would have been nice to find the man with the crooked nose, who looked an awful lot like an older version of Watly, and have a long talk. They could sit in an empty mess hall with two bottles of booze and put their feet up on the tables. They could talk about the Brooklyn days. Well, maybe later. Maybe after this was all over.

As it was, Watly was too preoccupied to fixate on this as much as he felt like doing right now. He was preoccupied with the passing time, preoccupied with getting to Second level, and preoccupied—once he stepped out of the Hosting Building and onto the street—with the sensation of being watched, of being followed.

There was a feeling of a person—or of *people*—being always just outside of his line of sight, just beyond the outer edges of his vision. Maybe behind him. Maybe in front. All along the shiny First Level streets toward the tubestop. Watly felt it. Passing the sleeping tenters it was there. Was it just paranoia? Or was there really someone out there? Who? If Sentiva had brought help along, surely they would have come to her rescue long ago. Then who? Had someone followed Sentiva to get to Watly?

12:25—Watly's buzbelt clicked off the time. He had to hurry. He had fifty minutes left.

Again the Subkeeper's expertly made cards did their job in the tube and Watly was on Second in no time, trotting along in the cool night air. Breathing in the freshness of Second Level, he felt quite at home in his jumpsuit and workervest. "Just like the old days." He laughed to himself.

A few people passed by, glancing at Watly with studied indifference. He kept his head lowered, wishing he had time to slow down and enjoy the richness of the air. Wishing he had time to think about the cleaning man. He didn't. He had to get back to the upper floors of the Alvedine Building—on Second Level called the Alvedine Donor Building—fast. Then, if all went smoothly, he'd break quietly into a donor room and get to work. As soon as he started "sending," Alysess would see his location, hook up his cable, and grab his signal. She'd be all ready by then. It shouldn't take her more than twenty minutes to insert the creosan wafers in Sentiva and to set up the hosting machine.

The Subkeeper had shown her how to prepare a hosting without a cuff, and he'd provided the proper override equipment: a two-pronged rod like Sentiva herself had used.

"Equipment and planning we will assist in," the Subkeeper had said to them. "But again, I cannot give you my people. I will not risk them for your little escapade. They are not expendable. They are for the Revy. You do this on your own. But . . ." the man had paused, "I wish you luck. Much luck, my children."

And so they were on their own. But so far, so good.

And if all continued smoothly Watly would shortly have the five to seven "donor hours" to make things right. His first and only stop once he "was" Sentiva would, of course, be the police. For a confession. To exonerate a certain Watly Caiper.

12:30, the buzbelt clicked. Alysess was probably almost done with the implant operation by now. Watly had to keep his part of the plan moving. He was on Second Level's Fifty-seventh Street, and there ahead was the Alvedine Donor Building, looming up larger than anything around it and garishly lit by surrounding buildings. It was a spectacular sight. Strange to think he had just left Alysess downstairs in this very same structure. The place was enormous.

As he neared, Watly's hopes fell. They fell hard. *Rape*. Cops. All over the place. The front of the building was swarming with them. Ten or fifteen of them easily. Maybe more. It looked as though they liked to hang out there, sitting on the brightly lit steps making conversation between shifts.

There was no way Watly was going to make it past them. No way to slip by. No bluff would get him around them for seven hours. The whole thing was sunk.

Watly turned slowly, trying to look confident, casual. He walked back around to the east corner, looking for another entrance. There was none. Just beautiful yellow brick, solid and smooth. Not even a window until three stories higher. The building was sealed up tight—no way in except the front door.

12:35

Well, that did it. It was over now. It Watly didn't get back down to Alysess fast, she'd just stand there waiting for a donor signal that would never arrive until Sentiva woke up. And Sentiva was not bound to wake up in a good mood. Alysess would have her hands full. Watly turned up Third Avenue back toward the tubestop.

It was finished. The whole raping mess. All this for nothing. The one decent plan they'd had, and here it goes falling apart right from the start. No confession, no baby, no future, no nothing. Watly was angry. Why the hell hadn't they taken this into account? Why the hell hadn't the Subkeeper come up with a way around *this* possibility? He was prepared for all kinds of *mechanical* obstacles: locked and sealed doors, alarms, booby traps, anxiety fields—he had a bagful of gadgets—but he wasn't prepared for *human beings*. They hadn't counted on that. Why did it have to be a cop hangout? Human beings. Why hadn't Watly himself thought of it? *Shit. So close, yet so far.* Somewhere down below, all prepped and ready a host was waiting to host. Sentiva Alvedine. A captive host needing only a donor. And here was Watly: the donor. But you can't *be* a donor if you can't get to a damn donor room. *Damn again!*

Watly was nearly back at the tube when the obvious answer finally hit him. It hit him almost like a physical blow, so powerfully he wondered why it hadn't occurred to him earlier. Yes. It was the alternative—the backup plan he sought. He had his solution. There was still a chance. If he was lucky, very lucky, and everything was still in place—if Sentiva had thought removing certain cables from her house would attract more attention and cause more suspicion than just leaving them be—then Watly *did* have a place to go. He had a donor room. He could turn the tables more exactly than he'd planned.

12:40, the buzbelt clicked.

The question was, did he have the time?

Did he have the time?

He started walking fast—a little too fast for Second Level standards. But he had to. He had to get to Seventy-second street between Park and Madison. He had to get to the Alvedine residence.

He was no longer aware of the sensation of being watched. He ignored the tickle at the back of his neck that warned of a follower. He blocked out the shiver of fear. He was too busy walking. Too busy trying to make good time.

CHAPTER 45

The buzbelt clicked *1:00* as Watly neared the two dark shapes of Sentiva's birdwing banisters. He was out of breath but happy that he'd made it this far and still had some time. The building was silent and ghostly; the only light Watly had to go by was a pale glow streaming in from the street outside. The door had been no problem, and the anxiety field combination was now easy to remember, although there was a brief moment as Watly first stepped down the hall when he wondered if it was really off. But it *was* off. That was just fear he was feeling. Pure, natural, nonsynthetic fear again. The place was creepy. The wicker furniture was now dark hulking lumps that watched him from the sides. Every shadow seemed ready to come alive and pounce. Any moment all the gray shapes around him would form monstrosities and attack. The place felt evil. Tainted.

Watly climbed the steps.

1:05

Watly stood in the doorway of Sentiva Alvedine's bedroom. The last time he'd been there she'd been lying naked before him

on the enormous bed. And he . . . he had not been himself. Not
at all. Now there was no one in the room but Watly. The tall
windows were wide open and the lacy white curtains billowed
ghostlike in the wind. In the dim light the pale canopied bed
looked much the same as before, piled high with pillows at the
head.

Watly stepped in. After a careful search he located a sealed
metal box bolted to the wall just under the right side of the bed.
Watly went at it with some of the Subkeeper's tools, working
mostly by feel. It wasn't long before he had opened the seal,
exposing a series of shiny ringlets within.

The donor controls. It was all still here.

The buzbelt clicked *1:10,* the click sounding too loud in the
darkness.

Alysess would be preparing for the hosting now. Just about
ready. Perhaps Sentiva was even groaning a bit, coming slowly
out of it as the doctor pulled the cables out and pressed the plates
against her new implants. *The timing,* Watly was thinking,
couldn't be better.

He pulled all the ringlets in the sequence given to him by
Alysess, one after the other, hoping that he understood the
machine's operation correctly. When he flipped out the final one,
he sat fully on the bed, feeling around in the pillows for Sentiva's
hidden donor plates. They had to be there somewhere. Perhaps
they were hidden deeper than—

"If you'd tell me what you're looking for," a voice came from
the doorway, "maybe I'd help you find it."

Watly froze. The voice was familiar. It was Fenlocki. Sergeant
Ogiv Fenlocki, cop extraordinaire. Watly did not turn to look. He
did not move.

"I'm looking," Watly said very slowly, his words measured,
"for a set of donor plates. Sentiva did the hosting from this bed.
She is your murderer."

"A long-distance donor, huh?" The sergeant coughed. "I
suspect"—his voice had that familiar tinge of humor—"that you
are looking for money."

"Money?" Watly almost laughed. He was still facing away
from the sergeant.

"How do you think I found you, my slippery fellow? Someone reports seeing a Second Level woman like Sentiva Alvedine traveling down to First and I wonder, what's up? You lured her down somehow, Caiper. I could figure that much. I follow her and I wait and what do I see? *Watly Caiper*, of all people, leaving the same building. Where does he go? Up to Sentiva's house. What does he do? Rummage here in the dark. No doubt he forced her to tell where she kept money—am I right? Maybe roughed her up a bit back there on First. I'll send someone over to have a look later. If you've killed her, that's too bad. But then, you can only be executed once for murder."

"Look in the pillows yourself if you don't believe me." Watly spoke without emotion.

"Why the sudden need for cash, Watly? Thought you could buy your way out of this mess if you had enough? Thought you could bribe your way out of the country, maybe? Head for mythical Europe, somehow? The outer countries? Too bad. You know, wherever you were hiding, you were doing quite well. You should've stayed. *I* sure couldn't find you. But here we are, then. Reunited at last."

The buzbelt clicked *1:15*.

It was time. Alysess would be waiting, searching for the donor signal. Watly flexed his right fingers. His hand was still in the pillows—nowhere near the chip pistol. What should he do? Fenlocki was not willing to hear the truth. He had all his answers already. Watly's only hope was still the plan.

The plan. In order to complete it, he'd have to try to kill Fenlocki right now—not just hurt him, but *kill* him. Watly needed to be undisturbed for the donor hours and then he'd have to get back to First. All secretly, no witnesses. With Fenlocki alive and knowing Watly was here, the plan was lost. But with Fenlocki dead . . . it could still work. And no one would know Watly killed him. A dead cop is discovered in Sentiva Alvedine's house. They'd figure it was her doing. Especially after she confessed to the Corber murder. And all the other crap.

"You've put up one helluva chase, Watly Caiper," Fenlocki was saying. "One *helluva* fine chase."

In the darkness, Watly eased his hand slowly out of the

pillows, inching toward his gun. "Are you going to kill me or
bring me in?" he asked.

Fenlocki chuckled. There was the click of a haver nerve gun
bolt sliding into place. "What would you do if you were me,
huh?"

Watly pulled his hand closer in, feeling the cold pistol grip with
surprising suddenness. He had it now. He gripped the gun firmly.
Funny how guns now felt comfortable in his hand. He had grown
used to them.

"I'd kill me," Watly answered. "And I'd kill me fast. With a
minimum of talking. And no fanfare. I wouldn't even let me turn
around."

Watly pulled the pistol up slightly, so it was free of the
bedspread.

"Good advice, my slippery captive. Good advice," the sergeant said respectfully. "But, in fairness to you and to my sense
of decency, I'd prefer you did turn. I need to kill a person, Watly
Caiper. I can't kill the back of a person." Watly started to swivel
toward Fenlocki. "Sorry for the nerve gun, Caiper. They issue the
damn things—"

Watly dove foreward on the bed and fired even before he
realized there were two of them. *Two* police! Not just Fenlocki!
His slug missed them both, sparking loudly into the upper
doorjamb as Fenlocki and Akral jumped to either side. Watly
rolled and dropped off the far side of the bed. Without waiting he
fired the unaimed gun behind him. Again the report echoed in the
small room. There were scrambling sounds as the two officers
found cover. *Two cops! Damn!*

"You all right, Akral?" Fenlocki shouted.

"Fine, sir."

Shit shit shit. Watly now had to kill them both to make this
work. Two cops. The plan was getting less and less likely.

The room lit up with the flash of a nerve bolt that streaked by
inches above Watly's head. He spun and fired back over the edge.
There was a dull thud as his slug hit wood.

Another bolt was fired, streaking into the corner of the
bedspread, glowing and then dying quickly. Watly heard more

movement. One of them was crawling around to the far side of the bed. Watly fired wildly again, hoping to scare them back.

Another bolt came—this one from the doorway—bursting across the room and landing right next to where Watly crouched. He rolled to the other side, trying to confuse them both. *Two against one. Nerve guns against a lowly chip pistol. Unfair, already.*

Another bolt flashed across and the whole place lit up as it looked for nerve in the pillows next to Watly's head. Watly leaned forward to fire again as a bolt streaked in and hit his gun barrel with a ping, lighting it up and making the gun almost too hot to hold. It climbed up the barrel seeking nerve, the ping still resonating through the handle. Watly almost dropped the pistol but the glow died fast before reaching his hand.

He stuck his head up again, adjusting his grip on the pistol. It was hard to see. There was nothing to shoot at. He pointed the weapon randomly and suddenly a dark shadow was flying toward him, sailing over the bed with gun extended. It was Akral, diving toward him. Akral fired forward as he leapt and the glowing bolt sprang directly at Watly. He ducked, dodging it by millimeters, feeling the rush of burning air as it passed his cheek.

Akral was upon him now. He hit hard with all his weight. Both guns were pointed wrong, over each other's heads. They struggled. Watly felt his bad arm giving out. A covering shot came from the sergeant and burned brightly on the window frame behind them for a moment.

Watly found the officer's collar and they both rolled back as one, crashing into the far wall. Akral's gun fired upward, the bolt lighting up the whole ceiling for a second. The cop was strong, his grip impossible. Watly felt his own hold weakening. His bad arm was no help at all, almost useless. The cop slammed into him again and again, wrestling for position, for leverage. Akral had him by the throat with one hand now. He was pressing against Watly's Adam's apple, just where it was most painful. Again Watly was choking. Like before with Sentiva. The blackness around got darker. He was losing peripheral vision, passing out.

Watly curled his feet up under him as they rolled, and kicked out with everything he had. Everything he had left. Up and out.

Hard! There was a resounding thump as Akral's head hit the wall. The officer slumped over on top of Watly, unconscious.

1:20, the buzbelt clicked.

It was too late. Alysess would be giving up. Sentiva might have woken up by now. She might have even—

"Akral?" Fenlocki whispered in the darkness. His voice came from the doorway.

Watly let his voice drop low, calm. He slowed his breathing. "Yes, sir." He carefully pulled his way out from under Akral's limp body. "I'm fine, sir. Just the leg," he said softly, imitating the cop's polite tones as best he could. Brooklyn tones. Orange tones.

"And Watly?" The sergeant sounded nervous, out of breath.

"He's out cold, sir." Watly answered, moving back to the edge of the bed and peering out. "Unconscious, I think."

Fenlocki stepped forward into the shifting blue light that came from between the blowing curtains. His gun was down at his side, his body relaxed. The glow of sweat reflected on his forehead.

"We've finally done it, my friend." Fenlocki's voice sounded human, relieved. "We've got the killer."

With that Watly sprang up onto the bed, his gun out straight. Fenlocki reeled back in shock—*his* weapon was still pointed to the floor. Watly aimed at the sergeant's face—just a few feet away. He could see the dampness on it, the twitch of the cheek, the wide eyes shining moistly in the darkness.

Now, Watly thought. *Kill him now.*

Now.

Pull the trigger and kill Sergeant Ogiv Fenlocki. And then shoot the unconscious Akral in the head. Kill them both. It's for the plan. To buy the five hours. For Watly's life, Watly's future. Selfish/good? Good?

Fenlocki stood still, looking up at Watly. Waiting for him to fire. His eyes, unless Watly was mistaken, were understanding. Resigned. Forgiving, even.

Now. Kill them both.

Now.

Watly did nothing.

Fenlocki's hand was moving now, very slowly coming up with the nerve gun.

Get him before he gets you, Watly. Kill yet another human being. One more. What's one more? What's the big deal? You've killed before. Kill this person . . . this cop . . . this officer. One of the good guys. Two. Ogiv and Akral. Cops trying to catch a killer. Protecting society. From a murderer. Kill the man, Watly.

Shoot him in the face.

Selfish—*what*? Selfish/*good*?

Fenlocki's nerve gun was almost up now. His eyes showed amazement that Watly had not fired yet. The sergeant was confused.

Watly trembled. He found himself lowering the chip pistol. Slowly pointing it to the floor. It was no good. It was all no good. *I have no right to hurt another person, I see that now. No right. Pepajer was right.*

Fenlocki's eyes flicked down to Watly's gun and looked bewildered for a second.

He raised his weapon up at Watly.

The buzbelt clicked *1:25*—a loud, single click—and Sergeant Ogiv Fenlocki, still looking astounded at his situation, hesitated a second, and then pulled the trigger on his nerve gun, humanely aimed at Watly Caiper's face.

The brilliant bolt flew out.

Right at Watly.

In a stupid move, an insane move brought on by reflex alone, Watly Caiper reached up with his hand to protect his face.

The whole room lit up like the sun for a second. This time the bolt found nerves. Watly shrieked. He let go of the gun, dropping to his knees on the bed. His hand was on fire, the nerves of his fingers glowing through the skin.

"I'm sorry, Caiper," the sergeant said.

The pain was worse than anything. The pain was worse than he'd ever imagined. Agony. Complete agony. Worse than death. Torture. Worse than life.

His fingernails were lit up from inside.

"I'm sorry, Watly," Fenlocki said again.

Watly stared at his hand. Tears were streaming down his face as the glow climbed up past his wrist. All he could think was, *I'm dying. I'm dying. I'm raping dying!*

"Thank you," Fenlocki said, his eyes warm. "Thank you for my life. I don't know your story, Caiper, or the story of why you did the murder, but you are not a bad man. I see that."

The bolts were nearing Watly's elbow. Watly cried out continually in pain. An achy, throbby, fiery pain. Echoing like a funny bone or a kick in the balls but a hundred times worse.

"You were a *person*, Watly Caiper. You had eggs." The sergeant held Watly's shoulders. "I will remember you."

Watly felt himself drifting some. A chill ran through him. The pain lessened as shock set in. He was removed from it—removed from his own screaming.

"I will remember you," Fenlocki said again. And Watly felt love for the man.

The pain was up to his shoulder now, growing stronger. But Watly felt it less. He was removed, distanced. *I'm dying now,* he thought. *And it's not so bad.*

Watly saw tears in Fenlocki's eyes. *Why are you crying?* he thought. *Why so sad?*

The pain moved in toward Watly's neck, enveloping him. *Pain can only go so far,* Watly thought, listening to his own screams. *And then you feel it less. This is good. This is how it should be.*

Watly's body was spasming. Shaking uncontrollably. The sergeant tried to steady him—helping him through it, holding him, guiding. Mothering.

Thump thump. Thump thump.

The sound of a human heart.

Watly saw death coming. Coming up fast. And he saw what it was. All that it was. It was no great mystery. It was nothing to fear. It was nothing to look forward to. It was nothing. Death is just the end of life. It is not something you experience. It is simply the end of all experience. A wall you do not pass beyond.

And that's all right.

Watly saw that it was all right.

Thump thump. Thump thump.

He felt more and more hollow. More distanced. Sleepy. His screams echoed far away. He felt his body fall back on the bed as if in slow motion. There was a new pain—far away—as the back of his head hit something hard, deep among the pillows. Two metal plates.

"You *will* be remembered," the sergeant said, still mothering through the death. And Watly thought, *That's nice. I hope so.*

The pain was far away now. In a neck and head he used to be closer to. In a body that was more immediate once. A wave of warmth washed over him. Dark warmth. Numbing warmth. Pleasant, comforting, sweet warmth. The end of pain.

One last thought that flickered through his head before his brain turned off—click, like a light switch—was: *I have not gotten my dream, but I have* tried *to get my dream. And that is enough. It is not the destination that matters, nor the journey. It is the road itself that matters. The road was my life.*

Thump thump. Thump . . .

And then . . .

Watly Caiper died.

His dreams, his memories, his hopes, his goals, his humor, his sadness, his lust, his joy . . . were all no more. There was nothing.

Watly Caiper was gone.

CHAPTER 46

Something was somewhere.

Something with thoughts and feelings existed, floated. Something with a sense of self flew, traveled.

It wasn't Watly. Watly was dead.

But something was somewhere. Flying, drifting. Something soared. Something glided high above everything, feeling the wind. Something banked and turned, reveling in the orange glow of sun. It felt feelings. It thought thoughts. It existed.

Something *was* somewhere.

An eyelid fluttered.

Then nothing.

Then fluttered again.

Two eyes opened slowly, groggily. They saw whiteness. The consciousness within was disoriented. There was a sense of confusion. Where? Who?

And there, nearby, a beautiful dark-skinned woman—clothes

torn and face bruised and bloody as if she'd been through a battle—looked on.

"Watly?" she asked the unfocused eyes.

"Watly is dead," a soft female voice responded.

The dark-skinned woman looked shocked, bewildered. Her lips tightened in disbelief. She straightened and inhaled deeply, moving closer. She smelled of powder and sweat. It was a nice smell. "Then who are you?"

"I am." The voice faltered, thinking. "I am Watly Caiper."

And so she was.

Trapped in the two creosan wafers was the projection of everything that had been Watly. His dreams, his memories, his hopes, his goals, his humor, his sadness, his lust, his joy . . . it was all there.

Watly's personality locked in Sentiva Alvedine's head.

Alysess's eyes were wet. "Watly is dead?" she asked, still not believing. Tears mixed with blood from the cuts on her cheeks. She must have had quite a fight keeping Sentiva still, keeping her pressed into the hosting plates.

"Yes," Watly said. "But it's okay. It's okay that way. Dying is not so bad. *Really*."

Alysess covered her face. Her shoulders shook.

Watly looked slowly down at her own womanly body. She too—Watly—was bruised and cut, perhaps even worse. But she was strong. She would heal. They would both heal.

Watly turned slowly to look at herself in the reverse-correcting mirror. She was, in spite of her injuries, beautiful.

I am beautiful, Watly thought.

It was interesting.

Alysess was truly crying now, sobbing freely, her head bowed. She was mourning the loss of her lover—of her poovus, perhaps.

Watly reached up to her with thin feminine fingers. They were strong, wiry fingers. Different fingers. "We'd better go, Alysess. We'd better go. Back to the subs. We've got a revolution to attend to."

Alysess looked up. "Are you really Watly?"

"I'm . . . I'm all the Watly there is now."

That answer didn't seem to satisfy Alysess. She squinted.

"But . . . are you *Watly*?" Her eyes were plaintive, almost begging.

"I guess I am. I'm Watly."

Alysess smiled slightly through the tears.

Watly smiled back—a real Watly Caiper smile. A Brooklyn Little-Watt smile. "Remind me," she said, holding Alysess's hands tightly, "to ask you later about your views on lesbianism."

Alysess laughed, sweetly, musically.

And so did Watly.

They rose to leave—slowly and very, very carefully. Watly looked down at her own breasts as she walked—her hips, her waist, her legs. She was shaky, unused to the body. Alysess supported her. They left the building cautiously and headed for the nearest sub entrance. They had to get back. It was time to keep their part of the bargain. Time to help in the revolution.

And somehow, Watly felt ready now. Ready to lead. Ready to care. Ready to be selfish/good. There were answers forming now, or at least the germs of them: how to fight without fighting, how to revolution without death. They'd been there all along, these answers. It had taken this long to realize that.

Pepajer would be proud. It wasn't really a secret. It wasn't really some special hidden truth. It was easy. You did it by thinking. By feeling. You did it . . . by *doing* it. That was the answer.

And maybe there would be more answers in the subs. Answers about Watly's mother. Answers about Watly herself. Answers from a tall man with a high forehead and a crooked nose and kind eyes. After all . . . there was hardly such a thing as family anymore.

Watly had to move gingerly as she and Alysess walked. She was unfamiliar with the body and how it worked. It would take time. But she would be okay, this new Watly Caiper. A part of her—a big part of her—was happy. In spite of the horrors that had just occurred—the trauma and death—and in spite of really being technically more a trapped *projection* than a real person, Watly found something to celebrate. So she was a deceased donor's projection. So whatever personality she now had came from two flimsy creosan wafers behind her ears. So she was, in fact, an artificial recreation of a dead man's mind. So what?

She was with Alysess again. She was ready to work for the revolution now. She was not a fugitive. She was alive. She was healthy. . . .

And, perhaps most important of all, Watly Caiper was pregnant.

ABOUT THE AUTHOR

PETER R. EMSHWILLER hails from a science fiction family. His dad, Ed "EMSH", started out as an sf illustrator, and his mom, Carol, is an sf writer. In Peter's thirty-something years, he has tried his hand as a journalist, an actor, a special effects technician, a comedian, an impressionist, a magician, a ventriloquist, a singer, an erotic-fiction writer, a filmmaker, an animator, a graphic designer, a makeup artist, a lighting designer, an artist/illustrator, a composer/lyricist, and a Managing Editor (for *Twilight Zone* and *Night Cry* magazines).

Though he still considers himself somewhat of a "dabbler," he has settled down to focus mainly on writing and performing. He lives in New York City with his wife, writer/actress/singer Margaret Mayo McGlynn, and their "three fabulous felines." Peter is currently at work on the sequel to *The Host*, entitled *Short Blade*, coming soon from Bantam Books.

For the summer's best in science fiction and fantasy,
look no further than Bantam Spectra.

SPECTRA'S SUMMER SPECTACULAR

With a dazzling list of science fiction and fantasy stars, Spectra's
summer list will take you to worlds both old and new: worlds as close
as Earth herself, as far away as a planet where daylight reigns
supreme; as familiar as Han Solo's Millennium Falcon and as alien
as the sundered worlds of the Death Gate. Travel with these critically
acclaimed and award-winning authors for a spectacular summer
filled with wonder and adventure!

Coming in May 1991:

**Star Wars, Volume 1:
Heir to the Empire**
by Timothy Zahn

Earth
by David Brin

King of Morning, Queen of Day
by Ian McDonald

Coming in June, 1991:

**The Gap Into Vision:
Forbidden Knowledge**
by Stephen R. Donaldson

Black Trillium
by Marion Zimmer Bradley,
Julian May and Andre Norton

**Chronicles of the King's Tramp
Book 1: Walker of Worlds**
by Tom DeHaven

Coming in July 1991:

**The Death Gate Cycle,
Volume 3: Fire Sea**
by Margaret Weis and
Tracy Hickman

**The Death Gate Cycle,
Volume 2: Elven Star**
by Margaret Weis and
Tracy Hickman

Raising the Stones
by Sheri S. Tepper

Coming in August 1991:

Garden of Rama
by Arthur C. Clarke
and Gentry Lee

Nightfall
by Isaac Asimov
and Robert Silverberg

Available soon wherever Bantam Spectra Books are sold.

AN217 -- 4/91